Advance Praise for
Lily in the Snow

"Set in contemporary Ontario, Lily in the Snow tells the story a young Chinese journalist who immigrates to Canada with high hopes but finds life in her adopted country far from easy. Through the eyes of her mother, Grace, we come to understand how hard it is for the generation that was brought up during the Cultural Revolution to understand and adapt to modern Western ways.

"Canada may be the homeland of Mao's hero, Dr. Norman Bethune, but Lily soon discovers that Bethune's name is barely recognized here. Many people in the expatriate Chinese community seek order and direction in the evangelical Christian churches, and Lily, with sharp perception and gentle humour, introduces the reader to a strong cast of immigrant characters, each with their own rich history.

"Central to the story is the often troubled relationship between Lily and Grace. Wide gaps exist in their expectations and views on childrearing but the author treats both mother and daughter with great tenderness and empathy as they struggle to fulfill their dreams."

— Jenny Kitson, Editor and Co-Director of the
Eden Mills Writers Festival

Lily in
the Snow

雪百合

by Yan Li

WOMEN'S PRESS
TORONTO

Lily in the Snow
Yan Li

First published in 2009 by Women's Press, an imprint of Canadian Scholars' Press Inc.
180 Bloor Street West, Suite 801
Toronto, Ontario
M5S 2V6

www.womenspress.ca

Cover images: ©istockphoto.com/stock-photo-8794745-tree-and-bench-in-the-winter.php; ©istockphoto.
com/stock-photo-5893911-woman-s-face

Canadian Scholars' Press Inc./Women's Press gratefully acknowledges financial support for our publishing
activities from the Ontario Arts Council, the Canada Council for the Arts, the Government of Canada
through the Book Publishing Industry Development Program (BPIDP), and the Government of Ontario
through the Ontario Book Publishing Tax Credit Program.

Library and Archives Canada Cataloguing in Publication

Li, Yan,
      Lily in the snow : a novel / Yan Li.

ISBN 978-0-88961-479-6

      I. Title.

PS8573.I21L54 2010   C813'.54   C2009-906639-4

Text design by Colleen Wormald

09 10 11 12 13   5 4 3 2 1

Printed and bound in Canada by Marquis Book Printing Inc.

For my mother,
close by or far away.

Chapter 1
Moving Sale

I

"What's good about Canada? It looks so dull!"

Grace was gazing at the concrete forests on the outskirts of Toronto's Pearson Airport from her window seat on the bus. In mid-winter, the vast wilderness under the pale, blurred setting sun was dressed up in patches of snow and dreary dark woods, a colourless painting suggesting not vitality but desolation.

Lily glanced at Grace secretly. During their eight-year separation, Mother had aged. Her sparse hair had all turned gray and her fine fair skin was marred by lines and dark blemishes. But her mind was still sharp and her eyes shone with the same critical light as always.

"There got to be something good, or I wouldn't stay." Lily replied, her voice low and her toes squirming in her shoes.

"Like what?" Mother seemed eager to understand.

Lily became silent. For seconds, her mind was busy with floating images, including a creamy painted old house surrounded by blooming white lilies, the swing of a bell tolling in an ancient church tower against the blue sky, and a skinny bald-head looking solemn and lonely as he walked through the windy fields. The corner of her left eye became moist, somehow, and the images

1

faded, before Lily was able to come up with a clear answer to her mother's question.

Ever since Grace had retired from her position as the editor-in-chief of a Beijing magazine a couple of years ago, she had repeatedly suggested coming to Canada to visit Lily. Despite Lily's effort in finding various excuses to put off the visit, Grace ran out of patience and finally purchased a plane ticket.

Aside from the issue of what was good about Canada, Lily's immediate worry was that Mother was not going to tolerate her daughter's disgraceful status once the truth became known.

II

That test came soon enough. Shortly after Grace's arrival in Mapleton, a city 300 kilometres west of Toronto, all the myths Lily had so carefully woven began to unravel.

Early on Monday morning, as Lily hurried over her breakfast and prepared to leave home, Grace watched. She stared at Lily when she was putting on a pair of old sneakers and asked suspiciously, "What kind of people dress this way in Canada?"

Lily looked at her red and gray plaid shirt and blue jeans, and the flowery overcoat, all used items accumulated from various garage sales. She was ready to head to the government Human Resources Office in downtown Mapleton.

"Students, probably," she answered in hesitation and then added, "but people can dress any way they like, Mother. Nobody will laugh at you in this country."

Grace was not easy to fool. "They look down upon you in their hearts!" she sneered. "What has happened to you, that you have become such a worthless and incapable person who has no sense of shame?"

Instead of working as a secretary for a private company as she had claimed in her letters home, Lily had been unemployed since she'd had Baby. Grace would not settle for the explanation that Lily could not find any job in Canada suitable to her skills. Lily had two master's degrees and had been a journalist for the prestigious government news agency in Beijing. Grace had heard many successful stories about her friends' children who had come to North America. It was painful to know that Lily didn't even need to dress decently in public.

An unfamiliar sound drew Grace's attention to Baby, who was sitting on the floor and flipping the pages of a Chinese cartoon book. The two-year-old boy, fascinated by the book Grace had brought for him, was happily murmuring to himself. Grace frowned. The aversion in her face exposed her conclusion that the boy was the biggest hindrance to Lily's career advancement.

Baby sensed the unusual stare and raised his little round face. Young as he was, he seemed to understand that he was not appreciated by this newcomer. He quickly lowered his head and became silent.

When Lily came back home at noon looking dismayed, she avoided Grace's eyes and let out a tired sigh, "Didn't find any new posts suitable for me today."

Grace opened her eyes wide. "Not even a secretary's job?"

"They often told me that I was overqualified."

"It's true!" Grace nodded. "If you chose to do your PhD degree at the University of Toronto instead of having a child, your road would be wider now!"

Seeing Lily was silent, Grace continued, "I'll bring him back to Beijing when I leave, and send him to a boarding nursery so you can concentrate wholeheartedly on a suitable career, perhaps to start pursuing your PhD now."

Lily raised her eyebrows at the suggestion. "No, Mother! In Canada, people don't send their children away at such an early age. It could damage their psychological development."

"Don't worry about him. He is big enough. Besides, the boarding nurseries in Beijing have very competent staff, much more qualified than you are! Your precious son won't suffer abuse there," Grace added sarcastically.

"Mother, I don't want my son to suffer the same trauma I experienced when young." Lily looked seriously into Grace's eyes.

"Why do you think of it as suffering?" Grace's face reddened as she raised her voice. "The boarding school you went to was a privilege afforded only to high-ranking officials! It provided an excellent education and prepared children for a successful future!"

"That's just Chinese philosophy. If you ask Canadians here, they will tell you such an arrangement is cruel!"

"But you are not a Canadian!" Grace sneered. "If you don't want to send him to a boarding nursery, I can hire someone to take care of him at home."

"Nobody can give a child the same love as a mother," said Lily in a sad tone.

Grace fixed her eyes on Lily, realizing the changes that had taken place in her daughter after eight years.

In the evening before going to bed, Grace came to a final conclusion. "I am going to stay in Canada for a good while to help you, since you are a brainless girl who always needs guidance. I didn't have the time and patience when you were small. But I have the time now."

She looked away from Lily and stared at the dim light through the blue lampshade on the desk, adding slowly in an unusually soft tone, "Besides, I also have a long-cherished wish to fulfill."

"What wish?" Lily asked.

Lily sensed something solemn in her mother's wish. That mysterious feeling actually emerged even before Grace's arrival, with her anxious insistence on coming. But what could it be? She searched her mother's face again, but the glisten in Grace's eyes had slipped swiftly away before Lily had time to catch it again.

III

The first guidance Grace offered was to move the family into a one-bedroom apartment in the basement of the same building so they could manage their limited financial resources independently. Ever since her maternity leave benefit had run out, Lily had been on social assistance, which allowed her and Baby to afford a two-bedroom apartment in this old, cockroach-ridden building. That was an unacceptable disgrace in Grace's eyes.

"I didn't raise you up to be a shameless beggar!" she declared. "I'll help you regain your long-lost decency."

As soon as their "Moving Sale" notice appeared on the building entrance, a flow of recent immigrants started knocking on the door. They all lived in the same U-shaped, four-storey brick building, nicknamed the "refugee camp," of downtown Mapleton.

A black woman took the coffee table. Two brown men carried away the old sofa. An ample lady bought the mirror dresser. A white boy, after two hours' hesitation, dismantled the crib for his pregnant girlfriend.

Finally, only one customer was left. She was a Vietnamese grandma with high cheek bones. Bare-footed, she curled up one leg in the chair, leaving a dirty pair of slippers on the floor. She was a neighbour from the fourth floor, with a large family.

Lily assumed that she had been a peasant in Vietnam. Outside the back door of the building, between the narrow walkway and the building wall, lay a two-foot wide, ten-foot long vegetable garden and a moss-covered rain barrel. In the summer, she had bumped into the woman watering the fresh green leaves of a tropical vegetable called Chicken Feathers with a tin ladle.

Her sunken eyes searched the almost empty sitting room and finally focused on the dark-gray woollen jacket hanging by the door. It was Grace's jacket.

The woman spoke no English, so held up a finger, dry as the winter cherry twig in the yard, indicating her offer of one dollar. Lily shook her hand to indicate, "Not for sale."

Misreading the signal, the woman thought Lily was bargaining for more money. She waved her hand, tilted her face sideways, rolled her eyes, stuck out her lips, and made a sound of contempt in her throat.

Lily remembered the bargaining skills back home in the Chinese markets and repeated her "that jacket is not for sale" hand gesture.

The woman remained seated, her mouth tightly shut but her eyes revealing a stubborn resolve. Again, she held out her dry winter twig.

Lily shrugged at the language block. She murmured to Grace, "I used to communicate with her well. Last summer, when I showed curiosity about the vegetables she was growing outside, she pulled out a large handful of greens and gave it to me!"

Grace cut Lily off. "Oh, well, let her have the jacket! I don't want it anymore."

After the neighbour left in smiles, with the jacket tucked under her arm, Grace gave a snort of contempt. "Did you notice that she was rubbing her toes all the time? She must have the beriberi disease. She had already fingered my jacket when she first came in! Oh, such a disgusting place! And the life you have chosen!"

Baby chose that moment to give a loud grunt. Seeing the boy standing with his legs parted and his little face reddened, Grace realized the trouble he was creating and turned her face away.

While Lily was cleaning Baby and changing his diaper in the bathroom, Grace sank into the remaining chair and sighed heavily. "You should have stayed with Prince ..."

Her voice was not loud, but the words hit Lily like a metal rod. Her brain buzzed as a pair of watery black eyes on a pale face flashed through her mind. She bit her lip and kept silent.

Why should I stay with that man when Mother is fully aware of his problems? Why was it that Mother always had such high expectations for her own daughter but didn't seem to care much about the quality of a son-in-law? Lily thought in dismay.

Chapter 2
Prince Charming's Tale

I

Lily first met Prince at the university she attended in China years ago. He was so nicknamed because many rated him the most handsome guy on campus.

He impressed her with his shining black eyes and his showy air, like a red tomato in a pile of muddy potatoes. Many mornings after breakfast, she would hide behind the bushes near the pathway to the classroom building, reciting new English vocabulary while hoping to catch a glimpse of his shadow.

At the start of summer vacation that year, Lily was on the same train as Prince. Both were travelling home to Beijing. They sat face to face across a tiny tea table. He looked at Lily flirtatiously, chatted in an enchanting bass voice and smiled with the charisma of a mature man.

Lily was five years younger than he, and totally enraptured. She sat stiffly in her seat, feeling as if she were performing a drama for the first time on stage under a blazing spotlight. Seized by a fear of spoiling this precious encounter, she talked little and didn't move at all until it turned dark in the carriage and Prince fell sound asleep, his face buried in his arms on the small tea table.

The train whistled through a long tunnel inside the mountains, and Lily stretched her numb limbs and relaxed. She looked at her watch, surprised to find that more than ten hours had passed.

A neatly dressed old man sitting next to her offered her a mug of water. "Have some water, girl!" Noticing her hesitation, he smiled kindly and continued in a lowered voice. "Don't worry! This is my own mug and it's absolutely clean. I can see you are a Muslim, too. Am I right? Of course we don't use their dirty mugs. I have been watching you. You didn't eat or drink anything offered on the train. Good girl!"

He seemed happy to find a strictly disciplined and faithful young Muslim. Lily touched her dry lips and blushed at his mistake. She had been too nervous to ask for the boiled water offered by the train conductor. Thinking now about Prince's self-indulgent talking and carefree sipping at his mug while totally ignoring her awkwardness, she felt that the handsome star had been somewhat selfish and herself pitiable. She looked at the old man with the warm water in his hand but hesitated still.

There were millions of Chinese Muslims. In her childhood, she had heard funny stories about them, such as one about a young Chinese man who loved a Muslim girl and was forced to drink a gallon of soapy water to clean his pork-contaminated intestines before marriage was allowed.

Though she didn't want to hurt his feelings, she had to turn down the kind offer with an apologetic smile, feeling deeply sorry that she couldn't comfort the old soul by pretending to be a Muslim.

II

It wasn't long before she discovered the following fact: an attractive face, just like those on movie star posters, if looked at daily, soon becomes as plain and blank as the walls behind it. Only a beautiful soul can remain attractive forever. Unfortunately, such a simple truth needed to be experienced to be fully recognized.

Lily dated Prince for more than a year, but her desire to marry him eroded day by day. Once their relationship became public, she received a number of visits from weeping girls who told her sickening stories of his lust and sin.

The night after she had broken off her relationship with him, Prince came to her dormitory, quiet and gloomy faced. He poked a fruit knife into his left wrist. "Say you won't leave me!" he said through clenched teeth. The knife shone viciously, and the blood was crimson dark under the dim light bulb hanging from the ceiling.

She was seized by fear, mixed with a complicated satisfaction, at the unusual way he demonstrated his love.

While working as a government translator in Beijing, she spent all her leisure time preparing for the entrance exams for graduate studies at the famous school of journalism in the Chinese Academy of Social Sciences. She planned to forsake her ill-fated relationship once she moved to a new environment.

She passed the six preliminary tests and was shortlisted to go through a final test plus a "political screening."

In the past, candidates had to be from politically flawless families, and that requirement had deprived many of the chance to enter the school. But now, in the mid 1980s, the political climate had changed, and the moral standards had also changed to fit a more open China. The school would screen out only those who had committed theft or adultery or had been involved with foreigners.

One young man, who had earned the highest marks in the preliminary tests, was dropped from the candidates' list after a background check reported that he had fallen in love four times with different girls during his university years.

Another candidate was dropped after his secret dossier, which was established for every Chinese citizen at age 18, revealed that he had sneaked into a hospital and peeped into the obstetrics ward to satisfy his curiosity about female bodies, when nothing like *Penthouse* or *Playboy* was available in China.

The most shocking news story was about a young girl. She had been observed by her neighbours holding dance parties in her home attended by people whose skin colours exposed them as non-Chinese. After being dropped from the candidates' list, she committed suicide.

Lily was terrified when news came that the school's admission committee had received an anonymous letter accusing her of having been the mistress of an American instructor back in her undergraduate years.

III

Lily had not even felt attracted to that hairy, bear-shaped American, whose square chest was at least twice the size as that of most Chinese men.

After China established diplomatic relations with the U.S., the man came in the early 1980s as the first foreigner ever to teach at Lily's university. The government paid him 600 yuan monthly to help improve the students' English. He was proud of his value as a "foreign expert," and boasted that he made more than Deng Xiaoping did. Indeed, the salary of the president of China then was 400 yuan.

But the foreign expert totally smashed the Hollywood image of the Western gentleman in everyone's mind, acquired through popular movies such as *The Sound of Music* and *Roman Holiday* introduced into China in the 1980s.

Lily blushed when the American bear asked how many girl students on campus were virgins. "Ninety-nine percent, at least," she answered, wondering why he wanted to know that.

"The Chinese government has cheated me!" the stout bear declared angrily, after learning that pre-marital sex and prostitutes were all forbidden. "China is a Puritan society! No one informed me of this before I came!"

After teaching his classes in American history and literature, the bear would practice weightlifting for hours at the sports ground, making loud and creepy roaring sounds the whole time the campus was quiet for the after-lunch nap. When asked why he tortured himself this way, he compared himself to a boiling teapot, using exaggerated gestures to convey his point to the surrounding audience. "The steam has to come out when it's boiling. Understand?"

Many students sneered at this foreign teapot theory and nicknamed him "the Flower Monk," meaning a lewd bachelor. They whispered in wonder, was it true that white men couldn't live without women?

To comfort the lonely bear, however, the school authorities discussed strategies for finding him a suitable wife.

At their initial suggestion that he should have a haircut and get his dirty jacket cleaned, the bear threw a sidelong glance and asked, "For whom should I look neat?" He also laughed out loud at their comment that he was old enough at age thirty-four to get married.

In the winter holidays, he flew to Japan, stayed there for three weeks and returned to school, declaring that his jaw was sore from too much kissing.

Despite the scandals surrounding the American bear, Lily treasured the rare opportunity of having a native English instructor, who was acknowledged by all as the best in the whole province. She took every opportunity to practice her spoken English with him, including accompanying him on trips to the post office and market place. She earned the best marks in all his classes.

When the bear left China a year later, he left all his English novels, scarce in China then, to her alone. He explained, "I would peep into the window and always found you studying alone in the classroom after lunchtime, when everyone else went to their dormitories to nap."

IV

The anonymous letter was clearly a result of jealousy. But the admission committee sent out a three-person team to investigate. The team travelled to all the places where Lily had stayed to ferret out any traces of immorality or treasonous activity in her history. The committee also called Lily in for an interview.

The atmosphere in the room was threatening and Lily felt her back wet with cold sweat as she awaited the first question.

"Could you describe what kind of person you are?"

"Someone with big ambitions but poor talents to achieve them," she said, knowing well that the culture regarded modesty as an important virtue.

After the interview, Lily was on pins and needles for two months before she finally received a letter of admission. Though the investigation found no evidence of her ever being immoral, the school authority warned her to be on guard about future activities, or she would be dismissed immediately.

Grace, having shared with Lily the acute anxiety of this period, was still worried. Grace well understood that Lily was no longer in love with Prince, but a breakup during this sensitive period would certainly jeopardize her career.

"You have to marry him, I am afraid," Grace's voice sounded reluctant, but firm. "Or the school will believe the accusation that you are an immoral person."

On their way to the government's office for marriage registration, Lily walked silently with Prince. As the heavy red gate above the stone steps came into sight, she had an urge to run away; the red gate seemed to her the entrance to a jail where she was to be locked up.

Prince, with a degree in political science, had been assigned to work as a clerk in a government office. His everyday work consisted of dining, dancing, partying, or having empty chats with other staff. At dinnertime, news of such activities would force its way into Lily's ears.

"I attended a social ball today at China's Friendship Association. Mr. Chang surprised everyone! He is in his sixties, but he's so good at the waltz and foxtrot! Oh, it made us young people ashamed!"

Or he'd describe a convention at the Great Hall of the People, complete with dragon livers, phoenix gallbladder, bear paws, and young stag's antler. Lily felt bad seeing Prince caught up in such shallow concerns. Once in a while, she would invite him to revise the articles she had written in the hope that he would shift his focus to something more worthwhile. But the awkward "golden touches" he left on her articles disappointed her even more.

At night, Prince would try to warm her up in bed by whispering lustful words in her ear. She would get gooseflesh all over as his fingers touched her skin and his wet lips smeared her cheek. The sight of the dark, ugly, filthy stuff between his legs made her sick, too. "It seems you know nothing else except how to get women into bed!" she grumbled.

Prince simply grinned at her complaints, his white teeth shining in the dark.

One day he came home with a new revelation.

"I bumped into an attractive woman today. She glanced at me as I went by. I don't know whether my clothes or my face drew her attention. Well, it must have been my hat, which is indeed unique with brown flannel and eight corners. Gee, the woman was so beautiful! I have never seen her before. I wonder which office she works in ..." Prince murmured all this while looking into a hand mirror and smoothing his shining black hair with his fingertips.

When he noticed Lily still concentrating on her newspaper, he carried on in an intoxicated tone. "She was quite tall. I made a rough estimate—she comes about up to my eyebrows. She was in a light gray cashmere sweater, and her breasts looked big. Her tight blue jeans hugged her bottom, which was as round as the westerners."

Lily's tolerance reached its end. "What else do you know, beside breasts and bottoms? Go to anyone you like, but don't bother me with such rubbish! I hope someone is merciful enough to take you away and leave me in peace!"

After that evening, Lily spent more time in the library, reading the literary works that had been mushrooming in the more liberal era. Gradually, she found herself seized by a new writer whose poetic style, laden with deep grief and sorrow, touched the most reclusive part of her heart.

While reading, her mind would naturally flow to a shadowy man whom she had tried hard to forget but never could. That was her father, a man jailed as a political prisoner and sent to a labour camp before Lily came into the world.

In bed, Lily would open her eyes wide and stare at the darkness. She imagined the man, whose face was always blurred, standing alone on top of a remote hill and gazing at geese flying south in the cloudless blue sky. She pictured him sitting on a rock looking pensively at the torrential Amur River, or writing at a crude simple table in an isolated hut. Before his starving body was frozen by snowstorms in the Siberian forest, had he ever dreamed of reuniting with his wife and embracing the daughter he had never seen?

When Prince approached her, she pushed him aside and talked about the stories written by the new author, whom she learned was a paralyzed man in a wheelchair.

"If only I were still single!" she concluded with a sigh.

"Don't forget the fact that he has no legs," said the man lying beside her.

"A man with a retarded body can be more attractive than a man with a retarded mind."

There echoed a dry laughter in the darkness. "If you had to clean up his dirty pants and lift him out of bed every day, I would like to see how much interest you had left in discussing literature with him!"

Common sense told Lily he might be right, but she had a reputation among her acquaintances as a star always seeking out unusual orbits.

V

By the mid 1980s, China had become even more influenced by the Western wind. Lily felt it was time to ask for a divorce, as suspicions aroused by the anonymous letter had died down with her dogged effort to appear as a woman of integrity.

Prince's face twisted. "You should never have gotten married in the first place if you want a divorce!"

"Then why is there a section on divorce in the state's marriage law?" Lily responded.

When she raised the issue again, he put a fruit knife on the desk. "Do you remember this? If you insist on divorce, there will be only death left for me this time! Tell me, should I end my worthless life right away?"

Lily gave a disdainful glance at the knife. Her thoughts flew to the day when she lost her virginity to this man.

It was during a summer vacation. Prince came every day for a whole month, pestering her with his desire. She had resisted until the issue became so tiring that she dropped her guard near the end of the hot season.

Deeply carved into her brain were the tearing pain, the pool of blood, her miserable cry, and the overwhelming regret. More distressing in her memory were the man's pretentious sorrow and clumsy show.

"I am so sorry, so sorry," he said amid her heartbroken sobbing, his hands holding his ugly organ. "It was all its fault! I will cut it off immediately! Can you find me a knife?"

Her aversion towards this man intensified as she caught his eyes avoiding the open kitchen door, where a big shining knife lay on the cutting board. Why not go and get it yourself! she thought in hatred.

The man was playing the same trick now. But she had matured. She folded her arms and focused her eyes on the white wall, where a fan of thirty-six peacock feathers displayed their dark-green silky spots. It had been a wedding gift just a year before.

The air in the room was stuffy. The man was hurt by her silence and look. "Fine, I am not going to scare you with blood. Shall I climb up your school's tall chimney and then jump, or shall I throw myself into the Imperial Lake so that my corpse remains in one piece? You make the choice!"

Lily examined him for a few seconds. "If you really want to die, and die heroically, I have a good suggestion for you. Last week I was asked to cover the story of a hero who is the first man ever to try to drift down the whole course of the Yellow River. He gave up halfway when he reached the notorious Dragon-Goat Gorge, where nobody so far has survived the rapids. You could go directly to the Dragon-Goat Gorge. I am sure you would create sensational news and become much more famous than that hero!"

He suddenly knelt down on the floor, held her knees, and started to cry: "Don't torture me anymore! To be or not to be, it's all because I can't live without you!"

Such words are sharper than any knife, any sword. Lily shut her eyes, and dropped the divorce issue again.

Prince had recognized the challenge of living with a sensitive woman and became more cautious.

He did almost all the household chores, cooking, washing, cleaning, and shopping, without being asked. In the hot summer, when Lily entered the yard on her bicycle, her face covered with dust and sweat, the man would rush out of the room, take the bike and lock it up for her. In freezing winter, when Lily came home covered in frost, he would immediately put a large mug of hot tea in her hands. Lily was fond of green leafy vegetables. At table, the man's chopsticks would never touch the dish of delicious greens near her plate, but left them all for her.

Lily felt guilty at those moments. Still, it was hard for her drifting soul to find peace.

VI

That was the era when the old Hollywood movies were rushing into China's opening door. One day when *Spartacus* was shown in the theatre, Lily vied with many people to get tickets, and finally was lucky in obtaining two. Prince joined her late that afternoon and they watched the movie with more than a thousand others in the audience.

Lily was deeply drawn to Kirk Douglas, who played the role of the leader of a slave uprising. When the movie was over, the couple walked out of the theatre in the stream of people. Lily was still lost in the heroic ending of the movie when the heroine, holding a baby, bids farewell to her dying husband who was nailed on the Roman cross.

Lily yearned to talk about the movie with someone. She looked at Prince. Always careful to make himself presentable in public, he hadn't neglected anything today either. He was neatly dressed, his back straight, his expression thoughtful.

He must also be moved by such a masterpiece, Lily thought. Just as she opened her mouth to make a comment, Prince touched her hips. Still looking straight ahead to keep his graceful manner, he said in a low voice: "Please get my bike for me." He raised his finger, pointing at the sidewalk a few yards ahead, packed with dozens of bicycles.

Lily's first reaction was disappointment that he wasn't even thinking about the wonderful movie. Then she felt strange. The man had never asked her to do errands for him. What was wrong today? She stopped and looked at Prince in confusion.

Prince put the key in her hand and urged her once again. "See it? It's under the tree."

Lily brought the bike over to him. When they reached the place where she had left her bike, she voiced her curiosity. "Why wouldn't you get your own bike?"

Prince explained patiently, "Didn't you notice that the sidewalk in front of the theatre is covered with fine sand? I saw it when I locked my bike there." He lowered his head and looked at his feet. Lily noticed that he was wearing a pair of bright white shoes. "I put on my new Nikes today. I don't want to get sand on them. It takes time to get it out."

As if someone had poured a bucket of cold water over her, all her passion vanished in a second. I am a fool indeed, Lily thought. How can I expect such a trivial man to be interested in discussing a tragedy?

Without comment, Lily rode away on her bike, leaving the confused man to scramble for his own bike. She hated to go home. Living under the same roof with such a man seemed unbearable. She bicycled around the city for hours through lighted avenues and dark lanes, Prince trailing behind her. When she rode faster, he would accelerate. When she slowed down, he would reduce his speed, always keeping a distance between them.

Around midnight, the whole city seemed to have fallen asleep. She came to the Forbidden City. She got off her bike and walked to the top of the marble bridge in front of the magnificent Imperial Gate, where Mao's huge portrait observed what was going on in the world without him.

Looking over the railing, she saw the dark water flowing silently underneath. Turning around, she spotted the man's shadow hiding behind the marble column about twenty yards away. She seemed to catch a cynical smile on his lean cheeks and felt annoyed. Why won't he come over and talk me into going home? The man is too weak to face challenges, or too lazy to figure things out. So the easiest way is just to wait for me to get tired and give up my protest.

She felt trapped. The world was large, yet there was nowhere to escape. She looked up at Mao's portrait hanging high above, but felt uneasy with those penetrating eyes seemingly staring back at her. At that moment, a couple of soldiers guarding the Square appeared from nowhere and questioned her. "What's your purpose lingering here at such a late hour?"

Early the next morning, Lily got on her bicycle and rode towards the north end of the city. The summer breeze tangled her long hair and flicked her light gray skirt, but soothed her disturbed heart.

Should I pretend I'm here for an interview, or tell him honestly that I have been admiring him for a long time? No, I can't let him know that I love him. As a married woman, it is shameful to declare that.

Lily's slim figure darted like a little fish through the old, narrow lanes. Her hand knocked at one wooden door after another in the area crowded with century-old flats. All shook their heads. Nobody had ever spotted a paralyzed writer in a wheelchair around the neighbourhood.

By the time the sun had risen high in the sky, Lily stood in disappointment by the street. Her courage melted in the smothering heat. She felt at a loss, surrounded by a world too materialistic and practical. Deep inside her, there had always been a thirst. But thirst for what? She wasn't quite sure.

VII

With exposure to more and more Hollywood movies and English magazines, many educated young Chinese sought to enlarge their perspective by studying abroad. Adventurous curiosity plus a wish to escape her life pushed Lily to join the current. While most of her friends selected the U.S., she was the only one focusing her eyes on the country Dr. Norman Bethune was from.

The Canadian doctor's name was known to almost every Chinese citizen ever since he died in 1939. His image as an ideal man somehow entered Lily's mind one night when she was a twenty-year-old young girl watching a movie about the Canadian man's life in China.

She felt deeply attracted to the man devoting himself to help the poor and the needy, during wartime. Many years had gone by since then, but she still remembered clearly that moonlit night when she stood alone in the very back of the open area where the movie was being shown to hundreds of industrial workers. It was the first time in her life she had felt a light feather brushing her bosom gently and wondered if that was the feeling of love.

After receiving a scholarship from a Canadian university, she busied herself in the exhausting battle to acquire a passport and visa. Since the government had strict control over highly educated people leaving China, bribery and debasement were required. She had sent cartons of cigarettes to the official who stamped permission letters to apply for a passport. She had also played the uncomfortable role of trying to be charming and flattering to a

Chinese soldier standing on guard at the entrance of the Canadian embassy, in order to get in and apply for her visa.

Prince begged to come to Canada with her.

"What's the point of you going there?" Lily said. "You are not interested in academic study."

"At least I can take care of you."

She looked at him with pity. Living under the same roof with him had never been part of her plan once outside of China. But she had always been aware of his strong wish to live abroad. Since being a student was almost the only way to leave China then, she promised to help him get accepted into an English language school in Canada.

Lily purchased her airplane ticket with all her savings. She scanned the set of furniture in the room, which still looked new, less than two years old, and told Prince to sell everything before he would leave. The money from the sale, she estimated, should be enough to buy him a one-way ticket to Canada.

When all had been arranged, Lily packed her suitcase hastily. Two hours before she went to the airport, Grace showed up. "Your going to North America is my dream come true!" she said, her eyes moist with a bittersweet happiness.

Chapter 3
Canadian Experience

I

With Mother now in Mapleton by her side providing free babysitting, Lily was able to focus on her job search. Within two weeks, she was hired as Warehouse Manager in a garment factory run by a Chinese man from Hong Kong.

Grace had become anxious watching Lily going out every morning to the employment centre and returning home empty-handed. As her expectations fell, the title of "Manager" sounded fairly attractive, despite the fact it was of a warehouse.

The next morning, Grace rose early, prepared breakfast and a lunch box for Lily, and watched as she pedalled away on her bicycle.

Lily soon figured out that the title of "Manager" was a trick, but she still worked hard in the warehouse, following the boss's order to keep her mouth shut like a docile mule. While sorting and piling up different sizes of jeans, she reminded herself constantly that this boring, back-breaking labour for minimum pay was free physical exercise, besides bringing bread to the table for the family.

Even so, she received a surprising notice at the end of the second week. "Fired!" just one plain word.

Grace's voice trembled with anger. "What? Fired? From such a job as that?! Why?"

Lily shook her head. Inside, she knew why.

All shop-floor employees had their purses checked before leaving the factory every day, in case they were stealing cloth. When she heard from her co-workers at lunchtime about this unwritten regulation, Lily found it hard to believe.

"Isn't Canada known as a country with one of the highest standards of human rights? It's insulting!" she declared.

"Lower your voice!" The Indian woman who worked as a sewer warned her, and whispered, "The video monitor watches everywhere, including the lunch corner."

At the end of the day, people were lining up by the exit. Lily watched with a heavy heart as the women, all new immigrants, opened their purses one by one for the factory owner.

It was her turn. Lily had made up her mind to challenge such humiliating treatment. Without looking at that morose face, Lily walked straight towards the door, head held high.

"You forgot to have your purse checked!" the Indian woman called from behind.

"I know!" Lily ignored the boss's frozen gaze and left.

That must be the reason, she figured. I was singled out as the black sheep and fired to prevent the spread of some dangerous thought among the docile donkeys.

II

Lily's wounded pride was soon healed when she found another job the next day.

The fashionable lady with a European accent welcomed Lily with a lovely smile. She showed her the kitchen in the century-old building in downtown Mapleton.

"Don't worry! I have plenty of jobs for you. You can decide how many hours you would like to work. The kitchen has never been thoroughly cleaned since I bought the inn twenty years ago. You can clean up the grease in here every morning until the kitchen staff arrives. Then," the European woman continued, leading Lily into a narrow, dark corridor and pointing out a few rooms, "you can shift to this area and clean those rooms."

It was hard to believe that the kitchen had escaped a cleaning for only twenty years. The thick layers of grease suggested centuries of cooking. Lily sweated for hours, but the result was hardly visible. Looking at the palm-sized shining island amid the dark grease on the stove surface, she rubbed her numb wrist. She wondered how long it would take her to make the huge kitchen area as shiny as the tiny island. Becoming a financially independent person now seemed illogical, if it meant she had to contribute to society this way.

A lyrical whistle circling around the ceiling cut off her thoughts. A young white man entered the kitchen, greeted Lily, and started banging things around. The deadly kitchen became alive with the cook's pleasant chat. "Are you Chinese?" he talked while taking meats out from the fridge. "I know how to cook oriental food, too, tofu, bok choy and lo bok ..."

The rooms along the hall were fairly clean compared with the kitchen. Yet the shock of the kitchen was mild compared to her experience in the hall one day.

Stepping into the hallway, she bumped into a blonde girl, naked from head to toe, standing by the door and chatting with a man in a carefree manner. The young cook, whose room was next door to hers, joined their conversation in a matter of fact way as if the girl was fully dressed. From the wide open door of the next room, Lily saw a purple-headed woman, also naked, sitting on the chair with her legs spread carelessly, smoking a cigarette.

Lily hurried down the staircase to the bar area and mentioned her discovery to the inn owner.

"Oh, dear! I told them not to bring clients to their rooms, but they don't listen! They are going to make trouble for me!" the European lady grumbled loudly, her eyes avoiding Lily.

Lily realized that the inn had a dance floor and that she had been cleaning strippers' rooms.

One late afternoon she sneaked into the dance room after work, her heart pounding fast with guilt. There she saw the purple-head exposing all her private parts to the curiosity of a few shouting drunkards. The girl's heavily rouged face remained cool as she leaped and spun to the loud music, inches from the grasping hands.

Lily's body stiffened as she watched. She could not understand why such evil would be allowed to exist in a beautiful country like Canada. The Chinese Communist Party had solved this social problem efficiently in the early 1950s. Over a thousand prostitutes in Beijing were arrested overnight, forced to give up their drug addiction, taught how to read and write, and then trained in production skills or matched with workers who were too poor to afford other wives.

When still in school, she heard from a professor that Canada had once benefited from a similar efficiency. About 200 years ago the French, killing two birds with one stone, cleaned up the streets of Paris and shipped the prostitutes to Canada to marry the farmers.

The more democratic a country becomes, the more difficult it seems to solve such social problems, she thought.

The next morning, Lily apologized to the purple-head as she came to clean her room. "I hope you don't mind that I watched you."

Purple-head shrugged indifferently. "I don't care."

"Can't you find any other profession?" Though hesitating, the words finally came out of Lily's mouth.

"Not one that pays so well." Purple-head noticed the sympathetic look in Lily's eyes and added, "I make more than 4,000 dollars a month. How much do you make?"

Lily was wordless, stunned. Expressing genuine sorrow to the warm-hearted inn owner, Lily quit the job the next day.

III

With more Canadian experience in her resume now, Lily quickly found work at a five-star hotel which was only half an hour's bicycle ride from her home. By comparison with the last place, the Crystal Palace struck Lily as a normal operation.

"Are you also a doctor?" the Jamaican lady asked, as she showed Lily how to tug the sheet properly underneath the mattress. On the first day, Lily had been assigned to the black woman for training.

"Why a doctor?" Lily was surprised at her question.

The Jamaican giggled. "We've already got five doctors from China working here, so I figured you must be the sixth."

Lily met the other five Chinese women at lunchtime. Two of them had been family physicians, one a pediatrician, and one a gynecologist. The oldest Chinese woman had a PhD in Earth Science. Like Lily, she had concealed her degrees to join the cleaning team.

Looking at the lack of expression on the faces around her, Lily saw her own image in the other people's eyes, particularly in that of the job interviewers. She suddenly realized why she was rated as "overqualified" for clerical positions. That characteristic unemotional look, with no trace of sunshine smiles, was suitable only for out-of-sight work, never at the front desk.

The Jamaican was indeed a good trainer. "Look! This way! No, you can't simply bend over. You've got to kneel on the floor and stretch your arms deep underneath the mattress to tug the sheets in tightly. Then they will not come off whatever the guests do in the beds. If you don't do it properly, the manager will ask you to do it again! If you don't learn fast, they might let you go!"

Seeing that Lily was not scared by her warning, the Jamaican admitted, "Well, I know, you Chinese are all intelligent and smart. This is only a temporary position for you. Sooner or later, you will all leave." She said, not looking at Lily, but throwing an empty stare at the blank wall.

The hotel's cleaning women were of three colours: yellow, white, and black. The Chinese staff, as the Jamaican said, were constantly moving, with some leaving and new ones joining every few months or even weeks, but the two white women had been at the hotel for years. A glance at them would convince people that the hotel was a charitable institution. One was a single mother, dumped by her man after her horizontal diameter surpassed her vertical one. The other was a silent lady with hollow cheeks and a glazed look in her eyes but no teeth. Lily felt strong sympathy for this lady after hearing whispers that her only son had committed suicide as a teenager. Her efforts to warm up the cold heart received no response, however, not even a glare.

It was hard for Horizontal-Great, sweating all over, to keep up with the others with the vacuum and bottles of cleaning chemicals. Lily would bend down to help her clean a bathtub when she had finished her own tasks. She had seen many people of similar size in Canada and was always curious why they would let this happen.

"Have you ..." she raised the question cautiously, "have you ever tried to eat less?"

Horizontal-Great was not irritated. "Of course I have," she replied between gasps. "But even if I drank water only, I would still be this way. It's in the genes."

The black workers seemed to be reliable long-time employees, regardless of their age, size, looks, and educational backgrounds.

When Lily praised the Jamaican's good English, her full lips trembled: "I studied child psychology in a college back home. My mother never taught me how to clean the bathtub and toilet. She expected her first daughter to be a teacher. I know she would be heartbroken if she found out what I am doing in Canada."

This reminded Lily of Grace's sad face. Her high expectations for Lily must now have been defeated by cruel reality. Despite the heavy feeling, Lily tried to look for the positive sides of working in a hotel. The lunchroom was always the hot spot. The cleaning women wasted no time during the half-hour break, gorging on the greasy and sugar-rich delicacies prepared for the hotel guests, with only two dollars deducted from their paycheques.

However, two weeks after Lily had enjoyed the exotic western dishes which she had hardly ever had a chance to taste before, she was shocked to notice that she had gained five pounds. The next day at lunch, she forced herself to ignore the tempting Italian pastas and walked directly to the fruit bowl.

She scanned all the fruits and found no perfect beauty. Probably leftovers from the hotel guests' dinner table the night before, she realized. As she picked up a green apple, she heard Horizontal-Great saying beside her, "That one has a bruise."

"But it also deserves a chance to be loved, doesn't it?" Lily responded.

Horizontal-Great gave her an understanding smile.

When they sat at the table and started eating, Horizontal-Great suddenly asked, "Didn't you ever get married?" Seeing the surprised look in Lily's face, she added, "You wear no rings on your fingers."

Glancing at the rings on Horizontal-Great's hand, Lily said, "It is not the Chinese culture to wear a ring to indicate your marital status. Women in China do not change their family names after their marriages, either. I met a Canadian professor who tried for years to get rid of her husband but had to keep his name even after the divorce, because she had academic publications under that name and didn't want people to forget her."

The Jamaican got her plate of food and sat by their table. "Today is my birthday. It's my sixth birthday in Canada. But I am not in the mood to celebrate," she said with a sigh. She lived with her two toddlers, after having kicked out her abusive partner with the help of the feminist organizations in town.

Lily looked at her clouded eyes, unsure what to say to comfort her.

"I have an idea!" announced Horizontal-Great. She put down her fork and lit a cigarette. "A new group is performing in the male strip club downtown. They are all handsome French boys from Montreal, I've heard. Why not celebrate your birthday there this evening?"

The Jamaican was thrilled. "Do you know how to get there, Lily? No? I'll draw you a map!" She jumped up from her seat and searched around the room for paper and a pen.

"Sorry. I am not going to that sort of place. Male strippers? How shameful!" Lily shook her head. She glanced at the other Chinese women sitting around, and saw no responses except from the gynecologist.

"I have long been tired of looking at human bodies, male or female. Not too much difference from a piece of meat." She joked and exchanged eye contact with the geophysicist and the family physicians. Lily could see how hard they were trying to conceal their contempt for such an idea.

"Come on, Lily. It'll be fun!" Horizontal-Great shouted with an encouraging wave and a suck on her cigarette. "You've got to enjoy life!"

"I am afraid it's not something I would enjoy." Lily decided to speak her mind. "To be honest, I would feel sad for those poor guys, making a living by abusing their parents' dignity!"

"Oh, no!" Horizontal-Great looked righteous, stubbing out her cigarette in the ashtray. "The men make fun of us. Why can't we make fun of them?"

The next morning, the Jamaican described every detail of their evening fun. She giggled and laughed, imitated and exaggerated, her dull look replaced by a youthful glow.

"The French guys are so handsome! They don't have any fat, but muscles all over! They took off their underwear and threw it into the audience. Were there many in the audience? Sure! There were people from the States, too! Only Canada allows them to take it all off! Too bad you missed it! One of the guys put a pair of sun glasses on his penis, which was erect of course, and moved his penis carefully up and down so the glasses stayed on! Oh, it was amazing! All the women threw money at him. And then he put the glasses on the nose of a white woman in the very front! ..."

"Did she take offence?" Lily asked.

"Offence?" the Jamaican stared at her. "I don't understand what's inside your Chinese mind!"

Chapter 4
Mother's Sorrow

I

On Saturday afternoon, Lily finished her shift early. As she and her colleagues took turns working on the weekends, tomorrow she was going to stay home and rest.

Before leaving, she turned down a hotel guest's invitation for dinner that evening. The man, who had emigrated from Germany twenty years ago, bragged about being the landscape supervisor for the government of a small city near Toronto.

"Remember, your own people are the last ones to help you!" His beer-tinted eyes gleamed as he warned Lily. "Come and look for me in the summer! I will pay you nine dollars an hour!"

His words reminded Lily of the cloth factory owner, the guy from Hong Kong. Nine dollars an hour sounded unbelievably high, plus his warm smile. Lily was considering the offer when she noticed the German winking at his male friend. She thought about his earlier comment that she "has a lovely moon face" and suddenly felt sick, as if finding a dead fly in her colourful salad plate. She walked away, leaving the winking guys behind.

"They must think we are brainless, easy prey!" commented the Jamaican.

Despite this unpleasant incident, Lily comforted herself on the way home by thinking that no matter how late she got home from work these days, there was always a hot meal ready on the table for her. Mother was making quick progress in learning how to use the oven, something never seen in households in China. One day she even baked a pizza. Though the look and taste were unique, with all kinds of vegetables mixed on top of a thick, burnt crust, Lily nodded to encourage her mother's efforts.

To allow Lily to live "cleanly," as Grace put it, she took over the heavy task of taking care of Baby when Lily was at work, so they would not have to apply for a childcare subsidy.

It always took Grace quite a while to get Baby's diaper on securely. She was convinced that he was not a smart boy at all, for children in China, she said, were all toilet trained before their first birthday. She also grumbled a lot about his mysterious silence. At two and a half, Baby was not talking yet. Grace found it hard to give him instructions.

"I cannot tell if he understands or not," she complained to Lily. "When I ask him to do or not to do certain things, he pays no attention at all, not even looking at me, as if he doesn't understand Chinese. But when I talk with you and happen to mention something about him, even though I don't say his name, he stops playing all of a sudden and stares at me."

Grace had little experience in handling babies. Lily had been sent away to her grandma as a one-month-old and didn't return to her mother's side until she was four. It was the same with her two younger siblings.

"As an intellectual woman, you are not supposed to waste your time on such worthless trivia," Grace had explained to Lily. "I am sacrificing myself to help you stand up! Once you are on the right track and can afford to send him to daycare, I will return to Beijing!"

Mother's plans always sound optimistic, Lily thought, with a heavy heart, while riding home on her old bicycle. "But do I have the ability to fulfill her wishes?"

As she went through the narrow entrance to the yard of their U-shaped building, she bumped into a man. He was eye-catching, dressed in the traditional black loose suit with tied trouser legs and handmade black cotton shoes, with a two-foot long knife slung across his back. It was her neighbour, Master Iron. He was obviously going to his workshop. They nodded at each other as they passed through.

The dark-skinned man with shoulder-length hair was one of the few Chinese living in the U-shaped building. He was, however, undoubtedly the most famous, because he was a coach at the Mapleton Kung Fu Academy.

The *Mapleton Gazette* had written about this man, who was regarded as a local celebrity. As a kung fu practitioner from China, he had played major roles in a few kung fu movies in the 1970s and 80s. Rumours had it that the master had had to escape China illegally since his martial skills were considered national treasures. Though he was not able to return to his homeland due to his betrayal, he seemed satisfied at establishing a school in Mapleton where he made a living teaching martial arts.

Lily had bumped into him a few times in the yard. He was often accompanied by a few of his fair-skinned disciples. Out of curiosity, Lily once approached him to chat. Master Iron gestured carelessly to his disciples and blurted out something vaguely English-sounding. A female disciple, dressed the same way as he, nodded politely, took a card out of her handbag, and passed it to Lily. Lily read it carefully and found more than ten titles printed under Master Iron's name, including "Prof. Iron," "President Iron," and "Dr. Iron." She felt that the world was becoming so title-obsessed that even martial arts practitioners were forced to follow suit.

Now as she watched Master Iron leaving for his work, in full confidence and with joyful steps, she started to wonder if she had made a mistake spending too many years in school reading empty theories instead of learning something practical.

II

While locking her bike inside the building entrance, Lily heard Baby crying in the basement apartment. She hurried in, opened the door, and found Baby sitting on the floor.

"What's wrong? What's happened?" She held him and tried to wipe away his tears. Once in his mother's arms, Baby cried even louder. Lily patted his back to comfort him.

Grace came out of the kitchen, a white apron around her waist, looking angry. "I found him opening the fridge door and touching the food inside. I dragged him away from the fridge only to find him doing the same thing a moment later. To teach him a lesson, I hit him!"

"Where did you hit him?" Lily asked in a shocked voice.

Grace was clearly annoyed at the question. "Where? Are you worried that I have damaged him? Don't I even have the right to educate him? You are simply spoiling a cheap thing as if it were a treasure!" She paused for a second. Seeing Lily kissing away Baby's tears, she sneered, "Sick! I feel sick to see you doing that sort of thing!"

Lily's hands shook. Then she realized that Grace had never kissed any of her own children and must feel uncomfortable at this scene.

"Mom, I think it is reasonable for a child to want to find out what's in the fridge. As a mother, I wouldn't stop him!" She tried to talk calmly but her voice rose higher.

Grace was even more irritated. "I would never have imagined that you could have declined so fast! You have forgotten all my expectations, wasted all your education, and abandoned your career simply to be a mother! But that job doesn't need any talent! Even a hen can carry it out perfectly!"

"Yes, even a hen knows how to protect her chicks, but not all mothers know how to love their children!"

"Aha," Grace gave a cold laugh. "You know how to love your son? You think I don't love you? That's because you don't understand what true love is about! A real mother cares most about her child's future. She will do everything to help the child fly high in the sky like an eagle, and not just hold the child in her arms giving kisses! Sick! It makes me sick!"

"If you don't like children, why did you give birth to us?"

"It wasn't my choice. I'd rather not have had any!"

Lily stayed stiff for a while before she decided to speak her real feelings: "Mom, how do you think we felt to be sent away so young, with the excuse that you had to devote all your time and energy to your career development?"

Lily paused for a second. Seeing Grace looking away, she went on. "You sent the three of us kids to boarding schools and nurseries and we saw you only once a week, once a month, or even at one point once in four years!"

"What was wrong with that?" Grace fought back. "You were trained to be independent from childhood on!"

"But you didn't even know what might have happened to me as a little child! You always complained that I was so skinny and looked yellowish but refused to eat any meat and oily food provided at the boarding school's canteen. I think I might have been suffering from hepatitis disease for years as a child."

Grace looked stunned for a second, but quickly denied it. "No! It was impossible! That was a first class school and any child's problem would be quickly noticed, if you had any."

Lily shrugged. "There were hundreds of children there. Who would notice if you had an appetite or not except the child's parents!"

"Had you had any serious disease, the school would certainly have notified me!" Grace argued. "Remember you were sent home once when you had a high fever?"

"Of course I didn't forget it. I was in Grade 2 then. My teacher took me home and phoned you. You came back, your face so impatient. You grumbled that you were so busy with your work and that I was sick at the wrong time. I felt so guilty that I didn't dare to tell you I had vomited a large amount of blood while lying in the school's separation room alone. Afterwards, you told me at least twice that you hated anyone being sick, since you believed that people claiming to be sick were just looking for attention. Now you often blame me for not sharing my thoughts with you. But you don't understand that this estrangement was formed right from my infancy."

Grace was bitterly hurt by her words. "Are you denying my whole life? Are you declaring that I am not a loving mother?" She pointed her finger at Lily. "Do you understand why I came to Canada, leaving your aged father at home unattended? For whom am I suffering this sort of life in this old, shabby building? You are such an ungrateful thing! My life was totally destroyed ever since I had you!"

Seeing her mother trembling, Lily became scared. "No! Mom, I didn't mean that! I have always hoped that we could share our true feelings with each other honestly. I don't want to follow the same path as you. I chose to be a mother before it was too late. I want to take care of my son when he is little and vulnerable and most needs a mother's attention. I believe that being a mother is certainly more meaningful than being the president of a country! I don't want a career if it only represents vanity and is meant to create jealousy!"

"Vanity?" Grace's fire was once again flaring up. "You were born during a time of sexual equality and you don't appreciate all the opportunities you have been enjoying! If I didn't work and earn enough income of my own, I couldn't have sent you to the first-class school to get a good education! You let me down! A pity!"

Lily felt speechless as she saw Grace's anger. "You and I are as incompatible as fire and water!" Grace declared. "Were it not for a wish I have yet to fulfill, I'd as soon pack up and leave this damn place at once!"

Lily wondered what kind of wish Mother had. This was the second time she had mentioned it since her arrival. Is she planning to travel to the large cities for sightseeing? But she must understand that I have no money or time to do so. At this moment, she suddenly felt Mother's stay in Canada to be an unbearable burden. Indeed, she thought, if Mother dislikes Canada and hates being with me, why doesn't she leave?

"I know you must feel tired looking after Baby day after day. But I couldn't afford to take you to travel around."

"Shut up!" Grace cut her off angrily. "Do you think I want to enjoy life in here? You stupid thing, you never could understand me!"

Lily regretted talking too much that night and making big trouble. It would take days of repeated apologies followed by cold rebukes before Mother's face would return to normal.

A knock at the door broke the awkward tension.

III

Standing at the door was a surprise visitor, Mrs. Rice, a Chinese lady with a round body and a fleshy pink face. She was an activist from the local Chinese Christian Church, and volunteered her time visiting many new immigrant families, trying to convert them.

Mrs. Rice opened wide her small, pea-shaped eyes and started in on Lily.

"It has been ages since you attended our Bible study! We got a lot of new sisters and brothers in our group and everybody is waiting for you to come back to the arms of the Lord!"

She took a breath and went on before Lily had a chance to say anything. "You live too far away from my home and it's hard for me to come over to check on you. A brother in our church drove me to the Chinese grocery this afternoon so I am finally able to drop by!"

"Well, I have been very busy just trying to survive," Lily replied.

"Busy?" Mrs. Rice raised her eyebrows. "It's okay without food for your stomach, but not okay without food for the soul!" She reached out her hand and put two boxes into Lily's hand. "These are puzzles based on Bible stories. My gifts for Baby!"

Lily was relieved that the tension at home would be softened with the unexpected visitor. She let Mrs. Rice in and introduced her to Grace. "Mom, this is Mrs. Rice. She is an immigrant from Taiwan."

Grace put on a polite smile quickly.

"You must feel lonely in Canada, don't you?" After a brief greeting, Mrs. Rice started right away to work on recruiting Grace. "You will find different Chinese organizations in a small city like Mapleton. I don't join any of them, because these groups are led by humans. The Christian Church is the only place led by God and that's where you should go!"

Noticing Mrs. Rice's eloquence about the church gathering steam, Lily thought Mother would lose interest, since people from Mainland China are mostly atheists. To her surprise, however, she found Grace listening attentively with great interest. Mom is just being polite, she thought.

While Mrs. Rice was chatting cordially with Grace, Lily went into the kitchen to finish the cooking Mother had left half done. When the meal was ready, she invited Mrs. Rice to stay for dinner.

Mrs. Rice stretched her neck into the kitchen, glanced at the stir-fried cabbage and rice porridge on the table, and shook her head.

"No, thanks. The brother is still waiting for me in the car and I am going home to eat the crab I just bought. The grocery store has live seafood from Toronto every Saturday. The crabs are fresh and taste great!" Mrs. Rice said, her mouth watering. "By the way, the church has invited a famous speaker from the States for this Sunday. Your mother wants to come to listen. Be a good daughter and bring her there tomorrow! Promise me! Afterwards you can come to my home for lunch. You will find out what a wonderful cook I've got at home these days!"

The echoes of Mrs. Rice's joyful voice vanished in the stairwell. Grace went into the kitchen, looked at the cabbage dish on the table, and asked Lily, "Did you put garlic in the dish?"

Seeing Lily nodding, Grace's face turned cloudy. "I never eat garlic, don't you know that?!"

Lily shook her head. Indeed, she had never known this. She suspected this was just an excuse of her Mother's to find fault with her.

"You don't even know what your mother likes and what she doesn't!" Grace complained. She took a bowl of porridge and carried it to the bedroom to eat dinner by herself.

Lily understood that Grace's action was meant to show that the dispute was not over yet. She hurried over her meal with Baby in the kitchen quietly, cleaned the dishes, bathed Baby and took him to bed. After he had fallen asleep amid her reading, Lily walked into the kitchen and found Grace sitting by the table writing in a thick notebook under the lamplight.

"It's late, Mom," Lily said in a low voice. "You'd better go to bed now."

Grace ignored her and kept on writing with an indifferent air. Lily bit her lips, and repeated her words in a humble manner to ease the tension. Grace finally put down her pen, took off her glasses, sat back in her chair, and closed her eyes. A few seconds went by in silence before she talked. "The word love has been applied so cheaply in so many unworthy situations by people who actually have no sense of what love is!"

Hearing no objection, she went on: "I have the urge to return to China immediately. You will appreciate everything only after I have gone!"

Lily nodded. "You know that, Mom, but I can't afford to let you leave."

Grace opened her eyes, still not looking at Lily, but said in a reconciled tone: "Go to bed now. I need to be alone."

IV

Lying in bed, Lily couldn't sleep. She pictured Mother writing with knotted brows under the dim lamplight. What is she writing about? Her sorrow that I am a shameful loser in the new world? That I have failed to be a desirable daughter?

My whole life has been destroyed ever since I had you! Mother's angry voice echoed and cut her heart again. Lily covered her face with the blanket.

From childhood on, she had been fully aware of Mother's disappointment in her. As the undesirable product of Mother's first marriage that lasted barely a year, Lily's existence had always served Grace as a negative reminder of the man Grace would rather forget for the rest of her life.

That sad story occurred when Grace was in the Air Force in the 1950s.

At the age of twenty-one, Grace was determined to build her own path by shedding her blood and risking her life. As one of the 200 volunteer soldiers recruited from her university, she was not sent to the battlefield in Korea. Instead, she was assigned to work as a sub-editor for the Air Force newspaper in Beijing.

There was no doubt about Grace's hard effort, her intelligence and her contributions. Year after year, her desk was piled with prize posters, award winning notices and medals. But all hell started after she married the army's rising star.

They first met at a conference sponsored by the army for award winners. He was the winner of a special grade prize and rose to fame quickly.

Grace attended one of his lecture seminars. He was by no means a Prince Charming in her eyes, merely an energetic young man with a plain face and a stout figure. As a matter of fact, she was impressed by him only once, at a Saturday evening party, when he was pushed by his comrades to sing a couple of popular revolutionary songs. Grace was surprised to find his voice very beautiful and even more surprised to see him performing a solo dance. His flexible jumps and movements on the floor, to the accompaniment of an accordion, were in excellent imitation of the Ukrainian dance seen in Russian movies.

The last time she saw the man, Grace had been seven months pregnant. In the dark jail where there was only a small window letting light in, she noticed the big changes in him over a short period.

Every happy incident flashed through her mind—when he was applauded at the big conference hall where his smiling face received admiration from thousands of people; when they attended a poetry-reading party in the wide courtyard of the Imperial Temple and danced to the music of Youth Waltz; when they walked along the main street lit up by lotus-shaped street lamps and discussed their new publications ...

And now, everything was turned upside down. How could a talented poet who was to have boundless prospects suddenly become a prisoner? A counter-revolutionary?

Her thoughts went back to the abrupt search of their home, a few months after they had married. As the man was taken away from the messy home, his lips trembled with anger as he shouted aloud to the army's men. Grace picked up the books and manuscripts thrown on the floor, shocked, but with the hope that all this was just a mistake.

A couple of months seemed ages long, amid her anxious waiting. The announcement from the army's Party's organization finally smashed her last hopes. He was accused as a member of an association of writers opposing the Communist Party's ideology. As a punishment, he was sent to a labour camp in a swampy area near the border of Soviet Siberia.

And now it had come to the last encounter between the couple. In the small room where the light was dim, Grace shivered with cold, though it was early in the fall and she could hear the tedious chirping of cicadas from the poplar trees outside the window. There were no more sweet smiles on her pale face. Her twinkling black eyes had gone dull. He was afraid to listen to what she was going to say, though he had anticipated the inevitable moment ever since he had been notified of the punishment. His self-esteem forbade him to show any weakness. Still, he collected his remaining strength and pleaded in a weak voice. "Please trust me. I am innocent, indeed. Believe me …"

Her heart shrank. She felt it cruel to leave him now. Though she knew that she had married him mainly for his fame, she could not forget his loving care. When she was pregnant and found it hard to fall asleep, every night, he sat beside her bed waving a fan gently until she was sound asleep. She also remembered him, sweating all over, riding a bike to look for ice all up and down the city under the burning summer sun, simply because she wanted to eat iced watermelon.

Should she yield to fate and remain his wife? The man in front of her looked so vulnerable and hopeless, with all his brilliance gone. She was surprised to find him incredibly common and plain, once the shining circles around him had faded.

"What kind of future could I expect with a man who had been pronounced politically guilty? The future was awful even to think about," Grace told Lily many years later. "As his wife, I would have

lost almost all my rights as a citizen, let alone my career prospects! And there was a child, still inside me, and her life would be completely destroyed."

Was that the punishment for my indiscretion in love and marriage? Grace asked herself and felt the baby inside her kicking harshly. Her lips trembled and finally released the decision she had thought over numerous times. "I can only trust the judgment made by the Party ..."

As she stood up and turned slowly towards the door, he reached out his arms in the air. Her eyes were blurred by tears. But she didn't slow her pace. At the door, she turned around and gave him a last gaze, before the door was shut.

V

Lily didn't really know how she came into the world. Grace's account was brief and flat. All Lily had learned was that she arrived on a fall evening, when the moon was bright. While the nurse complimented Grace on the little baby girl's pink cheeks and large black eyes, Grace was struggling over whether to send away the newborn to a childless couple or not.

Lily felt disappointed at the simple, emotionless account. She dreamed of a scene where a loving young couple in bed were checking into the dictionary for a name and debating over a number of carefully selected beautiful characters.

She also pictured her arrival in the world during a rainstorm night, as had happened with Baby's coming. The 36-hour-long struggle with escalating pain, the sleepless night when she was moaning alone in the hospital's observation room accompanied only by cold raindrops whipping on the window, her tearful pleas to the doctor for a C-section to rescue her from the torture, and her icy cold body with gallons of blood draining out of her veins.

She could understand Mother's calm reaction at seeing the new-born. Lily didn't taste the happiness of a new mother, either. When the Canadian nurse brought Baby to her and asked her for his name, she simply shook her head, with no strength even to say a word.

The next morning when she was still lying in pain, the nurse brought Baby to her and asked her to breastfeed the newborn. That day passed amid her awkward efforts in trying to get out of bed, her anxiety at not having breast milk, and Baby's hungry crying from morning throughout the whole night.

At that moment, she had felt the impulse to give up the boy and to get rid of the overwhelming problems. When the boy was exhausted from crying and fell asleep, she stared at his delicate features and searched for traces of the man who had created his life. The image of a man on a tractor moving among far-spreading meadows loomed in her mind, and she sighed.

Lily was studying at a university when she learned the truth about the man who was her own father. He had died long ago during a freezing winter and was buried in the snow-covered woods at an isolated labour camp deep in the Siberian mountains.

Grace's elegant oval face turned stern and her eyes as cold as a thousand-year-old glacier when she described her first marriage:

"I never felt regret about leaving him, never. He was a talented poet, indeed, and was famous at the time. But politically, he was wrong. He was anti-Party and anti-government and I trust the Party's accusation."

Such a statement smashed the beautiful fables Lily had woven over the years in her many secret dreams. Grace declared that the plain-looking man had unfortunately passed his plain features on to Lily, who would be prettier had she taken after her mother.

Lily's confidence was never built up. As time went on, Grace started to complain that Lily never told her the truth when she made drastic mistakes.

Indeed, Lily had concealed her relationship with Prince when they first dated, and kept Grace in the dark about her life in Canada—when she dumped Prince and got tangled up with Majesty. She now wondered if Mother could have led her onto the right track had she told her everything. She doubted it. Looking back on the path Mother had trodden, Lily saw overgrown weeds rather than blooming flowers.

Chapter 5
Echoes of the Nightmare

I

A heavy banging from outside drew Lily back from her nostalgic dreams to the reality of her current world. She heard water running in the washroom, Mother taking a shower. The running water soothed her restlessness and brought her into sleep.

She felt herself in the air, high above the ground, limbs pumping hard to keep her hovering like a bird. All of a sudden, she felt her feet tangled up, and she fell. Lying on the earth, she saw black snakes struggling underneath her back and shoulders, trying to bite her. She was seized by fear, but pressed down her shoulders hard in desperation, attempting to crush the wriggling creatures to death.

The next moment, she saw herself running naked, zigzagging down an old lane, chased by a group of men waving knives and shouting insults. The road was narrow and blocked by piles of red bricks. Her legs were heavy and her feet were so numb that she could hardly move. She waved her arms frantically, only to find she had lost the ability to fly. She wanted to cry for help, but could utter no sound. Hiding herself in the corner of an empty, shabby house, she caught her reflection from a broken mirror on the spider-web covered wall. Her hair had turned snow white and was falling out.

She touched her head in fear, only to find herself completely bald. Seized by horror, she moaned helplessly.

Someone was pushing on her shoulder. Startled, Lily woke up. "Wake up, Lily! Are you having a bad dream?"

She found Grace standing by the bed. "Oh, it's horrible, Mom."

"Some men are fighting over there. Did you hear?" Grace pointed at the window. The curtain was drawn a little bit open, and the lamp light in the yard shone in. "I have been listening for a while. They are speaking Chinese and arguing about money."

Lily heard the noises outside. The fierce quarrel was coming from the apartment a couple of metres away at the corner of the building, next to their bedroom window. The angry shouting at midnight was loud and scary.

Lily got up and checked on Baby, who was sleeping soundly on his small mattress on the floor. "Who are they?" Grace asked, while getting into bed.

"It sounds like the Mouse." Lily explained in a low voice. "He owns a buffet restaurant nearby and has hired quite a few workers. Some of them share his two-bedroom apartment over there."

"Do you know each other?" Grace was concerned.

Beside Master Iron, there were a few other Chinese men in the same building. Lily didn't know their names, but remembered a few who had unique features. One man had two protruding front teeth in his sun-tanned face, so she silently named him Beaver-teeth. Another one impressed her deeply with his sharp chin on a narrow pale face so she nicknamed him the Mouse.

The tension inside the small apartment had gone, with the help of the midnight quarrel outside. It was one-fifteen on Sunday morning. Lily felt cold under her thin blanket. She curled up and tried to go back to sleep. But remembering the nightmare, her mind again became alert. She lay awake trying to pick up the broken threads. Who were those men chasing her with knives? How come she was totally naked? As if in answer, memories buried deeply in her past began to slowly surface in her mind.

II

She was only ten when the Proletarian Cultural Revolution erupted, thrusting the whole country into chaos. The boarding school was closed, and she had to stay at home for months. She had seen violent mobs searching people's homes and innocent lives lost under fists and clubs.

There had been heavy rain in Beijing for seven days and nights. Mother came home that evening, after having disappeared for days. Her face looked cold and stern, and she started to shout at Lily. Lily felt wronged and reacted with words she had picked up on the street. "You are shameless!"

Mother was so angered that she started to tear off Lily's clothes. "I'll let you know what shame is!" The words were squeezed out between clenched teeth. When Lily was naked from head to toe, Mother pushed her out of the room into the hallway and locked the door from the inside.

Lily was horrified. This apartment was shared by two families, with one kitchen and one bathroom. Their neighbours, a family of four, had moved into the three-bedroom apartment at the height of the revolution, just a month before, and occupied the largest room. Shivering in the hallway, she could hear them talking in their room and was scared by the thought that they could come out any moment.

Lily pushed at the door desperately, hoping Mother would let her in. It remained tightly shut. When she heard the doorknob turning on the neighbours' door, she hurried into the washroom and locked herself inside. She didn't remember how long she had stayed inside the washroom. It seemed like ages, with every minute passing in loud, scary heartbeats. Finally, the neighbour knocked loudly on Mother's door and asked why the washroom was being occupied for so long.

Tears oozed out from the corner of Lily's eyes and ran onto the pillow. Mother, to this day you have always blamed me for not being decent. But do you realize that it was you who deprived me of my last shred of decency as a child?

She turned aside to face the window. The quarrel in the darkness had stopped, and the world, this foreign world, returned to its indifferent tranquility.

As years went by and the scars gradually healed, Lily had come to understand Mother better. Her whole life and her many talents had been wasted in decades of soul-destroying revolutionary campaigns. Her feminine gentleness had been hardened by the ordeals repeatedly imposed on her. She must have been desperate, humiliated by her own colleagues and betrayed by friends she trusted. When Lily was wandering through the streets in those days, she observed the mobs displaying "problem women" in public. Their scalps were shaved into monster styles and their faces were smeared with ink and spit. Mother was no saint, but it was an era when everybody was crazy.

Lily turned towards Grace, now lying still on the other side of the double bed, and listened to the slight whistling in her throat. From the light coming by the curtain side, she saw her mouth partially open as if she had difficulty breathing.

In sleep, Mother seemed suddenly old and fragile. Lily was seized by the saddening thought that one day Mother would also die.

She reached out her hand to close her lips. But halfway, she stopped.

Physical contact between her and Mother was something unfamiliar and awkward. Lily remembered the first and only time Mother had shown affection towards her.

It was the day after she had passed an interview and been accepted as a Grade 1 student at boarding school. Outside the school office,

standing in the vast, vacant playground, Mother grasped Lily's tiny
hand in her own palm, shook it, and then looked up at the cloudless
blue sky, sighing.

The summer sun beamed brightly overhead, turning Mother's
brown hair golden, and her fair skin shone smooth as ivory. She was
as brilliant as a marble statue, and her palm soft, gentle, and warm.

An unfamiliar thrill shivered through Lily from head to toe. She was
seized by the feeling and could hardly move. Then she heard Mother
sighing in a melancholy tone, "Oh, you have become a student, Lily!
What a hard journey I have travelled!"

Mother lowered her head and gazed at Lily, her eyes full of complicated expressions—love, hope, sorrow, and regret.

Somehow, Lily felt that Mother was not looking at her but at someone else. That impression was engraved in her mind for decades.

III

Lily had always wanted to discuss with Mother openly about her
father and hoped to find out if Mother had ever loved him, which
would make Lily's own existence less pitiable.

She also wondered if Mother really loved her stepfather, who
started to take care of Lily when she was a four-year-old. He was
a very nice, highly educated government official, with all the qualifications worthy of Mother's respect. But their relationship was
brought to the edge of divorce several times.

Lily was never confident sharing her thoughts with Mother. She
was always intimidated by her high expectations.

Mother had shown her what humiliation meant when she was in
Grade 3. That year, Mother was separated from Father. That was
their second or maybe third separation, after their disagreements
had become irreconcilable. Mother was living in a dormitory room
in the office building where she worked.

Lily stayed in her boarding school and would spend every weekend in Mother's room, which Grace shared with an unmarried young woman. Knowing nothing about Mother's first marriage then, Lily thought she was Mother's favourite child. Why else would Mother always take her with her and leave the two younger children at home with Father?

During this year-long separation, however, Mother seldom talked with Lily; each Sunday she spent in gloom. While Lily sat reading and writing at the desk, Mother lay on her pillow, staring numbly at the ceiling.

At the end of that term, after examining Lily's school report card, which included the unacceptably low score of 80 in math, Mom ordered her not to step out of their room on the third floor for the rest of the weekend. "Just think, what will you say if someone asks you about your marks!" Mother said.

This attitude was in sharp contrast to the previous time, when Lily had a good report card. Mother had taken her to the first floor canteen for lunch. When lining up for food, she greeted her colleagues eagerly and exchanged information with other parents.

"Hey, Mr. Chang, what did your son get? All 90s? That's great! How about your daughter, Mrs. Wang? 95 and 98? Isn't she smart? ... Lily? Well, she got an average of 99.5! Isn't that funny!"

There was no doubt Mother cared about her and loved her, but she lacked the skill to express her affection.

During one summer holiday when Lily was at university, she could no longer tolerate Mother's complaints and left home just before dinner. The next day, she was stunned to see Mother on campus. Mother had endured hours riding on the train just to bring her the roasted chicken cooked for her the day before. Outside Lily's dormitory room, Mother put the chicken into her hands, with no word, no smile, but a complicated look. Then she turned, walked away, and disappeared down the staircase.

IV

The first light of dawn penetrated the curtain. Lily rose quietly, walked into the sitting room, sat in front of the desk, and turned on the computer.

The blue light on the screen drew her into a world cut off from the depressing reality of her life. For years, this had become the only place where she could seek temporary release for her captive soul and peace for her troubled mind.

The project was brewed a long time ago in Beijing during her final year in the journalism school. She had been recommended by her professor to work for a woman writer from America as her research assistant, interpreter and translator. For a period of six months, Lily interviewed people, did research in libraries and collected information from newspapers published in the early 1920s. She happily earned 400 dollars, a sum which helped to pay for her air ticket to Canada.

At the writer's request, Lily also wrote a fifty-page rough memoir of her family. The writer was deeply impressed by the story and encouraged her to turn it into a book. "When you finish it, I can recommend you to my agent so you can publish in America!" she told Lily.

A year after she came to Canada, she started seriously on her novel. But progress was slowed as her life became complicated. She continued, however, like a snail crawling persistently, searching for something unknown on the other side of a peaked mount.

Literature was a holy and magic world. She could not find any other field where she could create and feel great.

The room was bright with sunshine. She noticed Grace's reflection on the screen.

"What are you writing about?" Grace murmured, staring at the screen. She could hardly read the English words on it. But she had noticed Lily's fondness for the computer shortly after her arrival.

Lily's hands turned stiff. "Nothing important." She tried to turn aside.

"But what kind of unimportant stuff?" Grace wouldn't give up.

"It's ... something about China."

"Specifically?" Grace dug further.

"The life of ordinary people."

"What kind of people?"

"Good people and bad people, and people who are neither bad nor good."

"What's the point of writing about them?"

"To understand why the world has no hope."

"Let me remind you," Grace raised her voice, clearly unhappy at Lily's ambiguity, "that an honoured writer will never jot down anything detrimental to her nation and people!"

"I just want to write out my feelings about life truthfully."

"But truth is often ugly and disgusting!"

Lily turned off the computer and changed the subject. "I am not working today. Shall we take a walk after breakfast?"

Grace frowned. "Have you forgotten that you promised Mrs. Rice last night to bring me to the Chinese church today? You are not old yet. How can you be so forgetful?"

After a simple breakfast of cornmeal porridge and pickles, the family got ready to go. The church was only a 45-minute walk so they decided to go on foot. Grace first put on her black pants and beige cardigan, but then changed into her dark gray pants and purple cashmere sweater, and asked Lily if she looked all right.

Lily was putting a diaper on Baby. Seeing Mother look in the mirror and comb her hair, she realized Mother's enthusiasm for this outing. Staying at home with a silent little boy every day must be extremely boring for her. Life in this small city was too peaceful, and the church was almost the only place that provided some social activities for non-English visitors.

"You look beautiful, Mother!" Lily praised, sincerely. When dressed up, Grace always presented herself as a professional and elegant looking woman.

Grace grinned proudly, "I won't be the same as you." She put on her well-polished, flat-heeled leather shoes. "Are you going out like that?" she questioned Lily in a disapproving tone, finding her in her usual jeans and sneakers.

"Nobody knows who I am anyway," Lily replied.

Chapter 6
Peacocks on Show

I

Once outside, they found there was still a chill in the air. At Lily's suggestion, Grace returned to the building to find her warm overcoat.

While waiting for Grace in the sunny area near the entrance of the yard, Lily was startled by a tiny figure suddenly appearing beside Baby's stroller. It was the Mouse, with a cigarette in his fingers. He greeted her and they started to chat. He told her that he used to be a colonel in the Chinese army and had escaped to Canada a few years ago with a large amount of money belonging to the Chinese government.

Then he shouted all of a sudden, "I let the people down, and I let the Party down!"

Lily gave a little jump at his outburst. "Then why did you do it?" she inquired, feeling rather silly.

Under the bright sunlight pouring between the U-shaped buildings, the Mouse-colonel narrowed his eyes and nailed his blank stare to her forehead. She was anticipating heroic clichés such as, "I took the money to support the democratic movement abroad," as many criminals claimed.

He surprised her with an honest statement. "The country is in a mess. If I didn't do it, somebody else would have done it anyway. I am but a small operator. There are many fatter rats in today's China."

Lily wondered why he was so bold in telling his stories to a practical stranger. The anxiety of hiding like a chased mouse for more than five years must have driven him crazy, she thought. The cost of successful stealing was not a low one. He seemed to have no friends, no social life, and was not even able to walk around with his head held high like Master Iron.

Seeing Grace coming over, the Mouse-colonel turned his back to move away. "It's time to work in my restaurant now."

As they walked onto the street, Lily told Grace the story. When Grace showed her surprise, Lily added, "About four thousand corrupt officials have escaped China and many of them are harboured in North America. Rumour has it that in Toronto and Vancouver, hundreds of them live close to one another in million-dollar houses. They stay inside their houses during the day and go out only after dark, just like mice. The Chinese government has difficulty getting them back because they are well protected by Canadian law. The colonel is better than those people, for at least he works."

"You should avoid such people anyway," Grace warned her.

Few cars or pedestrians used Mapleton's Sunday morning streets. Lily noticed the lawns becoming green among the snow patches, and some small yellow and purple flowers shivering in the chill wind by the doorsteps of the houses along the roads.

"What kind of flowers are these?" Grace pointed at the tiny flowers.

"They might be some sorts of lilies."

Grace breathed deeply the fresh air and insisted that the flowers in Canada had brighter colours than those in Beijing.

Lily wasn't sure if that was true. She wondered if she had been in Canada too long to notice its bright side. Her eyes caught a shining spot on the sidewalk. She stopped and bent over to look at it. It was a penny. She reached out her hand, but heard a voice, "No!"

Embarrassed, Lily withdrew her hand and stood up. "Never do that again!" Grace looked at Lily straight in the eyes. "It's cheap."

Lily felt awkward. She wanted to explain that picking up a penny in Canada was regarded as good luck, but she swallowed her words. She pushed Baby's stroller hard and walked on in silence.

When they turned onto the main street, Grace looked excited to see a number of church buildings along the way, in classical style or post-modern architecture. She slowed down her pace and watched with great interest. "Are these churches for Canadians only?"

The enthusiasm in her face struck Lily as odd and she wondered why Mother would be so drawn to this scene. Lily pushed the stroller forward and urged Grace along. "The Mandarin service in the Chinese church starts at ten-thirty and we have to hurry up!"

II

At the Chinese church, Lily saw a lot of new faces in the hall and felt surprised that the congregation had grown so fast during the past few months. The Chinese community in Mapleton was a small one, about three percent of the city's population. The church functioned naturally as a community centre, attracting the attention of many newcomers.

"Hello!" Mrs. Rice's high-pitched Mandarin greeting rolled out before her full figure came in sight. She shook their hands warmly. "I am so glad you have kept your promise to come! God works in you!"

Lily's eyes were immediately drawn to the woman beside Mrs. Rice. It was hard to tell her age. The shining, jet black hair was pulled into a ponytail decorated with a black and white spotted hairpin. Her honey-coloured face was a perfect oval, and her cheeks and cherry-shaped lips were carefully rouged. Most attractive were her sparkling black eyes. She wore a pair of high-heeled shoes, a pink cashmere sweater and a brown leather skirt, her slim figure strikingly emphasized.

Mrs. Rice appeared a pathetic foil, standing beside such a woman. Her shortcomings stood out so much that one might wonder if her legs could still be called legs and her waist really a waist.

"Let me introduce you." Mrs. Rice pushed the woman towards Lily. "This is Camellia. She is like you, also from Mainland China. She has an abusive husband and son, so she is staying in my house for the time being." Just at this moment, Mrs. Rice noticed someone she knew from the crowd. She apologized quickly and vanished.

Camellia exchanged greetings with Lily and Grace. She noticed Baby and bent down to touch his cheeks. "Is this your son?" Camellia's voice showed her surprise. "He is such a good looking boy! Who does he look like? Your husband? Is he here today?"

"No, I left him a long time ago," Lily answered reluctantly.

"Did you really?" Camellia showed great interest in her reply. She raised her head, blinked her large eyes, and asked, "How long have you been in Canada?"

"Eight years."

"So long! Then you must be familiar with everything. I am sure you can help me. I have been here for only a year."

"What kind of help do you need?"

"I want to divorce my husband. But I don't know any English. Maybe you can help me find out how I can get divorced, since you have gone through the divorce issue in Canada."

Lily realized now why the woman was so interested in her. "Hasn't Mrs. Rice helped you at all?" she kicked the ball back.

"No!" Camellia shook her head and made a face. "She is a Christian, you know. How can she support my wish for a divorce?"

Lily nodded with understanding. "How long have you been married?"

"Twenty years."

Lily could hardly believe her ears. But when she looked more closely, she could see traces of age in Camellia's perfect face. The muscles at the corners of her mouth were a little bit slack.

"If you have already spent more than twenty years with your husband, why can't you tolerate him now?"

"I have never loved him!"

"Never? Then why did you marry him in the first place?" Lily still had the journalist's habit of digging into details.

"I had no choice then."

This kind of answer needed more time to explore than they had at the moment. Then Lily remembered what Mrs. Rice has said when she introduced them. "And ... he is an abusive man?" she said softly.

Camellia's eyeballs moved around, searching for a reply. "What is abusive? He never used his fists, but he tortured me mentally, and asked my son to beat me up."

"What? How dare your son beat you?"

"He seized my hair, kicked me, and hit me with the soup bowl, the teacup, the telephone. Just crazy! Look!" Camellia rolled up her sleeve and exposed the big blue bruises on her upper arm. Then she lowered her head and parted the thick hair to show the scar underneath.

"No!" Lily and Grace exclaimed at the same time. "Didn't your husband try to stop your son?"

"Stop? No!" Camellia opened her eyes wide. "He encouraged him instead! He said, 'Good! Justice is done! Why not simply beat her to death! You are helping to relieve my sorrow!'"

Lily shook her head. "If you are in such a situation, why not call the police and seek help from the government?"

"No, I don't want them to arrest my son. They will put him into jail, and spoil his future! He is going to university in the fall, you see."

"A typical mother!" Lily sighed. "So what are you planning to do now?"

"Once I get the divorce settlement, I'll return to China immediately!

Life in my home city, Yangchow, is much more comfortable than here. Why should I stay here and suffer?"

Lily sensed a rosy colour in Camellia's plan. Impulsively, she said, "I guess you must have someone you love in China!"

Grace threw a critical glance at Lily for her bluntness. Lily realized with embarrassment it was improper to be so straightforward when meeting someone for the first time.

Camellia didn't seem to mind her directness, however. She blushed a bit but nodded with a smile. "Yes, you are right. He is looking forward to my coming back—day and night!"

III

Before the sermon started, Lily left Baby in the children's Sunday school class in the side wing, where a couple of teenage girls were trying to teach the toddlers a song entitled, "The Precious Blood of Jehovah Washed Away my Sin."

Lily looked at the Chinese character "blood" and wondered if Baby would understand the meaning of the word since he could not even say "milk" yet. She wanted to suggest to the girls to teach a children's song to the toddlers instead, but remembering that this was a church and seeing Baby playing happily, she left without any comment.

After Lily sat down with Grace in the back seats of the spacious assembly hall, the speaker of the day, a short, round-faced man with a flat nose and thick glasses, appeared on the platform. He was originally from China and currently a biology researcher at a U.S. university. He attacked Darwin's theory of evolution, using archeological discoveries and legends related to Chinese myths to prove that the universe was created by God. He also detailed the long emotional process of how he had been turned from a stubborn Communist atheist into an honourable Christian.

Everyone in the audience seemed captivated. Lily found his words fresh compared to the dry, over-fried sermons delivered by Mr. Wong, the church's minister, an immigrant from Taiwan.

When the scientist finished amid warm applause, Minister Wong stepped onto the platform. He was a handsome tall man in his early 30s, with a long face, fair skin, and a pair of gold-framed glasses. Even more impressive was his vibrating metallic voice, an indispensable tool for his job. Standing in front of the microphone, he raised his palm into the air.

"Brothers and sisters, please lower your heads and pray now ... Yes, all lower your heads ... Okay, after listening to our esteemed guest speaker, if you are touched and therefore believe that Jesus Christ is your only saviour, please stand up! If you are willing to follow our Lord, please stand up! If you are willing to open your heart to our Lord today and be saved from death forever, please stand up! ... One ... Two ... Why? Not anyone else touched by today's speech? Four ... Five. Thank you, my Lord! Any more? Any more? Please, open your heart to accept the light from God! ... Any more? ... Eight ... Nine ..."

Lily could hardly control her curiosity, so she looked up to see who were the newly recruited. She saw only five people standing before she heard Minister Wong's warning, "Keep your head low and do not look up! Pray hard! Those who have stood up can sit down now ... Any more? ... Any more? ... Ten, eleven ..."

Lily noticed Mrs. Rice sitting in the row ahead of her standing up all of a sudden and pulling up Camellia next to her. "Twelve, and thirteen!" Minister Wong's voice was bright with triumph.

Lily felt her neck getting sore and was relieved to hear the announcement that the recruiting marathon had finally ended. Altogether, thirteen people were invited to step onto the platform to receive Minister Wong's congratulations. Eleven were women. Seeing Mrs. Rice also on stage, Lily realized her cooperation must have been prearranged to help with the show.

"Volunteers please stay behind!" Minister Wong shouted. "Please take the new recruits to the basement for individual guidance sessions. Attention please! Each pair must be of the same sex, not the opposite sex!"

Hearing this instruction, some men who were walking towards the platform came to a halt and looked at each other awkwardly.

Lily laughed. "How funny!" she commented to Grace. Hearing no response, she looked at her mother, and found her gazing at Minister Wong, her eyes shining.

IV

When the service was over, Lily went to the Sunday school class to get Baby. He was sitting on the floor with a few other children playing with puzzles of the Bible stories. Lily looked at the puzzle he had finished and found it was a picture of Adam and Eve under an apple tree in the Garden of Eden.

When she came to the hallway with Baby, she found Grace standing in a corner with Mrs. Rice, who was telling her the story of Minister Wong.

Minister Wong had been a star in his high school years in Taiwan. His eloquence and good looks made him outstanding in drama and speech competitions. Unfortunately, he failed for years on end to pass the university entrance exams. Finally, at the suggestion of his teacher, he applied to the Bible College, which had easy entrance requirements, and became a clergyman. Years before, when the situation in Taiwan had become tense with escalating conflicts among various political powers, Minister Wong had applied to immigrate to Canada, where his profession was in high demand due to the increasing numbers of Chinese immigrants. Not long after his arrival in Toronto, he was sent to Mapleton since the previous minister of this church had recently died.

"He and I are alumnae, you know. I am also a graduate of the Bible College in Taiwan." Mrs. Rice told Grace proudly.

"Does he know many other Chinese ministers in Canada?" Grace asked.

"Sure he does!" Mrs. Rice nodded to confirm this. "Why do you ask?"

Grace blushed. "I ... well ... I ... "

Camellia came out of the washroom and greeted them. Lily noticed that her lips were freshly rouged.

"Did you drink from the cup during the service?" Camellia asked Lily. "I thought it would be wine. But it turned out to be sweetened water!"

"It was the blood of the Lord!" Mrs. Rice corrected Camellia. She then invited Grace and Lily to come for lunch at her house, only a fifteen-minute walk away.

"Camellia is a wonderful cook! I love the duck fat pancakes she made last week! Let's ask her to make them for us again today!" Mrs. Rice licked her lips as she turned to Camellia. "How do you like that idea?"

Camellia replied quickly with an embarrassed smile. "It takes time to make duck fat pancakes. Shall we eat something else instead?"

But Grace turned down the invitation, explaining that she was tired and must go home to rest. Mrs. Rice insisted warmly that the family must come for dinner another time.

Saying farewell, Camellia smiled beautifully at everyone. But Lily sensed a hint of anxiety in that smiling face.

What was the relationship like between Mrs. Rice and Camellia? she wondered.

Chapter 7
Camellia Stuck in the Rice Hole

I

Back home and after a quick lunch, Camellia was cleaning the dishes when Mrs. Rice yawned and went upstairs to take a nap.

With the kitchen work done, Camellia spent half an hour in the bathroom, first making her ponytail into a coil at the back of her head, and then into two pigtails decorated with yellow and pink beads on both ends. She looked at herself in the mirror sideways and grinned, seeing a young girl of sixteen. With a last satisfied glance at her new hairstyle, she sneaked out of Mrs. Rice's home and took a bus to the largest mall in west Mapleton.

Spending a long morning in church was tedious, she thought on the bus. Were it not for Mrs. Rice's ardent insistence, she would have gone shopping this lovely morning instead of sitting in the church. There was one pleasant moment, however, she thought with a smile, when she was standing in the centre of the platform and receiving so many admiring or jealous looks from the audience below.

Every time Camellia came to the mall, she would linger at the jewelry stand. The owner was an immigrant from Hong Kong who had opened the store in Mapleton about a year ago. The first time Camellia spotted her, with shining jewels in her ear lobes, on her fingers, and around her thin neck, she silently nicknamed the lady "Madam Jewelry."

Now she greeted her with a smile. "I spent a whole morning at the Chinese Church. It was so boring! Have you ever been there?"

Camellia pointed at some earrings and Madam Jewelry took them out for her to try on.

"Yes, I've been there a couple of times. I don't agree with some of the practices in that church. You know what other people think about the place? It's a matchmaking centre!" Madam Jewelry twisted her lips, showing her contempt.

"Matchmaking?" Camellia thought of the men she had met in the church and laughed. None seemed worth her attention.

"Hey, Camellia!" Someone was calling her from behind.

Camellia looked back. It was none other than the woman she had just met this morning in the church. "Well, Lily! How come we meet twice in a day!"

"God must have sent me to watch out for you." Lily joked. "I heard a familiar voice, but hardly recognized you. You changed your hairstyle!"

"Don't you like this?" Camellia felt her two pigtails, looking seriously at Lily. Lily just smiled.

Seeing her subtle disapproval, Camellia blinked her eyes and asked her opinion about the earrings on the counter.

Madam Jewelry greeted Lily, her eyes sweeping through Lily quickly. "Don't you want to pick a necklace or ring for yourself? I have got new stock in just this week."

Lily just nodded politely at the shining items Madam Jewelry presented under her eyes one by one.

Camellia pointed at a diamond ring and said that her lifelong dream was to own a ring with a whole carat diamond.

Lily looked confused. "If artificial jewelry looks the same, why would you spend your savings on the authentic stuff?"

"Oh, poor Lily! Don't you know that diamonds reflect a woman's status? Fake diamonds don't mean a thing! And anyway, who would purchase a diamond ring with money from her own pocket, except an ugly woman?"

Madam Jewelry had long recognized that the two women were simply gazers instead of customers, at least for the time being. So she relaxed and picked up the topic of church again.

"I worship God and follow only what God wants me to do. Because of God's blessing, I have three boys who are all top students in their classes." She leaned forward and confided, "Everything in the world is created by God, including my life. I won't hesitate if God wants my life! Okay, take it, I say!"

Lily was impressed by her enthusiasm and smiled. "You seem to be a very faithful Christian. Which church do you go to?"

"I am with no particular group. A Christian is always Christian as long as you pray in the right way."

"What is the right way?"

"Let me tell you." Madam Jewelry nodded, pleased with Lily's interest. "I had not been a faithful Christian until one day, when I found I had suddenly acquired the ability to pray in a language I had never heard before. This language is called 'the Tongue.' Many people in my church in Hong Kong can pray in the Tongue once they have been inspired by the Holy Spirit. I believe that God is calling me to spread the Tongue to more people in Canada. When I have more time to be involved with the local church, I'll certainly teach more people how to pray using the Tongue!"

Lily and Camellia both urged her on. "Could you demonstrate the Tongue to us? Please!"

Madam Jewelry nodded, lowered her head, shut her eyes, and started meditating. A few minutes passed. Both Camellia and Lily held their breath and waited patiently until the lady suddenly shivered and uttered a string of strange chirping sounds accompanied by weeping noises in her throat.

Camellia opened her eyes wide and asked Lily in a whisper, "Is this English? No? What could it be?"

Lily shook her head. Madam Jewelry's demonstration reminded her of the traditional Chinese witch performance, which had been banned for a long time. When Madam Jewelry stopped her praying and returned to normal, Lily asked, "Do you have to practice hard to acquire the skill?"

Madam Jewelry shook her head. "No, it's not hard at all. Everybody can do it …" Her words were interrupted by a customer and she quickly adopted her business manner and worldly smile.

Lily left with Camellia and decided to sit down for a coffee together. Once they were settled, Lily asked Camellia to tell her story.

II

Camellia had met Mrs. Rice through the help of the Chinese church, when her escalating domestic troubles forced her to seek refuge outside her home.

There was an extra bedroom in Mrs. Rice's large house by the lake. After learning about Camellia's situation, Mrs. Rice announced heroically, "Move into my house right now! Don't worry! Everything is free for you there!"

Camellia had been deeply touched. A free room and free meals? That would save a few hundred dollars every month! To show her gratitude, she offered to share some housework. Glad to know Camellia was good at preparing Southern Chinese dishes, Mrs. Rice said, "I am a straightforward person so let's be frank! There are only four members in the family, my three kids and me. You can be in charge of cooking for the family. But please offer different menus each day to stimulate everyone's appetite and keep us healthy!"

Mrs. Rice had solid theory to support her actions. "It's important that we eat well. You know, for women entering their middle years, the lack of proper nutrition might accelerate the aging process. Are you envious of my skin? It's smooth and fair, without a single spot, isn't it? Well, there is no secret but eating well!"

Mrs. Rice was indeed a generous person. She never tried to hide her beauty therapy from others. After Camellia moved in, Mrs. Rice entertained her friends and her friends' friends at her home three times a week. At the dinner table in front of all her guests, she would praise Camellia's excellent cooking, with exaggerated facial expressions. "Don't you think Camellia could put the chefs in Toronto's five star hotels to shame?"

Camellia was so encouraged by the high praise that she made an even greater effort, racking her brain to produce more enchanting menus for the endless dinner parties.

Mrs. Rice clapped her hands when she learned that Camellia could make sweet dumplings—a traditional food made of rice flour with sweet stuffing, usually eaten during the Lantern Festival each year. An excellent idea struck her and she suggested, "Why not make some dumplings as gifts?"

Camellia hesitated, since it was not the right season. Besides, making them would take up almost all her spare time. But she was not the type to question why, particularly when she needed that room and board.

In the following days, hundreds of sweet dumplings rolled out of her flexible fingers. The various stuffings smelled good: red bean, lotus seed, chocolate, minced dates, black sesame and pine nuts. There were fifty in each pack, neatly wrapped.

Mrs. Rice counted the boxes, murmuring happily. "This one will be sent to my second daughter's piano teacher. This one is for my oldest daughter's math tutor. That one is for my son's swim instructor. And these will be delivered to Minister Wong and the church volunteers. And the rest? They will find their way into the houses of Mrs. Chen,

Mrs. Tang, Mrs. Lee, and Mrs. Pan. Well, what a good idea! Now I will be able to pay reduced fees to the children's instructors. And the debts of gratitude I owe to the ladies will be paid! And, besides, I am contributing to God's work as well! Aren't I a smart person, Camellia?"

Two weeks later, however, Camellia became fed up with her role. What's the point of coming to Canada if I have to dress in an apron and dance with a wok around the fire from sunrise to sunset? she fumed to herself. Everyone in China envies the wonderful, luxurious life in the capitalist world. They don't know what a hell it is!

Think about the life I used to enjoy in Yangchow, where Dwarf hired a young country girl to handle all the housework. I was never expected to dirty my fingers with any sort of chores. All I had to worry about was what dress to wear and which restaurant to go to!

But look at me now! My tender hands have become rough and dark like bark on an old pine. All the elegant silk dresses and high heel shoes I brought to Canada for parties and balls are lying at the bottom of my chest!

Ah, how stupid I am, abandoning all the pleasures in China and crossing the ocean to become a servant in a strange land! No wonder Dwarf always says that I am a typical woman, with long hair but short intelligence, a creature born to be bullied. Mrs. Rice claims that she is helping me, but God knows who is helping whom! So many ads in the Chinese newspaper offer a housekeeper free room and board, plus eight hundred dollars monthly!

Despite the bitter thoughts brewing in her mind, Camellia was still a brand new immigrant from China. She had not been in Canada long enough to learn the frankness of the new continent. As a Chinese woman, all she could do was conceal her disappointment, and continue to put a smile on her face.

Another thing Camellia found hard to appreciate was Mrs. Rice's tongue, flexible but hard to chew, just like the roasted oxtail dish Mrs. Rice enjoyed eating so much.

Mrs. Rice had graduated as an honour student from the Bible College in Taiwan. Spreading the Gospel to the heathen naturally became a part of her life's work. But her actions, in Camellia's eye, seemed ridiculous and even stupid.

At breakfast time, the three children sat up straight in their seats around the table, listening to Mrs. Rice's prayers, before they picked up their chopsticks. Camellia understood that she was in Rome, and smartly imitated the Romans, with her fingers crossed in front and chin tucked in.

With her eyes half open, Mrs. Rice uttered her wishes: "My Lord, thank you for giving us such a rich breakfast to enable us to work and study with plenty of energy!"

"My Lord, my older daughter is going to have a math test today. Please remove all obstacles and all difficult questions in the test for her!"

"My Lord, my son has caught a cold this morning, with a little bit of fever and discomfort. Please relieve his pain and let him be well and alert as usual!"

"My Lord, my second daughter has been impatient with her piano lessons recently and intends to drop out. Please cool her down, give her wisdom, and keep her interested!"

"My Lord, Camellia has gotten up early in the morning to make this delicious food for all of us. Let's be grateful for her work!"

"My Lord, Camellia cannot digest dairy products. Please fix her stomach so she can benefit from this rich nutrition!"

While listening to all these detailed demands and thanks going on one by one, Camellia couldn't help but feel impatient to start the meal. The soybean milk in the bowls and the steamed buns were all getting cold and wouldn't taste good any more.

What's wrong with Mrs. Rice, begging favour from the lord for such trivial matters? Look at the way she acts! As if there is really a lord somewhere in the sky! But where is he? The French song, "The

Internationale," clearly states "there is never any lord, nor can we depend on God or emperors. It is ourselves who should be relied upon to create happiness for mankind." Hasn't she ever heard the song? Well, maybe not. The song was popular only in the communist world.

Suppose there is indeed such a lord in the sky? Well, I bet he would get completely tangled up with all these demands if everybody bothered him the same way she does!

Camellia's silent rebellion didn't escape Mrs. Rice. She added new contents to her endless prayers at once: "My Lord, Camellia's eyes have been blinded by Satan and cannot see the mighty force of you. Please throw light into her reclusive heart and allow her to see you! My Lord, it makes my heart ache to think of Camellia and her family members suffering horribly in hell! Please rescue them and show them the way to Heaven!"

III

Late that afternoon, Camellia returned home from the mall. As soon as she opened the door, Mrs. Rice's sharp voice echoed in her ear.

"Why did you leave home without telling me?" Mrs. Rice complained.

While Camellia busied herself in the kitchen preparing dinner, Mrs. Rice, watching her as she worked, started describing to her the horrible scene in hell, the disastrous moment when the end of the world comes, and the urgent necessity of becoming a Christian at once.

She waved her fleshy palms and talked excitedly. "The fire, big, red burning flames, will destroy everything in the world! People, animals, trees, and buildings—everything becomes ashes in choking black smoke. And only we Christians, under the blessing of God, will follow our Lord to rise into the sky, amid beautiful music, and live forever in paradise. Forever! Have you got it? That means we will never die! Aren't you afraid of death?"

Camellia stopped chopping meat and faced Mrs. Rice. "When will the end of the world come?" she asked in a suspicious tone.

"Well, pretty soon! It will arrive in no time, probably around the year 2014. Some people have done an accurate calculation. So you see, there isn't much time left for you. You'd better hurry up and be baptized so you can come with us! If I didn't love you so much, I wouldn't talk my mouth dry to bring you to Heaven. I would simply leave you down here in the fire!"

Camellia hesitated, but finally decided to speak her mind: "If you already know that everything is going to be destroyed in an unavoidable fire, then why was it necessary for you to buy such a large new house? Isn't it a pity that this beautiful home will be burnt to ashes in just a few years?"

A slight smile tugged at the corners of her lips as she spoke. She left unsaid her real thoughts: Who are you trying to fool? Do you think I am a three-year-old? Your description sounds as if you have seen doomsday with your own eyes! What a pity that the Bible, like Buddhist and Taoist theories, which might be well-intentioned, is ruined by this amateur's poor interpretation!

Nothing could escape Mrs. Rice's small yet penetrating eyes. "Don't you believe me? Look! Without the blessing of our Lord, disaster will fall on your head sooner or later! I warn you, you'd better be careful. You may have a car accident one day or cut your finger off, wham, like this, while cutting meat!" Mrs. Rice suddenly hit Camellia's wrist hard with the edge of her palm.

Calluses started to grow in Camellia's ears from Mrs. Rice's constant preaching. She was even more annoyed today at the woman's cursing and the hit on her wrist, which made her nearly cut her finger.

IV

That night after she went to bed, Camellia found it hard to fall asleep.

Are you afraid of death? Mrs. Rice's question crept into her mind again. Of course I am. Few Chinese believe in the possibility of life in the other world. That is why everybody is trying to enjoy every minute now.

The moon cast the shadow of a maple tree on the beige curtains. Her mind was swamped in thoughts of the mysterious universe, the theory of "heaven and hell," and the short journey of life. The more she thought, the more she was seized by fear.

"Life in Yangchow is surely better than here," she whispered into her pillow. She turned her face towards the wall and shut her eyes. The city is too old and the streets noisy with crowds of people and streams of bicycles, but still, people there don't feel lonely. And they never have a quiet moment to reflect on Gods or ghosts in the constant hustle and bustle.

Gradually, her mind became confused and she was lost in a world of colours. All of a sudden, however, she saw a pool of blood accumulating on the cutting board on the kitchen counter. Scared, she heard a sharp whisper in her ear: "Camellia!"

She woke up at once. Cold sweat covered her back, her heart thumped fast in her chest. She felt her arms and hands. Thank heaven it was only a dream. The wristwatch by the pillow pointed to two o'clock. The large house was dark and quiet. Camellia stared at the ceiling, trying to concentrate on her dream.

Did I cut my hand? Whose house was that kitchen in? It didn't look like Mrs. Rice's kitchen. Then, where was it? Is this dream trying to tell me something? What's the time in China now? Early in the afternoon. What would Dwarf be doing at this moment? The whisper in the dream was undoubtedly his voice! What does he want to say?

She wanted to call him in China at once! The phone was in the sitting room. But Mrs. Rice had difficulty sleeping and could be startled by a mouse yawning. The last time Camellia was sending kisses over the phone at midnight, she had been shocked to find Mrs. Rice standing behind her in her nightgown! Camellia then had to confess everything and face Mrs. Rice's attack on her morality for days.

To avoid the lessons in morality, Camellia had made the acquaintance of a Chinese student at the university and went to his home to make her calls. She promised to talk for only ten minutes, and prepaid him in cash. But the calls were hell! Worried about the bill, the man stood right next to her, looking at his wristwatch all the time, afraid she would talk one second more! She was too embarrassed to say anything intimate to Dwarf, though he kept on interrogating her.

Without her, he would be spending his time in bars, playing mahjong and flirting with other foxy women. Last time, when she had heard rumours and questioned him, he just provoked her: "Are you jealous? Then, come back to China! Once you are back, I will send the others away!"

Come back? Easier said than done! Not everyone is lucky enough to have permanent residence permission in Canada. I've got it, and how could I be so brainless as to give it up! In two more years, I can become a Canadian citizen. Once a citizen, I will be totally free to fly anywhere in the world. Dwarf is too selfish. I am sure the heartless man must let other women sleep in our bed! Every piece of decoration in that apartment is soaked with my love and imagination. How can he allow those cheap women to leave their stain on them!

Camellia's heart twisted in jealousy. Dwarf's vigorous, laughing face, her husband's waving gray hair, her son's violent screaming, the blazing laser lights in the bars, and the swishing of silk dresses and exposed legs on the dance floor all twisted like a roll of tangled yarn in her mind.

She turned over and over in her bed until the furniture in the room became visible in the early dawn.

After breakfast Mrs. Rice said she was going to visit some new-comers to Canada and would come home in the afternoon. "Please stay home and read the New Testament. As for lunch, you can make fried rice with scrambled eggs for yourself. That's simple and won't take you much time. We will talk about what to eat for dinner after I come home."

Camellia nodded anxiously until Mrs. Rice was out of the door. Then she picked up the phone immediately.

V

A few days later, Lily brought Grace and Baby to Mrs. Rice's home for dinner. Camellia prepared drunken chicken and sweet and sour fish, both famous dishes in her hometown. At the dinner table, Lily told Camellia about an English as a second language program spon-sored by the government for new immigrants.

Camellia was happy to hear about this free program. Obviously, it was more practical and worthwhile to learn English than to study the Bible in this new land. After Lily helped her with registration the next day, she started school at once.

It was an effort to start learning a language in one's forties. Though Camellia's attention was more focused on the Canadian teacher's jewelry and the different dresses she wore each day than on the boring repetitions of the English sounds, she tried hard to manage an hour or so after supper to review what she had learned in class before going to bed.

However, Mrs. Rice found this new situation hard to appreciate. One morning after breakfast when Camellia picked up her school bag and walked towards the door, Mrs. Rice reached out and stopped her. "You don't need to go to school!" she announced.

"Why not?" Camellia asked with a wary frown.

"All you want is to learn English, right?" Mrs. Rice asked. Camellia nodded. "All right then. It's not necessary to go out every day. You can stay at home and learn with me. I am good in English, too!"

Camellia wondered whether Mrs. Rice's English would be as good as that of the Canadian teachers in the school. But she didn't want to hurt Mrs. Rice's pride, so she put down her bag. Mrs. Rice sat beside her at the dining-room table and taught her how to read "How are you," "Thank you," "Good morning" and "Good night." She was serious and meant to prove herself a capable teacher.

Fifteen minutes went by and Mrs. Rice's enthusiasm waned. There was no doubt it was a boring task, repeating and repeating those simple phrases suitable for daycare children!

"Well, let's take a break now! My throat is burning." Mrs. Rice put down the textbook, leaned back in her chair and yawned.

Camellia quickly rose and went to make some tea for the tired teacher.

"I know you are not yet ready to accept the Bible right now," Mrs. Rice sipped at her jasmine tea and started talking again. "Let's change the topic today. I'll tell you my success story instead."

You are only a housewife staying home all year round. What's there to boast about? Camellia questioned silently. But she had to show interest, as Mrs. Rice displayed great eagerness to share her secret. She needs a rest and I'd better relax as well, Camellia thought, and wait for my next English lesson.

Mrs. Rice was so involved in her own story, stuffed with so many details, that hours passed and she had covered only her success history from her birth until she was thirteen and had her first menstruation.

"Oh, dear!" Mrs. Rice looked at her watch and cried out. "It's already twelve o'clock! No wonder my stomach is making noises! Camellia, turn on your brain and think about what we should eat for lunch! Don't let me eat the same thing as usual. Think about something fancy and give your hard-working teacher a surprise! Come on!"

The following day passed exactly the same way. As she recalled the heated period of life as a teenage girl, Mrs. Rice's success story became exceptionally detailed, told not year by year but day by day. When she had finally reached the age of twenty, it was time for lunch again!

She was carried away by her own story. After lunch, Mrs. Rice skipped her usual nap and dragged Camellia back to the table to continue the account of her golden age.

By the third day, Mrs. Rice's reminiscences approached the glorious climax, where under the mighty power of her Lord, she had defeated all her rivals and finally won the man who took her down the aisle of the church to the sound of triumphant music!

Camellia, having waited anxiously and pretending to hang on every word, now saw the light of a conclusion to this boring history and grasped the chance quickly. "You are really smart, Mrs. Rice. Your success story has certainly proved that!"

"Be patient, please! I am not finished yet! There is much more valuable experience you need to learn from! The wedding is just the beginning of a long march. Taming your husband requires more talent! Do you know how to control your husband's heart?"

Dwarf's face with striking wild features flashed through Camellia's mind. She shook her head. "No. I really don't know."

"Fine, then! Now let me teach you how." Mrs. Rice nodded her double chin firmly. "But this is my patented experience. It's so valuable that I seldom reveal it to anybody unless she is my closest friend. You understand how much I love you, don't you? That explains why I am willing to do you this favour."

She bent over and lifted the wedding album from the tea table. "Don't you think my husband is handsome?" Pointing at a man, she said. "He is, definitely! But not only that, he makes good money, too. He has been working as a senior electronics engineer in an American-owned company in Taiwan for many years. Such an attractive man! But when he comes to Canada next time, you can ask him: has he ever dared to say 'No' to my face? Never! No, never! I have tamed him to be a faithful dog who will only look in my eyes and follow my instructions."

"How?" Camellia showed genuine interest this time.

"First of all, you have to win his respect for you as a loving wife. You know very well that I enjoy gourmet foods. But when I pre-pared something special in the kitchen, I would always feed myself secretly there. When I brought the dishes to the table finally, I would just advise my husband and children to eat whereas I myself hardly touched the delicacies. Wouldn't he see me as a perfect wife?"

Camellia saw no novelty in this trick, an old practice she had used many times. So she pushed further. "But it must be hard to control a man when you are far away."

"Take it easy," Mrs. Rice assured her. "You can understand that it was for the better education and future of our children that I immi-grated to Canada with our three children. My husband was left alone in Taiwan to make money and support the whole family, like many families in Taiwan and Hong Kong do. But do you think I would be so foolish as to leave this big fish at large to feed the many greedy cats around him? Aha, no! I have a way to remote control him!"

"What's your secret?" Camellia clicked her fingertips on the table, urging her to talk.

Mrs. Rice took a mouthful of tea and went on. "I convinced him to purchase a new car and large properties both in Taiwan and Canada and thus put him heavily in debt. This way, he has to worry his head and busy his body day and night to make money every way possible to pay the debts. How can he ever spare a single moment to date other women? He would never be in that sort of mood!"

"Didn't he ever ask you to work to help with the finances?" Camellia was curious.

Mrs. Rice smiled. "You know, I am a smart person and speak good English. I would have no trouble finding a job here. But I won't. I told my husband: If I ever go out to work, that would mean that I have lost my confidence in your ability. Of course I phone him almost every night, saying 'I love you,' and 'You are the greatest husband and dad in this world.' He is constantly reminded of his responsibilities."

Camellia nodded carelessly, her mind drifting away. This sort of trickery wouldn't work on a man like Dwarf. Money flows easily into his pocket and allows him plenty of time to fool around with women.

Her thoughts were interrupted by a pat on the shoulder. "I tell you, Camellia, you are far from being smart and there is so much you need to learn from me. You are skilful only with your hands. You can do many things, I admit. But whatever you do is only serving other people. As for me, though my hands cannot compare with yours, my brain functions very efficiently and so I can make others work for me! You have heard Confucius' saying, 'Those who work with their brains rule and those who work with their brawn are ruled!'"

Camellia was speechless. She blinked her long eyelashes and reflected upon Mrs. Rice's words. All of a sudden, Mrs. Rice sensed that she had been carried away by her success story and made an unwise comment. Her mind whirled fast and threw out a new topic to distract Camellia.

"Sexual life between a couple is a no less important means of taming the husband, too. What I have been practicing in our sex life is never to allow him a regular three meals daily. I keep his stomach empty to make his appetite strong. When he is so hungry that he can wait no more, I throw a piece of meat to him. In this way, he enjoys his food very much, whatever it is, and feels grateful to me for letting him eat."

When she caught Camellia's eye sweeping her overweight body, she added, "Yes, I am not slim, according to current standards, but because I am clever, I never have to do any exercise like my Canadian neighbours do, to keep themselves attractive in their husbands' eyes. You see? Well, what about you? It's your turn now. Tell me something about your sex life."

Not expecting such bluntness, Camellia twisted her hips uneasily in her chair.

"How often do you go to bed with your husband?" Mrs. Rice refused to let her off the hook. "Do you have an orgasm each time?"

"Well, it's ... Oh, you know, who has never experienced that?"

"Do you still have sex with your husband since he discovered your affair?"

Camellia blushed, murmuring. "He tried to, but, you know, I won't let him ... I can't."

"No? Oh ... Then, what was it like when you were with Dwarf in China? I guess he must be a lot better than your husband?"

Camellia nodded, but then quickly shook her head again, with an embarrassed smile.

"Oh, come on!" Mrs. Rice pushed her. "There is nothing to be ashamed about! Why not tell me? You see, I am not going to be able to help you unless you give me a clear and complete picture!"

"As a matter of fact, I don't care much about a man's sexual ability." Camellia finally found a way to make her point. "I look for other things in a man."

"But sex is important throughout one's life!" Mrs. Rice hit her palm on the table to disagree. "My parents-in-law are in their eighties and they still carry on their sex life. It has become a routine for my father-in-law, just like daily meals. But that is a heavy burden on my mother-in-law. She is old and that area is too dry. Of course it isn't comfortable for her, you know that, right? Guess what I sent to Taiwan as her birthday gift last year? Vaginal lubricating cream! Wasn't that a wonderful idea?"

Chapter 8
Unicorn with Jade

I

Though busy with her new role as an English teacher, Mrs. Rice didn't neglect any of her old buddies on her evangelical list. On the night of Good Friday, Lily received a call from Mrs. Rice, reminding her to bring Grace to the supper party at the church on Saturday night. "It's free!" she emphasized.

Lily looked at the drizzle outside the window and wondered if the rain would stop at daybreak. Grace was excited to hear the good news and expressed her interest to come anyway, rain or shine.

On Saturday morning, Lily drew the curtain aside and saw the bright sunshine. Ever since she had come to Canada and learned the story of Jesus Christ, she had noticed the strange phenomenon that every Good Friday was a cloudy, miserable day, while the following Saturday and Sunday were always clear and bright.

It reminded her of China, where people joked about the fact that on March 8, International Women's Day, when female state employees were given the afternoon off, the morning would often be cloudy and the afternoon clear and bright. This coincided with the ancient yin-yang theory, which labelled females as half of the

Grand Terminus, and also illustrated one of Mao's slogans in the new China: "Women hold up half the sky."

Though several Canadian friends shook their heads at this Chinese-style superstition, Lily hoped the mystery about the death and rebirth of Jesus Christ was not just a well-intentioned fable.

Late in the afternoon when the family left home for the church dinner, Grace again showed her curiosity as they passed through a downtown church. She watched the many people walking towards its entrance and commented, "I saw some Chinese-looking people coming into this Canadian church. They must all understand English. Have you ever been there?"

Lily nodded. She had walked into this church once out of curiosity. She was warmly greeted at the door by a well-polished old man with oiled hair and shiny shoes. Despite his wide smiles, Lily was taken aback by his breath, strongly perfumed mouthwash mixed with denture odour, and quickly escaped into the assembly.

Throughout the one-hour sermon that day, Lily had focused her attention on the penguin-shaped minister in snow-white shirt and ink-black suit. He stood gracefully, whispering like a gentleman into the microphone one moment, and then jumping vigorously around the platform like a provoked bull the next. One minute his voice was as soft as a buzzing bee, but the next as loud as a roaring lion. He smiled sweetly, exposing his whitened teeth, sobbed miserably, though without any trace of tears, knitted his brows into knots, twisted his body in unbearable pain, and stamped his feet with fury at those who were still stupidly blind to God's light.

All the people in the congregation stood up, emotionally waving their arms, while singing along with the rock and roll on the stage. When the penguin finished his show and stepped down from the platform to shake hands with a few newly recruited, Lily came to the front to observe him more closely, with a couple of questions ready on her lips. Though he had a refined smile on his well-nourished pink face and greeted warmly all who reached for him, she kept her questions to herself. For an inconspicuous moment, she had caught the gleam of a worldly expression suggestive of satiation after a greasy wine banquet instead of the "holy" tint.

II

"Come this way!" Mrs. Rice waved at Lily as soon as they showed up in the basement church hall.

Tables were set out in rows. The air was filled with the good smells of deep fried chicken wings, and stir-fried noodles and rice, contributed by members in the catering business. People were chatting heartily around the tables before eating started.

Mrs. Rice pointed the seats for the family to sit by her side.

"Did Camellia come today?" Lily asked.

"No. She is working," Mrs. Rice said. "I told her that she doesn't have to work, but she won't listen!"

Lily was about to ask more questions when the meal started. After Minister Wong thanked God in a loud voice, everyone started eating.

At that moment, a couple walked into the hall.

Mrs. Rice waved her chopsticks to the late couple to come over and introduced them happily to Lily. "This is Unicorn, and this is Jade, his wife." Before she finished her introduction, however, both Lily and Jade exclaimed in surprise.

"Lily! I didn't know you were in Mapleton!" said Jade.

"It's you, Jade!" Lily was also excited. "I stopped coming to church for a few months due to the cold weather. I didn't know that you'd arrived!"

After Lily introduced Grace to the couple, Jade explained to Mrs. Rice, "We were schoolmates in the same journalism program in Beijing. Lily was then president of the Graduate Students'

Association and I was the Communist Party's group leader in my class!"

"It is indeed a small world, isn't it?" Lily held Jade's hand and examined her old friend carefully. "We have all changed so much over the years since we left school. I don't think we would have recognized each other if we'd met in the street!"

Though Jade had wrinkles in her delicate face now, she had kept her slight figure and her pleasant, silvery voice. Her narrow, slanted eyes sparkled with excitement, and she spoke animatedly. She was as warm and active as ever.

Her husband, Unicorn, on the other hand, was a silent man. Except for an initial nod at Lily, he had said not a word. He was short and plain, with the unhealthy skin colour often seen in colitis patients, and his partially gray hair stood thick and straight like the spikes of a porcupine. One of his eyes was much smaller than the other one, but both shone with stubbornness. Like an ant in a muddy hill, this man would easily skip police attention had he been a criminal. But Lily also caught a kind of determination in the firm set of his lips which suggested something other than those superficial impressions.

"When did you come to Canada?" Lily asked Jade. "I remember you were assigned to work at Radio Beijing after graduation."

"Oh," Jade sighed, "It's a long story!"

Mrs. Rice pushed her shoulder and whispered. "You'd better get some food first or the good stuff will be gone soon! Some people are getting their second helpings already! You can talk later, while you eat."

III

Jade had worked at Radio Beijing as a news editor until the June Fourth Incident in Tiananmen Square in the summer of 1989. Because of her active involvement with the political dissidents on the government's list, she was ordered to write self-confessions periodically even for years after the incident. The pressure reached its peak one day when her home was abruptly searched by the state security bureau. Upset and irritated, Jade made the bold decision to cross the border and escape to Russia with her husband. Arrangements were made by an anti-government network.

However, life in Russia, where the communist system had been replaced by capitalism, was hellish. They spent three years living like tramps in the Moscow streets, suffering from the freezing cold and constant hunger, isolated by the language barrier, and constantly worrying about the dilemma of what to do next. Murders were committed around them almost every day. Jade had to lock herself inside their apartment while Unicorn wandered the streets to look for some way to make a living. She forced herself to read, but no book could hold her attention as she was always on the alert, glancing at the doorknob nervously whenever there was the slightest noise in the corridor.

Their little son had been left in China with his grandparents. Jade missed him day and night, but returning home was impossible, since they had left China illegally. She had almost reached the end of her rope when she met two Chinese men in a Moscow street who greeted her in perfect Mandarin. Like drowning sailors seeing the mast of a ship at sea, the couple threw themselves warmly into the arms of the Christians sent by the church in Canada. Eventually, they arrived in Montreal.

"How did you turn into a Christian after being a staunch Communist Party member?" Lily asked, with great interest.

Between hasty mouthfuls, Jade recalled the earlier times in her life. She was only fifteen when she lost her mother, a dedicated high school teacher in Beijing. Her mother had been brutally tortured by her students when the Cultural Revolution erupted in 1966, and had been made to watch the lynching of the school's old principal, but nobody came to arrest the murderers. It was too much for her mother and she chose to die one night by taking an overdose of sleeping pills.

As the only child of a suicidal anti-revolutionary mother, Jade received all sorts of abuse at her school's denouncing meetings. It was a girls' school, but all the girls behaved like beasts then. Her former friends came onto the platform to spit at her, kick her, and pour ink and glue all over her. "I almost wanted to follow my mother to the other world!" Tears burst out of her eyes even now, at the memory.

Lily passed her a tissue and patted her.

"The Cultural Revolution has been over for many years, but the nightmare often comes back to me." Jade continued. "Whenever I think about my mother, I feel miserable. After I became a Christian, I felt even worse. Had she known there is a mighty God and cherished any hope, she would never have chosen death ..."

After they arrived in Montreal, the couple could not find decent jobs for two years and had to rely on welfare to survive. Unicorn used to be an engineer but ended up delivering pizza in Montreal. As the months went by, he became hot tempered. They quarrelled frequently and she started to go to church and pray hard for God's help. The church in Montreal sent people to her home to help calm Unicorn with advice from the Bible. Almost every visitor sent to her home was convinced that to convert Unicorn would mean smashing a rock with an egg.

But God always worked in his own miraculous way. One day when Unicorn was delivering pizza on a country road, driving at high speed, his car crashed into an oncoming car and killed the old lady driver. Unicorn survived. He was out of the hospital a week later, after a surgery leaving him with different sized eyes. The accident made him ponder: could this be a warning from God? Had he been denying the messages sent from God's visitors?

Two months after Unicorn had started to read the Bible carefully, he received a letter from Mapleton University inviting him to continue his scientific research. Since then, he had been reading the Bible conscientiously every night.

IV

"What a long road you have travelled to get to Canada!" Lily said.

"What made you abandon your wonderful job to come to Canada, anyway?" Jade asked.

Lily thought for a few seconds before she replied with a smile, "A real man."

"So it was for love." Jade also smiled. "Who is this real man?"

Lily laughed. "Fundamentally, I came for the spirit of Norman Bethune."

"Is that so?" Jade claimed, making a face. But after a moment's thought, she nodded. "Well, I believe it could be a good reason."

"Sorry, which real man?" Mrs. Rice was at a loss. Chewing on a chicken wing, she looked at Lily with curiosity.

Lily was not surprised. She had become used to the ignorance people in the hero's country have shown about him. In Canada there was hardly anyone who knew his name, though in China there was hardly anyone who wasn't familiar with the name of this Canadian. As someone from Taiwan, it was quite natural that Mrs. Rice had never heard about this communist hero.

"You can tell her about Norman Bethune," Grace said to Lily encouragingly.

Lily told Mrs. Rice that in China everyone in her generation could recite the article written by Chairman Mao about the hero, just as almost everyone in Canada had read about the Bible.

"What did the article say?" Mrs. Rice showed curiosity.

Lily started to recite: "Dr. Norman Bethune was sent to China by the Communist Party of Canada."

Unicorn and Jade both joined her. "He made light of travelling thousands of miles to help us in our War of Resistance Against Japan. He worked in China for two years and to our great sorrow died a martyr at his post. What kind of spirit is this that makes a foreigner selflessly adopt the cause of the Chinese people's liberation as his own? It is the spirit of internationalism, the spirit of communism, from which every Chinese Communist must learn ..."

Lily stopped, forgetting her lines. The couple also stopped. They looked at each other, and laughed. Lily found tears in Unicorn's eyes. She felt a warm current in her bosom.

"What are you laughing at?" Mrs. Rice shook her head. "There is nothing interesting in those words. It's kind of boring, in my opinion."

The opening paragraph of the article "In Memory of Norman Bethune," written by Chairman Mao in 1939, brought Lily back to the years when she was a schoolgirl. The words in the article were dry, indeed, compared with the movie about the hero. She described whatever she could remember about Bethune to Mrs. Rice.

In the mountains and plains of North China, the strange name shone over mud huts and caves. In Chinese characters, Bethune meant White Seeking Grace. In villages where no doctor had ever been seen, peasants spoke with pride of the doctor who had come to them from the remote world to make the dying live.

Norman Bethune trained many Chinese medical workers and created the first hospital in that region, built in a Buddhist temple but flattened by Japanese bombardment two months after its birth.

On high mountain trails and through long valleys went his portable "operating theater," transported by two mules. Sleeping in hollows in the biting night cold, the strong-minded man with flashing eyes led his caravan to wherever there were wounded.

He travelled to the battlefields to tend casualties under heavy Japanese shellfire. He drew his own blood to rescue dying soldiers and then completed the operations.

Unfortunately, the forty-nine-year-old doctor cut his own finger during an operation and developed an infection. Bethune was dying when the hard-to-get penicillin arrived. He had finished his will, leaving all his belongings to people who had worked for him and with him. His last wish was to save the precious medicine for other people.

"Because of all this, Chairman Mao concluded, at the end of his article, that 'Bethune was noble-minded and pure, of moral integrity, with love and sympathy, and of value to the people,'" Lily said.

V

Mrs. Rice shrugged, sneering, "Sounds as if he was Jesus Christ! I doubt it!" She put down her chopsticks, wiped her mouth, and changed the topic by asking Jade, "Tell me, how was your home visit this afternoon?"

Jade shook her head slowly. "Not so pleasant."

"Tell me what happened." Mrs. Rice stretched her neck in full attention.

"We had been talking cordially until I started telling them about God's kingdom. The couple suddenly cooled down and treated me as if I were trying to sell them drugs!"

"Well, you can't pour hot soup down your throat! Next time, you must not reveal your purpose at the very beginning. Make friends first and start to spread the gospel only after they begin to trust you."

"But I have already visited this family three times and this was the result!" Jade frowned. "I feel so weak and need support from our organization dearly."

Lily was amused by the word "organization." It sounded just like the Communist Party. One of the party's iron rules was to require its members to report everything to the "organization" and follow whatever instructions given by the "organization." Does a church function the same way as a political party?

She watched Jade, who was listening attentively to Mrs. Rice's teaching and nodding with a trusting look. Just like me, Lily thought, Jade was brought up in the collective-styled communist society. Though we all had a hard life and wanted, at least theoretically, to get rid of the dictatorial system, we had actually become accustomed to its style: a life of unity, collectives, instructions, orders, control, and mass mobilization. Psychologically, we were still afraid of being isolated and being independent.

Jade, Lily thought, had not been in Canada long enough to appreciate its culture of independence. She desired strong fellow comrades who all shared a common goal. She was thirsty for all-encompassing instructions from a powerful organization and wished to swim in a collective environment. In Canada, however, there was no place except the church where she could find the familiar atmosphere she was so used to.

On an impulse, Lily asked Jade if she and Unicorn had been baptized.

To her surprise, Jade replied, "No, we haven't."

"Oh, why not, if you are already so faithful in your belief?"

Glancing at Unicorn, Jade answered, "I am ready, but he still has some problems."

"What kind of problems?"

"I am still looking for the real church," Unicorn explained. "I have tried a few different ones, both in Montreal and Mapleton, but I could not find the right one to baptize me."

"What kind of church are you seeking?" Lily asked. "I have tried different ones as well, Baptist, Presbyterian, United Church, Catholic, and Jehovah's Witnesses. But the more I compare, the more indecisive I feel. In Canada, we are given too many choices, and nobody tells us the correct way, quite the opposite of China."

"Well, I am looking for one where the majority of the converts behave in the way that is described in the Bible," Unicorn looked serious.

Lily grinned. "How do you feel about this church?"

Unicorn was about to say something but stopped when Mrs. Rice waved to Mr. Wong, who was walking over towards their table.

Minister Wong reached out his hand to Grace and said warmly, "I have heard from Mrs. Rice about your coming to Canada. We welcome you!"

Grace stood up from her chair, blushed and smiled shyly when she shook hands with Minister Wong. As Minister Wong turned and was about to leave, however, Unicorn put down the chicken leg in his hand and put out his arm to stop him. "Just a minute, Minister Wong. May I talk with you for a second?"

"Yes, what can I do for you?" Minister Wong asked politely, carefully avoiding Unicorn's hand. He was in a fashionable new suit today, a Pierre Cardin.

Unicorn wiped his mouth with a napkin and stood up to talk with Minister Wong. He was at least a head shorter than the Minister so he had to look up. "I have a few suggestions for your service."

Minister Wong blinked his eyes. "What are they?"

Unicorn said, "First of all, I don't think it is right for you to attack other factions of the Christian church in your sermons. You think only your church is the authentic one and all others are heresies. To me, however, each church has its merits as well as its weaknesses, and no church should be regarded as the sole correct one."

"But," Minister Wong disagreed, "if you study the Bible more carefully, you will be able to see the heresies."

Unicorn shook his head and continued. "I have also noticed that each time you give a sermon, you end up by saying, 'May God bless all of you,' and 'May the peace of God be with you forever!' I think this is wrong."

Minister Wong replied with a confident voice, "There is nothing wrong in this! It is written in the Bible."

"Alright!" Unicorn suddenly opened his good eye wide. "But who said this in the Bible?"

"Jesus Christ, of course." Minister Wong shrugged, showing impatience.

"Yes," Unicorn nodded, and went on, "I know it was Jesus Christ. But who is he? He is God, isn't he? Sure, he can speak that way. But how can you, an ordinary person, speak the same way as God? The problem lies here. You regard yourself as God and not the same as the rest of us. The correct way for you to say it should be as this: May God bless all of *us* and may the peace of God be with *us* forever!"

Minister Wong's face flushed. But Unicorn tried to explain further. "I have always felt it odd when you talk that way. So I checked the Bible carefully to make sure this sentence was spoken by Jesus Christ. I am telling you my opinions honestly because I sincerely hope that our church will be led in a healthy way."

Minister Wong looked around hastily to see if there was anyone paying attention to the conversation. He took off his glasses and cleaned them with a piece of cloth, trying to cover his uneasiness.

Lily felt sorry for him and looked away to avoid embarrassment. She had heard from Mrs. Rice that Minister Wong, proud and hot-tempered, had expressed a bias against people from Mainland China. People who grew up in a communist world, he once complained to Mrs. Rice, seemed to enjoy debating issues and question why. Besides, they were generally not as wealthy as those from Taiwan and Hong Kong and couldn't be relied upon as a major income source for the church.

Lily worried that Minister Wong was irritated by Unicorn's comment. Just as she expected, as Minister Wong calmed down, he responded to Unicorn with an ironic smile: "Well, as you are

from communist China, there is still a long way to go before you
can really recognize what makes a healthy Christian church!"

Unicorn laughed. "I have plenty of knowledge for understanding
that, because Christianity is similar to Communism in many ways.
If it isn't, I won't accept it!"

"It's totally insulting to put the two together!" Minister Wong
raised his voice. "Communism is an evil system! In a free society, you
can say whatever you like, but in a country like China, if you dare to
criticize the President today, you are finished tomorrow!"

"Ignorant!" Unicorn waved his hand. "You are simply repeating
propaganda from the U.S. government!"

Minister Wong was about to attack Unicorn further when he
noticed that they were already drawing attention. He held back
his words and forced out a thin smile. "No more argument. I must
attend a meeting now."

As he walked away, Jade, looking worried, whispered to Mrs. Rice.
Putting down her drink, Mrs. Rice stood up hurriedly and followed
Minister Wong to his office. Lily hoped she would be able to smooth
things over.

Grace had watched the argument attentively, obviously trying to
conceal her nervous excitement. She felt relieved seeing the Minister gone and murmured to Lily, "I hope he is not offended."

Her words were interrupted by Baby who was nibbling at a piece
of carrot but putting another one in front of Lily's eyes with the
Chinese words, "Mom" and "eat."

Lily was glad to see that Baby had started talking, ever since he
had participated in the children's Sunday school. Altogether, he was
able to say about ten words now.

"He is so lovely!" Jade touched Baby's head and said to Lily, "He
reminds me of my son when he was a cute toddler." Then she was
silent, clearly lost in thoughts of her son back in Beijing.

"Have you applied for him to come to Canada?" Lily asked.

"Yes." Jade looked happy again. "We sent an application right after we acquired our permanent status in Canada. He should join us soon if nothing goes wrong. Where is your husband? Is he in Canada?"

Lily simply answered, "No," picked up a napkin, and cleaned Baby's face and hands.

Grace's face turned gloomy. She gave Lily an accusing stare and looked away.

As a sensitive woman, Jade knew that something unhappy must have occurred in Lily's life. "Well, I have talked all the time about my experience. But I haven't heard anything about your life in Canada yet. What have you been doing all these years?"

Lily looked up in the ceiling as if searching for something in the air. Seconds later, she shook her head with a dry smile. "Nothing worth mentioning."

Chapter 9
The Remaining Soapy Bubbles

I

Lily's earliest memories of Canada had flown away like bubbles blown from a child's mouth. Most disappeared promptly before she could fully appreciate their shapes and shades. A few remained vivid and alive.

On her first day in Canada, she feared that the ways exemplified by Dr. Norman Bethune, the real man she had been looking for ever since she was twenty, had long disappeared in Canada.

When her airplane landed at Pearson Airport, it was almost midnight. As the passengers walked through the long passageway leading to the arrivals area, she was behind a group of middle-aged white people. They talked loudly but moved slowly, totally blocking the way. Lily was anxious to find out if there were still buses going to Mapleton at this late hour. She walked faster, care-fully moving past the heavy lady in front of her. As she passed, however, she heard the lady yelling, "No!" She hesitated briefly, but didn't slow her pace. As she passed another one in the group, however, someone kicked her ankle hard and she almost fell. She looked back in shock, and saw a man with gray hair and a narrow red face staring at her and roaring: "Excuse me!" The group burst out laughing. She shuddered and felt deeply humiliated, but failed to find any vocabulary she could apply in dealing with idiots. The American Bear didn't teach the students how to swear. His hairy image loomed in her mind, now as a real gentleman.

Her initial shock wore off quite quickly, though. When Helen, her graduate advisor, asked her what courses she would like to select, Lily was at a loss. It dawned on her that she was in Canada and there was no more Party organization to arrange things for her now. At age thirty, she had to learn how to make decisions for herself.

For a few nights she was invited to sleep in Helen's living room, while taking her first step towards independence: finding her own place. As she started hunting, she learned that a math professor owned a house near campus with fair rent for students.

"I have seldom seen an Oriental woman as tall and fair as you!" the math professor exclaimed as Lily entered his office. He also praised her fluent English and suggested that he take her to dinner where they would discuss the rent.

The professor drove his car onto the highway and out of the city, finally stopping at a red-roofed restaurant surrounded by farm fields. Entering the exquisitely decorated dining room, she wondered why he would bother to drive so far for just a meal.

They were the only customers. The meal lasted two hours. Though Lily was very hungry, she had little time to enjoy the dishes, as she had to deal with numerous questions from the professor. He inquired in detail about China, everything from politics and history, to culture and the economy. In this country, an invitation to a free dinner must mean payment with a free lecture, she thought.

After the meal, the professor drove the car back to the city and pulled in by the riverside. "I want you to enjoy the best scenery in Mapleton!" he told her.

Lily would have preferred to go back and have a rest. But fearing she might offend her host, she pretended to be happy.

There were quite a few cars by the riverside. She felt odd as the professor parked the car in the back row, with all windows tightly shut, and continued with his endless questions.

She didn't see the promised great scenery from inside the car, except for some yellowish lights across the river on the American side. She felt dizzy and headachy as the air got stuffy in the hot summer night. She also needed to go to the washroom, but was too shy to say so.

Another hour went by, but the professor's enthusiasm grew and his interest eventually shifted to personal matters. It was hard to carry on such an overlong conversation and she looked for an opportunity to end it. He didn't seem to understand her deliberately briefer and slower responses, but accelerated his questions and shortened the intervals between them, leaving no chance for her to say "let me go."

She felt caught in a thick web, the situation suffocating. She waited and hesitated until it became intolerable. Finally, she decided to abandon her Chinese-style politeness and said bravely, "Sorry, Professor, I am suffering from a headache and cannot stay here any longer. Would you please take me back?"

He glanced at her, an elusive smile on his face. She felt guilty. I must have been rude, interrupting the host's show of goodwill.

As he started the car, she let out her breath. It suddenly dawned on her, "Well, it turns out that foreigners don't understand subtle hints. Everything has to be stated frankly and straightforwardly!"

She kept silent all the way, afraid of triggering any unexpected suggestions. Not until after she got out of the car did she dare to bring up the original issue: "What about your room for rent?"

Another ambiguous smile loomed. "Well, I'll think about it and give you a call this week!"

II

The next day, Lily found a notice on campus advertising a place with low rent.

She entered the dark, narrow basement of a house and was warmly welcomed by an Egyptian. He introduced himself as a PhD student and said he was looking for someone to share the small two-bedroom apartment.

As the Egyptian happily showed her around the rooms, Lily looked at the man, his hair permed in a fashionable style, off his forehead and curling down the back of his neck, like a seahorse.

Though the idea of sharing an apartment with a male was hard to accept, Lily tried to convince herself that this was the Canadian way. Other Chinese students who had arrived in Canada earlier had set the example when males and females squeezed into one small apartment to save money.

She decided to leave, however, when her eyes fell on cockroaches running in all directions as she opened the closets and drawers in the kitchen.

The seahorse held up a couple of bottles. "Don't worry about that! I have ways to deal with them."

She retreated politely but firmly.

Back at Helen's home, she was told she had to find a place as soon as possible.

"I'll have a visitor next week," Helen said, her face turning pink.

Helen mentioned that a colleague at school might have a place for Lily and drove her to the house immediately.

It was a nice house by the woods. The couple, who taught Hebrew, was near retirement age and planning to resettle in Israel. The wife showed Lily the extra bedroom she could move into and explained the arrangements, "We both like Chinese food very much. If you cook for us every day, you would pay us only $100 monthly for the rent."

Lily was still working on the math when Helen expressed concern on her behalf. "I am afraid Lily won't have time to cook for the family every day. She will need more time to study, particularly in her first term."

The next morning, Lily phoned the math professor again.

"There is indeed a vacant room in my house," the math professor confirmed. "As for the rent, well, everybody else pays $200 monthly, but I can make an exception for you. You can live there free!"

"Free?" Lily thought he was joking.

"Yes, free," he paused for a second, "if you will have dinner with me once every week."

There was a sour flavour in his tone, as unpredictable as his smiles by the riverside. Without hesitation this time, Lily turned down his offer.

III

Lily finally found a place near campus. The original shape of the house was typical for a Canadian family house, with three bedrooms upstairs and a dining room and sitting room on the main floor. When seven graduate students from China had moved into it a couple of years before, they had divided the entire house with curtains, making a private corner for each of them.

When Lily moved in, she was lucky to get the former sitting room. Her neighbour in the former dining room was a girl from Shanghai. People from that city had a reputation in China as being streetwise. Lily was grateful to have this wisdom, particularly in an economics student, close at hand.

In the hot summer, when the rooms felt humid and stuffy, the Shanghai girl bought an electric fan. A month later as the weather became cooler, she took the fan back to the store on the last day of the refund period.

Seeing Lily rushing between classes, the library, and her bedroom every day, the Shanghai girl grinned, "If Bs can guarantee you next term's scholarship, why should you abuse your precious youth in getting As? Don't you understand that men appreciate your flesh rather than your brain?"

The Shanghai girl had made up her mind to marry a "foreigner" instead of a Chinese. "Students from China are too poor! They can only afford to date you in their offices. Talking and talking until their lips become dry, they do not even offer a cup of coffee!"

As part of her scheme, the Shanghai girl never cooked at home. "Cooking makes you smell greasy," she told Lily. "And you lose the precious opportunity of bumping into rich men in restaurants."

Every morning, she would dress up neatly and walk into the Harvey's down the street. A cup of black coffee and a small order of onion rings would keep her there for half an hour while she waited for any big fish to appear.

Not long after, Lily noticed that the Shanghai girl was surrounded by a few "foreigners." Among them was the Seahorse.

The Shanghai girl told Lily that she liked Seahorse better than the others, since his parents were well-to-do capitalists who owned a middle-eastern grocery store in Toronto.

"But aren't you afraid that he will eventually marry four wives?" Lily teased her. "That is legal in their culture."

The Shanghai girl was not put off. "If that happens, I will ask for a divorce and get half of his property. That is the Canadian law!"

But one midnight, Lily was wakened up by a knock on the door. The Shanghai girl entered her room and started to cry: "I have finally seen through him! He brought me to his place after we had dinner in a restaurant. He started kissing and cuddling and eventually demanded sex. I told him that the Chinese do not accept pre-marital sex. He lost his temper immediately and complained that it was not fair that I would eat his dinner but not go to bed with him.

I said that he was totally unreasonable to value a dinner the same as a woman's virginity!

"But he said since we were in Canada, we should follow Canadian custom. In a Canadian store, you can try on any clothes you like before you buy, and you can easily get a refund if you don't like them. A marriage is a lifelong investment, so of course one has to try it before making decisions.

"I made it clear to him that a woman is fundamentally different from a coat. Once you have tried her on and decided you don't want her, nobody else would want her!

"He was irritated when he failed to convince me. He asked me to get out of his sight at once, since my presence had become torture for him!"

When the Shanghai girl found a young white "foreigner" visiting Lily, she could hardly conceal her jealousy. "How did you get such a good deal?"

Lily explained that Kevin, a new professor in philosophy, was simply interested in learning the Chinese language with her. Kevin was a China fan. Besides learning Mandarin, he was also enrolled in the local kung fu school to learn Chinese swordplay. Sometimes when Lily finished her tutoring, they would walk to the campus, where Kevin, dressed in loose black pants tied at the ankle like an old-style Chinese peasant, would display his newly acquired skills proudly to her. "I wish to become a Shaolin monk one day," he declared.

Lily was amazed that Kevin would know Shaolin, the most famous Buddhist temple in China that had a tradition of more than 1,500 years training its monks in the martial arts. His knowledge and enthusiasm about Chinese culture added to his value on Lily's scale.

Though she denied the Shanghai girl's probing, she actually couldn't deny her liking for this "foreigner." It was a pity that Kevin's dream was to become a Buddhist monk.

One evening before suppertime, when Kevin was practicing in the meadow at dusk, quite a few passers-by stopped and watched his graceful movements in admiration.

"I should start a class on campus!" Kevin felt pleased, nodding at Lily.

At that moment, a Chinese man laughed loudly, commenting, "You still have a long way to go to be a master!"

Before Lily had a clear view of this rude intruder, he walked out of the small crowd of observers and said to Kevin, "What you are performing is simply for display, but no good for practical usage." He then showed Kevin a few movements, which he explained were the authentic Shaolin style kung fu from China.

As she watched, Lily's initial dislike of the proud man vanished. She was drawn by the man's quick, forceful movements and started to appreciate his handsome features. He was nicely proportioned, an eye-catching type not commonly seen among Chinese men.

When they parted that evening, he told her to call him Majesty, a nickname he had acquired from childhood friends.

Lily's impression of Majesty as a "real man" was deepened when the Tiananmen Square Incident took place in the summer of 1989.

The Chinese students on the Canadian campus gathered together around the TV, watching the tanks and armed soldiers rushing into the Square and bloody bodies being removed on bicycles amid the sounds of gunshot. At dawn, Lily joined the students for a big rally in Toronto, where tens of thousands of people gathered to pay tribute to the dead.

During these events, Lily observed with admiration the way Majesty organized student meetings, talked bravely to interviewing cameras, and called for donations for families of the dead. He is a brave man, she concluded.

It took three years, however, before Lily finally started to question the bravery of this man.

Chapter 10
The Cat on the Swing

I

On July 1, Majesty and Lily, sitting side by side, watched the fireworks from the hilltop by the river. People around them yelled happily as the night sky was tinted green, yellow, purple, and red.

"It's the birthday of the Chinese Communist Party as well as the birthday of Canada. Don't you think we should have a celebration?" Majesty asked, taking a bottle of Scotch out of his bag and waving it in front of her eyes.

They returned to her place and sat on the floor in front of the TV Lily had picked up from the street. They opened the bottle. Lily sipped and frowned, "Oh, my, what a horrible taste!"

Majesty tried it and shook his head too. "Of course, no foreign liquor can compete with the Chinese ones. The aromas run into your nostrils as soon as you open the top!"

Lily found some pickles to go with the drink. As they talked about the famous liquors at home, the strange flavour of the foreign drink became milder.

"It's boring, just to drink this way. Let's have a contest!" Lily suggested. "Isn't it the Chinese tradition to combine liquor and poems in one?"

Majesty was enthusiastic, too. "How about reciting Mao's poems? The loser will be fined with a mouthful of liquor!"

The poems flew out of their lips like a running stream. The highly romantic and heroic sentences composed by the late Chairman in his prime had become popular throughout China during the Cultural Revolution. In less than an hour, they had finished the nostalgic recitation. The liquor in the bottle remained untouched. No one was a loser.

Majesty lit up a cigarette and inhaled deeply. "Things we experience when young are not forgotten easily!" His black eyes under the thick brows focused on the soft lamplight. "But those crazy years buried our youth alive!"

II

When he was sent to the Inner Mongolian Steppes he was only eighteen. He carried his luggage and kung fu stick on his back to the railway station, where he saw many parents crying as their children were forced to go far away from home. He didn't cry, for he believed Chairman Mao was right in sending high school graduates to be re-educated by the peasants in the harsh rural areas. The slogan sounded convincing—washing away the bourgeois ideology with sweats and forging a new generation physically strong and morally sound.

In the small village where he was assigned to stay, he was elected by the other nineteen youths as their leader. They lived in a large mud house with two big rooms, one for males and one for females. At the beginning, the youths and the peasants got along well. They worked in the cornfields and herded horses with the villagers during the day, and taught the peasants to read Mao's works and government documents at night. Some of them were assigned to be teachers in the village school. Some who received three months of training became the so-called "barefoot doctors" and practiced acupuncture and provided simple medical care for the peasants.

In the small village far away from town, it was hard to get the latest newspapers. The youths read Mao's *Little Red Book* over and over because there were no other books available. On the walls and ceilings of their house, old newspapers were pasted as wall-paper. Majesty read each line on the old newspapers repeatedly and changed his body position constantly, sometimes lying flat and sometimes upside down, so as not to miss a single word.

One day, a young man returning from a trip to a town a hundred kilometres away shouted to all about his discovery. "Hey, we are all backward snails! People in town nowadays are studying the philosophical works of Mao, Karl Marx, Frederic Engels, and Lenin, but we are still reading the *Little Red Book* in this isolated village!"

They experienced snowstorms, earthquakes, prairie fires, mountain floods, and man-made social disasters. Over many sleepless nights they pondered the road their lives seemed to be taking. As more years went by their enthusiasm faded. Everyone tried hard to find ways of leaving the village. Once in a while, a quota was assigned to the village to recommend someone to study in a university or to work in a factory. To get recommended by the villagers, everybody worked hard to please the peasants.

From the very beginning, the peasants knew that the city youths were not going to settle there forever. Despite the initial government subsidies, the youths' existence threatened the already meagre resources in the village. Gradually, the peasants started to regard them as headaches. There were a lot of disputes, such as fighting over the distribution of meat and fuel. One winter when their house was freezing cold and the villagers refused to give them enough cornstalks, Majesty led the youths in grabbing a whole wagonload of stalks from the warehouse during the night.

"It was stealing, I admit," Majesty said. "But we were forced to do it, to survive."

They usually had no meat unless an ox became sick or too old to work and had to be butchered. The scene of butchering was very sad. The ox understood what was happening, but could not talk. It kneeled on the ground, tears dropping from its eyes, pleading. Majesty watched with complicated feelings, but then everyone in the village would have a share of its meat. When there was no meat for months, some young men would kill the hens and dogs the villagers had raised privately. While the young people were cooking the meats by their stove, the villagers would stand by the door swearing loudly.

"Well, those stupid days! It has been twenty years now, and a whole generation has gone by!" He finished with an emotional sigh.

Lily listened to his account and was lost in her own memories too. She had escaped being sent to a remote rural village. At the age of sixteen, she joined the navy, on the basis that she was good at singing and dancing. In the 1970s, when propagating Mao's thought was the priority of the government, the army, the navy, the air force, and all large government companies recruited young people who had artistic skills to set up performing teams.

"You were luckier than we were," Majesty commented. "At least, you were entitled to a fixed income and medical care and didn't have to worry about your future."

"My suffering was different. The political pressure and the strict discipline in the navy almost drove me insane!" She recalled her futile struggle for three years to be accepted as a member of the Communist Youth League. She always failed because of her innocent outspokenness.

When they found it was already midnight, Majesty stood up. Outside, he stopped on the porch, breathing deeply the night air filled with the fragrance of roses blooming by the moonlit fence. Lily stood behind him, wordlessly. The smell of a man, a mixture of sweat and smoke, was intoxicating. She held her breath. Her heart thumped fast.

III

Lily's ill-fated marriage had been brought to a full stop before she met Majesty.

Prince arrived in Montreal three months after Lily left China. She managed to get him accepted into an English language school in this city far away from her.

Lily refused his plea to join her in Mapleton but insisted that he should face the challenge and learn to overcome all difficulties by himself, just as she had. She also reminded him of her decision to get a divorce once he could stand on his own.

"Please be merciful!" he begged in his letters. "I feel lonely in this cold city with knee-deep snow most of the year and foreign voices every day."

His letters never failed to depress Lily. She felt guilty about having sent this weak soul into a helpless situation, while at the same time, the psychological torture reinforced her decision to leave this wretched man.

She had applied for permanent residency shortly after her arrival in Canada. She waited for a year until her application was approved, and Prince's also approved as her spouse, to bring up the divorce issue again. Though still reluctant, Prince was grateful for her help in obtaining his permanent status, which made his life easier in Canada, and finally agreed to a divorce.

While signing the papers in the Chinese Consulate General in Toronto, she bit her lips and avoided looking at the man whose face was smeared with tears. When her bus left Toronto and was running along the wilderness dyed yellow and red by autumn wind, she burst out crying and wept all the way during the five-hour trip home, mourning her buried youth and repenting her role as a deserter who caused the weak and vulnerable to suffer.

In Prince's last letter to her a week later, he wrote,

I knew you were a very special woman from the very beginning and thus decided to dedicate my whole life to you. To make sure you were mine, I took you against your will. I am fully aware of the hurt in your heart and therefore tried my best to heal up the wound and to melt the ice during our brief life together.

It's a pity that you cannot appreciate my love. The more effort I made to please you, the more you treated me as a dirt. There were moments when I saw you happy, which always reassured my heart. But often, the smiles were brief and would disappear as your eyes became fixed. I knew what you must have remembered at those moments and I had to remain dumb.

Under your critical eyes, I could never raise up my head high. You have defined me as a shallow person who doesn't deserve a "deep" thinker like you. Now you are leaving and I don't have to act humble in front of you any more. I want to tell you that I am deeper than you have imagined, but unfortunately your limited view prevents you from realizing that fact.

Here's a simple example. You felt bad that I had had sexual experiences with two other women before I met you. That shadow never disappeared from our marital life. You have always regarded me as an immoral person, and looked down upon me with contempt as if I were a released criminal.

But I don't think I was wrong in what I did. Chinese society is extremely narrow-minded in judging premarital sex. Now that we are in Canada, I believe you have observed with your own eyes how open people are here. Don't you see that I am just a victim of the pre-modern ideology in China?

*I hate to lose you but understand there is no choice. I realize that my
love, unfortunately, can only be proved by allowing this cruel divorce,
which you so desperately desire.*

*You are free now. However, you will eventually find out that I am
the most suitable type of man in this world, for a woman like you.*

*To heal your psychological wound, I will treat you fairly. I promise
I will wait for six years for you to recognize the serious mistake you
have made. We were together for less than three years. Is three years
enough to judge a man? In six years, then, you can try two different
men. If you find out that I am actually better than the others, please,
then, come back.*

After reading the man's final letter, Lily's heart was sprinkled with a
mixed spice of bitter, sweet, hot, and sour. For the first time, she felt
this man had some value, but she shut her eyes and forced herself
to ignore the feeling.

IV

On Majesty's 38th birthday, Lily planned to give him a surprise.
Though never interested in cooking, she busied herself for hours
that afternoon and managed to put four dishes on the table.

He came and sat down, took out a picture and a toy cat from his
bag and sighed. "My daughter's birthday is close to mine and I forgot completely about hers. But she still remembers mine and mailed
this birthday present. I am a bad father, very bad!"

He touched the toy cat, which dangled on a swing, and then gazed
at the picture for a long time, completely ignoring the dishes on the
table as they became cool and then cold.

Lily looked at the picture. "How old is she? Six? She looks like a
naughty boy."

"What? Do you think she looks like a boy? Why? How come I

don't see it?" Majesty dug in, his eyes shining. Clearly, he was more eager to discuss every detail about his only daughter than to enjoy the birthday dishes.

A flush of jealousy dampened Lily. But she forced herself into a patient study of the picture, to please the man she liked.

Majesty moved into this house when the Shanghai girl had moved out to live with a PhD student from India.

Lily asked if the Indian had promised her marriage after the trial period.

"Who cares?" the Shanghai girl replied, in a defeated tone.

The fear of being alone has taken over her sense of pride, Lily thought. Many of us reluctantly give up our long-cherished values when we are thrown into a society where people are supposed to be independent.

Ever since Majesty had moved into the Shanghai girl's former room and become Lily's next-door neighbour, he had gradually reduced the number of letters he wrote back home, though not the amount of money he saved from his meagre pay.

Lily understood that his concerns about his wife and daughter in China had not diminished a single bit. He was just giving himself a testing period to check his capacity to make a cruel decision.

The woman far away in China didn't seem to notice any of the obvious changes taking place in her man. Every once in a while, the familiar red and blue envelope with pitiable handwriting would appear in the mailbox. The intrusion of the innocent letters served successfully to revive his guilt. There were intervals when Majesty would deliberately avoid Lily for a few days.

The three-year-long, awkward relationship with Majesty helped Lily understand the truth: for people with a conscience, to abandon was more painful than to be abandoned.

Sometimes when they were taking a walk after dinner around the well-shaded streets, Majesty's confident laughter would suddenly stop as his eyes fell on a little Asian girl passing. Always at those moments, Lily would have to be very cautious in her conversation, lest her own joyfulness might be offensive to the sorrow of the poor father.

One evening, Lily got supper ready in the kitchen. She called Majesty a couple of times but had no reply. She put down the dishes and walked into his room, only to find him standing by the window, looking worried. Her eyes quickly swept his room and caught the familiar light green, square-lined paper on his desk. She picked up the letter, read it, and located the source of his loss of appetite.

> *Yesterday I tried to get our daughter registered in a school. I went to a number of places, but found all the good quality ones are full and won't take her. Tears came out of my eyes and dropped onto my shirt . . .*

Lily could not understand why this woman, a few years older than herself, would be so vulnerable in facing just a little trouble. Not only did she overreact by shedding tears, but she also wrote her tears down and mailed them to the helpless father on the other side of the globe. He was successfully beaten down. Probably, tears were the most powerful weapon in attacking a good-natured man.

Where did you get so much cat's pee? What's the use of crying? Mother's comments about Lily's tears sneaked into her mind. She wondered if Mother ever understood the power of tears.

Majesty responded to the cat pee by sending more money back home and instructing the woman to bribe school principals with expensive gifts.

V

Neither Majesty nor Lily was rich then. Each of them lived on a $5,000 yearly teaching assistant's salary. To save money, they never bought any fresh vegetables and fruit, putting only the reduced items into their cart when shopping.

They also discovered a new way to save further. In the farmer's market on Saturdays, they found some vendors dumping leftovers in the garbage cans at closing time. From the so-called "garbage," they could pick out plenty of good produce. They would collect boxes of vegetables and fruit, enough to feed ten people for a whole week.

Majesty would pile up four boxes of the fragile produce on the back rack of his old bike. He carried the hardier things, such as potatoes and carrots, in a big sack on his back. While he pushed the bike forward, Lily helped hold the boxes steady at the rear. Once home, they kept enough for themselves and sent the extra to other Chinese students.

Sometimes when they were pushing the fully loaded bike home, Lily noticed passing cars slowing down beside them. They were often Lily's professors and friends. She had to turn down their kind offer of a ride because of Majesty's stubborn insistence on self-reliance. "I hate to beg anyone for help!" he declared.

She didn't appreciate his overdeveloped pride. It only made her suffer with him under the hot summer sun for hours, on display to many observing eyes. But he was used to being stared at, having been a professor in China for eight years, and was impatient with her discomfort.

Her self-esteem was deeply hurt one day when she was driven away by an old vendor at the market. "Get away from here, you garbage collector!" The man waved his hand and sneered at her in contempt. Her blood froze as she painfully realized her nasty image now in the market. When she complained to Majesty about their shameless deeds, however, he only criticized her for acting like a petty bourgeois when her vanity was injured.

Now she wondered which was worse—Majesty's down-to-earth, practical manner, or Prince's dandy-type vanity?

"Do you really love me or not?" she questioned, her voice stern. "Why don't you care about my feelings at all?"

"Only a petty man would whisper sweet things in your ears all the time and pay attention to such trivial stuff," Majesty always replied in an all-correct manner. "A real man takes care of you at crucial moments and on significant events."

"Then, why do you insult me by not divorcing?" Lily cornered him. "Do you think that is something trivial?"

Majesty looked at her anguished eyes and fell silent. A moment later, he let out a heavy-hearted sigh.

"I have deliberately prolonged the process, to get her more prepared. You know she is weak. Besides, there is the child. If her mother went insane, how could we live happily? On the other hand, if you are smart, you should appreciate that I am a serious man about important decisions. If I can treat her so carefully, I would do the same to you ..."

VI

The situation had gone on this way for two years. Majesty had stretched the intervals between his letters home from three to six months. But when he was idle, he would lean against his bed and stare at the swinging cat he kept on the desk.

The red and blue envelope never failed to arrive in the mailbox with its monthly report. The contents were forever the same: repeated reminding about his eating habits and clothing care from a loving wife.

 · Doesn't she ever feel suspicious? Lily thought she must. That would explain why she sent her daughter's photos regularly, but never included her own image. She must have guessed everything. But by pretending to know nothing, she cleverly shifted the responsibility for a showdown onto the man's shoulders.

Though the woman didn't have much schooling, she had naturally inherited in her blood the essence of traditional Chinese philosophy. Her display of the Taoist survival strategy of non-struggle, tolerance, submissiveness, and to never be the first proved the ancient principles effective in "conquering the hard with softness."

Majesty said with a heavy heart, "The most difficult thing in the world is to hurt an innocent. Sometimes I even hoped she would act like a shrew, crying at the university office where I worked, ruining my reputation among my friends and colleagues, and shouting at my parents and relatives. If she had done that, I might feel better ..."

Lily looked at him with pity, wondering who was weaker, the man, or the far away woman.

Majesty's father used to be a senior official in the old government. He was labelled as an anti-revolutionary after the communists took over China. She could imagine how hard it must have been for Majesty to get out of the Inner-Mongolian grassland.

After herding horses for six years, he was the last one of the youths to bid farewell to the villagers. He hoped to return to his home in the large city, but was assigned to work as a coal miner in a place a few hundred miles away.

As a bachelor in his mid-twenties, Majesty was supposed to get married. His aunt introduced him to a girl who worked in the large city. According to the law, if Majesty married her, he would have a legal reason to move into that city.

He met her in his aunt's home during holidays. She didn't attract him at all, being plain and dull. Every time they went out, she just listened to his talk and never responded to anything. He made a decision to stop seeing her and told her so.

He wasn't prepared for her tears, though. She sobbed, saying, "Please don't make a hasty decision. You haven't discovered my worth yet! It takes longer to appreciate it."

He was surprised to see such a dull log in tears, and he felt pity for her. But in literature, he had read the beautiful and enchanting love stories of other people, and he didn't want his own love to be like chewing rubber.

The woman was his first love, if it can be called love. When he was in the grassland, there were village girls who were probably interested in him. They sometimes sang flirting folk songs behind his back after a day's work in the cornfields as they were walking home against the setting sun. It was hard to deny that their lively giggles, like a gentle breeze in the autumn fields, had blown ripples in the pool of his youthful heart. But he knew he had to leave, and marrying a peasant girl would keep him in the grassland forever, according to government policy.

Back at the mine after his holiday, he received a letter from his father. His ideas reflected the marriage values of those years.

About your marriage, your mother and I share the following opinions about the girl your aunt has introduced:

1. Politically sound. She is from a family of industrialized workers, the most revolutionized category.

2. Job security. She works in a state-owned machinery factory and is guaranteed lifelong employment.

3. Sound health. She is healthy and good health is the most important factor for a happy family life.

4. Strategically correct. According to government policy, married couples living separately should be given priority in job transfers to cities. The girl's older brother has told your aunt that he would help you transfer to this city if you marry his sister first.

5. Disadvantages. The girl has finished only Grade 6. However, many of our state leaders have never been to universities. Many workers and peasants are illiterates. But that doesn't stop them from making huge contributions to our motherland.

6. Our great leader Chairman Mao taught us that one must know

*one's own limitations. Our family has a disadvantaged political
background. Therefore, you cannot be picky in looking for a spouse.*

In 1977, with Chairman Mao gone and Deng Xiao Ping succeeding
him, China started its reforms. When the government announced
its decision to resume the system of university entrance exams
abolished by Mao, Majesty's long-buried dream of going to university revived. Like many young people, he had been deprived for ten
years of this precious opportunity.

He spent all his leisure time reviewing textbooks and took part in
the nationwide exams. When the results came out, everyone in the
mine was surprised to see Majesty as the number one candidate in
the province, recruited by the prestigious Beijing University.

As he was packing up to start his new life in Beijing, news came
that the girl's sick mother had passed away. Though they had seen
each other only a few times, custom regarded her as his girlfriend.
While helping the family with the funeral, he was deeply struck by
the girl's desperate sorrow.

"Don't worry! I am always ready to help you," he promised her
with heroic feeling. Needless to say, his farewell words served as
the best medicine, not only for that moment, but also for the future.

Majesty was a prominent figure at Beijing University. Girl students
admired him as a major player on the school's basketball team. In a
university where every student was the top one from his or her native
province, Majesty's uneducated fiancée was like an empty sack. But as
a man who valued traditional virtues, he stuck to his word.

Four years later at graduation, he was assigned to teach at the
university in his home city. Majesty saw his fiancée again. Though
reluctant, he knew he had no choice but to marry her, since the girl
had been waiting for him patiently for four years and was becoming
an old maid.

VII

"People in those years were innocent," Majesty said. "It sounds funny today to say that I never held her hand, not to mention there never being any serious incident like kissing, from the time when we were introduced until our wedding.

"Our relationship, for more than ten years, was like drinking plain water, tasteless but indispensable. I had always felt it a great pity that I would die without knowing what love was like. Then I met you.

"When I was in my office or in the library, I couldn't concentrate on my work at all but kept on looking at the door or the aisle, expecting your shadow ... Never before had I tasted that kind of feeling ... Now, looking back, I realize that I had never loved her ..."

"But," said Lily, fixing her eyes on his, "she must have been very grateful to you and treated you like a king."

Majesty lowered his head and became silent again. After a while, he nodded, avoiding her eyes.

"Sure. She did. She was certainly tired after working in the factory for a whole day. But she did all the household chores. And after the baby was born, there was much more work. We didn't have a washing machine, so she had to wash the diapers by hand every day and dry them on the coal stove at night. When the baby was three months old, she started sending her to the daycare every morning before she went to work. She couldn't ride the bike with the baby's carrier tied on the back. So she simply pushed the bike for the one-hour trip, summer and winter. She never complained, though I seldom lent a hand. Our incomes were small. When we had something good to eat, she always let me and our daughter eat first. We were assigned to live in a small one-bedroom apartment. I often had to work late. She would make sure that the baby kept quiet the whole night.

"My little girl is really smart. She demonstrated her talents when she was only a baby. If she came home early from the daycare, she would hide herself behind the door and give me a surprise. Oh, you don't know how much I miss her! That kind of feeling can sometimes drive me crazy. Well, it's hard for you to understand, since you have never been a parent ..."

Lily moved her eyes away from his guilt-ridden face. It was torture, being forced to share a man with another woman, even mentally. She struggled hard not to blame Majesty, knowing his pain was no less than hers. As a matter of fact, she had felt guilty about their relationship from the very beginning. The constant pressure of moral judgement seriously hindered the closeness between them.

What, after all, has pushed me onto this thorny road, against my moral sense? Love? She knew that in the mind of a North American, that sole word was enough to protect anyone from anything. No other defense was necessary. But her taste of love had proved that love was as vulnerable as a sand castle and brief as the blooming flower, compared with the stronghold of family, built with flesh and blood, and glued by selfless sacrifices.

Chapter 11
The Severed Love

I

"I feel so ashamed to be with you!" Grace said to Lily, as they walked home from the church after the Easter dinner.

Though it was fairly late, Lily turned down an offer from one of the parishioners to drive them home. She wanted to walk with Grace and Baby under the shining moon of the beautiful spring night.

Baby was tired and soon fell asleep in his stroller. Grace's voice sounded angry, as she had felt disgraced when Jade touched upon the tender part of Lily's life during their reunion. "Had you told me the truth, I would have stopped you from jumping into this stupid affair and destroying yourself totally!"

Bit by bit, Lily had confessed everything in detail to Grace after her arrival in Canada. Grace had clenched her teeth and let loose at Lily with all the nastiness she could summon. Lily received her words quietly, understanding that those malicious terms were actually prepared for Majesty, should he ever stand in front of Grace.

"I have been afraid of you since childhood, Mother," Lily replied. "Particularly when I have to tell you something negative."

"Afraid of me? Your mother? Then why were you not afraid of those bad men?"

120

Lily sorted her thoughts before she answered. "Perhaps I never got enough care, as a child. So I have been over-sensitive to any little sign of love or care from people, good or bad."

"Are you trying to blame me for your own faults again?" Grace cut in.

"Mom, if you had shown that you loved me and cared about me, I would have had more self-confidence as a child and wouldn't have been so easily trapped by worthless suitors."

Grace sneered. "The problem is, you were not an attractive child at all, and displayed nothing which could arouse affection and love, even from your own mother! Had you been a pretty-looking, soft-tempered, and easy-going little girl as many others, people might have liked you."

Lily felt hurt and became quiet. Her memory swam back to the early scenes when she was a four-year-old and met Mother for the first time in the labour camp. Grace and other political dissidents were there planting rice and wheat for two years as a punishment for their outspokenness.

Oh, why did you bring her to me? That was the first thing Mother said to Grandma when she brought Lily to the farm.

You haven't seen her since she was one month old. I am afraid you are missing her. That was Grandma's reply.

How could I miss her? Am I in the mood to miss her?

Unfortunately, as a four-year-old, Lily remembered everything: the conversation, and the anxiety in her mother's eyes. Even now, half a lifetime later, she had to breathe deeply the moist night air mixed with the fragrance of new leaves to try to get rid of the unpleasant feeling aroused by the memory.

"In my opinion," Grace went on with her comments, "if one cannot find the ideal love, one should remain single throughout one's life."

"Really?" Lily looked at Grace. "Do you regret getting married and having us three children?"

"Sure." Grace's reply was cold and firm. "I shouldn't have cared about other people's expectations."

Lily remained silent for a while before she asked again. "Didn't you ever love anyone in your life?"

Grace avoided answering it directly. "As a matter of fact, you don't understand what true love is like!"

"What is true love like?"

Grace stopped, looked up into the starlit sky, let out a long breath, and shook her head. "A person like you wouldn't understand it, even if I told you."

"Why wouldn't I?" Lily also stopped.

"Because you don't have the soul to appreciate a lofty type of love."

Lily knew that was Mother's way to make her feel low. But suddenly she didn't care. The tranquil and relaxed Canadian night seemed to provide them with a good opportunity to share their deepest thoughts. "Tell me, please!"

"A true love is pure," Grace said slowly, choosing her words carefully, "without any physical desire, without any selfish demands, and involves only spiritual pursuits."

The dim lights from the houses below the hill blinked with romantic and mysterious signals. Grace's voice became gentle and emotional under the soft wings of the spring night, bringing Lily into a remote world full of nostalgia.

II

Everything looked and smelled fresh, as if it were only yesterday that Grace was a sixteen-year-old high school girl.

Her hometown, Hanzhong, was an ancient city in central China, famous for historical events and legendary heroes vividly described in classic novels. Scattered among the mountains and rivers were the remains of temples and palaces tracing back more than two millennia. In the prosperous valley, life was easy and slow, with abundant rice, fish, and poultry, and fruits and vegetables grew all year round in the mild temperatures.

Grace was a celebrity in the local high school. Her father was the richest landlord in the county. However, wealth and position didn't have the same sparkle for her as they did in the eyes of ordinary people. From childhood, she had seen too many of the evils that come with privilege.

When the Japanese occupied the whole of the East China coastal area during the Second World War, many universities moved west to the inner territories. Several chose this ancient town, protected as it was from the outside world by natural barriers.

It was at the time when the concept of "free love," choosing your own mate rather than marriages arranged by parents, started to be popular. The students from large cities were especially attractive to the teenaged girls.

English was first introduced on campus when a young university graduate was hired as a teacher by the local high school. Grace found English to be an interesting new game, a lyrical poem, when it first came to her as a serenade of twenty-six letters enunciated by the baritone standing in front of the blackboard.

The young teacher, tall and slim, with a pair of gentle black eyes behind his round, clear-framed glasses, attracted everyone's attention with his elegant smile. He was confident and optimistic, talked in a gentle manner, and emphasized, whenever possible, "God's immense love."

Grace remembered clearly the evening her heart strings were truly plucked. It was early in the fall, when the setting sun was dyeing the western sky orange-pink and the dusk was filled with the floating sweet scent of osmanthus blooming in the campus yard. The other girls in her dormitory had gone out after supper, leaving Grace alone in the room.

She was lying on her bed, reading a novel, *The Woman in the Pagoda*, a modern love story that was a bestseller. The ridiculous romance had misled many young hearts with its call for extraordinary "love," where the young heroine had sacrificed her whole life to live in a nunnery in order to take revenge on the man who had refused her love.

She was tearfully buried in the miserable ending when the sound of a man's singing drifted through the open window. It was an English song, exotically beautiful, bearing a tinge of sentimental sorrow.

She later learned that the song was called "The Last Rose of Summer." The desolate and mysterious melody was to linger in her mind for the rest of her life.

Grace went to the window. Across the bushy lilac and peach trees shading the schoolyard, once an old temple, she gazed at the paint-peeled wooden door where the young teacher lived. He was from Chingdao, a coastal city in East China. As a former German colony, Chingdao was famous for its European style red-roofed, white-walled houses, hilly streets of stone, the best beer in the nation, and a variety of Christian churches. He had come to inner China with his school after his hometown was taken by the Japanese. He had planned to go to England for graduate studies in theology, but was unable to leave now, as the seaway was blocked. Teaching, he was waiting patiently for the war to end.

Grace was his favourite student. He was not only pleased by her witty responses in class, but was also struck by her blooming peach-like beauty and spontaneous personality. She was slim, taller than ordinary Chinese girls, and impressed everyone with her vivacious black eyes. She was astonishingly brave, too, often commenting frankly when most people would be afraid of offending. A thorny rose.

In this traditional town, it was improper for a young woman and man to be by themselves. Therefore, the only happy time they spent together was group dating.

On bright, sunny spring days, he led his young students, hunting guns on their shoulders, into the wilderness. In the golden fields sprinkled with dandelions, he was entranced by Grace's laughter, which echoed in the air when turtledoves were startled into the blue sky by the crisp fire of the guns.

On hot summer evenings, they took walks along the quiet riverbank overshadowed with weeping willows and waving bamboos, picking up coloured pebbles, enjoying cool breezes from the river, and they would always stop to admire as the setting sun kissed the water's surface.

When autumn winds painted the woods with yellow, brown, and crimson strokes, they were drawn by ox cart into the tangerine orchard, intoxicated by the floating aroma while sipping green tea under the old gardener's straw shed.

When frost covered the sparse woods, they went hiking deep in the mountains, following traces of thousand-year-old paths dug across the cliffs, to burn incense in the temples and at the old shrines to legendary heroes.

Everything in the secluded town was imbued with ancient simplicity and the fragrance of nature. In all outings the young teacher displayed his charisma. He talked in a relaxed manner, with confident smiles and meaningful gazes, engraving his image on innocent hearts.

On rare occasions when Grace came to his office to hand in homework, he would chat with her, while leading her eyes with a gesture to his calligraphic work hanging on the wall: "Golden beach, blue waves, my beautiful dreams ..." As he read the words in an emotional tone, she was lost in imagining the mysterious beach and waves of the sea, so unreachable from her limited inland life.

III

He was fully aware that Grace, his sixteen-year-old student, had fallen in love with him. Grace implicated herself only with sudden blushes and sparkling eyes when she bumped into him. While he enjoyed the pleasant feeling of being admired by a pretty girl, it was painful to think about the next step.

He was already engaged to a former classmate. She was a faithful Christian, just like everyone else in his family. His fiancée paled compared to Grace. As the only son of a well-known pastor in his hometown, however, he had been brought up with a strong sense of sin.

Weighing his feelings on the scale of morality, he decided to remind himself constantly to hold back the dangerous flame and act just as a big brother.

The young teacher's lukewarm, ambiguous attitude only added to his charm. To her, his unusual style, nourished with Christian culture and marked with European influences, formed a sharp contrast to the decaying atmosphere of the ancient town, mouldy with opium pipes, bound feet, greasy restaurants and noisy teahouses.

She tried her best to impress her secret love. She played a leading role in every field—in class, on stage, in sports and speech competitions.

On Christmas Day, the young teacher invited all his students to the local Protestant church. It was only the second time Grace had ever entered a church.

Christianity, a foreign religion that had been introduced to China less than a century ago, was not widely accepted by the people who had worshipped the Buddha or followed Confucian doctrines for thousands of years.

The other church in the city had been built by the Catholics. Grace, despite adult warnings, had walked into that church one day as a curious seven-year-old. She was welcomed by a Chinese-speaking white man who led her to the backyard where she tasted sweet milky grapes picked from the vine.

She didn't die and her eyes and liver were not made into medicine by the green-eyed, red-haired foreign devils, as local rumour warned, but she was given a serious beating at home that evening.

Grace did not accept this unreasonable punishment easily. She crawled underneath her father's smoke bed and gulped down handfuls of opium ashes to commit suicide. Such a method had been used successfully, she had heard, by women in times gone by in this huge compound shared by the families of four brothers.

Grace was saved by having fresh urine from little boys forced into her mouth, the traditional treatment for stomach poisoning. When she came back to herself, she saw her mother crying and remembered abruptly the mysterious voice she had heard during her coma: "You are too young. You are not supposed to die yet. Go back to the human world ..."

She had never walked into a church again, as her memories of church were linked with cruelty and ignorance. But now she was sixteen, rather, almost seventeen, and she was going at the invitation of her beloved teacher.

She stood with her friends and looked curiously at the high ceilings and the decorations on the platform while searching secretly in the crowd for the figure she wanted most to see.

She was wondering where her young teacher might be when an old man with a white beard and a red robe suddenly loomed in front of her.

He put down the bag from his shoulder and took out a parcel for each of the students, saying: "Happy Christmas! Happy Christmas!"

"It's you, my teacher!" Grace was thrilled, recognizing the familiar voice. She moved a few steps away from her friends and opened her parcel secretly. It was a notebook with a finely embroidered silk cover. The front page was inscribed in that beautiful, finely wrought calligraphy: "How I hope you will become a member of our Lord's family one day!"

A member of his family! She raised her head and received the warm look. Her heart melted in trembling sweetness. The whole night she chewed over and over the unwritten messages in the sentence.

The next Sunday morning, Grace went to church again with the young teacher and a few other girls. She stood in the front row and watched with admiration as her teacher led the singing of the hymn. She listened attentively when the pastor gave a sermon and the Christians prayed. She imitated their actions and wished sincerely that the Divine her beloved teacher loved would also shed light in her soul.

She remembered the mysterious voice which told her to return to the human world during her suicide attempt as a child. Would that be the same Divine worshipped by her teacher? She doubted it. The skinny, sad man nailed on the cross on the wall of the church looked totally different from the plump, happy Buddha in the local temples.

To her disappointment, however, no matter how hard she tried during the following weeks, she could not feel any hint of the existence of the Divine.

"Don't despair!" he comforted her, his eyes shining with power. "As long as you are always opening your heart to God, you will sooner or later feel his mighty love and care!"

Speaking these words, he felt himself to be a patient pastor guiding his lambs, thus the burdens of his soul lessened and his troubled feelings purified.

IV

The eight-year war ended with Japan's surrender in the fall of 1945. When the fields were blooming with dandelions, the young teacher got a letter from the theology school in England. Before leaving on his long journey, he invited Grace to meet him secretly by the wild creek outside of the city's western gate.

Along the winding trail shone with moonlit, spring wind blew up the reed catkins and soothed Grace's troubled heart. She lost her usual confidence as she walked side by side with her beloved teacher, alone, in the quiet night.

> *Beside the ancient pavilion and along the old trail,*
> *Touching to the sky are the endless green meadows.*
> *Evening wind blows up the willow and interrupts the flute whistle.*
> *Gentle rays of the setting sun spread over peaks of the hills.*
> *Far away to the edge of the heaven and corner of the ocean,*
> *My beloved, go.*
> *A cup of rice wine washes down my sorrow.*
> *Tonight in cold darkness, I shall dream of you.*

This popular farewell song from his depressed voice deepened the sorrow in her disturbed mind. She blushed, as he reached out his hand and carefully picked the reed catkins on her hair and shoulders.

On their way back to school, they found a small store still open late at night. Under an oil lamp, Grace's eyes were caught by the plastic combs. They were new to the city and referred to by the local people as "chemical combs." Their bright colours and fine shapes immediately defeated the plain traditional combs made from peach wood and ox horn.

With his encouragement, she chose a crescent-shaped elegant comb that was ivory in colour.

"For you, as a souvenir." He paid and put the comb into her palm. "When you comb your smooth, fine, shining hair every morning, you will be reminded of me, I hope."

Grace was totally taken by this unexpected display of romance. She felt that the moment she had been looking forward to for so long was taking place right now, though pitiably at the eve of his departure.

His gentle voice continued. "If you don't mind, I'd rather you give me a wisp of your beautiful shining hair. I will carry it with me everywhere in my journey around the world ..."

Grace was engulfed by an overwhelming tide of happiness that almost stopped her breath. In her naïve young heart, the words he had just uttered were nothing less than a solemn oath. Her chest swelled and her throat constricted, she nodded shyly, wordlessly.

The young teacher borrowed a pair of scissors from the store owner, a sleepy old man. As his slim fingers touched her hair tenderly, near the neck, an unprecedented current struck her from head to toe. Large tears rolled out of her eyes and dropped onto her bosom.

In her dizziness, she felt the warm air from his mouth and heard his whisper clearly in her ears, "I will convince my family members. I will overcome all obstacles, eventually. Trust me ..."

Chapter 12
Evangelical Momentum

I

The pair of lamb-like black eyes and a crescent ivory comb stayed in Lily's mind. What happened after the young man went to England? Though Grace's recall was reluctant and in broken pieces, Lily collected the colourful silk threads and wove them into a fanciful tapestry with vivid scenes.

When they came to the U-shaped building it was late at night. The whole yard lay quiet in darkness. They stopped talking and walked in silence.

A noise from the garbage area, however, scared Lily. With the help of the street lamp, she saw a skinny man standing on top of the dumpster. It was Beaver-teeth, holding a beer bottle in one hand and a garbage bag in the other. Seeing that Lily was looking, Beaver-teeth put the bottle into the bag and quickly bent his back.

As Lily and Grace walked towards the building entrance, Beaver-teeth called from behind.

"Hey, there is a couch. It's in good shape." He said with an awkward smile, still holding the garbage bag in his hand clicking with bottles. "Do you want it? I can help you get it out."

Lily hesitated, looked at Grace, and turned down his kind offer.

As they stood in the yard talking, Lily noticed a figure through a ground floor window, which had no curtain. A man with his upper body naked was doing exercises. From the familiar long hair on his shoulders, she recognized him as Master Iron, the kung fu instructor in town. He was hitting his fist repeatedly against a bag of sand hanging on the wall. She was seized by the scene when Grace tugged on her elbow. She excused herself to Beaver-teeth and they headed towards the front door.

Entering their basement apartment, Lily found the answering machine on the desk flashing with a message. It was from Mrs. Rice. "I forgot to remind you in the church that we are going to have the Bible study in my home tomorrow evening. Please come with your mother to enjoy tea and other goodies! You have missed this study group for too long and it is high time to return to the Lord's army!"

II

On Sunday afternoon, when Lily finished her hotel work and got home, Grace told her that Baby had been asking the whole day to go out. "He must have tasted all the fun from outside!" Grace said. "But I am so tired from yesterday's activity and didn't take him out."

Lily would have rather have stayed at home and rest, but seeing Baby standing by the closed door and watching her silently with expectation in his eyes, she decided to take him to the Bible study after dinner.

Mrs. Rice's landscaped home was in the city's wealthy neighbourhood. She greeted Lily warmly in the spacious hallway with its cathedral ceiling. In the large living room, Lily met a few people who were relatively new to Canada. She didn't know any of them, since Mrs. Rice's guests changed frequently. Few stayed in her Bible study group for more than a couple of months.

"Jade is busy visiting homes," Mrs. Rice replied to Lily's inquiry, while taking out a Bible theme puzzle for Baby to play with on the floor. "Camellia is working in a downtown restaurant now. She leaves right after breakfast and comes home just to sleep. Ever since she got that job, she has a good excuse to skip the Bible group studies."

While Mrs. Rice was preparing tea and snacks in the kitchen, Lily was amused by the conversation between two guests sitting on the sofa next to her.

"What can I do when zealous Christian missionaries harass me at my door?" asked the young lady.

"Put a sign saying 'No God' on your door!" suggested the young man.

"Then there will be someone coming every day to explain to me that there *is* a God!"

"Tell them that you believe in the Buddha or something else."

"But the Buddhists might come!"

"There are hardly any Buddhists in Mapleton, and they don't try to convert you."

"Come on! Just tell me what I should say to get rid of the door knockers."

"You can say this: I will believe in Christianity when wars are no longer started by Christians." The young man laughed, proud of his own wit.

Lily suspected that they must be the so-called "rice Christians" who came to seek practical help rather than faith. The task facing Mrs. Rice was a tough one.

"Have you ever been bothered by such visits?" asked the young lady, noticing Lily was listening.

Lily nodded. "An old Canadian lady and her grandson used to show up at my door on Saturday mornings. They always came uninvited and sat down to talk for a couple of hours, trying to convert me."

"How did you get rid of them?"

"Why should I? She was so pious and devoted all her energy to her beliefs. She would feel sad if I simply asked her to leave. I always tried to spare an hour for her. Discussing issues in the Bible, I practiced my English and she also felt that she had her day—"

She was interrupted by Mrs. Rice, who was putting snack foods on the coffee table. "You must be talking about the Jehovah's Witnesses, Lily. They are not real Christians and you should drive them away next time or you will be led astray ..."

When the snacks were almost finished, Mrs. Rice led the group in reading a passage in the Bible and then asked everyone to make comments. There was silence.

Seeing nobody respond, Mrs. Rice started. "I'd like to give you a witness of God's mighty hand! My father is eighty years old. He was diagnosed with cancer last year. A fist-sized tumour was growing in his liver. The doctor said he would live only a few more months. But after my father declared to be a Christian, a miracle occurred! The tumor in his liver shrank to the size of a walnut and he is still alive today!"

The young man asked, "Didn't your father use any medication, such as traditional Chinese herbs, etc.?"

"Of course, every patient in the hospital has to use medicine. But without God's blessing, no medicine works well!"

A few people laughed. Mrs. Rice was unpleasant at their attitude, so she commented. "It's a wiser policy to just take it for granted and get baptized. Think about it. You will lose nothing if you find out there is no paradise when you die, but you will certainly be a winner when there is one!"

Lily looked at her watch and found it was close to nine o'clock. She had to get up early for work so she left before the discussion was finished. Pushing Baby in the stroller, she walked towards the bus stop. As she turned the street corner, however, she bumped into Camellia.

Camellia was excited to see her. "I found a job as a kitchen helper! I meant to tell you about it but I always get home very late these days and couldn't call you." She told Lily that she was actually off that day. But to avoid the Bible study she went to a friend's home and spent the day there. "Please do not tell Mrs. Rice this. I am tired of her interrogation every day!"

"What kind of interrogation?" Lily asked.

Camellia turned around and took the handle of Baby's stroller, saying: "Let me walk you home so we can talk on the way."

III

Camellia had been at the English as a Second Language school for a couple of weeks but then quit when someone helped her find the job at Fatty's Wok. This was the first full-time position she had been offered since coming to Canada. Needless to say, she was excited and devoted herself totally to it.

One afternoon, Mrs. Rice had phoned her at Fatty's Wok.

"Camellia my dear! I am craving roasted duck today. Your boss makes good barbecued meat. Would you please bring some for me when you come home tonight?"

From the barbecued meats hanging in the restaurant window, Camellia selected a roasted duck with crispy, light brown skin and paid seventeen dollars for it.

Mrs. Rice took a piece of greasy duck breast into her mouth and purred, "Hmmm, it's delicious!" She nodded, her voice blurred by chewing. "How much was it?"

"Not so much. Forget it!" Camellia replied in the proper way a Chinese person would respond, confident that Mrs. Rice would push her further for the price and then force the money into her hand.

Much to her surprise, however, Mrs. Rice seemed to be fully naturalized into Canadian culture. She took Camellia's polite gesture for granted and omitted the correct Chinese response.

Camellia waited and waited, but they washed the dishes, said good night, and went to their bedrooms as usual. Mrs. Rice never mentioned paying for the duck again!

Has she forgotten? Or has she been in Canada for too long, five years now, and learned the foreigner's way? Doesn't she remember that as a Chinese person, she is not supposed to take my polite rejection seriously?

Camellia wondered as she lay in bed. Her heart ached thinking about the seventeen dollars. Does that money come easily? I have been cutting frozen beef all day with a big heavy knife, and my fingers and wrists are as stiff as those of a corpse. But little is left after paying for that damned duck!

A few days later, Mrs. Rice called her at work again. "Camellia, my dear, you know that I am fond of deep fried shrimp balls, don't you? Remember to bring some home today, okay?"

Mrs. Rice was fully aware of the rules in the restaurant. The restaurant supplied a free meal to its employees. If an employee missed her supper because the restaurant was busy, she would be allowed to take home a box of leftovers.

Camellia felt that Mrs. Rice's demand was pretty difficult. "Shrimp balls are always combined with other things in a dish, Mrs. Rice. There are no more than a few shrimp balls in each dish," she explained.

"Silly girl! Why not talk to the boss nicely and ask him to add a few more to your box? Use your brain!"

It was not her brain, however, but her nerve that didn't function so well. Fatty's hot temper was known to all employees. When business was slow, he would grumble and anxiously burn incense to the shrine of the Wealth God by the door. When too many customers rushed in, however, he would shout at the "clumsy" workers.

Camellia had no idea what Fatty had gone through to become a big boss today. As a young man, he had come to Canada with only his two hands to get him ahead. Twenty years later, Fatty owned six restaurants across Ontario, and each one brought him a net profit of $60,000 annually. But she could not understand what the point was in being a millionaire if Fatty kept the same lifestyle he had when he was penniless. Saving money seemed to be his only purpose in life. Keeping the diligent and thrifty tradition of a Chinese peasant, Fatty never allowed any leftovers to be dumped. Camellia had once seen him taking food out of the garbage can and swearing at a kitchen helper for bankrupting him.

With a man like this, Camellia felt hesitant about opening her mouth to ask for more free shrimp balls. Shrimp balls kept well and could be served in the restaurant for days. But she was not willing to purchase the balls either. Most likely, Mrs. Rice wouldn't pay her back.

To be entitled to bring home a box of food, she deliberately missed supper that day, busying herself with chopping and washing. At the last minute before everyone left the restaurant, she finally worked up the courage to ask Fatty for a box of shrimp balls.

"They're not for me. Do you know Mrs. Rice, the Taiwanese lady? She likes your shrimp balls so much!" Camellia smiled at Fatty to minimize her unreasonable demand.

Fatty frowned. Camellia met his sharp stares and felt embarrassed. The smile stiffened on her face. She knew her female tricks would not work with a guy like him.

Of course Fatty had met Mrs. Rice quite a few times, and each time she had talked to him about her God. However, Fatty had faith in the Chinese gods who performed different tasks in the world, such as the earth god, the river god, the door god, the kitchen god, and the goddess who would bring you many sons, if she was pleased. In all his restaurants, Fatty placed an incense shrine for the most important of all gods, the wealth god. He also had strong faith in the old saying passed down for generations in his hometown: ugly wife, nearby field, and night soil are the three big treasures of a farmer's life. To him, beautiful women were the source of disaster, wrecking men like a relentless typhoon. For that reason, he chose a plain woman for himself, but hired good-looking ones to empty the wallets of other men.

A few more embarrassing seconds went by in silence. Fatty recognized that Camellia was a hard-working employee. There were bandages on her hands, burnt over the frying pan. Very few good-looking women would be willing to stay in that hot, greasy kitchen. If Camellia had been able to speak some proper English, Fatty would have put her out front.

Finally, he picked up the plate and counted four shrimp balls into her box. On second thought, he added four more, for eight is a lucky number representing a flood of money.

"Tell your friend that she should pay for this if she wants to eat next time," he said coldly, ignoring her sweet smile.

IV

At the breakfast table, Mrs. Rice continued her prayer to the Lord by asking the mighty God to save Camellia's sinful soul. At night, as she enjoyed the food Camellia had brought home, she carried on a worldly conversation, with a new focus.

Is this the first job you have ever had in Canada? No? Where else have you worked? As a babysitter? In whose home? For how long? How much money have you saved? In which bank have you deposited the money? What kind of account do you have? How is the interest calculated?

How much does the restaurant pay you per hour? How many hours do you work each week? What, you aren't sure? ... Of course I know there are deductions like income tax and employment insurance. But just tell me the net amount on your latest paycheque. You don't remember that either? Well, show me the pay stub and I can tell you!

You have brought some money with you from China? What kind of money? Chinese money or US dollars? How much? What's the exchange rate for Canadian dollars now? Where did you deposit it? Does your husband know this?

How much money can you get from your husband if you divorce him? Do you have any idea how much he earns and how much he has in savings? You don't know? You silly head! You are not supposed to trust men! He has probably hidden some savings from you, maybe an RRSP! What is an RRSP? Well, you see, you have plenty of things to learn from me ...

Camellia wasn't dumb and she could sense that Mrs. Rice meant to remind her of the following facts: You are no longer cooking three meals a day for the family. But you are still occupying a bedroom upstairs! Now that you have a steady job and a monthly income, it's high time you start to pay the rent! Or I could easily rent the bedroom out for $300 a month during the school year! Haven't you ever heard the Canadian saying that there is no free lunch? Do you know that my hydro bills went sky high after you started working in the restaurant? You don't like the greasy smell in your hair, but what's the point of spending an hour under the hot shower every night just to get greasy again a few hours later! Besides, you have never purchased your own toilet paper, soap, and laundry powder! You are simply taking advantage of my kindness!

Although Camellia could read Mrs. Rice's mind, she was not willing to spend her hard-earned money. Therefore, she just pretended not to understand Mrs. Rice's implications. Camellia had learned in her English class that in Canada, nobody is supposed to dig into other people's privacy, asking them their age or how much money they make. Didn't Mrs. Rice know this? Does she think it's easy for me to make the few dollars? You are rich! Why should you care if I live here for free? Besides, have you totally forgotten about the roast duck and shrimp balls?

As Chinese women, however, neither would state their feelings frankly. Therefore, Mrs. Rice's zealous concern made Camellia's face change colour frequently, pale one moment, red the next. She was tempted to tell Mrs. Rice to stop questioning her like a judge in a criminal court. But she had never learned how to pull a long face at others or refuse improper demands. She was trapped in this "cordial" relationship where any type of non-cooperation would seem offensive.

The awkward situation was brought to an end one night when Mrs. Rice showed her the telephone bill and asked her to pay twenty-eight dollars for long distance calls she had made secretly to China. This abrupt, non-Chinese behaviour tore away the restraints between them. Finally, Camellia realized that this free room and board was not free at all.

"I think I will have to move back to my husband's home soon," said Camellia, before she parted from Lily an hour later near the U-shaped building. "I can no longer tolerate Mrs. Rice."

"But, didn't you struggle so hard earlier to escape your husband? Think carefully. Make sure you are not leaving the wolf's den just to fall into the tiger's cave."

V

Out of Mrs. Rice's large gardened house and back in the one-bedroom apartment in an old building, Camellia had the feeling that she was Cinderella returning from the prince's gorgeous palace to her stepmother's rat-running basement. Everything seemed intolerably dirty, messy, and stuffy.

Her husband, Old Chia, occupied the queen-sized bed in the bedroom, and their twenty-year-old son, Dragon, had a single bed in the living room. There was no other choice for her but to sleep on the couch beside Dragon's bed.

Old Chia pretended to be indifferent to her coming back. But she knew that he actually felt relieved. Whatever had happened, he would always prefer that she stay home rather than live elsewhere and air the family's dirty linen in public.

At night, Old Chia would go to bed and leave the bedroom door ajar, silently suggesting that Camellia, still his wife, could come in any time. Through the open door Camellia could hear him turning frequently in bed and sighing heavily. There came his moans: "Oh, Mom ... Mom ... Why did you leave me in this world ..."

The moans became sobs. He seemed to be mourning his long deceased mother again. Camellia found it unbearable torture. At the same time, she felt pity for him and a sense of guilt for the suffering she had brought him. She pulled the blanket up around her head.

Will you stop torturing me? Camellia prayed silently. She bit her lip and tried hard to suppress the sorrowful tide in her chest. I know I have hurt you deeply. But how can you blame me for not loving you and respecting you, when you are so weak and fragile! You are not like a man, not at all! You miss your mother, but I lost my father when I was very young, too. I have always wanted to have a strong man as my husband, someone who could take care of me and be relied upon. But you have totally disappointed me! I have acted for twenty years as your mother and I have had enough! Am I wrong not to want to be your mother for the rest of my life?

Old Chia had been unemployed for quite a while. He had a PhD from China, but that degree didn't help him much in the Canadian market. After two years working in a high-tech company, he had been laid off for no particular reason.

He felt deeply humiliated. It was not easy for him, at fifty, to maintain the same energy as his younger colleagues. In China, everyone took a two-hour nap during the lunch break. Old Chia found it hard to break this habit and often dozed off early in the afternoon. To catch up on his work, he would get up early and go to work at dawn. The whole city was quiet at that hour. The only sound was the lonely clicking of the chain of his old bicycle, interfering with many sweet dreams along the street. Still, he finally lost the job.

He had sent out hundreds of application letters but received only one interview request. A company in Toronto was looking for a Chinese manager with Canadian experience. The night before the interview, Old Chia clumsily dyed his gray hair jet-black. And early the next morning, he changed into his best clothes, a dark blue woollen suit purchased for four dollars in the Salvation Army store, and stepped onto the Greyhound with shaky legs.

His meagre hope diminished as soon as he entered the company office, where he found more than twenty people, young and energetic, seeking the same position. He was completely beaten. During the day, he would sit numbly in front of the computer and stare at the screen, his brain blank. At night, he would lie in bed, chew over the miserable fate brought on by his foxy wife, and sob.

VI

Mrs. Rice's concern for Camellia seemed sincere. Each morning, as soon as Camellia woke up, the telephone would ring every few minutes.

Is that you, Camellia? Are you up now?

Are you brushing your teeth? ... Sure, I can tell from your blurred voice.

Are you eating your breakfast, Camellia? What are you having today? Steamed buns and rice porridge? Oh, you make my mouth water!

Are you ready to go now? Why so early? What time do you start work today? When are you going to finish? ... My, so late!

It was always Mrs. Rice's considerate voice on the other end of the phone line.

The ringing phone often disturbed Dragon's youthful rosy dreams. Again and again he was forced to return to the unpleasant reality of home.

One morning, he was boiling with rage after a sweet kiss was relentlessly cut short by the annoying rings. Without telling anyone, he turned off the ring function on the phone.

As Camellia was chopping chicken breasts in the restaurant around lunchtime, Mrs. Rice phoned.

"What happened to you, Camellia? Thank God you are still alive! I made at least ten calls to your home this morning but nobody answered! I was really scared. I thought they must have murdered you! Oh, poor Camellia, she has been killed! The more I thought, the more fearful I became. But you know I don't drive and could not go over to see what had happened. I made a number of phone calls to friends who can drive. I explained to them one by one the mysterious and horrifying situation in your home and asked them to go there and check for me. I don't know if they have been to your home yet or not, but you have really scared me to death! Camellia, you know how much I care about you! Now you must promise that from tomorrow on, you will never fail to give me a call in the morning and let me know you are safe and sound. My heart won't rest in peace unless I know you are alive! …"

Camellia was concentrating on Mrs. Rice's long-winded complaint, when a thunderstorm suddenly exploded over her head.

"How long are you staying on the phone? You are preventing food order calls from coming in! Remember, I am not going to tolerate idle workers in my restaurant! Go and wash the rice now! Are you blind? Can't you see that we are out of steamed rice?"

Camellia hung up the phone hastily. For heaven's sake, Mrs. Rice's imagination is so rich. And she spread news about my private life to everyone she knows. How can I ever live as a normal person in Mapleton now?

Camellia's mind was fully occupied by these troublesome ideas, and she lost count of the number of bowls of rice going into the steamer. Half an hour later, when Fatty's eyes fell on the harder than usual steamed rice, his big face turned red. Pointing his finger at Camellia's nose, he let loose a string of roars in Cantonese at her.

When giving instructions to his employees, who were mostly from mainland China, Fatty managed to speak Mandarin, with a stiff tongue. Though his Mandarin was anything but fluent, Camellia could usually make out half of it through gestures and guesses.

When angry, however, Fatty naturally returned to his mother tongue to gain fluency. He talked so fast that Camellia could understand only one word of Fatty's howling. That word emerged repeatedly and sounded like "old mom." She figured out that he must be swearing at her, for the word "mom" is universally applied when expressing rage.

After this incident, Camellia checked the telephone ring function at home constantly to make sure Dragon hadn't turned it off. And she always remembered to make the "safe and sound" report to Mrs. Rice every morning immediately after she woke up, even before she used the washroom, lest incoming calls wake Dragon and create more chaos.

On one of her days off work, Camellia decided to spend the day at a friend's place, to avoid the cold faces of her husband and son at home.

In the evening after dark, as soon as she entered the door of her own home, she heard the telephone ringing loudly.

Dragon frowned at her and shouted, "Hurry up, get it! It's for you, no doubt! It's been ringing the whole day and driving me crazy!"

Camellia ran over and picked up the phone. Yes, it was none other than Mrs. Rice.

"Oh, Camellia my dear, you finally came home! Tell me, where have you been today? Seeing a friend? What kind of friend? You met in the English class? Male or female? Why didn't you tell me about her before? What did you do together for the whole day? Nothing in particular? You should have let me know where you were going today! You see, you have made me worry about you the whole day! Listen! You are not supposed to make friends carelessly. It could cost you your life if you bump into a bad person! ... Of course I know you are lonely. But why not come to our Bible group study? You will find plenty of nice sisters and brothers here."

VII

The next time Camellia had a day off, she knew she had to alert Mrs. Rice in advance. Mrs. Rice advised her that she should spend the day properly.

"You are working almost every day now and hardly have any time left for English studies. You must have forgotten all the English I taught you. What a pity! Come to my home tomorrow morning, as early as possible! I'll help you review all the lessons!"

The following morning, Camellia arrived at Mrs. Rice's home shortly after breakfast. Her eyes immediately focused on the white bandage wrapped around Mrs. Rice's left hand.

"What happened to your hand?"

"Oh, I cut my finger yesterday when I was preparing dinner. It's still hurting a lot!" Mrs. Rice raised her hand close to Camellia's eyes. She made a painful face and clicked her teeth.

No wonder you phoned me last night inviting me to come here. I cannot have any rest on my day off now, Camellia thought bitterly. But instead she said, "Since you are not feeling well, let's not study English today. Your injured hand cannot touch water. You can let me take care of any housework that needs to be done. I will help you."

"Wonderful! I do need your help! The laundry must be done before the children run out of clean clothes. After that, you can wash the rice and pork ribs in the kitchen. Let's have soy sauce roasted ribs for lunch. By the way, it has been so long since I had the duck fat pancakes you make! And I am certainly missing them these days!"

It was a time-consuming project to make duck fat pancakes, involving several complicated steps—peeling off the fat from the duck, heating the fat into a liquid and mixing flour into it, all by hand. When the pancakes were finally piled up in a plate, Camellia looked at her watch and was shocked.

"Dear me, it's five in the afternoon! My son has invited two schoolmates home for dinner tonight. I have to rush home now to prepare it."

As Camellia was washing her hands, Mrs. Rice said, "Well, I have nothing to do tonight. I'd better come with you and spend the evening in your home."

The suggestion was shocking. Camellia hesitated, responding to her enthusiasm reluctantly: "Of course … I'd like you to come with me. But who is going to look after your children at home tonight?"

"Come on, Camellia! They are all teenagers! Who needs to be looked after? The duck fat pancakes are ready for them on the plate on the kitchen counter. This isn't Mainland China, where each couple is allowed only one child and all children are raised like little emperors! My children are not spoiled. They know how to get food from the plate for themselves."

While talking, Mrs. Rice had put on her jacket and shoes, ready to follow Camellia out. Just at that moment, there was a knock on the door. A couple of young men entered the hall when Camellia opened the door. They were members of Mrs. Rice's Bible study group.

Mrs. Rice was stunned. She had totally forgotten the activity scheduled that evening in her house.

But Camellia was relieved at their arrival. It gave her a chance to get out of there alone. "Well, what a pity Mrs. Rice. Now you will have to stay home with your guests. I am afraid I must go by myself. See you next time. Bye."

"Wait!" Mrs. Rice had already had an idea in two seconds. She waved her injured hand to the newcomers. "Let's go to Camellia's home to study Bible tonight. I know she has at home a jar of *Longjing*, one of the best green teas from China. We will all have a chance to taste it this evening. What good luck you guys have."

Camellia panicked. "I … I … I'd love to invite you all to my home for *Longjing*. But what a coincidence that I happen to have some other friends coming tonight. How about we choose another date for your visit?"

Mrs. Rice was surely not boasting when she claimed she was born with a good brain. She responded without losing a beat, "What's the problem if you have other friends? Introduce them to me, and your friends will become mine too. Let's go, everyone!"

VIII

Camellia was not the only target. Ever since the weather got warmer, Mrs. Rice had intensified her evangelical visits to Grace and Lily.

She was happy to see Grace's enthusiasm in all the church activities, in town or out of town. Last Sunday when a famous preacher was giving a talk in Toronto, Grace took the long bus trip with other young people. Mrs. Rice was confident the church would soon baptize another communist.

Shortly after Lily got home one afternoon, she received a phone call from Jade, her old schoolmate. "Good news, Lily! I got a Chinese version Bible for your Mother. Can I send it over to you tonight?"

"Well …" Lily's first reaction was to put off her coming. She had just finished her hotel work and was tired. "You don't need to take a special trip just to bring it. Bring it over another time when you come to have tea with me."

"Mrs. Rice felt that you need more guidance. She realized that you are kind of hard to deal with and she asked me to help answer your questions."

"I'd rather try to understand everything on my own."

Jade was a sensitive person. "Yes, I have also warned Mrs. Rice not to chase you too closely so we don't scare you away and spoil the whole thing."

"Aha! Are you treating me as a big fish ready to take the bait?" Lily joked, while feeling displeased that Jade clearly regarded Mrs. Rice as her comrade now.

As soon as Lily had washed the supper dishes, the evangelical team arrived at the door. Unicorn had recently purchased an old car for $600. It made noises everywhere except for its horn.

But Mrs. Rice defended the car. "The Lord knows that I don't drive, so he sent you to Mapleton. Now we can get around much more easily to spread the gospel!"

They sat on the couch and sofa Lily had acquired recently from people moving out of the building. They brought not only the Chinese version Bible and a few more boxes of puzzles, but also good news to Grace, about a one-week program called "The Success Camp" held in northern Ontario in the summer. The trip was subsidized by the church headquarters in Toronto and only a minimal fee was charged. Participants were expected to be close to the threshold of God's kingdom. The camp planned to invite famous Chinese ministers from all over North America, with the aim of converting a large number of atheists in a limited time.

Grace's eyes lit up when she heard that Mrs. Rice had recommended her for the trip to Minister Wong. But who would help take care of Baby if she went to the camp?

Lily caught the eagerness in Grace's face. She understood that Mother needed some social life to relieve the anxiety building up inside her. "Mom, you can just go. I will find a babysitter."

"I can help you, Lily," Jade offered. She and Unicorn were not qualified for the trip since they had already announced themselves to be Christians.

While Mrs. Rice gave Grace more information about the camp, Lily chatted with the couple. "Have you ever thought of becoming a church minister?" she asked Jade, knowing she had been looking for work unsuccessfully since coming to Canada. "Your experience in China as an anchor would be very helpful."

"I would like to," Jade replied. "Unfortunately, the church will not allow females to be ministers."

Lily shook her head. "That regulation differs from that of the Communist Party. Otherwise, it seems that the church is quite similar to the Communist Party's organization and you would fit in it perfectly."

"You have hit the point, Lily!" Unicorn suddenly cut in. "I have also noticed a lot of similarities between the Communist Party and the Christian churches, in their theories, forms, and organizational structures."

"Yes!" Lily nodded in agreement. "They all hold up an idealized world, and people need to work hard to make it reality. The targets attacked by Mao, such as the injustice between the rich and the poor, the oppression of women, and inequality of all kinds, were also stressed by Jesus Christ. Remember the standards set for New Communists when we were children? They were almost the same as the Ten Commandments. The only difference is that we were required to confess our sins to Mao during those years, while in Canada the message receiver is God."

"Jesus Christ was undoubtedly the first communist in human history." Unicorn smiled, which made his gloomy face pleasant looking.

"The idea in Karl Marx's *Communist Manifesto* was borrowed from the Bible!"

"A true communist should also be a true Christian, just like you two!" Lily pointed at Unicorn and Jade, and laughed. "You should get yourself baptized without hesitation!"

Unicorn also laughed. "The problem is that I think true faith should be about giving instead of asking and getting, just as was expected of Communist Party members—sacrificing your own interests for the benefit of others. But the pamphlets circulated in the church often carry stories about so and so praying hard to God for a job or a house, and their material wishes were granted. It sounds selfish and sullies the purity of faith. You know, if your prayer for employment is granted, it means that somebody else loses this opportunity."

Mrs. Rice stopped talking with Grace and turned her face to Unicorn. "Hey, it's not selfish. God only takes care of his own."

Lily supported Unicorn. "Your pursuit of faith is on a higher level. But the majority of people are willing to accept only a faith which will bring benefits to them."

The room fell quiet. Both Unicorn and Jade thought about her words seriously. Baby was murmuring to himself while playing with the new puzzles. Lily looked at the puzzles and found among them pictures of Eden, the burned Sodom city, and Abel offering his baby son. She was excited when she figured out the sounds from Baby's mouth were something like "Hallelujah, Hallelujah." He was able to link syllables together now. What progress! She wanted to share the good news with the others. But realizing nobody else in the room was paying attention, she controlled herself and stayed quiet.

"You are right, Lily," Unicorn resumed. "Communist ideology and Christianity are different. The former requires all of us to sacrifice our own interests unconditionally, for the benefit of all mankind. It is the highest request of the human soul. On the other hand, to adopt the Christian faith is easier. So long as you are willing to believe in God, you are promised life in Paradise after death."

Lily nodded. "Yes, human nature is selfish and greedy and the Christian faith is closer to human nature."

Jade felt a little bit uneasy at her comment and argued. "Whether a religion is perfect or not, a faith always has its positive aspects. China under Communism during Mao's time was an atheist society, but Marxism and communist ideology actually functioned as a religion in controlling the whole country."

"But Mao was doing a harder job, because he had shut off the door to Paradise and promised no life after death, therefore making his ideas less attractive!" Lily insisted.

Grace, listening all this time, joined their discussion. "It's also a pity in today's China that Deng Xiaoping has opened up the exit of Hell and let out all monsters! There is no functioning moral standard to guide the people."

"The authorities only try to stop people from accepting heresies," Lily said. "Actually they should try to provide the hungry souls with healthy spiritual food, such as Christianity."

"Absolutely right!" Unicorn hit his palm on his lap and said, "Ironically, don't you think that Mao has actually prepared China for Christianity during his rule by smashing all traditional values? What I am doing in the school lab is just meaningless. It would be much more significant to spread Christianity in China instead!"

"But didn't you say that you still have some problems with the principles of Christianity?" Lily reminded him.

"Yes, I do," Unicorn nodded. "That's why I would like to study in a theological institute. Since the Bible has been translated a number of times from its original language into different ones, I am pretty sure many of its initial concepts have been distorted in translation. If I could study Hebrew and Greek, I would be able to read the original version."

Lily asked, "Are you serious?" Seeing Unicorn nodding, she asked Jade. "What's your opinion?"

Jade hesitated before she answered. "He is getting more and more frustrated with his research in the lab, since he has not been on good terms with his professor. He may have to leave the lab sooner or later, I am afraid. As a matter of fact, he has started sending inquiry letters to a few theological institutes. It seems there's little to prevent him being admitted, except for financial assistance and his status as a non-baptized Christian ..."

Mrs. Rice looked surprised at this information, "How come you didn't tell me anything about this?"

Jade gave her an apologetic smile. "We don't want too many people to know when it is still undecided."

Mrs. Rice patted Unicorn on his shoulder and said, "So it is all the more important that you get baptized first!"

Unicorn shrugged. "But the question is, how many people in our church have followed the way of Jesus Christ?!"

"Darn!" Mrs. Rice pulled a long face. "You just want to be in love forever, but never get married! And it's odd that you don't want to marry the lovely girl just because her relatives are not lovable!"

Everybody laughed at her comparison except Unicorn. "A marriage concerns relations between humans only, while a faith deals with relations between the human and God. I can tolerate an imperfect marriage but not—"

Mrs. Rice stood up. "Come on! I don't want to listen to your complaints about our church again. We've got to go to Camellia's home now."

Jade looked at her watch and asked in hesitation, "It's ten. Isn't it too late? Shall we find another day to visit her family?"

Mrs. Rice shook her head, "No, I need to talk with Camellia's husband tonight. My daughter will go to university in the fall and she needs a math tutor. Old Chia is unemployed and has nothing to do at home anyway. He can help my daughter while I can help improve his relationship with Camellia. It benefits everyone."

Chapter 13
Breast Says No

I

Days before Grace would take her exciting trip to north Ontario, hot summer had already signalled its early arrival in Mapleton with sensational headlines, including a demonstration by a local Canadian women's organization. They were planning to march bare-breasted in public on Sunday to protest a law against such a display.

Although Grace found the logic hard to understand, when Lily explained the how and why to her, her curiosity was aroused and she wanted to watch this absurd foreign behaviour with her own eyes.

On the morning of the breast demonstration, Grace put on a dark purple short-sleeved silk blouse she had purchased in Beijing before coming to Canada. Looking in the mirror, she grumbled, "The sun's rays in Canada are too strong. If my skin had not been tanned from walking with Baby outdoors daily, the purple colour would be just perfect for my fair skin."

Hearing her complaint, Lily couldn't help wondering why her mother cared so much about her appearance. "Who knows you any-way, in this small corner of a foreign world?" she said carelessly, while dressing Baby.

"I know you don't care. All you care about is your precious son!" Grace fought back.

On their way to the city park, Grace was amazed at an animal show. A flock of Canadian geese was crossing the road while cars from both directions stopped and waited patiently. Led by one of their parents, five cute newborns were walking slowly across in a straight line while the other parent stood in the middle of the road like a crossing guard.

While Lily was deeply touched by the lovely scene, Grace was more impressed with something else. "Oh, the Canadians!" she exclaimed with appreciation. "They give wild animals the same respect as human beings!"

Lily told her that the news reported that many cities were frustrated by the overwhelming numbers of geese. The government gathered thousands of them into trucks and transferred them to. unpopulated areas.

"That's so silly!" Grace laughed. "They can be made into meat to feed people who depend on the food banks!"

II

Walking into the city park and over a hill, they saw Moon Lake, its mirror surface ablaze with the golden beams of the scorching sun. The usually quiet park was swarmed with thousands of people. And more were entering the park from all directions. There were families coming with their babies in strollers, loaded with diapers and milk bottles, ready for a day's free entertainment. Adults fully equipped with cameras and camcorders were on alert to catch the historical moment. Smart business people had located their hotdog and popsicle stands along all strategic paths.

It was hard to get a clear view of the demonstrators standing by the lakeside because the crowds blocked the view. Grace and Baby stopped a distance away in the shade of the trees. Lily, failing to get a good view, turned her attention to the observers and was surprised to find them silent, serious-looking, and somewhat embarrassed. With so many people around, the quiet in the park felt odd.

At twelve o'clock sharp, there was a buzz in the crowd of human flesh. Lily jumped up and caught sight of a number of women taking off their shirts in the centre of the crowd. Many in the crowd craned their necks and moved into position to get good camera angles.

Only seconds later, however, a few fully armed policewomen squeezed into the crowd and led the demonstrators into the waiting cars. They were mostly young women, walking through the crowd with an indifferent air. Lily waited to hear them shout heroic slogans, such as the scenes often shown in Chinese revolutionary movies, but she was disappointed. She also failed to catch the lofty expression of martyrs sacrificing their lives for the cause of justice for humankind.

After the police cars sped away, the crowd became noisy. The arguments of some people around caught Lily's attention. One man complained that the demonstration had been so brief that he didn't even have a glimpse of bare breasts. The lucky ones who stood in the front rows didn't seem to be satisfied either. A couple of them made negative comments about the women's bodies, surprised at how the women could feel proud showing unattractive body parts like those in public.

A well-dressed lady said it made her sick to see such bodies, and she could well understand why the law would forbid it in public.

A young man with shoulder-length hair and a bushy beard responded to the lady's attack. Good looking or not, if breasts were a natural part of the body, there was no reason the law should ban showing them in public, he argued.

His challenge roused more comments from the lady and her friends. They asked him if he would like his wife or girlfriend to bare her breasts in public, and if he would like to show his penis and let people comment on its size and shape, since it was also a natural part of the body. The lady also declared that Canadians aren't supposed to act like uncivilized tribal women in the African jungle.

The young man was not giving in. Had he had a girlfriend, he declared, he would fully support her in fighting for justice. He also warned the ladies about racial discrimination in their insults towards African women.

Lily listened and laughed and told Grace what she had just heard.

Grace found the arguments interesting. "However liberated, women in China would not want to fight for such a right!"

"In China, the issues relating to women's rights are so different from those in the West," Lily said. "While European and North American women are fighting for equal rights and equal pay, feminist workers in Mainland China are seeking the return of rights for the family and the right to feel like women again, to be treated and respected like women. Western feminists criticize the Chinese feminists as backward, while the Chinese claim themselves to be more advanced. Equal pay and rights at work? The things Western women are fighting for are rights that Chinese women acquired long ago."

"But don't forget that equal status for women is the result of decades of communist rule," Grace disagreed. "For thousands of years, Chinese women were at the bottom of society."

Lily questioned, "But don't you think women's liberation has ended up with women taking on men's responsibilities in addition to their womanly roles? No wonder a feminist worker in China has complained that women's emancipation has finally emancipated men."

"What's bad about that, then?" Grace asked.

"Don't you see that both genders in China have become neutralized, with men becoming increasingly weak and vulnerable, and women tough and strong?" Lily argued.

Grace uttered a dry laugh. "You have been away from China for eight years, and the wind has changed again. With the government's new economic policy, equal pay and equal opportunity for women have started to disappear. Private enterprise and a market economy mean that income gaps are reappearing and the old capitalist evils are reviving."

Lily admitted that she had heard such reports, too.

"I miss the old times when the Communists first took over China in the early 1950s," Grace said with a nostalgic look in her eyes. "They brought in fresh air. Rascals and hooligans were arrested. Men who had more than one wife were urged to choose one and let the rest go. Women were encouraged to go to school and to work. Prostitutes were arrested and turned into part of the working class. But since the 1990s, prostitution has returned, together with other old sins such as keeping concubines and smuggling women. So, in what direction do you think feminists in China should go now?"

III

After leaving the park, Lily and Grace made their way home. The early afternoon sun was still strong. To avoid sunburn, Lily led Grace to a community trail winding through dense, dark woods. The air in the woods was cool and fresh. Grace slowed her pace and breathed deeply. Lily, pushing Baby's stroller, felt good to see her mother starting to appreciate more and more about Canada, the respect for animals, the humane treatment of demonstrators, and the abundance of natural areas around the city.

Baby suddenly raised his small hand and pointed his finger to the woods on the left. "Mom, she!" he burst out.

Alerted, Lily stopped and looked. She saw a black-haired woman bending over to pick herbs growing under the thick layer of fallen leaves. When the woman raised her head, Lily saw it was Camellia.

She was surprised that Baby had recognized her, as he had only seen her a couple of times.

"Hey, we have a surprise meeting again!" Lily waved to her. "Aren't you working at the restaurant today?"

"I'm off today."

"Why are you always off on weekends when the restaurant should be busy?" Lily wondered.

"Fatty asks his son to work on the weekends so as to save money. The boy is only eleven years old. Oh, the rich!" Camellia shook her head, and showed the greens she held. "So I come here to pick some wild leeks."

"Wild leeks?" Lily came closer and examined the inch-wide, foot-long green leaves. "Are you sure they are not poisonous?"

"No! They taste just like Chinese chives. But the chives sold in the store are very expensive, about three dollars a pound. Many Chinese families come here to pick these for free. There are so many in the woods around Mapleton."

Lily smelled the strong aroma of the wild leeks and suggested to Grace that they might also try some.

Camellia happily told her that there were many more things they could collect for food. "There is an alfalfa field down the roadside. You can pick the tender leaves to make stir-fry. Last fall I also found a lot of mushrooms in the meadows and soybeans in farm fields," she said proudly.

"Mushrooms?" Lily asked. "Could you tell which ones are good and which ones are poisonous?"

Camellia nodded confidently. "Of course. I can recognize many types of edible mushrooms. By the way, where have you been this morning?"

When Camellia learned about the breast demonstration, she stamped her foot with regret for having missed the marvelous show. "I love to have fun. But there aren't many enjoyable activities in this small city, and life is so boring. I don't understand English and am often blind and deaf to what is going on. Next time there is something interesting, let me know."

She tied a bagful of the wild leeks onto Baby's stroller handle and said, "Take this with you. I've got plenty. You can stir-fry them with eggs, or chop them fine and mix them with minced pork to make steamed bun stuffing. My son likes them very much and eats a lot of them. Old Chia enjoys eating them too."

Lily wondered if Camellia's relationship with her family had become smoother lately, with Mrs. Rice's home visits. She was just about to ask when suddenly an old white man appeared behind them and shouted loudly at Camellia. "Why are you here again? Didn't I tell you last time that it's illegal to dig anything in the city woods? It's illegal! Do you understand?"

Camellia stared, her eyes round, unaware of what the old man was saying to her. After Lily translated the old man's message, she looked embarrassed and apologized to him in Chinese. "Sorry, I didn't understand what you said last time. I'll never come again."

"If I ever see you in here again, you will be fined one thousand dollars!" the old man warned her angrily as the women left in a hurry.

Once out onto the street, Camellia asked to go home with them, for she wanted to make a private phone call. "I'll pay you when the bill comes," she promised, her eyes pleading.

Lily figured Camellia must want to talk to her lover in China. Thinking about Camellia's happiness a moment ago when she mentioned her son's and husband's good appetites, she felt sorry about the woman's complicated life.

While Camellia was making the phone call, Lily and Grace stayed in the kitchen preparing for supper. Minutes later, Camellia opened the kitchen door, looking worried.

"Nobody answered the phone. He is not home, at this hour! Long past midnight! Where could he be?" She seemed to be talking to herself, her large eyes shadowed with suspicion.

"You can wait for a while and try again," Lily comforted her. "Perhaps he is on his way home."

Camellia nodded. Seeing Grace snapping the ends off the wild leeks, she sat in a chair and joined her at the table.

"I've heard you say before that you have never loved your husband, so why did you marry him in the first place?" Grace seemed interested in exploring this topic.

"Oh! It's a long story." Camellia let out a heavy sigh. She put down the wild leek, sat back in the chair, her arms folded, her eyes fixed on the ceiling.

Chapter 14
Camellia's Story

I

I was barely three when my father died. He left no impression on my mind. But my mother said he was a handsome, strong man, good at everything: shooting, riding, driving, and wrestling.

When the Japanese surrendered in 1945, he was a regimental commander in the Nationalist Army. Nobody had predicted that the Nationalist government would be defeated so quickly by the Communists. When the Nationalist troops retreated to Taiwan, my father didn't go with them. He became an instructor at the Military Institute and married my mother. They had three children. The year my father died, the third child was still inside my mother.

My mother said that during the campaign in mid-1950s to eliminate anti-revolutionaries, the Military Institute asked all ex-Nationalist officers and instructors to confess their crimes. My father was suspected of being a spy for the government in Taiwan.

My father didn't come home for days. At lunchtime one day, Uncle Bay, my mother's older brother, suddenly showed up at our home. He said he had been called to the Military Institute and told that my father had committed suicide. He cut his left wrist. A pool of blood stained the floor of the room.

Since my father had died by his own hand, he was classified as a "guilty anti-revolutionary," even though, in traditional culture, suicide was understood to be the best way to declare one's innocence.

During the day and in front of other people, my mother was deadly silent, with no words and no tears. One moonless night when the sky was dark as black ink, my mother took my hand in her left hand, carried my one-year-old brother in her right arm, and walked slowly with her pregnant belly to a nameless graveyard in the city's hilly suburbs. She found my father's tomb, took out a pair of white linen shoes and tied a piece of white linen around her head. After dressing properly in the traditional funeral style, she knelt down in front of the tomb and let out a long anguished cry.

Two months later, my mother gave birth to my second brother. My mother was only twenty-six. She was a high school teacher, smart and pretty. Quite a few people wanted to marry her, but she rejected all. She told me later that if we children had all been girls, she might have remarried, but since there were two boys whom she wanted to bring up proudly for my father, she decided to remain single for the rest of her life. As surviving family members of an anti-revolutionary, we received no financial aid from the government. So we relied on my mother's limited income and grew up in poverty.

II

When I finished Grade 9 in 1970, the government policy was that all graduates who could not find jobs in the city had to resettle in rural areas as new peasants. My mother begged several of her former students and, finally, one of them found me a position in a small factory.

From my first day as a worker, my mother warned me again and again not to fall in love with anybody in the factory. "Your father and I were both university educated. But you are not able to go to university because of the political climate now. This will be forever a hurt in my heart and I will see you at least marry a university graduate before I can rest in peace!"

The chance came the year I was nineteen. A few factories in the city were holding an exhibition and I was asked to be the show receptionist. I met Old Chia there. He was a technician, and I asked him to help fix my broken radio. When he came to my home with the repaired radio and chatted with my mother, my mother felt he was an ideal choice. He was twenty-five, a university graduate, and the only son of an old widower. My mother analyzed the situation. "He is an honest person with skills and knowledge. And, to be frank, he is somewhat simpleminded and therefore easy to control. Besides, his mother died a long time ago, so there is no mother-in-law to find fault with you. You will have an easy life once you are married into this family."

But what about my wishes? From the time I was seventeen, I had never lacked suitors. I had the best figure in at least half the city. When China's Vice-President selected a wife for his only son from all the girls in the nation, I was on the short list. When a film studio was recruiting new stars, I was also recommended. But each time, I was dropped once they learned about my father.

I liked one young man very much. He was a trumpet player in the army orchestra, a handsome man with sparkling eyes and a straight nose, tall and square-shouldered. When I watched him marching as a soldier, I imagined that my father might have looked the same way. When we were together in the street, we attracted much attention. He was very proud of me, of course.

However, my mother was strongly against my dating this man and she pushed me to date Old Chia instead. I didn't like Old Chia from the very beginning. He had no class at all. He couldn't even speak one complete sentence when conversing with others. Once when he was standing in my home and chatting with me, he turned around in a complete circle, for no reason! A jerk!

My mother made fun of me to my face. "Well, that trumpet player is good-mannered and looks a real man. But has it ever occurred to you that the army will never allow him to marry you, because of your father? He is certainly aware of that regulation and is simply playing with you."

I knew my mother was right. There was almost no possibility of marrying the trumpet player. But that did not make Old Chia any more attractive. As soon as I saw his shadow at the front entrance, I would sneak out the back door. But he would come in, sit, and chat patiently with my mother.

My mother asked Uncle Bay to help convince me. He had a conversation with Old Chia, to judge his qualifications. Throughout the hour-long meeting, Old Chia never raised his head to look at Uncle Bay and said no more than five sentences. He was concentrating on smashing a few peanuts into fine crumbs with his fingers, rubbing them into cracks in the table, and then running his hands over the table to smooth the surface. Uncle Bay concluded that he was a little bit slow, but a very honest man.

III

During this period, I got involved with Big Brother. He was my next door neighbour, nine years older than I was. We had grown up on the same street, but I hadn't seen him much since he had graduated from university and gone to work in Shanghai. I met him that year when he came home on vacation. He looked surprised to see me. "You have grown up into a young woman now, Camellia!" He didn't hold my pigtail and tease me any more, as he had done when I was a little girl. But I still trusted him as a big brother. I told him about my sorrow at being forced by my mother to date Old Chia.

Big Brother comforted me patiently. I enjoyed very much being with him. He was good at the violin and calligraphy. He had read so many novels that there was never an end to the stories he could tell me. It was under his influence that I grew to love reading.

When he finished his vacation and returned to Shanghai, I suddenly realized that I could no longer live a single day without seeing him. We started to write to each other, a letter each day. Sometimes I would receive two letters from him in one day! There are about 400 letters from him, all neatly packed in a large trunk in my mother's home now.

One day when I was working in the factory, the receptionist came over and told me there was a long distance phone call for me. Who would call me?

"Camellia, I miss you so much!" His voice made me tremble. For the rest of the day, I felt so energetic and happy that I was oblivious to the dull roar of the machines.

Big Brother came back to Yangchow more often now, almost every holiday, just to see me. My mother discovered our love and told me not to see him any more.

"He is not suitable for you," she said. "First, he works in Shanghai. You know it is almost impossible to get a residence permit for a large city like Shanghai. If you married him, you would have to live separately. Second, his family background is also a very bad one, a capitalist one. If you marry him, your children will also be trapped and never able to hold their heads high, for both of you belong to the disadvantaged classes. If you marry Old Chia, you will surely benefit from his sound, proletariat family background. You will be given all the opportunities for education, promotion, good employment and so on, and nobody will dare to bully you!"

Since my mother forbade Big Brother to see me, we worked out a code. When he came home to Yangchow, he would secretly draw a line in chalk at the corner of my front entrance. I would add a vertical line to it, making a cross, to indicate I had seen the message. Then we would find ways to meet.

That spring, we walked hand in hand along the bank of West Lake. We sat in the ancient pavilion where a famous thirteenth century courtesan had died young and was buried by her lover. He read the poem written on her tomb and held my hand in his warm palms. "Do you know what my biggest wish is, Camellia?" he whispered into my ear. "I will die without regret if your hand is still in mine when I become a gray-haired old man!"

Things went on like this for three years. Finally, I steeled myself to face my mother with the news of this forbidden love. My mother was strongly against it, but seeing that my determination to marry him was irreversible, she had to give up her fight.

When my mother told Old Chia about my decision, he was totally crushed. He had believed that his patience would eventually win my heart. He became sick and lay in bed for months, unable to go to work or even come out the door.

Old Chia's father rushed into my home one day, pointing his finger at my nose and swearing loudly. "Goddamned whore! Bitch! Man-killer! Dregs of the Nationalist government! You have destroyed my only son. If he dies, you will pay with your life!"

My mother and I were scared to death. The father then went to my factory and complained to my boss. Rumours spread everywhere quickly, portraying me as an immoral woman who played with men's feelings and "stepped into two boats at the same time." Everyone either stared at me or looked away. I knew that even if I had ten mouths, I could not explain things to everyone's satisfaction.

But I knew I was justified. From the very beginning, I had never agreed to be Old Chia's girlfriend. But he still dropped into my home to chat with my mother once a week. That was his decision. Why should I be blamed?

I felt very depressed and looked forward to Big Brother's coming home. However, for two weeks, I received no letter from him. I worried that something had happened to him.

One evening as I was going home on my bike in a heavy rain, I was so heavy-hearted that I bumped into another bike coming towards me on a narrow stone bridge. I fell and hurt myself seriously. When I got up, managed to walk home, and looked at myself in the mirror, I cried.

That weekend, Big Brother came back. I didn't want him to see my bruised face, so I hid in my home. My mother wouldn't let him in, regarding him as the source of all the disaster that had fallen on my family. He left.

A few days later, his letter came from Shanghai. He said that Old Chia's father had been to Shanghai and talked with his employer. His boss warned him not to seduce another person's fiancée or he would be punished. To clear matters up, he had come home but had been unable to see me. He heard the gossip from the neighbours, who accused me of being an immoral girl who flirted with every man, and had been given a serious beating by a group of rivals.

At the end of his letter, he wrote,

After careful consideration, I have made the decision to part with you. I am thirty now and my parents want me to marry as soon as possible. There are insurmountable obstacles to our love and it looks hopeless. At my age, I am no longer dreaming of romantic love and will be ready to accept the arrangement of fate. You are still young and I hope you will eventually find someone who will satisfy both you and your mother.

After reading his letter, I lay paralyzed in bed. I had always regarded him as a loving father who cared for me, gave me warmth and power, and protected me as an innocent, vulnerable little girl. I had become used to relying on him, listening to all his instructions and worshipping him as the indispensable sun in my life.

I became seriously ill. My hair started to fall out and my skin touched my bones. I avoided the mirror, afraid to look at my ugly image. I lay in my small bamboo bed day and night, wondering about the meaning of life.

My mother worried terribly. She was afraid I would follow my father's path and commit suicide. She brewed herbal medicines and forced me to eat. Every night when the lights were turned off, she would tell me stories in the darkness about historical and legendary figures and about her own life and sufferings, just to take my mind off things. Her old, hoarse voice went on and on in darkness accompanied by crickets chirping in the corners, and the sorrow in my heart was becoming thicker and heavier.

IV

A few days later, Old Chia came to see me with a dying hen in his hand. My mother thought about the disaster he and his father had caused and turned a cold face to him. "What do you bring that thing here for? A gift?"

His father started to drop in as well. His attitude had changed completely and flattered my mother all the time. He was a foreman in charge of a factory's security. People joked that he was good only at catching adulterers and fawning on the leaders and nothing else!

One night, my mother sighed repeatedly before she finally found the courage to speak. "Old Chia's father has chased after me for quite a while and asked me to marry him. He said we would be one big family this way.

"I told him no. I lived with your father for only three years, but I've never wanted to marry again. I would like to face him again as his wife one day. But I am getting older and will leave you sooner or later. I hope to see you married so I can join your father peacefully. Old Chia is different from his father, anyway. It's not easy for a man to wait patiently for so many years. I am sure he will treat you nicely all his life."

During the New Year's holidays, I had a few days off. Old Chia said he wanted to take me to his hometown in the country for sight-seeing. My mother was happy to hear this and urged me to take the trip. We planned to take a boat down the Grand Canal, which would leave the city early in the morning. Since the Chia family home was closer to the wharf, it was arranged that I would spend the night there to be ready to catch the first boat.

Upon arrival, I found that the Chias shared a house with three other families. The Chias occupied two connected rooms upstairs. I saw a double bed in the inner room and a single bed in the outer room. I asked, "Where am I going to sleep tonight?"

The old man replied, "You will use the single bed, and we will use the double."

However, after supper in the evening, the old man quickly took off his clothes and spread out in the single bed! I waited for him to get up. When I heard him snoring finally, it was already eleven-thirty. The buses stopped at eleven o'clock. There was no taxi then, and I was stuck. I decided to sit up until daybreak. I found a novel and sat under the desk lamp reading. Old Chia sat at the other end of the table, also reading a book. At two o'clock I became very sleepy and yawned repeatedly. I looked at Old Chia. He was still concentrating on his book. I walked to the double bed, lay down silently, and quickly dozed off.

I had no idea how long I had slept when I felt someone moving my body. I woke up in darkness and found that Old Chia had already untied my pants and shirt. Alarmed, I screamed out, "What are you doing? No, No!"

Old Chia's hands stopped. At that moment, his father's voice came from the outer room. "Stop shouting, you shameless thing! Do you think you will feel honourable if the neighbours are awakened? You

may end up being laughed at as a cheap whore who has offered herself at our door!"

Hearing this, I dared not shout anymore. Old Chia, encouraged by
his father, resumed his activity at once. He fumbled up and down at
my body, and gradually I became weak and vulnerable.

No, I didn't fight back. Why not? Well, I was young then, and
had never experienced that mysterious thing between a man and a
woman. I admit that I was curious about it. So with these complicated feelings, I gave in to Old Chia's advances.

However, with the first morning light, I suddenly woke up and
realized what had happened. I had lost my virginity! This had been
a trap. How could I have been so foolish? I got up, put on my clothes,
ignoring Old Chia's questions, and ran out of that insidious house.

When my mother saw me at the door, she was surprised. "What?
Didn't you go to the wharf?" I said nothing, but threw myself onto
my bamboo bed and cried aloud. My mother seemed to understand
what had happened. But she didn't seem very upset. She said, "Since
you have lost your virginity, who else would want you? You'd better
marry Old Chia now."

For a month, I desperately sought some escape, but I could think
of no way out. Then I missed my period. The test showed I was
pregnant! I was doomed to marry him!

I had my son, Dragon, near the end of the year. From the moment
he was born, I gave up my dreams of romance and felt peace in my
heart. My son was like my own life, where I set all my hope and joy.
There was no space for anything else. For him I sacrificed everything, including my love for Big Brother.

Four years after I had lost contact with Big Brother, I received
an unexpected letter from him. He said that he had never forgotten
me for a single day during those years. He felt guilty and sorry that
he had abandoned our love, no matter how heavy the pressure had
been, and that he was going to feel regret for the rest of his life.

Reading his letter, I felt the smothered fire in my heart suddenly rekindle. I sent a telegram to him at once asking him to meet me at the railway station in Shanghai.

My son was then three years old. During the day he was in a daycare, and in the evening my mother helped with babysitting. I worked two continuous shifts to get a day off, and took a night train to Shanghai.

During the three-hour train ride, I sat carefully on the seat to avoid making wrinkles on my new cotton dress purchased for the trip. It was dark-blue with tiny white rose buds embroidered along the edge. I wondered what I might look like in his eyes, though I had successfully got myself back to shape after my pregnancy.

The train entered the Shanghai station. While people were getting off the train, I looked at myself in the window glass and smoothed my hair, blown around by the wind. Abruptly, someone covered my eyes from behind. I touched and felt his hands. My body started trembling at once!

From that time on, I often worked two shifts and took the night train to Shanghai. We would go to a famous European style restaurant and order a dish or a drink every two hours so we could stay and chat there for the whole day. When the sun was setting, we would part reluctantly. I would catch the train home and start a new shift. Nobody ever noticed my absence. Big Brother told me he was not on good terms with his wife. Though they had a daughter, he would still consider a divorce and he wanted me to divorce Old Chia and join him. I wanted the same. But whenever I pictured my little son falling into the hands of a stepmother, I was torn.

With this divided mind, I continued the secret dating with Big Brother until he went to the U.S. a few years later. I saw him off at the airport. Since then, we have not seen one another.

Chapter 15
The Dark Tunnel

I

Camellia finished her story, her eyes gazing blankly into the distance.

Grace seemed deeply touched, staying motionless in her chair. Lily caught the same complicated expression she had seen before in her eyes.

"Are you going back to Yangchow to join Big Brother in the future?" Lily broke the silence. "Did he return from the U.S.?"

"Well, he is still in New York and single now. His wife left their daughter to him and ran off with an American."

"Then, you will be able to join him finally!"

Camellia shook her head slowly. "No. It's impossible. Everything has changed." Noticing both Grace and Lily were looking at her with many questions in their eyes, she sighed, "What you have heard is just the first part of my story. There is a second part."

Lily raised her eyebrows. "The first part was already complicated enough. And there is a second part?"

Camellia smiled, looked at her watch and stood up, "I should make another attempt to reach China now."

It was almost four o'clock in the afternoon. That meant four in the morning in China. Lily was very touched by the tale of Camellia's unfortunate life and she hoped the poor woman would be able to find the man she loved this time, whoever he was.

A moment later, Camellia came back into the kitchen, her face cloud-ridden. "He is still not home. Where could he be?"

"Have dinner with us and phone him afterwards," Lily suggested.

"No, I have to go home now." Camellia picked up her bag of wild leeks and walked towards the door. "If I am too late, they will be suspicious and make trouble for me again."

II

Lily put onto the table a dish of the stir-fried wild leeks and said, "Let's try nature's delicacy!"

Grace tasted a little bit and her face twisted in anger. "Didn't you know that I don't eat garlic?" she hissed.

Lily was shocked. While putting the bib on Baby, she replied, "I am sorry I forgot. But garlic is healthy. You may try it."

Grace's eyes snapped with rage. "No, garlic tastes horrible! I told you before but you still put it in the dish. Do you intend to torture me?"

Lily was stunned to see Mother react so strongly to such a small matter. While the family was eating their supper in awkward silence, she tried to ease the tension and shift her mother's attention by chatting. "It was sad to hear Camellia's story. I feel so sympathetic for her!"

Grace sneered, "You'd better feel sympathetic for yourself, for living a shameful life!"

Lily was hurt by the cruel words, but controlled herself. "What is the matter? I don't understand why you are so angry. Can't we ever discuss anything peacefully, Mom?"

"It's impossible to talk peacefully with a stupid mind!" Grace raised her voice. Glancing at Baby at the table, she went on. "A smart woman will never allow herself to be a single mother without the protection of marriage!"

Lily shook at the sting. She put down the chopsticks in her hand, cleaned Baby's mouth with a towel, and forced herself to speak with a smile. "I no longer wonder whether I have been a moral person or not. I just consider whether things are worthwhile or not. To me, for a child like Baby, all my sacrifice has been worthwhile."

"You simply have no self-awareness. You have been trapped repeatedly and are in a pitiable situation because you have never realized how stupid you are! You don't mind to live in shame, but what about me?" Grace's eyes were burning with rage. "Why do I have to tolerate the disgrace at my age? You make me ashamed to face everyone! My life would have been much easier without you!"

"Mother, do you know how you can help me become an ideal person in your eyes?" The last trace of a smile disappeared from her face, but Lily still tried to talk calmly. "The best way is to tell me how good I am, instead of how bad I am! That's the theory I have learned here."

"You want to listen to beautiful lies, but I don't lie!" Grace banged her rice bowl loudly on the table, declaring, "I hate liars! I hate hypocrites! I hate you, too, I hate you to death! You are my lifelong enemy! Now you know my true feelings!"

Baby, scared by the loud explosion, stared in fear, twisted his lips, and started to whimper.

Lily stood up, took Baby from his chair, and left the kitchen. She sat on the floor in the sitting room, picked up a cartoon, and tried to read to Baby, though her voice was broken and trembling.

Grace walked out of the kitchen, went into the bedroom, and threw herself on the bed.

Lily understood Mother was waiting for her to come and apologize. But she was so anguished at the sudden eruption that she didn't want to give in this time. She held Baby in her arms and tried her best to concentrate on the joyful life of rabbits and bears in the fairy-tale jungle.

A minute later, she heard something hit the floor heavily. It was a mug. Baby shook in her arms, and she stopped reading.

"You want to challenge me, don't you? Fine! Let's see who's in charge!"

Lily's mind went into a blank panic for a moment, but she clenched her teeth, held Baby tightly, and tried to continue reading.

Her refusal to surrender drove Grace crazy. Bang, bang, bang. One by one, books, newspapers, then pillows and blankets, were hitting the bedroom door and flying into the living room.

Baby's lips quivered and he finally burst out crying. Shaking, Lily stood up, took Baby's hand, and walked out of the apartment, leaving the disastrous scene behind.

III

Walking along the streets at dusk, Lily met the smiling faces of an old Canadian couple sitting on their front porch. "Hi, Sweetie Pie!" They waved to Baby in the stroller.

Lily forced herself to smile at them, though her mind was overwhelmed with sorrow.

I hate you, hate you to death! The stinging sentences chopped her heart into pieces. Why? Why would Mother lose her control to such a degree, when I didn't say anything to irritate her? The garlic? ... Or Camellia's story, which reminded her of something unforgettable, unforgivable, involving cheating and betrayal, in her past?

A bottle of bitter wine must have been brewing for decades, since her young teacher had gone, Lily mused. Perhaps Mother values her first love more than her first child, particularly when the child was not from the man she loved. Yes, not only have I been disappointing to her all these years, my very existence has constantly served as a reminder of the man who had destroyed her otherwise happy life.

Ever since Lily had learned Mother's love with her young teacher, she stopped blaming Mother for leaving her father. As Mother had stated calmly one day to her, "true lovers would be faithful to each other for their whole lives long. Those harsh political storms simply provided opportunities for unhappy couples to separate."

To outsiders, Mother always maintains her image as a well-educated and fine-mannered woman. But the bitter juice inside her has to be diluted once in a while by the tears of her ill-fated daughter.

Probably, Mother has become anguished, seeing no light ahead in the long, dark tunnel. Indeed, no relatives, no friends, and no money, I am the one lacking all these tools to climb out of the dark tunnel.

She pushed along the stroller, thinking of how she had left home in China in a hurry, in such a hurry that she hadn't even glanced back at the land where she was born and raised. She was courageous, or bold, astonishingly bold, to be a lonely woman walking in the dark. But where was her light?

She had crossed oceans and mountains, over rivers and bridges, and then had vanished like a raindrop in the vast sky, all for the image of Dr. Norman Bethune, an ideal man who, as she gradually found out, was not even recognized as a hero in his homeland. Helen, her graduate advisor, blamed that on the Cold War mentality, for casting all communists in North America as monsters. Lily had figured out, ironically, that Bethune's unusual deeds might simply be a real Christian's behaviour.

In her years in Canada, Lily had often had dreams in which she was looking for her home. The homes in her dreams had always been different, some familiar, some exotic, some with her family members, some with strangers. Her search brought her to a windowless Muslim mosque, to the bank of the Ganges River, to an incense-burning Chinese temple, and the crowded stone monuments of a Catholic graveyard. She wandered about in those dream places but found no sense of security there either. Waking up, she would often sink into her fears of homelessness and feel at a loss.

But she stayed. She felt something glittering, waiting for her in some unknown, obscure place. She couldn't tell what it was, or exactly where. All she knew was that she had stayed because of that blurry feeling of promise.

Lily stayed outside though it was totally dark. Stars covered the night sky, and lights had been turned off in houses, one by one. Baby had fallen asleep, dogs stopped barking, and the old wheels of the stroller sang with a tedious, rhythmical squeak.

She measured her heavy paces step by step, from this end of the quiet street to the other, and then from that end to this, watching silently as her lonely shadow grew and shrank from short to long, long to short, under the cool light of the street lamps.

Under one of the lamp poles, she spotted a discarded pot. She stopped and examined it and found it was a dying asparagus plant. It was so dry that the tiny fine leaves fell like snowflakes at the touch of her fingers. She stared at it for a while, then tucked it tightly under her arm.

Chapter 16
Dragon Boat Festival

I

The morning Lily noticed a fresh green bud growing out of the dying asparagus plant, Grace left Mapleton for the "Success Camp."

Seeing Grace off at the church, Lily learned from Mrs. Rice that the dragon boat festival was to be held at the city park the coming Saturday.

Lily wasted no time in telling Camellia the exciting news, but Camellia had already heard about it, since Fatty's Wok would be selling food there and she had been asked to work that day.

On Saturday morning, Lily brought Baby to the park. Hundreds of people gathered around Moon Lake, where colourful boats bobbed on the surface of the water. Squirrels jumped from tree to tree above the din of music from drums and loudspeakers, and excited shouts of the crowd. The smell of barbecued meats and hot dogs permeated the air and bushy hills.

One food stand attracted Lily's attention with a savage display— a baby pig turning over flames, sizzling as the fat turned flames into thick smoke. She thought about the heated arguments over dog meat in the "civilized world" these days, and wondered why the same people would crave butchered piglets without feeling guilty.

179

Over the hill, her eyes fell on the only Chinese food stand, Fatty's Wok. She caught sight of Camellia's slim figure inside the tent. Camellia was frying spring rolls while Fatty and a young boy were busy dealing with customers lining up for the food.

Camellia noticed Lily and gestured for her to come to the back of the tent.

"Why didn't your mother come?" she asked, stirring the spring rolls inside the pot.

"She has gone to northern Ontario for a week-long program organized by the church," Lily said, her mind flying back to the sleepless night. By the time she had returned home with Baby it had been well after midnight. After she had picked up the stuff littered on the floor, and lain down in bed, Grace asked her to get up. They came to the living room and debated until four o'clock in the morning until Lily was so exhausted that she had finally agreed that Grace was a great mother.

"A summer camp? Why didn't Mrs. Rice tell me about it?" Camellia looked disappointed. "She only asks me to come to boring sermons, but never interesting trips like this."

"Perhaps she thinks you are still too far away from God's threshold," Lily joked. "You are not even a member of the 'Faith Searching Group' yet."

There were three groups of Bible study organized by the church. There was Mrs. Rice's entry-level "Faith Searching Group," the intermediate level "Soul Growing Group," and the advanced level "Apostles Forging Group" led by Minister Wong himself.

Camellia shrugged and looked around. When she found Fatty and his son fully occupied with customers, she took a handful of roasted almond flakes from her pants pocket and quickly thrust them into Lily's hand. "I took these for you. They're delicious," she said in a low voice.

Camellia must have taken them from Fatty's restaurant without asking. Lily felt embarrassed, not knowing what to do with the almonds in her hand. "They're expensive!" Camellia said, extracting the spring rolls from the boiling oil. "The boss always keeps us working till eleven at night, but he pays us only till nine! Put them in your pocket, quickly!"

Just then, Fatty shouted in the front. Camellia shuddered and brought the rolls to the front hurriedly.

Seeing the almonds in Lily's palm, Baby reached out his small hand for them. Lily felt awkward and decided to buy a couple of spring rolls. Coming to the front, she bumped into Mrs. Rice and her younger children who were waiting in the line for food.

"I saw you talking with Camellia in the back," Mrs. Rice whispered. "Did you ask her for some free rolls?"

"Oh, no, no!" Lily blushed and changed the subject. "Where is your first daughter?"

"I left her at home. Old Chia has come to help her with her math today," Mrs. Rice said. When it was her turn, she pointed at Baby and asked Fatty to add a couple of more shrimp balls in her plate. Glancing at Baby, Fatty did. Lily thanked him and walked down the hill towards the lakeside with Mrs. Rice.

"Are you still in touch with your ex-husband?" Mrs. Rice asked. "It must be hard for you to bring up a small child by yourself, if he does not send you any money! There is a government organization that helps look for missing husbands."

Lily nodded at her kindness, but showed no interest in pursuing the topic, afraid that such a discussion might lead to embarrassing moments.

II

Standing on the beach, Lily had a good view. The Dragon Boat Festival had originated in China around the year 276 BC, in memory of a patriotic poet who drowned himself in a river at the loss of his country. But this was the first such festival in Mapleton. All together, thirty-two teams took part in the competition, some coming from as far away as Toronto.

The team from the Mapleton Kung Fu Academy caught Lily's eye. Most of the people on this boat were fair-skinned Canadians, dressed in black T-shirts. The leader of the team was Lily's neighbour, Master Iron. Standing in the very front of his boat, his long hair waving in wind, Master Iron beat a drum and shouted himself hoarse. He was repeating rhythmically in English, "Quick! Quick!" blue veins jumping on his forehead.

Master Iron needs no makeup, Lily thought. He looks just like the malicious warrior he has played in the movies. "I didn't know that Master Iron was good at rowing, too, besides playing knife and sword," Lily said in surprise.

"Who?" Mrs. Rice asked. "Oh, you mean that kung fu master?"

Lily nodded. "Yes, we live in the same building, but we seldom talk to each other. He doesn't seem to be friendly with other Chinese in the building either. I guess he is interested in Canadians only."

"But when I bump into him in Chinese restaurants, he is always asking people, including me, to introduce him to a Chinese girl to marry!" Mrs. Rice giggled. "I heard that a few of his white disciples had been attracted by his skills. But nothing comes out of it. You can imagine what it would be like to live with a man who has to hit an iron bar 1,000 times per night to keep fit!"

Lily thought about the night scene from a window show she had spotted and smiled. "How old is he?"

"He claims to be thirty-eight."

"How come he never gets old?" Lily laughed. "He said he was thirty-eight at least five years ago!"

Mrs. Rice nodded. "I think he must be close to fifty." As the words flipped out of her mouth, however, she suddenly changed her tune, observing Lily's face cautiously. "Well, it's hard to say. He is dark and skinny, and that could make him look older than his age, don't you think? He might not be much older than you, Lily!"

III

When the first round of competition was over, the loudspeaker announced that the Mapleton Kung Fu Academy had won first place. The group in black T-shirts shouted in excitement.

"I will be back in a minute," Mrs. Rice said to Lily, and walked hurriedly through the crowds towards the group in black.

Lily was not clear what Mrs. Rice was going to do. From a distance, she saw Master Iron greeting Mrs. Rice warmly. He was waving his arm vigorously in the air and talking proudly to the disciples surrounding him.

Lily suddenly remembered Kevin, the professor who used to learn Chinese with her years back. She had lost contact with him when she started dating Majesty, who'd had a strong aversion to her seeing other men for any purpose. Years ago, she heard that Kevin had quit his position at the university and become a Buddhist monk, as he had always wanted. Lily thought she could ask Master Iron if he knew anything about the whereabouts of Kevin, his former disciple. Urged by the idea, she moved through the crowds with Baby towards the black group.

As she came near, she heard Master Iron's loud voice. "I told you that I believe in no God and no ghost but myself. Don't tell me you are the way, the truth and the life! ... What? Girlfriend? Sure I want to have a girlfriend! What kind? Of course someone young, fair, and slim. And tall! Do you know someone like that?"

"Yes, I know a good girl. Her education is much better than yours ..." Mrs. Rice said, having no idea that Lily was standing behind her now.

"Come on! I have a PhD in martial arts and I am a professor." Master Iron cut her off. "Do you know I have been to the U.S. three times to receive prizes given only to the world's most famous people? I was required to dress in a tailcoat when receiving the prizes. My portrait has been hanging on the wall in the City Hall for months. It's even larger than my real head! Have you seen it? No? The Canadians call me the Lion King! Well, with my qualifications, who do you think I don't deserve? Anyway, how old is she?" Master Iron finally stopped to catch his breath, spittle accumulating on his lips.

"She is ..." Mrs. Rice's voice hesitated, but went on. "She is in her late thirties, and a single mother with a—"

Lily frowned, withdrawing a few steps to hide herself from view.

"Well, forget it! I am a virgin and I will marry a virgin only. And, if she is already in her thirties and has a child, how can you call her a girl?"

"At your age, " Mrs. Rice was pushing, "you should be realistic and keep your eyes away from those twenty-year-olds. "

"Why shouldn't I look for a young girl? It's true I am not that young, but my body is not old at all. When I am practicing kung fu, I look harsh and may scare away a lot of women. But when I am not practicing, I am soft and gentle as silk and over-cooked noodles. If you don't believe, just feel my hand. Come on, feel it."

Lily heard Mrs. Rice's joyful giggles.

Master Iron went on. "You may think I don't know how to please a woman. Honestly, it's me who needs to be pleased. When I went to New York to perform, I impressed everyone with my fast knife. After I finished, some young girls rushed over and kissed my cheeks! Remember, they were American girls. But you know, I will marry a Chinese girl only, since I want my children to be purebred ..."

At this point, Mrs. Rice seemed to have seen another old acquaintance among the crowd. She excused herself to Master Iron and walked away hastily.

Lily and Baby were suddenly exposed in front of Master Iron. He greeted her with a confident smile. Lily stepped forward, congratulated him, and inquired if he knew anything about Kevin.

"Kevin? Yes, he was my student, but changed his master years ago."

According to Master Iron, Kevin had started suffering leg pains after practicing kung fu for a few years with Master Iron. No medical diagnosis could find the source of the pain. He walked into a Buddhist temple in Toronto one day and found his talk with the old monk there soothing and relaxing. When he became more involved in Buddhism, an inexplicable thing happened. His pain would disappear as soon as he walked into that temple, but reappear when he returned to his own house. After this phenomenon was interpreted by the monk as a sign that he was predestined to be attached to Buddhism, Kevin abandoned his academic career.

Lily sighed at this confirmation that Kevin had followed his dream to become a Buddhist monk. She remembered that he had also declared that he wanted to create a novel in which the heroine from China was looking for western values while the young Canadian man she met ended up going to China for oriental philosophies. Did he ever think of her now? she wondered.

The loudspeaker announced the start of the second race and the crowd gathered again. Lily walked away from the beach and up the hill with Baby.

She sat under the shade of a pine tree and looked down at the beach. While Baby was poking at tiny flowers and ants, she lost herself in thought. Her mind stayed with Kevin's pensive look, his flexible tai chi dance with a sword in his hand, and a crippled shadow walking into a Buddhist temple.

She wondered if Kevin would have become part of her life today if Majesty didn't interfere with his kung fu display on the campus meadow that day. Kevin had broken up with his fiancée after becoming involved with Lily. She still felt guilty, for she knew that the beautiful PhD candidate at Harvard University could have been the best choice for Kevin. But she had fallen for Majesty. The gloomy faced Kevin walked into her office and dropped the ultimatum letter on her desk. "If you keep on being childish like this, you will be endangering our friendship," it declared. She had hesitated for a couple of days but finally tore the message into pieces.

Another tide of hails and drums spread from the water surface towards the woods. She saw the black boat leading in the front. As her thoughts came to Mrs. Rice's failed attempt as a matchmaker, she almost laughed out loud.

Do I really need any man in my life, anyway? At this moment, she saw Mrs. Rice and a middle-aged Chinese man walking down the hill. She saw her trembling, heavy breasts and heard her shrill voice as she talked with the man and walked towards Lily, waving her hands. Suspicious that Mrs. Rice was trying to make another match, she frowned and started to put Baby into his stroller.

"Mom, no, no ..." Baby twisted his lips in protest. He had developed a love of staying outside and hated the idea of going back into the U-shaped building.

Her heart was seized when she looked at Baby's little face. It reminded her of the painful expression of a deeply troubled man with knotted brows.

That night, with Mother away and Baby asleep, Lily's mind drifted to thoughts of her love with Majesty, amid a rare moment of peace.

Chapter 17
Deer Valley

I

It was at hidden away Deer Valley that they travelled the last part of their doomed-to-fail journey.

As their blue Chevrolet came to the end of the stone wall and turned into the driveway, Lily gasped, "Wow, what a place!"

Majesty slowed down as they passed over a concrete bridge above a running stream far below. Yellow daffodils swayed beneath old firs lining the driveway. Rolling green meadows merged into apple orchards far away. A sudden flight of honking geese created ripples in a pond, fragmenting the surface reflection of drifting clouds and dancing willow.

Perhaps startled by the car, two long-legged, light brown animals suddenly bounded out of the pines and fled towards the dark woods at the farther end of the meadow. Their bushy white tails waved up and down like silky flags in the air.

"Look! Are they deer?" Lily grabbed Majesty's shoulder excitedly and exclaimed, "I don't remember ever seeing deer with that sort of tail at the Beijing Zoo!"

"There are many types of deer," Majesty explained. "Since you are an ardent nature admirer, this might be a very suitable job for you."

At the curve of the driveway, they caught sight of a magnificent white building on top of a hill. They continued to the end and stopped their car by the fountain in front of the building. There they got out, and looked at the closed doors of the quiet house and the charming surroundings. On both sides of the building were geometric-shaped gardens divided by neatly trimmed shrubs and connected by mosaic pathways.

"What a waste!" Lily said. "Such beautiful nature and such a huge space enjoyed by only one person. Just think of the crowded parks in Beijing, where three couples have to share one bench!"

"Stop! Thank God nobody understands Chinese here, or you would fail the interview because of your communist ideology!" He looked at his wristwatch. "It's time. Remember, don't talk rubbish!"

The door at the corner of the house opened with a click and out shot a short-tailed Doberman with shiny black hair, fast as an arrow. Lily screamed in terror.

Majesty quickly scanned the ground but found no potential weapon. He raised his foot, but withdrew it just in time as a woman's quivering voice wafted across the air.

"Come back, Victor!"

Standing in the open door was a white-haired old woman in pink flowered pyjamas.

She walked slowly to the side of the fountain, the dog now docile at her side. "Don't be afraid! Victor is welcoming you!" The creature nuzzled at Lily's shaking hand.

"Oh, Victor? Well, he's a beautiful dog, indeed!" Lily's heart was still pounding fast, but she forced a smile. She resisted the urge to wash her dog-saliva-smeared hand in the fountain, rubbing it hastily on the back of her blue jeans before she shook hands with the old lady.

Lily had graduated more than a year ago. She had been admitted into a PhD program at the University of Toronto. After some hesitation, however, she had finally chosen to stay in Mapleton to be with Majesty while he was doing his PhD. Her painful decision had brought her no luck, however, for so far, she hadn't been able to find a suitable job. Two days ago, she had found this position in the paper and had passed the initial phone interview with the employer. It would be a great pity to lose a job because of a dog.

"The old housekeeper and gardener were with me for more than ten years. We got along very well. I hated to let them go when they asked to retire," Mrs. Fortune talked slowly, in the flat voice typical of aristocrats in the movies. "Please come and look around the house before you decide whether you want to work here." Her gray eyes held a confident smile.

Lily and Majesty walked silently through the ground floor, as Mrs. Fortune explained, clearly a proud tour guide, the function of each gracefully decorated room.

When Lily stepped into the library, she could hardly control her surprise. "Oh, so beautiful!"

Mrs. Fortune looked at her. "Do you like this room?" Seeing Lily nodding, she smiled. Among the twenty applications she had received, she had somehow picked out this Chinese couple. And now her choice was confirmed. People who loved books made her feel safe.

Lily was enthralled by the beauty of the private library. Bookshelves extended from floor to ceiling. Hardcover books, many very old, were neatly arranged on the shelves. The thick carpet stretched to the other end of the room and up two steps to a platform. On the platform were a few antiques. The most interesting was a large globe, its fine smooth surface shining with a light-brown, oily tint. On top of a rusty iron stand was an open encyclopedia. An exquisite crystal chandelier hung from the centre of the ceiling, reflecting the rich colour of the crimson curtains. Everything in the room, even the cold remains of the logs in the fireplace, spoke of dignity.

Lily's eyes fell on the big carved desk in front of the window. "May I put my computer here?" she asked tentatively.

"Of course, you can. Nobody is going to use the library anyway."
Lily was touched by her generosity and liked the old lady at once.

Mrs. Fortune opened the door to the back porch and led them out. Across the wide lawn was a long marble railing. At both ends were stone steps leading to the deep river valley below. Hearing laughter, Lily leaned over the railing and looked through an opening in the dense trees along the river. She spotted a couple of young people in a canoe floating downstream. The sound of their carefree voices mixed with splashing water echoed over the lawn and faded into the woods.

Majesty pointed at the dozens of blooming flowerpots on the railing and asked: "Did you plant all these yourself?"

"You must be kidding." Mrs. Fortune twisted her heavily rouged lips and waved her hand in disdain.

Lily noticed the protruding knuckles on her fingers, sure signs of hard work, and wondered about the old lady's background. She felt pity for her little affectation and started to get a flavour of what it might be like to be a servant of the bourgeoisie.

II

But Lily did not find her new position unpleasant. The nicest part, perhaps, was the daily trip to the mailbox at the edge of the estate, accompanied by Victor.

At two o'clock in the afternoon, she would let Victor out of Mrs. Fortune's bedroom to do his business in some bushes near the cottage, his favourite washroom.

Past the rose garden and the oak woods, the old abandoned cottage was nowadays a paradise for raccoons and their families. It stood high above the spot where the stream joined the river. The door was off its hinges, leaning against the outside wall. In the centre of the hall was a small tractor, and some tools were scattered on the floor. There was a fireplace and a couch in the living room.

Inside the small room on the left were a few pieces of bedroom furniture. Everything was drab, and the air smelled moldy.

On her first exploration, a continuous rumbling sound led her to the door at the corner of the hall. It opened onto a long deck suspended in the air. Lily stepped carefully, fearing the aged structure might crash at any moment. Looking through the broken screen, she saw that the stream became a waterfall into the river below.

When Victor finished his business, they would walk down the winding driveway towards the entrance. Mini-sized cabins were dotted here and there along the road. They had been built for animals by the owner's husband decades before.

Victor treasured dearly his romps in the woods. He took off after squirrels and chased them up the trees.

Mrs. Fortune told Lily that she had bought Victor when he was only two weeks old. She had had him trained for everything except fighting. "I want to bring him up like a nice boy, not a vicious street dog!"

Lily wasn't sure if Victor was indeed a kind-hearted creature, but she agreed with Mrs. Fortune's claim that the seven-year-old dog's IQ equalled that of a five-year-old child.

But Majesty disputed this. "A five-year-old's IQ is a hundred times higher than Victor's!"

But Mrs. Fortune was not easily defeated. "You have no experience raising a child, so how can you prove that?"

Majesty looked at the old lady and then at Lily. He clenched his teeth and forced the words back into his mouth. Seeing his expression, Lily steered the conversation in another direction. They had answered the ad as a childless couple, concealing the fact that Majesty was a father.

Mrs. Fortune had explained the child issue to them once during her routine vodka evening. "What I wanted most but couldn't have was a child of my own. My husband already had grandchildren when we married, and he didn't want to be a father again. When he passed away, my chance was gone. I'd trade all my property for a son, a big son of my own! I used to have a Yugoslavian couple working for me. When the wife got pregnant, I let them go. I couldn't tolerate the sight and sound of a baby, at my age. Do you understand?"

The old lady used to recall emotionally the glory days when she and her husband entertained Paul Martin in this big house. "Of course, I mean the senior," she said, as her faded blue eyes lit up. "Not the young one in Ottawa now."

Victor was immediately drawn to the newcomers. Besides the daily trip with Lily to the mailbox, he also loved joining the young couple in their after-dinner walks in the gardens. While Lily held Majesty's arm, talking and laughing, Victor would run back and forth around them.

After the walks, Victor always tried to follow them into their bedroom. Lily pointed to the other end of the corridor and said, "Go back to your mother now!" She felt that the dog understood Chinese after only a few months of hearing it.

But Victor would simply sit on the carpet outside their door, eyes fixed on her. She always ignored his stubborn protest and closed the door.

One night, she felt thirsty after reading in bed for hours. She got up to get a drink. When she opened the bedroom door, she found Victor still sitting outside the door. As if he understood what she wanted, he rushed downstairs to the kitchen ahead of her. She brought a cup of water upstairs and again closed Victor outside. However familiar she had become with the animal, she could not tolerate the idea of dogs running around her bedroom. She had grown up in an environment without animals.

Tuesday was laundry day. Lily gathered Mrs. Fortune's clothing and bedclothes. The thick black hairs on the snow-white sheets, pillow cases and pyjamas never failed to remind her of her shock when she had first seen Mrs. Fortune and her pet snuggled in the king-size bed. She always washed her own clothes first, then

Majesty's, then the living-room and dining-room linens, then the kitchen towels. Only then did she put the dog-hair clothes into the washer. When they had been washed, she would run the washer empty with clean, cold water to ensure that her own clothes would not be contaminated by those disgusting dog hairs.

When dinner was ready and she brought Mrs. Fortune's tray into her bedroom, putting it on the stool in front of her sofa chair facing the TV, Victor would jump over, saliva dripping from his mouth, and gobble up a piece of meat held out to him on her fork.

"No hurry, darling! Watch your table manners!" Mrs. Fortune reminded him gently, while putting a piece of meat, full of dog saliva from the fork, into her mouth.

As Lily watched, she lost her appetite. She had to look away so that her disgust wouldn't show.

"Oh, God! How can she ever eat anything with a dog?" she sighed to Majesty as she returned to their dinner table in the kitchen.

"If you had ever finished the leftovers on your baby's plate, you would understand such feelings," he said. Majesty's voice was not loud, but Lily felt its weight.

Mrs. Fortune's motherly love was genuine. Each week when they went shopping together, she always let Lily pick the human food for the following week, while she herself would linger in the pet food area for half an hour, enjoying choosing carefully like a doting mother choosing baby food. She insisted that Victor have different snacks daily, chicken, beef, pork, liver, all in turn.

Lily had once accidentally violated Victor's dignity when she helped to pick out a few man-made bones. Mrs. Fortune sneered at the three-dollar bones, replacing them with the five-dollar ones.

"What's the difference? Why not donate her extra money to hungry people? There are plenty of them in the world!" Majesty grumbled in Chinese.

III

Victor was so annoyed at Lily's cold-blooded behaviour in shutting him out of her bedroom every night that he took revenge. When Lily came out of the bedroom one morning, she found the rug in front of her door turned upside down. During the following days, she had to fix the rug every morning. She kept silent until one day she found Victor's BM on the rug.

"The dog is indeed intelligent!" she told Majesty. "He knows that my job is cleaning and he did this to punish me."

Majesty threw the dirty rug into the basement which was full of century-old mysteries. The cold war between the dog and the servant continued. One day, Lily didn't close her bedroom door tightly when she left. As she returned an hour later, she found the door wide open and shreds of toilet paper spread everywhere around the room. There were deep tooth prints in the remaining toilet paper, suggesting his mounting hatred.

Angrily, Lily ran out of the bedroom. But Victor was nowhere. Looking at the tightly closed door on the other side of the quiet corridor, Lily imagined Victor smiling contentedly under the armpit of his drunken mother.

She rushed into Majesty's study where he was working on his thesis. He listened impatiently to Lily's description of the event and waved his hand, frowning. "Well, you'd better stop now! Aren't you afraid that you will be degraded to a dog's level if you continue your battle of wits with him? Besides, there's his mother!"

As Mrs. Fortune was constantly comforted by her vodka, she seemed unaware of the silent battles going on in the old house. An experienced drinker, she would often finish a forty-ounce bottle in less than two days. Quite different from alcoholics in China, the Canadian lady required no food to go with her vodka, just ice cubes.

Since she discovered Mrs. Fortune's secret, Lily had worried about the harmful effect of the alcohol and wanted to discuss it with her. At the beginning, Mrs. Fortune had tried conscientiously to conceal her hobby from her servant. When she was running low on stock, a deliveryman would bring a brown paper bag to the house. Mrs. Fortune hurried downstairs, with unsteady steps and shaking hands, to take the bag to her room herself. She would avoid Lily's eyes. Noticing her guilty look, Lily would hold back her impulse to discuss the matter.

Though Mrs. Fortune declared she had long ago stopped going to church and hesitated to confirm Lily's inquiry if she was still a Christian, that didn't prevent her from using the Christmas season as a good excuse for self-indulgence. After finishing six bottles of vodka within days, she fell down the staircase one afternoon and hurt her head. Lily found her, in pink pyjamas and messed up hair, lying on the Persian carpet stained with blood and vomit, smiling and singing softly in a dreamy voice.

Lily's heart was filled with sympathy and sorrow.

After Mrs. Fortune was taken away by ambulance, Lily discussed the matter worriedly with Majesty, who had just come back from school. "She must feel great pain for making the wrong decision in choosing wealth and giving up motherhood. So she has to anaesthetize herself with alcohol."

"Nonsense!" Majesty sneered. "People like you who have majored in arts always tend to explain everything in the world in a romantic way. Just like Freud, who related everything to sex. An alcoholic indulges in liquor simply because he or she likes the taste, and gradually gets addicted. Her stomach would feel itchy without it. That's all!"

One night when Lily and Majesty were in their own bedroom, there was a gentle knock on the door. Lily was leaning against her pillow reading. Wondering if Victor had acquired the new skill of knocking like a human, she didn't move. The knock came again. Majesty put down his newspaper, walked over, and opened the door.

To his surprise, it was Mrs. Fortune standing by the door in red pyjamas. She held a silver tray with two crystal glasses filled with liquor and decorated with fresh lemon slices. "Room service!" she said with a charming smile.

Majesty looked bewildered. But seconds later, he got it. "Thanks!" Laughing happily, he took a glass from the tray, sipped at the unknown liquor, and praised it politely. Lily declined, so Mrs. Fortune took the second glass herself and toasted with Majesty. Satisfied with the result of her efforts, Mrs. Fortune returned to her own quarters with Victor.

Cooking for Canadians was very easy. Mrs. Fortune and Victor's food was so simple: coffee, fruit, and toast for breakfast, nothing for lunch, and baked stuff for supper. Since the lady insisted on a healthy diet, no seasoning was allowed in the food. There was no need for cutting either. A lump of meat was put into the oven and the knob turned on. Monday beef, Tuesday pork, Wednesday chicken, Thursday mutton, Friday fish, Saturday and Sunday onion, carrots, and potato.

Majesty could no longer control his temper after eating such food for a week. "These are not meals for humans! It's almost like feeding the pigs!"

Since then, Lily had prepared two separate meals every day. To satisfy Majesty, she would make typical Chinese food, such as steamed rice, tofu, and stir-fried vegetables. Lily didn't enjoy spending her time cooking, and she found Majesty's picky appetite a burden. Lily found the drunken lady easier to live with than the sober one. Besides, cooking duties were simplified when the vodka was flowing. It was only when the hostess was embracing her beloved vodka that Lily's burden was lightened. Mrs. Fortune required no food then, just ice cubes and black coffee.

Majesty seemed unaware of Lily's feelings. He quoted something from a French philosopher he had read when he was young: "When a man comes into his home and sees his wife knitting or sewing, he feels relaxed. But he feels unrest to see her reading."

She was not familiar with men's feelings either. As a matter of fact, she had never tried to understand what men like or dislike. "What do you like to see, then, when you come home?" she inquired seriously.

Majesty avoided her eyes. "I, like all men, share the same views as the author."

Men are different, she concluded. She remembered her university days when Prince congratulated her with admiring smiles. "I saw your name again on the school bulletin board! How do you manage to be among the top three students in your department every year?"

She became uneasy now if Majesty walked into the kitchen while she was reading. She would quickly put down the book or newspaper, tie an apron around her waist, and go to the sink, trying to look like the ideal woman in his eyes.

"You will eventually discover that I am the most suitable type of man for a woman like you." Once in a while, Prince's farewell words in his last letter tinkled in her mind, and poked her heart.

At those moments, she would remind herself that Majesty was a decent man, insightful, never made obscene comments, and was therefore worth her sacrifices.

IV

Majesty had not finished his PhD thesis yet and often felt worn out from his work on the estate. Mrs. Fortune acknowledged the situation. "There is endless work in Deer Valley. We need a whole army, actually!"

Around Thanksgiving time, Deer Valley turned into a fairy-tale world, with colour everywhere. Lily enjoyed herself immensely as she picked apples and pears in the orchard at dusk, watched geese flying towards the southern sky and fallen leaves floating away in the golden stream.

She would sing loudly in the empty vastness, thrilled at the echo of her own lonely voice, her eyes becoming moist with a mysterious fear of nature's silent power. Once, she had dropped all the fruit she had just picked, turned around, and run indoors, away from the terrifying tranquility.

For weeks, Majesty rode on the tractor with the blower, driving the fallen leaves inch by inch into the stream. As he finished one part of the meadow, it would be covered with a new sheet of golden leaves before he finished the next. He saw no sense in the environmental theory of Canadians. To prevent the smoke from burning leaves on a bonfire, people created smoke by burning fuel to run machines.

As Lily came out to wave him in for dinner, Majesty stopped the tractor, jumped off, and brushed the leaves off his clothes. "This work is not for human beings! Victor should be tied to the seat to run it!"

Before all the leaves had been blown into the stream, snow started to fall. Majesty was about to celebrate his farewell to the torturous tractor when he found himself bound to the huge, heavy snow plough. Each morning as he looked at the dancing snowflakes outside the window, his face would become even more overcast than the sky.

V

The month before Christmas was the golden season for the local stores. Almost every day, Mrs. Fortune asked Majesty to drive her in the Cadillac to shop. She would spend hours in the mall buying one sweater, only to return it the next day.

One snowy afternoon, Mrs. Fortune went to The Bay again, making another effort to find gifts.

"Aren't you buying any gifts?" she asked Lily.

Lily shook her head. She had no one to send any gifts to, in this vast land. She accompanied the lady the whole afternoon until she was settled on a large, light green vase.

Mrs. Fortune, dressed in a heavy fur coat, stood among the people crowded in front of the mall entrance. Lily held the large vase carefully beside her. She watched anxiously as Majesty tried to squeeze the Cadillac in among the other cars. When he finally managed to get the car parked by the curb, he got out and held Mrs. Fortune's arm, walking carefully on the slippery ground.

Glancing proudly at the two servants, Mrs. Fortune got into the car. Majesty frowned at her snobbish air, but Lily was sympathetic to the old lady. Certainly not a highly educated woman, she had married wealth and had eventually become a slave to wealth. Having servants from a developing country who had a much better education than she had, wealth and vanity were the only weapons she had to protect her dignity.

After dinner that evening, Lily went into the library. She planned to light a fire in the fireplace, make a pot of jasmine tea, turn on her computer, and work quietly writing her book by the cozy winter fire. Before she turned on the chandelier in the darkness, however, her eyes were caught by the view out the window.

The snowstorm was over and the whole world was tranquil. The meadow under the bright moonlight shone like a crystal garden. The big cedars by the house breathed silently as they stooped under the heavy snow bending their limbs. She caught her breath, entranced, as a red fox snuck out from behind a tree and jumped onto the fountain edge. Looking around, it caught sight of the figure inside the window. Startled, it fled. A trail of footprints was left on the snow.

In the snow-lit library, Lily's memory was drawn back to the songs she used to sing as a teenager. She was particularly fond of pieces eulogizing the epic Long March, when communist-led troops strove hard for a whole year to survive the government slaughter in 1934. There was no doubt that the heroic revolutionary romance had influenced her generation to an unforgettable degree.

An impulse to sing became stronger and stronger. Eventually, she could no longer resist and opened her mouth:

The snow-covered wildness stretches with no end.
Food has run out in the freezing highland.
The Red Army soldiers are iron men
refusing to bow to the snow-capped mount ....

Her voice swelled, echoing against the ceiling in this vast room.

Majesty followed sound of her voice to the library and joined her singing:

Wind and rain soaked our thin clothes,
but forged our bones stronger.
Wild herbs filled our empty stomach,
yet nourished our will ....

One song after another, they sang in high spirits and excitement, totally forgetting where they were. Then Lily's voice faltered as something touched her leg. She lowered her head and saw Victor.

Outside the library door was the white-haired lady in her dressing gown, standing still as a marble statue in the sudden silence.

For many sleepless nights, Lily had come downstairs and sat for long hours in front of her computer. Her focused writing in this quiet library nourished her thirsty soul, allowing her precious moments to escape the hollow, blank life in the vast estate.

The memoir she had started on the suggestion of the woman writer she had worked for so long ago in China had somehow changed into a work of the imagination, and now she travelled freely in the world she had created, full of lively men and women, dreams chased and dreams within grasp.

VI

The winter was exhaustingly long, almost six months. The meadows turned green again only after Easter. Two weeks later, the whole estate of Deer Valley was dyed golden by a sea of blooming dandelions.

Majesty stood in front of the fountain, looking pensively at the rolling meadow beneath his feet, the buzzing bees and butterflies dancing around him. Nostalgia filled his heart and his thick-browed eyes became moist.

The charming scenery in Deer Valley had not helped to ease Majesty's guilt. Earlier that year, he and Lily watched a Chinese show on video. The program was about a single mother raising her handicapped daughter all alone after being abandoned by her husband. When the mother was speaking on screen, Majesty turned stiff. Lily heard surreptitious snuffling noises, and when she peeped at him out of the corner of her eye, she saw something shining on his cheeks.

The long struggle between love and morality had been detrimental to the man's good nature. His impatience and paranoia came from the deep sorrow and conflict in his heart, and his hot temper had become worse and worse as time went on.

"Why don't you divorce him?" Mrs. Fortune asked, having found Lily weeping in the kitchen a couple of times. "You have everything, and you deserve a much better man. A Canadian man!"

A Canadian man? Kevin's image waving a shining sword on the moonlit meadow somehow came to mind. Then her mind shifted back to the image of her old love, the ideal Canadian man.

VII

Lily's hot admiration of Norman Bethune was dampened in the man's homeland. Most people shook their heads, telling her they had never heard of him. Others irritated her as they described him as a "drunkard" or "swashbuckler." She would tell them that people in China often swore at the Americans, but never the Canadians, all because of this man.

Shortly after Majesty acquired his driver's license a year before, they drove to the old lumber town, Gravenhurst, the birthplace of the hero.

The creamy-coloured old manse stood among blooming white lilies, looking simple, neat, and clean, and it welcomed her with its quietness. Her eyes were moist as she stood still in the room laid out the way it had been when Norman Bethune was a small boy. The frame church down the road, the lake he had loved to swim in, the hills where he had chased butterflies, the forests and the summer skies that delighted him—all lingered in her mind.

The caretaker lady informed them that the memorial house had been set up for visitors in 1970s with funds from the Chinese government. More than ninety percent of the visitors were from China, and five percent were from Spain where Norman had also volunteered during the war. But to the local residents, the communist doctor meant very little, even less than his parents.

Norman's mother had been a missionary. She was filled with a vast love for mankind and a firm determination to save the heathen and spread the word of Christ. Norman's father, the minister in Gravenhurst's Presbyterian church, won more than ordinary recognition for his powerful sermons.

Although Norman Bethune's statue was seen in many places in China, the erection of his statue in his hometown had been a controversial issue. His complex personality and unconventional behaviour aroused criticism. His frustrations, built up over the years before he came to China, were eased after he arrived in the ancient land.

In a letter to his friend, he described his feeling: "Life here is pretty rough and sometimes pretty tough. But I am enjoying it … I am tired, but I don't think I have been so happy for a long time. I am enormously content. I am doing what I want to do. And see what my riches consist of! I have vital work that occupies every moment of my time. I am needed.

"I have no money or the need for it. I have the inestimable good fortune to be among and to work among people to whom communism is a way of life, not merely a way of talking and thinking.

"The stoic Chinese indeed! Here I have found comrades who belong to the very hierarchy of humanity. They have seen cruelty, yet know gentleness; they have tasted bitterness, yet know how to smile; they have endured vast suffering, yet know patience, optimism, quiet wisdom. I have come to love them; I know they love me too."

It was hard for Lily to understand why his wife, a pretty British woman, married him twice but twice divorced such a respectable man. Although she might have had reason. Norman once became acquainted with a single woman, a Christian missionary sent from New Zealand to an isolated mountain village in North China. Lily felt jealous when she read of the girl having dinner with Norman in her missionary compound under dim oil lamps. His eloquence and irresistible charisma won over the woman to the cause of the Chinese revolution. In a long letter to Norman, she wrote about her venture into the Japanese-occupied areas to purchase medicine for the Chinese wounded. Lily sensed the unwritten romantic message between the lines.

When he was dying in a small village and writing his will, Norman didn't forget his divorced wife. "I am fatally ill. I am going to die. I have some last favours to ask of you," he wrote to the Commander of the Chinese Communist Army. "I should like you to ask the China Aid Council to remit some money to my divorced wife, on my behalf—perhaps in installments. My responsibility to her is undeniable, and I cannot leave her cut off simply because I myself have no money. Tell her that I have been very happy ..."

After dividing his belongs, such as fountain pens, shoes, boots, trousers, cases, surgical instruments, and blankets, among his Chinese friends, Norman wrote:

"Give my everlasting love to all my Canadian and American friends. Tell them I have been very happy. My only regret is that I shall now be unable to do more. The last two years have been the most significant, the most meaningful years of my life. Sometimes it has been lonely, but I have found my highest fulfillment here among my beloved comrades. I have no strength now to write more ... to you and to all my comrades, a thousand thanks ..."

Bethune's body was carried on a stretcher along the barren hills from village to village on cloudy, cold winter days. For five days, they tried to find a place safe from the Japanese bombardment to bury him. And for five days, the stretcher was escorted by hundreds of weeping Chinese men, women, and children.

Gazing at Norman Bethune's statue and the gray pigeons hovering over it against the cold autumn wind, Lily solemnly lit a piece of incense in her heart for the man who really deserved her love.

VIII

"A Canadian man? Where can I find such a man?" Lily's voice sounded hollow in the spacious room.

Mrs. Fortune's lips moved, but made no reply, her eyes staring blankly at the birds jumping among the willow branches outside the window. Like Lily, Mrs. Fortune had also become the victim of Majesty, a servant who often forgot his role.

Once when the old lady had asked him to empty the garbage can, Majesty, concentrating on finishing his thesis and disliking being bossed around, simply turned a deaf ear. Irritated, she went into the garage, dragged the garbage can into the house, and left it in the pantry connecting the kitchen and the dining room.

Majesty stopped Lily as she was trying to move the heavy garbage can back to the garage. "Leave it there! Do you hear?" he shouted in a loud voice. "She wants to make me embarrassed? Okay, let's play it out. We'll see who is going to be more uncomfortable."

The three people under the big roof shared the house in extreme awkwardness for three days and nights. Lily's nerves were stretched to their limit when Majesty finally moved the stinking garbage can back to the garage.

Each of them realized now the ill-fitting roles they were playing in the house and such an inharmonious relationship had to be brought to an end. Majesty had completed his PhD and secured a position in an expanding satellite company in the U.S. The time had come for them to move on.

IX

After breakfast in the morning, the two servants at Deer Valley submitted their notice to the old lady.

"Why?" Mrs. Fortune's wrinkled eyes opened wide in shock. She turned off the TV, sat straight up on her sofa, and asked in a trembling voice, "Why would you leave me alone? Why can't you stay? We get along so well." Tears welled in her eyes. She held Victor's neck tightly, buried her gray head in his black hair, and started sobbing.

Lily was struck with pity and almost wanted to withdraw her resignation. She had not expected the old lady to be so upset.

She took out a Kleenex for the old lady and patted her shivering shoulder. "Don't worry. You still have Victor with you."

Mrs. Fortune stared at the gauze curtains wafted by the moist breeze from the river down below. The air in the room smelled of earth. "Victor? ... Well, you know about his disease. The doctor told me he is not going to survive the summer."

Majesty stood by the sofa, silently watching the vulnerable lady and her dog. A number of times in the past year, he had driven them to a famous animal hospital in Toronto for checkups.

"Here you are!" The doctor would always hand her a prescription and say the same thing. "Keep giving him these pills. He has another few months in him yet ..."

The pills were kept on the kitchen counter. It was Lily's task to feed them to Victor every morning.

Lily read the bottles carefully and found the medicine was just vitamins. Majesty thought the doctor was simply creating some tension to scare the rich lady, but Lily believed that the doctor's prescriptions did something to ease the old lady's mind.

Mrs. Fortune rubbed her eyes with the tissue and murmured, "Ever since my husband passed away, I have raised four dogs. But one by one, they all left me behind. They are now buried under the apple trees in the orchard. Victor is going to be my last dog. I am not going to have any more. It was so sad, so painful, to part with each of them. I am getting old, and I can't go through it any more. I have made a will. After Victor has passed away, his urn will be kept in my bedroom and buried with me."

The next morning, Majesty went downtown and brought back a video camera. He spent a couple of hours in his own room reading the brochure and then went into Mrs. Fortune's bedroom.

"Please get dressed. Let's go out in the garden. I am going to make a video of you and Victor, together. In the future, whenever you miss him, you can always play the tape in the VCR."

During the following weeks, Mrs. Fortune successfully restrained herself from the bottle to carry out interviews with new servants.

After screening dozens of applicants, she finally selected a decent looking middle-aged white couple, who had been custodians from Newfoundland and claimed to be related to Prince Charles of England.

X

On the day they left Deer Valley, Majesty drove Lily to a house downtown where she had rented a room. He took out her luggage, put it at the front door, and they waited in silence for the landlord to show up with the key.

Lily stood on top of the steps of the narrow old Victorian rooming house. Her eyes scanned the scraggly front yard, the cherry bushes along the fence, the heavy clouds in the sky, and finally settled on Majesty, who was leaning against the car and smoking silently. His eyes avoided hers.

The last night at the estate had been a starless and windless early summer night. Noisy frogs sent their repeated chorus into the open windows. There was no light in their bedroom. The tiny red spot from the cigarette in Majesty's hand flared when he took a puff.

Lying in bed, they finalized their plan: bid farewell together to Mrs. Fortune and then separate in the city. Majesty threw away the cigarette and touched her hand. "Oh, your hand is so cold. Are you not feeling well?" He moved his hand to her forehead. "Well, I guess you are fine, right? ... Why do you just keep silent? ... You make me feel bad."

Lily felt her heart being eaten away bit by bit by the crying frogs. She wanted to cry out, but found her strength drained away. There were no tears either. The riverbed in her soul had long ago dried up.

Majesty's fingers touched her hair, eyes, nose, lips, held her cheeks gently. He stared at her and said, finally, "She is not as good as you, in every respect. But life is beyond our control. When we are desperately in need of experience in love and marriage, we are still young and don't have it. Once we have gained the experience, however, we actually don't need it any more."

"Whatever I do, it is impossible to satisfy everyone. You are a strong-willed woman. I know you will feel pain, but you will never fall down. As for her, she is a typical weak woman, and her survival depends on other people. I love you, but I feel pity for her. I am like a piece of bread during the starvation. If I give it to you, I would give you more energy. But if I give it to her, I would be saving the life of a dying woman and an innocent child."

Chapter 18
Shepherd in Her Soul

I

"Join the army of our Lord!" "Be a fully devoted child of Jesus Christ!"

The large-print slogans on the wall were certainly eye-catching. The group of famous ministers were servants of God indeed, influencing and convincing with their charm as they took turns giving intense sermons throughout the week. There had been eloquent lectures in the daytime and romantic bonfire discussions at night. The Success Camp ended brilliantly, with more than ninety percent of the participants having declared their willingness to believe in the Lord.

However, Grace felt disappointed as she packed her simple luggage and stepped onto the bus back to Mapleton.

The blood-red setting sun was being nibbled away by heavy gray clouds. The monotonous noise of the bus engine on the highway was deafening and nauseating. She felt dizzy and shut her eyes, leaning back in her seat. The young people in the bus started singing, led by an enthusiastic choir leader.

The Lord is my shepherd, I shall not want.
He maketh me lie down in green pastures;

He leadeth me by the quiet waters.
My soul he doth restore again ...

Dusk gradually wrapped the world and blurred everything outside.

"My soul ... he restore ... the path of righteousness ... " Grace repeated the words silently as she drifted into a reverie of the past. A pair of lamb-like black eyes blinked and blinked, emerging in her mind like the bright, twinkling morning star against the curtain of the descending night.

II

Grace received dozens of letters from the young teacher. The first one he wrote on the bus as he left the mountains. Grace could still recite from this letter decades later.

Adieu, adieu, the tranquil river and green hills, the welcoming town and the charming girl ... During sleepless nights, I am longing for you. Grace, Grace, I couldn't deny my calling ...

In the early days after the young teacher had left, Grace went home every day from school to check for letters before anyone else could find them. Love between a teacher and a student was not accepted by custom, and she had to hide her sweet feelings in the dark.

Reading his letters, she felt she was travelling with him—in the bus on the winding road through the mountains, in the small inn of the provincial capital city, on the train leading to the coast, and on the ship leaving the seaport.

Although she was fully aware that he was getting further and further away from her, Grace always had the strange feeling that the young teacher would reappear unexpectedly in front of her eyes one day, just as he had on Christmas Eve when he surprised everyone by showing up as a white-bearded, red-robed old man.

Grace had never been interested in needlework, but one day, she went into the largest silk store on the city's main street, and selected a piece of fine, pale blue material. She hid inside her room for a whole afternoon working out a satisfactory design. For days, she spent all her spare time on the handkerchief. She embroidered differently shaped, tiny white flower buds along the four sides of the fine material. In one corner she stitched a flying reed catkin.

On the eve of boarding the ship to England, the young teacher received the handkerchief. In his letter he wrote,

I pressed my lips against the reed catkin, soaked with the innocent breath of a young maiden, as I bid farewell tearfully to my motherland ...

III

Grace stared at the misty drizzle in the gray sky, lost in thought. It had been months since she had last heard from him. He should have arrived in England long before, but there had been no letter.

The lilac tree in the yard seemed to weep, the drops of autumn rain wetting its leaves. The wooden doors behind the tree were tightly shut, and moss had grown on the front steps. The melodious English song, "The Last Rose of Summer," drifting in the fragrant air a year ago had disappeared like a memory of a dream.

Grace trembled. Suddenly, a strange feeling struck in her heart: he is coming back to me today! Yes, this time, he is!

She was thrilled at the sudden revelation. She hastily put on her favourite apple-green, short-sleeved shirt and tucked it inside a pair of white pants, looked in the mirror and combed her hair, then rushed out the door.

She jogged to the bus station outside the northern city gate. As she approached the red brick building, she saw an old bus arriving. Her heart jumping into her throat, she quickly hid inside the waiting room. Through the window, she watched the passengers getting off the bus, one by one. And then the bus door was shut.

She let out a breath, left the window, and sat on the bench, waiting for the next bus. She was met by a couple of acquaintances who asked why she was there. She said that she was waiting for a relative, all the while worrying about what she would do if the young teacher arrived at that moment.

The whole day passed, her enthusiasm being eaten away bit by bit. Grace didn't realize that dusk had already fallen until the clerk came out of the ticket office. When he told her there were no more buses that day, the whole universe felt blank.

Tired, hungry, and cold, she stepped dispiritedly out of the waiting room and stood under the eaves. The drizzle had turned to rain drops, falling from the gray sky and chilling her bare arms. She had chosen to wear the apple-green shirt and snow-white pants especially for him, having seen the admiring look in his eyes when she wore them before, but they looked out of place now in the gloomy autumn evening. She shivered, held her arms tightly, and stepped onto the muddy road.

From that day on, Grace was altered. She withdrew from all after-class activities and resigned her position as editor of the school journal. People no longer spotted her slim figure on the sports ground and seldom heard her carefree laughter. She was often seen gazing pensively from the dormitory window. In class, she would stare at the blackboard, her mind vacant. She saw those black gentle eyes everywhere, on the wall, on the ceiling, in the air.

Christmas Day came again. When the ancient city was covered in darkness, Grace sneaked out of her home and walked to the Christian church.

In this mysterious world, would she find a trace of him? She opened her eyes wide and searched among the moving shadows in the candlelight. She waited and waited, but the old man with the white beard and red robe never showed up as she had expected.

She stood in the last row of praying people, her eyes fixed on the man nailed on the cross high above. The organ sent out a soft tune and the people started singing.

"Silent night, holy night, all is calm, all is bright ..."

The mysterious yet familiar music echoed against the high ceiling and saddened Grace's heart. Her eyes became moist as she remembered hearing the song a year ago standing beside the young teacher. The face of the nailed man blurred in the dim candlelight.

Is that him? She opened her eyes wide and couldn't believe what she saw. The young teacher was there, looking down silently at her from the cross above, his gentle black eyes filled with tears! Thrilled, she reached out her hands.

"I am here! Do you see? I am here!" She burst out crying and waved to him tearfully!

The other parishioners cast anxious glances at her, but then averted their eyes respectfully, continuing with the hymn.

"Son of God, love's pure light. Radiant beams from thy holy face ..."

Her uncontrollable sobbing poured like a flood to join the high notes of the choir.

IV

His last letter finally came from England, a year after his departure from the ancient town. Grace could never forget that Friday evening. She was having supper with her whole family in their country home when a male servant came in and handed her a thick envelope.

As soon as her eyes fell on the English address on the envelope, she dropped her chopsticks on the floor. She left the table hurriedly and ran to her own room in the backyard.

Under the cozy light of a red candle, Grace opened the envelope with shaking hands. It was an eight-page letter, describing in detail the scenery, food, clothing, and people in that exotic land. She giggled happily as she read the humorous wit flowing from his pen. Her smile froze, however, when she came to the end.

I am writing to you with complicated feelings. After careful consideration, I have finally made up my mind to remain single all my life. I have informed my parents of my decision and I am sure they will support me to dedicate my life to the Lord. If you can forgive my delay in writing to you for so long, I hope we can continue our pure friendship ...

Her eyes stayed fixed on the last lines. The sky fell upon her.

"Pure friendship ... Pure friendship? ..." The words turned over and over in her mind, sawing her heart into bleeding pieces. Was everything just friendship? The comb, the lock of hair, the poems, his solemn promise? ... Have I been a fool? Or has he simply changed his mind?

She sat in the chair motionless, cold and stiff as a plaster statue, until finally she sank in bed, her mind vacant and paralyzed.

The red candle on the table exhausted its last drop of tears and went out. The room fell dark. A cat sneaked through the eaves and left a chilly, prolonged sigh in its wake. The moon hid its cold face among the leaves of the old osmanthus tree.

A long time passed before she came to herself.

There was no misunderstanding. He loves me truly, and I saw it in his eyes, Grace convinced herself. But his love for God comes before everything. Yes, he stressed "the pure friendship" just to ease my sorrow at his decision. Maybe his parents will disagree with his decision? Or maybe there will come a day when he changes his mind and comes to look for me again? What should I say when I reply to his letter? Do I wish to maintain this "pure friendship"? No, I can't!

The diplomatic phrase was insulting, coldly denying the most precious feelings! It must be hard for him, too, to tear me out of his heart, using a method so cruel ...

While sunk in overwhelming pain, she also began to feel a deeper respect and admiration for the young teacher. She saw a sage ascending higher in the sky, brilliant and lofty, leaving behind crowds of ants in the dirty secular world.

V

History intruded more quickly than she could digest. The Civil War broke out and lasted for three years, ending with the Communist takeover and China being cut off from the rest of the world.

Grace ignored all signals of love time and again and missed a number of good prospects who could have brought her a happy life, patiently waiting for the revival of the true love denied.

Consciously or unconsciously, she had imitated the heroine of *The Woman in the Pagoda*, burying her youthful beauty in hopeless waiting to punish the one who had betrayed her innocent youth. When alone, she often indulged herself in imagining the intoxicating moment of their reunion and was brought to tears by the sorrowful scene in which he stared at her with guilt and regret, seeing the tragic fate she had embraced for his sake.

She would have liked to follow her teacher's path, too, to devote her life to a holy cause instead of wasting her talents. For more than half a century, the pair of lamb-like black eyes had accompanied her during many bright and dark moments.

At the start of the Land Reform Movement, she led her family in turning over all their property and wealth to the government for redistribution among the poor, tasting the feeling of self-sacrifice and dedication promoted not only by the Communists but also by her dear teacher's preaching from the Bible.

When the Korean War broke out, she left the university to be a volunteer soldier, fully prepared to prove her value by shedding her blood and risking her life. When she stepped onto the stage and read aloud a heroic poem in front of a large audience, she felt her young teacher's appreciating gaze like warm sunshine.

She was already twenty-seven when she married, an unusually late age at that time. The decision was made reluctantly, after waiting in vain for ten years for the return of the disappeared reed catkin.

She was seven months pregnant with her daughter when her husband, a writer, was arrested as a political prisoner. She left him without hesitation to show her support for the government. Had she ever loved the man, her decision would have been a different one.

Her second marriage had lasted just over a year and her son was only one month old when she was declared a Rightist. She was sent to a farm for three years to do back-breaking labour, a method adopted by the Communist Party to remold the brains of intellectuals. She always took the hardest task, struggling to demonstrate her willingness to atone for her "crime" and to keep her second marriage alive.

When she was condemned, humiliated, and tortured during the Cultural Revolution in the late 1960s, she was tempted to commit suicide to prove her innocence. It was the pair of lamb-like eyes that drew her back to life from the edge of death.

Her trial of devotion was a long one. She lived this way for twenty-two years, humiliated as a second-class citizen until Mao died in 1976 and his successor turned the verdict.

Though her prime had passed, she tried her best to make up for the loss of her youth in the few years left before retirement. Yet time had changed, and life played a big joke. When she finally swore solemn allegiance to the Communist Party and fulfilled her lifelong wish to be a party member, everyone else in China had abandoned

Marxism and was eager to embrace the capitalist dream of becoming rich overnight.

Now, the only thing valuable which remained was the secret, sweet and bitter first love she had protected so well deep inside. Decades had passed, but the strange devotion refused to leave her despite her efforts.

One sunny morning, when I happen to turn my head, she would say to herself, the young teacher will be standing behind me with his charming smile.

VI

The reed catkin blown away by merciless winds long ago resurfaced in an unexpected way. At an alumni party a few years ago, the young teacher's name had penetrated her eardrum like a sharp arrow. Her heart almost jumped out of her throat as she inquired in a casual way and finally obtained the address of the teacher's younger sister, a medical doctor in Beijing.

The doctor responded to Grace's letter. "Yes, my brother was a teacher in an inland high school during the war. He left for England when the war was over and eventually became a minister in a Christian church in North America." The doctor said she would pay a visit to Grace in her home the coming weekend.

Grace read the one-page letter over and over, but reached no conclusion about whether the sister had any clue about the "big secret" between her brother and his former student.

On that summer evening when the doctor was expected, Grace sent everyone in the family away and waited nervously at home. She had cleaned everything, tried on several different dresses, and weighed repeatedly the proper words and attitude she would use in case the doctor had already learned about the role Grace had played.

Had the doctor contacted her brother before she suggested the

visit? Grace examined herself carefully in the mirror and wondered. She hoped the doctor had. Then it must be the brother's wish
that the doctor come to see her.

But what will the doctor think when her eyes fall upon me, a
withered woman with her youthful glow eroded? And how is she
going to describe me to her brother after the visit?

Grace froze at this thought. She locked the door and fled her home
five minutes before the doctor was to arrive.

VII

Ever since she had retired from her position as editor-in-chief for
a Beijing magazine, her lifelong dream had become more and more
consuming. The trip to Canada finally enabled her to begin her
search for a needle in a big haystack.

She took every opportunity to trace him. During the day when
Lily was working at the hotel, she would push Baby's stroller and
walk as far as she could along the streets of Mapleton, looking
closely at every Chinese-looking man who passed by. She knew he
must have aged, but it was hard for her to imagine his looks now and
her eyes always fell on impossibly young men.

She would stop at all the churches on her way, observing people
coming in and going out, hoping to catch sight of the familiar black
eyes.

She would attend all trips organized by the Chinese church and
listen carefully to the conversations among the converts, in case his
name would jump out.

Fully aware of the vastness of North America, she believed her
faithful search would be rewarded, if there was indeed a loving gaze
in the eye of the almighty, as her beloved teacher had said.

Chapter 19
Tiger Power Pill

I

The young people's singing echoed in the bus and vibrated in her ear.

He maketh me lie down in green pastures;
He leadeth me by the quiet waters ...

"I will find you, I will." Grace stared at her gray-haired image in the dark window and murmured silently, "I am sure you are still alive and waiting to see me, under God's caring eye."

The bus dropped Grace outside of the U-shaped building late in the evening. The compound was bathed in a strange chorus of exotic music, foreign language from videotapes, vegetables sizzling in woks, and crying babies. Without air conditioning, all the melodies poured out of the open windows and echoed around the narrow yard.

Grace didn't frown as she used to when walking through the stuffy hot air. The week-long stay in the cool mountain camp with the large group of Christians-to-be had softened her. She had forgotten the tense atmosphere she had left at home and anticipated that something good might have happened to Lily during her absence.

When she bumped into the Vietnamese neighbour pouring a bucket of water into her narrow strip of vegetables, she exchanged smiles with the lady.

Her instinct was proven correct as soon as she entered the basement apartment. Life had taken a dramatic turn for Lily. Mrs. Rice had introduced Lily to Mr. New, a Cantonese-speaking businessman who had come from Toronto.

A former accountant in Hong Kong, Mr. New had immigrated to Toronto in the 1980s and later set up an immigration consulting office. Mrs. Rice had been his client when her family applied for immigration to Canada a few years before.

Mr. New's business was soaring high in recent years as many people from China were trying to come to North America, with China opening its doors to the outside. As a result, he had a few branch offices around Ontario. Mapleton was his next spot and he was looking for someone to run the office.

He was impressed with Lily's qualifications. Without much hesitation, he agreed to hire her for a trial period of three months.

"God opened his eyes!" Grace said emotionally, her voice trembling. "I prayed so hard for you in the camp and it worked! When are you going to start the new job?"

"In a few weeks. The boss is looking for office space in downtown Mapleton now."

"We should invite Mrs. Rice for dinner some day. It was so nice she introduced you to Mr. New!" Grace suggested. On second thought, she asked in doubt, "Well, why didn't Mrs. Rice try to get this job for herself?"

"I heard that she doesn't want to work," Lily said. "She thinks that if she had any income, her husband in Taiwan would not work so hard to support the family and he might become spoilt."

"Is that so?" Grace grinned disparagingly, but didn't comment.

"The pay for this job is ten dollars an hour, much better than the hotel work," Lily told her more. "Mr. New had received more than a hundred applications after putting the ad in the newspaper."

Grace's smile faded. She warned Lily, "You must treasure this hard-to-get opportunity. Don't forget how you lost your job in the cloth warehouse."

Lily smiled. "Don't worry, Mom! Mr. New looks very gentle and nice …"

Grace felt better. She remembered Baby now and looked around. "Is Baby sleeping? Did Jade help take care of him while I was away?"

"Yes, Unicorn picked him up every morning and brought him back in the afternoon when I got home. Jade read Bible stories to him and took him with her when she visited homes."

"Does Baby understand those stories?"

"I don't know. But he does say a lot more new words these days, such as 'Yes' and 'No,' and …" Lily stopped when she realized Grace wasn't paying attention.

"It's hard to find kind-hearted people like them these days," Grace said. "We should invite them for dinner, too. Let's find a good day."

"I don't think they would care about a dinner. The best way to reward them is to join their Bible Study Group. The couple has just started it in their home to serve more newcomers from China," Lily said and then remembered something important.

She turned around to retrieve an envelope from her computer desk and showed it to Grace. "Well, Mother, this envelope arrived with a cheque for thirty dollars from the Chinese newspaper *The World Journal*, published in New York. There is a note inside, saying it is for an article written by someone named 'Disappointed Heart'…"

Before she finished, Grace looked at the cheque and said happily, "Oh, I didn't expect they would pay so much for my article!"

"So, you are Disappointed Heart?" Lily asked in surprise. "I thought they made a mistake in mailing me this cheque. When did you write for them, and what did you write about?"

"You always tell me you can't find a decent job in this country. I just wanted to demonstrate to you that as long as you make an effort ..." Grace could hardly conceal her pride as she searched for a folder she had kept in the bedroom. Among the articles she had cut from *The World Journal,* she found one and showed it to Lily. "It was published a few weeks ago. I meant to show you later..."

Lily's eyes were immediately caught by the title, "Voice of a Mother." She scanned it quickly and realized that the article had been inspired by the vehement quarrels between Mother and herself.

The author, Disappointed Heart, recalled the painful efforts Chinese women had made in their struggle for liberty in the past century, including vivid descriptions of the life of her mother and of herself. She then took issue with her daughter's complaint about being made into a strong woman who had to rely on herself for everything.

The article ended with questions. "Why doesn't my daughter appreciate all the rights won through the fierce struggles of many women? Why doesn't she realize that what I have given her is crucial in her life? Could it be that the women's liberation movement in the world has gone too far and the younger generations are tired of it?"

Lily remained silent. Mother had found the right place to let out her frustration. She glanced at Grace, who had been waiting all this time for her reaction.

"Congratulations, Mother!" Lily cheered her. "It's well written. You have still kept your youthful sharpness. You can probably make a living by writing in Canada!"

Grace smiled. "Since I don't have a bank account here, I arranged for the cheque to be payable to you."

"What would you like to buy with this money? Some gourmet food, such as live fish?" She knew very well that Mother liked fish, but they had never purchased any because of its cost.

Grace looked at Lily for a while before she said, "I think you should have a haircut. You are going to work in an office now."

Lily touched her waist-long ponytail. She had kept the same hairstyle for many years, first for Majesty, who said he loved long hair, and later, just to save money. At her age, close to forty, it might be time to cut it short.

"Yes, Mother." She nodded. "We will go to a hairdresser tomorrow. You also need to have your hair done by a professional."

"Yes, let's treat ourselves for once," Grace agreed gladly. Her gray hair had been clumsily cut by Lily a few times and had no style at all.

II

The next evening after supper, the family went to the plaza nearby. They found a small but fairly pricey hairdressing shop inside a large department store and waited in line. Their hair was cut and styled by a young Cambodian girl. After tipping her, Lily put a five-dollar bill into Grace's hand.

"That's all that's left from your writing income, Mother," she said jokingly. "You can see what else you can do with the money."

When they returned home, Lily examined herself in the mirror. With her long hair gone, she found her image unsettling. "Do I look much older, Mom?" She asked in a doubtful voice.

Grace assessed her. Obviously she felt the same way. But she comforted Lily with an encouraging smile, "No, I don't think so. The new hairstyle makes your round face narrower. It's better—"

Grace's words were cut off by a sudden knock on the door.

Lily glanced at her watch and confirmed again it was well after ten. Who would come to visit at this hour? Surely it must be a Chinese person. Since few people in China had a telephone in their homes, it became an accepted custom to visit others without informing them first. The images of Mouse-colonel, Beaver-teeth, and Master Iron loomed in her mind. She was alerted.

The knocking resumed and Camellia's anxious voice came from outside. "Lily, it's me! Please open the door!"

Camellia stepped into the apartment hurriedly. "I can't stay in that home any longer!"

Lily was shocked at the sight of her. Her face was purpling with bruises around both eyes, and her hair, usually so sleekly arranged, was a mess. "What happened to you?"

Camellia had found an ad in the Chinese newspaper a couple of days before for a position as a housekeeper in Toronto. She phoned the family and made an appointment for an interview that morning. The night before, she could not sleep well, planning to get up early to catch the bus to Toronto. Around two o'clock in the morning, she woke up to some rustling sounds. In the darkness, she saw Old Chia sneaking to the sofa where she was lying. He took her purse, which was tucked in beside her pillow. She kept silent. A moment later, he returned and replaced it.

When she got up in the morning, she found that her passport and immigration papers had disappeared from her purse! Without them she could not look for employment in Canada. When she asked Old Chia to return them, Dragon rushed in, holding the immigration papers in his hand, and shouted at Camellia, "You acquired your permanent residency status through my father. Now that you want to divorce, we will not let you keep your legal status! And we will not allow you to find a job away from us!" As he spoke, he tore the papers into pieces.

Though angry, Camellia left home to catch the bus. Upon arrival in Toronto, she was supposed to take the subway. But she didn't know where the subway station was and didn't even know how to say *subway* in English. With a map in her hand she stopped a man who looked Chinese. When she found he didn't understand Chinese, she pointed at the ground under her feet and imitated the whistle of a train. The man realized at once what she wanted and showed her to the subway entrance. However, when she finally got to the place, the family refused to hire her because she could not provide any legal documents. No matter how hard she tried to explain, they were suspicious that she had been smuggled into Canada.

Back home in the evening, she cooked the family's favourite dishes, trying hard to please them. After dinner, she begged them to apply for replacement documents for her. They started to blame her for everything, including Old Chia losing his job. But the telephone rang at the wrong time. She knew who was calling and stood up to get the phone. Dragon was faster, however, and grabbed it. He pushed her away when she tried to take the phone. Suddenly, he lost his temper and hit Camellia on the head with the handset! Camellia hid herself in the kitchen, but Dragon rushed in and took the big knife and started to chop at the wooden cutting board. Old Chia grabbed him and held him back, and Camellia seized her chance and ran out of the apartment.

"That's horrible, he could have killed you! But why was he so angry? Who was on the phone?"

Camellia's eyes widened. "Remember I told you some of my story before? I guess I will have to tell you the other half before you can really understand."

Lily sensed it was going to be another long story. She asked Grace to put Baby to bed, and boiled the kettle for tea, preparing to stay up late.

III

In the early 1990s, Old Chia finished his PhD in China and came to Canada to explore new opportunities. The idea of the adventure was initiated and encouraged by Camellia. Many of her acquaintances had left China. Their extravagant life in North America never failed to make her jealous.

One source of jealousy was her next-door neighbour, a foxy girl. She was ten years younger than Camellia and had taken advantage of the chances offered by the new Reformation Era. All the neighbours watched with envy when the girl married a fleshy, Buddha-like businessman from Hong Kong and started buying her parents expensive appliances, a colour TV, a washing machine and a refrigerator, items rarely seen then in ordinary homes.

After a few years, the foxy girl astounded the community again by divorcing the Buddha and marrying a Canadian war veteran. Although the neighbours tried hard to control their giggles as they watched the shrunken veteran, a red feather quivering on his black hat, stepping into the girl's home on his shaking legs, they couldn't help but admire the girl's far-sightedness.

Two years after the girl had left her home for Canada, her mother proudly showed her neighbours pictures of the girl's happy married life on a beautiful farmhouse in southern Ontario. Everybody was surprised to see the withered bridegroom replaced by a chubby white man. It turned out that the impotent veteran had dissolved their marriage and presented her as a gift to his former boss.

When Old Chia was pushed into applying to go to Canada, and finally boarded the airplane, Camellia felt she had accomplished a big task and only had to wait for the day she would join him in the West. Since Dragon had become a high school student and no longer needed her care, she had a lot of free time. After work, she would change into high-heeled shoes and a silk dress, and go to the newly opened bars and entertainment centres that had been strictly banned during Mao's time.

She found the dance floor the most exciting place to be. As she whirled around in a waltz, tango, or foxtrot, she noticed admiring glances from all over the ballroom. She was pleased to see that her charm was still appreciated, though her prime might be past.

Within a short time, Camellia was known throughout the city as the queen of social occasions. She kept up with the schedule of all the dances around the city and adjusted her work shifts not to miss any of them. As she indulged herself in her new life, she found Old Chia's father even more annoying than before.

If she stayed in bed in the morning after an exhausting night, the old man's swearing would burst out of his bedroom door and chase her until the moment she left home. If she got home late in the evening to cook dinner, he would refuse to eat the leftovers she hastily brought to the table and grumble about her neglect of her womanly duty.

Friction between the two escalated without Old Chia there as mediator. One early morning Camellia was wakened by a loud sound. The old man had poured his night soil on the floor in front of her bed, in protest at her delay in emptying his chamber pot. For days, she had to put up with the foul smell issuing from the cracks in the wooden floor.

After Old Chia had found a job in Canada and started sending money home, she quit her job, and would leave home early in the morning, banging the door on the old guy's crazy screaming, and stay out as long as she could.

Her encounter with Dwarf occurred at the mah-jong table attached to a dance hall. She was playing with a few girlfriends when a stout man entered the room. Glancing at him, she continued with her game. But the other girls all left the table and surrounded the man. Camellia realized she had made a wrong judgement.

A friend whispered in Camellia's ear the legendary myth surrounding the man.

In the mid-1940s, at the end of the war, not long after the Japanese had surrendered and left China, a month-old baby boy was found abandoned in an empty Japanese camp. The boy was adopted by a poor Chinese couple living in the same street.

The baby grew up into a stereotypical Japanese-looking man, with a large head, small eyes, thick arms and short legs, and hence earned the nickname Dwarf. Although Dwarf's school report was disappointing, his distinctive shape didn't escape the teachers' eyes. When he finished Grade 9, he was selected as a weightlifter on the city's sports team.

Because no record was ever broken by him, Dwarf remained obscure. His real talents finally came to the fore after the government permitted free enterprise in a market economy. Though his inquiry letters to Japan didn't turn up any of his relatives, Dwarf took advantage of his status as a Japanese orphan in China and acquired interest-free loans from state banks. Touting himself as the heir of a doctor of traditional medicine, he claimed to know a miraculous therapy to cure male impotence, a nationwide problem. "Tiger Power Pills" earned him huge profits in a short time. It was hard to substantiate the effects of the pills, since nobody who tried them was willing to go public. But in the liberated atmosphere after Mao's puritan regime, numerous men, impotent or not, were tempted into secretly paying the high price for the pill to discover the joys it promised.

Dwarf was a smart businessman and a warm-hearted friend. He helped every friend in need and bribed all the key officials, and was thus able to obtain continuous state investments and to change his wife three times without any trouble.

The story of Dwarf aroused Camellia's curiosity. Her attention was drawn to the crowd around the rich man. It turned out that Dwarf was offering 5,000 Chinese dollars for any girl who would strip for him. After some hesitation, three volunteers came forward. Dwarf didn't seem satisfied with their potential and looked around the big hall, hunting for better prospects. His eyes fell on Camellia, lingered for a few examining seconds, then moved away.

Camellia's face paled at the insult. Comparing herself with the much younger girls, she realized sadly that her prime had already passed. As Dwarf flirted and laughed with them, Camellia sat motionless in her seat, her heart boiling with vinegar. Biting her lips, she made up her mind: I will show you who is the real catch in this city!

To defeat the youthful girls, Camellia demonstrated to Dwarf her womanly tenderness, motherly love, and her striking beauty under careful makeup. Though it was sometimes exhausting to compete with all the foxy women around Dwarf, she found great pleasure each time she won and her value was proved.

Her moral stronghold was not hard to conquer when she tasted the unknown pleasures money could create. Despite her initial contempt for Dwarf's vulgar looks and poor education, it didn't take long before she found herself attracted to the man's wild vitality, his witty eloquence, his uninhibited personality, and his generosity. Even the way he treated his women, with melting kisses and honey-soaked whispers one moment and loud, abusive swearing the next, seemed full of elusive charisma. Dwarf deserved to be called a "real man," she felt.

Stepping out of Dwarf's brand new Toyota, she enjoyed being the recipient of jealous looks. But the sweetest moments for Camellia were sitting on Dwarf's knees, holding his bull-shaped neck, and telling him her childhood stories or making other girlish chatter. Like a pampered little girl in her father's arms, she murmured "my little daddy," feeling that her long-cherished dream of being with her father had finally been realized.

The strength of her new love was challenged when Old Chia's application for permanent resident status for her and Dragon was granted by Immigration Canada. While Camellia was reluctant to leave Dwarf's arms, her hesitation met with reproaches from all, including her mother.

On the day of her departure to Canada, Dwarf saw her off at

the airport. "It will be interesting to see how that worthless book-worm supports you in a foreign land. If you find life in Canada intolerable, come back to me fast. You can't expect me to wait for you long."

IV

"So, it is for this Dwarf that you want to leave Old Chia?" Lily asked, making no attempt to conceal her disappointment. "Well, what about Big Brother? Don't you love him anymore?"

Camellia shook her head. "After experiencing the love with Dwarf, I felt the love I had with Big Brother was just as blank as water. I still phone him in New York sometimes. But I no longer feel the passion I did when I was young."

Lily thought for a while before she said, "I just wonder if that Dwarf is really worth your desperation. He sounds like a man with-out any morals."

"Oh, dear!" Camellia sighed at her comments. "You've been left behind, Lily. What's moral and what isn't? The lifestyle in China has changed immensely since you came to Canada. Apart from the fact there are men who have several wives illegally, women are also adventurers. I am fully aware of Dwarf's problems, but I can't stop loving him even if he is Satan. Life with Old Chia is unbearable after having tasted love with Dwarf. I told Old Chia that I wanted a divorce, after living a loveless life for twenty years. Now Dragon is grown up and there is nothing left for me to worry about, I told him, please give me my freedom and let me go. I want to enjoy the second half of my life."

Lily nodded slightly in understanding. But she still felt there might be something wrong in Camellia's decision. "Old Chia doesn't sound like a bad person. He loves you very much, too, in his own way, doesn't he?"

Camellia shrugged. "What's the point of his love? He treats me as if I were a housekeeper."

When they were in China, Old Chia was incapable of helping with any housework. One night at home, he was boiling some water for tea and noticed the flame becoming weak, a signal that there was not enough propane in the tank. But he didn't say anything about it. The next morning, he got up very early and left home hastily without even having breakfast. Camellia asked him to eat something before going to school, but he wouldn't stay a minute longer. His behaviour seemed odd, but Camellia didn't figure it out until she turned on the stove and the fire went off in a second.

No breakfast could be made. She had to put five-year-old Dragon on the handlebars of her bicycle, thrust a cookie in his hand, tie the empty propane tank on the back of the bike, hold an umbrella in her left hand, and go out in the rain. She took Dragon to daycare first, and then went to the propane station for a full tank. She brought it back home and then went to work on an empty stomach.

She couldn't understand why he wouldn't have just told her the propane was out the night before. Was it because he didn't want to go out and buy a new tank? Was he afraid of hooking it up? She had to hold Old Chia's hand every step of the way before he would even attempt anything new. When he prepared to take entrance exams for his PhD, she took him to the professor's home to ask for reading materials. When he graduated and looked for a job, she begged people to accept him. When he planned to come to Canada, she bought expensive gifts to bribe his boss before Old Chia was allowed to leave China.

"I am tired of being a mother to three generations of men." Camellia let out a heavy sigh. She drank the tea, already cold, and went on. "But if I divorce him and leave them unattended, I can imagine how miserable their life will be and I would feel guilty. Old Chia is not a sociable person and has not a single friend in Canada."

One winter day when Camellia was on a bus going home, she happened to see Old Chia riding an old bicycle in the same direction. His gray hair was blowing in the chilly wind, his back bent, his cheeks carved with deep wrinkles. Camellia's heart was filled with sorrow.

"Even though they have been abusive to me, I still wish the best for them. I hope they won't be crushed by my leaving ..." Camellia started sobbing.

"If you feel sorry, perhaps you should stay."

Lily's words shook Camellia out of her sentimentalism. She stopped her sobbing and went on with the negative side of the picture.

V

Before Camellia arrived in Canada, Dragon had already written to Old Chia about her affair with Dwarf. Old Chia had no courage to question Camellia about it. Instead, he asked Dragon to sell the fur coat he had bought for Camellia from the Salvation Army Store in Canada.

After Camellia came to Canada and asked him for a divorce, he brought out a piece of paper he had prepared. There were four conditions for divorce listed on the paper. First, to avoid public shame, Camellia should not go to court. Second, Camellia could take only her clothes and no other property. The gold ring given to Camellia for the marriage must be returned to Chia's family. Third, Dragon belonged to Old Chia and would not go with Camellia. And last, Old Chia's father, then seventy-nine years old and living in China, would be taken care of by Camellia.

"Don't you think the conditions are absurd?" Camellia shouted. "Of course I would never accept them! I told him that I had worked like a slave for this family for twenty years and must be given some money. I know how much he has saved in his bank account. He has purchased retirement savings as well."

Old Chia's reply scared her, however. "If you take a penny from me, I will kill you. Canada has no death penalty, so what do I have to be afraid of? The worst that could happen is that I would spend the rest of my life in jail. But I wouldn't have to work, and I would get free meals and lodging. I have heard that the jails in Canada are cleaner and much more spacious than university student dormitories in China. The jails are equipped for all sorts of sport activities and the prisoners also get paid to do work."

Lily shrugged. "It sounds attractive. I should go to jail instead of working in the hotel."

Before she finished, the telephone suddenly rang, loud and scary. Lily looked at her watch. It was already two in the morning. Something told her that the call was related to Camellia.

She picked up the phone and heard a nervous male voice. "May I ask if Camellia is at your place?"

"Who are you? And how did you know my telephone number?" Lily asked.

"Well, I am Old Chia." His voice faltered. "Camellia has been away from home for hours. I am afraid she is in trouble so I am phoning all her friends."

He must have found Camellia's notebook, Lily thought. But the man doesn't sound like an evil person. "If you hadn't abused her, I bet she wouldn't have stayed out so late! ... Yes, she is at my place now. But I want to tell you, wife abuse is against the law in Canada."

"No! Don't listen to her rubbish!" Old Chia was clearly in a panic. "She is a liar! She often lies! Nobody has abused her."

"No? Then why is her face black and blue?"

"That's, that's ... She bumped herself. Her blood platelets are always low and she gets bruises easily. It looks scary, but actually it's nothing serious ... "

"You had better remember that if you hurt her again, she will call the police!"

"She ... if she ever dares to call the police and destroy our future, we ... we will die together with her!" The man's voice trembled and he started sobbing.

Lily hung up the phone. She didn't know what to say.

"I have made up my mind to divorce him now, even if I can't get any money from him!" Camellia said. "Can you help me find a lawyer and interpret? I want to do it immediately and go back to China!"

"It's very late now and we need to rest. I have to go to work at six-thirty in the morning." Yawning, Lily stuffed a pillowcase with clothes for Camellia so she could get some sleep on the couch.

VI

After lying down beside Grace in the double bed, Lily couldn't fall asleep for a long time. Gradually, she felt herself riding in a cloud of mist. A huge, black shadow with strong wings hovered first above her, then below, her body rising, falling, tossing around. The trembling touch of the wings and the gentle, warm breath of the creature surrounded her.

She found herself landing in a familiar place. It was a small home in a yard full of blooming oleanders near the ancient city walls of Beijing. The layout of the furniture was the same as before. The large mirror on the cabinet reflected a fan of dark-green peacock feathers against the white wall and the thick bamboo root penholder on the desk. The teapot on the iron coal stove was whistling with white steam and gray pigeons were cooing on the windowsill.

The atmosphere was cozy. But ages seemed to have gone by since she had been there, and she had returned with her soul full.

Prince's shadow loomed by the mirror across from the queen bed, his face pale and blurred. His silhouette in the mirror showed him as young and handsome as before, with thick black hair and in his favourite dark wool sweater. He remained silent and emotionless. She felt the rush of a gentle, warm current around her. "I am back ... I am tired ... " she whispered, her eyes moist.

She was sure she caught an ambiguous glittering in his black eyes. She moved towards him and closed her eyes. The shadow reached out his arms and laid her on the soft pillow embroidered with white chrysanthemums. She relaxed.

"It's too late!" a voice burst out. She turned and saw a slim young woman with long, shining black hair blocking the doorway against the blue sky.

"Get out of my bed!" the young lady screamed.

Lily raised her head and looked at the shadowy man, expecting him to put a stop to the rude intrusion. But he seemed numb and indifferent. Her heart crumbled and her throat choked. She felt betrayed and sobbed in pain.

The ring of the alarm clock brought Lily back from dreamland. The bedroom was bright with morning light. She found her mouth half open and her throat dry. Did I cry out in my sleep? she wondered. Probably not. Nobody seemed to be awake.

She closed her eyes again and combed through her dream. Strangely, this was the first time she had ever dreamed about Prince. Undoubtedly it happened due to a phone call she had made a few days before during Grace's absence.

That afternoon when she was alone with Baby at home, she had suddenly remembered Prince. What could have happened to the man? Had he finished his studies in Montreal and found a job to support himself? She thought about the six-year waiting period he had given her in his last letter and added up the years since she had left him. More than seven now. He had probably found a new woman and might be a father, too.

She had a sudden impulse to call him, but hesitated at the idea ...

What for? The affections or sentiments, sweet, bitter, or sour, once lost, would never taste the same. During those years, Prince's shadow would loom in her mind once in a while, sometimes showing kindness in his smiling eyes, sometimes with a greedy and selfish look.

After a struggle, however, she couldn't resist the strong urge and finally picked up the phone. Her hand trembled when she dialled the number he used to have seven years before.

"Who are you looking for?" a young woman's tender voice asked in Chinese.

She realized at once what had taken place. "I am ... Lily ... Probably you have heard about me." She tried to sound calm, but her body was shaking.

"Oh ... Yes ... I know ..." the young woman's voice stammered, betraying her uneasiness.

"Are you new in Canada?" Lily cut in directly. Beating around the bush was never her style.

"Yes, just a few months."

"I hope you are enjoying life in Canada."

"Hum." The woman made no reply.

"What is he doing now?" Lily asked further.

The woman hesitated for a few seconds before she answered, "He is under training to become a truck driver."

Lily felt sad, though this didn't come as a surprise.

The young woman misinterpreted her silence and added, "I don't like what he is doing. But he told me we would have a lot of money. He had been unemployed for a long time when I arrived in Canada."

"How did you get to know him?"

The woman grumbled. "When they introduced him to me, they didn't tell me what he was doing in Canada! I wouldn't have married him had I known!"

Then you must have married him for his permanent residency status, Lily thought. After a pause, she said, "Would you please tell me your address? I might be able to help you when my situation gets better."

As Lily wrote down the address, which was exactly the same she used to know, her nose twitched.

Hanging up the phone, she fell into bed, still shaking. Her eyes fixed on the ceiling, seeing a lonely figure in an old apartment in downtown Montreal for seven years, waiting in vain day and night for a repenting call which never came. She genuinely hoped that the young girl was a good choice for him, someone who would not intimidate the poor man with her restless soul.

Though Lily had left her phone number with the girl, Prince didn't call back. Does he still hate me? Perhaps I shouldn't disturb him anymore.

Grace moved beside her and asked, "Did you hear the alarm? Probably you don't need to go to the hotel any longer."

"I still have to go," Lily replied, "until it's definite that I have the other job."

Chapter 20
Diana's Hall

I

Entering the cleaners' room in the hotel basement, Lily learned the news that two of the Chinese doctors in the team had quit their job.

The geophysicist started a new career arranging the adoption of baby Chinese girls into Canada. The adoption business must have grown fast in Canada, or she would not be quitting her stable job at the hotel, Lily thought.

The other doctor was the gynecologist who had just secured a research position in a health study lab at Mapleton University. Dealing with dozens of poppy-seed-sized mouse ovaries daily might be a challenge for many others, but not for her, she said. It was easier than her medical work had been in China, and without the psychological burden. Working in a hospital in China, she had carried out hundreds of tubal ligations on women every year.

As the co-workers talked about the resignations, Lily caught the gloomy look in Jamaican's eye.

"I have nowhere to go and have to stay here forever," she grumbled as she threw a bundle of new towels into Lily's hands. "We should be promoted as loyal employees, shouldn't we?" Lily nodded and wondered how the woman would react when Lily's turn came.

The routines in the guest rooms didn't feel suffocating anymore since she knew there was an end. She even started singing a Chinese folk song when she was dusting the fake tree in the hallway. The crude lyrics created by peasants generations back somehow slipped into her mind and came out of her mouth, smooth as a running stream and fresh as morning dew.

The first time I looked for you, you were not home.
Your mother hit me on the back with a heavy ladle.
I miss you so much that my hands are weak,
and I picked up the chopsticks but failed to hold my bowl.
I long for you so much and my heart is so muddled,
that I threw garlic into the boiling water instead of potato ...

She was so carried away that her singing got louder, vibrating in the room and the hall.

"Your voice is so beautiful!"

She stopped singing and turned her head. A hotel guest, a white woman, was standing in the doorway with a smile on her face.

Lily thanked her, but then blushed when she realized she knew the woman. It was Helen, her graduate advisor at the university years back.

Helen recognized Lily, too, yet she blinked her eyes, trying to conceal her surprise awkwardly. "Well, I didn't know you are working in here ... I thought you had left Mapleton, like other graduate students. Have you been in contact with them since then?"

Helen said that she came to the hotel for a conference organized by the Royal Society of Canada. From her business card, Lily found that Helen had become the Dean of Graduate Studies at the university.

Lily felt embarrassed that she had let her advisor down so she quickly explained that she was about to start a new job in a consulting office, which might make her school knowledge useful. Helen smiled, with obvious relief.

II

When Lily got home after her shift, Grace told her that Camellia had just phoned and asked for her help. Lily picked up the phone and dialled the number Camellia had left.

"I don't know where I am and I don't understand anything these people here are saying to me! Please come and help!" Camellia sounded as if she was drowning.

It turned out that Camellia had gone to the English school in the morning. Ever since she started working in Fatty's restaurant, she had missed many classes. Now with her landed immigrant papers destroyed and her determination to get divorced, she had remembered the teachers at the school and hoped to get their help. As soon as she walked into the classroom, the black and blue around her eyes caught her teacher's attention. The teacher drove Camellia away to some building and left her there with some other women.

Without changing her sweatshirt and jeans, Lily took off on her bicycle again. Half an hour later, she found the building. It was a large gray construction with an inconspicuous sign reading "Diana's Hall."

After being led through three locked entrances and a maze of hallways by a white woman with hair in inch-long spikes, she was finally led into a tiny windowless room. Camellia was brought in. She reached out and held Lily's hands.

"Thank heavens you have come! I have been trying so hard to communicate with them. They gave me a few papers to sign. It seems they want to help me, but I don't know what the papers say so I won't sign them. I took out my Chinese-English dictionary, found the word *divorce* and pointed to it. But they talked so much I got totally confused!"

Lily found out that Diana's Hall was a government subsidized organization where abused women were allowed to stay free for four weeks while receiving counselling and legal advice. Short-hair questioned and took notes while Camellia described what had happened. Lily acted as their interpreter and noticed that Camellia was concealing the fact that Dragon was the one who actually hit her, and instead made Old Chia the scapegoat.

The workers would help Camellia bring her husband to trial, based on the information she had provided. But Camellia's only wish was to get a divorce.

"No, I don't want to bring my husband to trial. Not at all. It will destroy their future." Camellia grasped Lily's arm in anxiety. "Please, Lily, please tell her that I regret coming here and will go home!"

"We can't let you go home. We are responsible for your safety," Short-hair stated. "Since your husband has abused you, you are not allowed legally to live in the same place with him."

"But I have to work in the restaurant! This place is too far away from downtown." Camellia tried to find excuses. "Besides, I don't speak any English and it's hard to communicate with you."

When Short-hair informed Camellia that she had to live separately from her husband for a whole year before she could apply for a divorce, she was stunned.

"A whole year? That's too long!" Camellia looked panicked and said, "I have always slept on the living room sofa and Old Chia slept in the bedroom. Does that count as a separation?"

Short-hair bit her lip and hesitated. "Well, it depends. It's hard to prove if there has been any sexual activity or not."

Camellia shook her head quickly. "No, no! Of course I don't let him do it." She turned to Lily and whispered. "Dwarf would kill me if I did."

"How could he know even if ..." Lily stopped half way, realizing it was an improper comment.

"Dwarf has made a secret mark on me and he would surely find out ..." Camellia didn't finish either.

Lily was even more confused. How could a man make a sign on a woman's body that would reveal such a thing? she wondered.

Short-hair had no idea what was going on and suggested, "To qualify for the separation period, you may need to stay here for a few weeks and then start looking for a place for yourself."

"By the way," Camellia asked, "can the previous time I spent in Mrs. Rice's home also be counted as part of the separation period?"

"Maybe you can go back to Mrs. Rice's home and stay there to qualify for separation," Lily suggested to Camellia.

Camellia shook her head, explaining that Mrs. Rice had asked Old Chia to be her daughter's math tutor. He had been going every weekend for almost two months. Not only did Mrs. Rice not pay him a single penny, she didn't even ask him to stay for lunch after teaching in her house.

"Can you believe that? Not even once!" Camellia said. "I am not a fool, and I know the rate for a tutor is at least twenty dollars an hour for someone with Old Chia's qualifications. He has a PhD!"

Lily smiled, "But if he doesn't care, you don't have to care either!"

Camellia patted her thigh. "For Heaven's sake! If she doesn't want to pay money, at least she could appreciate Old Chia's contributions. But do you know what happened last week after she got the news that her daughter had been admitted to the University of Toronto? She thanked God repeatedly for helping her daughter realize her dream. She talked and prayed tearfully, but never mentioned a single word about Old Chia."

"I will find out what I can do to help you." Lily stood up, ready to go home. "Please call me if you need my help tonight."

III

Late in the evening, Lily phoned Jade. She knew the couple had recently rented a two-bedroom apartment near downtown, close to Fatty's Wok. Their son would soon be coming from Beijing to join them. She wondered if the couple would let Camellia use one of the rooms temporarily as a solution.

Nobody answered the phone, however, and Lily thought that Jade might have been visiting new immigrants' homes while Unicorn might be still working in his lab.

The next day when Lily finished her hotel work and got home, she phoned Jade again. Still there was no one at home. Hanging up the phone, she rode on her bicycle again and went to Mapleton University to look for Unicorn.

When she finally reached his lab in the zigzagged building, she found the door was locked. She sighed and walked downstairs. As she passed by the café at the corner of the main floor, however, she spotted Unicorn sitting by a table with someone.

Lily stopped and waited by the entrance. She thought he might be meeting with his advisor for something unpleasant, since Unicorn looked unhappy and was talking in an excited voice.

It was five o'clock. Lily could smell the sweetness of the doughnuts on the shelf nearby. She looked at the beautiful sweets, in various styles and coated with chocolate or coconuts, and felt hungry. She forced herself to look sideways though, unwilling to waste any money for her luxurious desire. But she struggled at the thought whether she should buy one for Baby, since he had never tasted any sweets.

At this moment, however, she was shocked. She saw the cafeteria worker, a young woman, taking the remaining doughnuts in the baskets and dumping them into the garbage can.

"Oh, no!" She let out a cry and opened her mouth wide. "Why do you throw them away? Have they gone bad?"

The worker felt odd at her questions, but explained patiently. "This is the company's policy. We have got to dump all the unsold doughnuts before we close each day."

"Why?" Lily kept on digging in. "You could reduce their prices by the end of the day."

"We tried to reduce the price by half after one o'clock, but people simply waited till after that time to buy and we made no profit. So we decided to discontinue that practice."

Unicorn came over, obviously having heard their conversation. "The unsold doughnuts should be given to the poor for free instead of being dumped!" he commented. "Such a waste!"

"Absolutely right!" Lily nodded at him. "Why don't you try to find the boss in charge and give him the advice? At least the unsold food can be brought to the student residences on campus."

"When I was a child, I heard about the American capitalist's sin for dumping overproduced milk into the sea to keep the price high. We saw it with our own eyes today!" Unicorn said, and waved good-bye to his advisor.

Outside of the café, Lily described Camellia's situation and asked if she could stay in their home temporarily. She noticed the anxious look in his different-sized eyes and was surprised to see his lips peeling, too dry. "The workers at Diana's Hall will not let her leave unless she has a safe place to go," she added.

Unicorn said he was willing to help but he needed to talk to his wife first.

IV

In the evening, after Jade and Unicorn picked up Camellia from Diana's Hall, they drove to her home to get her belongings.

The small apartment was packed with furniture and boxes.

Relieved that Dragon was not home, Camellia hurried to pack two suitcases of clothes while Old Chia sat in front of his computer and pretended not to pay any attention. His eyes stayed fixed on the screen while his shaking hand moved the mouse aimlessly. Jade and Unicorn tried to carry on a polite conversation with him, but Old Chia was too upset to speak anything.

Camellia wrote down a telephone number on a piece of paper, put it beside Old Chia's hand and said, "If you and Dragon need to contact me, you can call this number."

Old Chia stopped moving the mouse. His lips trembled, but he said nothing and didn't look at his wife.

Unicorn looked at him sympathetically. "Call me if you need my help!" he said to him in a low voice as he took Camellia's suitcases.

By the time the couple had brought Camellia to their home, it was already dark. Camellia piled her luggage hastily in the smaller bedroom, neatly furnished with a single bed, desk, and chair, and went into the living room.

"What a long day!" she said as she sank into a chair, letting out a heavy sigh. "My stomach is making noises. I bet you are all hungry, too. What would you like to eat for supper? I will cook for you."

Jade was impressed with her enthusiasm to help. She glanced at Unicorn, who was leaning against the couch, with his eyes closed.

"Will you eat something tonight?" she asked.

Unicorn opened his eyes, shook his head, got up from the couch, and walked into the bedroom.

"Well," Jade told Camellia, "let's make some instant noodle soup for tonight."

It took less than ten minutes. When Camellia went to serve the noodle soup, she was surprised there were only two bowls on the table.

"Unicorn will not eat or drink anything on Thursdays," Jade explained.

It turned out that Unicorn had read in the Bible that the ancient Jews used to fast as a way of showing their pious devotion to God. This inspired him to start a self-imposed fast every Thursday, the day most suitable for his schedule.

"Unicorn is so skinny. Is this good for his health?" Camellia asked in doubt.

"I advised him to give it up. I said that nobody in our church fasts, not even Minister Wong. They just pray to God. But Unicorn is a very stubborn person. He said 'I am different from them!'"

Jade was not as strong-minded as her husband. She tried fasting with him a couple of times but found it too hard. To support him, anyway, she usually cooked nothing on Thursday, but just drank water and ate a little bread.

Camellia controlled her urge to laugh out loud. She put on a serious air and asked, "Does he feel anything special from his prayers after the fast?"

Jade nodded. "Sure. First of all, he was able to give up smoking without much difficulty, a bad habit he had had for fifteen years. Besides, he also feels he can communicate with God better and understand God's messages more clearly."

"What kind of messages?"

Jade had thought for a while before she responded. "For instance, Unicorn and I have applied for graduate studies at a famous theology institute in California. Yet without financial assistance, it will be impossible to go. He felt his anxiety about the situation was eased after praying to God ..."

Camellia had heard from Mrs. Rice about the couple's intention to study theology. Though she felt it was a stupid idea, she was smart enough not to hurt their feelings. "Does he pray on Thursdays only?"

"No! We pray together every night after reading the Bible. Unicorn insists that we read the English version instead of the Chinese version. He believes that every time the Bible was translated into another language, additional errors were made and it got further away from its original meaning. He also bought an English version Bible tape and plays it in the car when he drives."

V

An hour later, Unicorn came out of the bedroom with a Bible in his hand. He passed it to Camellia and said: "This is for you, a Chinese version Bible."

Camellia looked at Unicorn carefully. His face was pale, his lips dry, and the area around his eyes sunken and dark. He looked sick.

"Do you want a cup of tea? I can go and boil some water," she asked with concern.

"No." Unicorn shook his head, looking straight in her eye. "God does not want you to divorce."

She looked away from him and asked sharply, "What does *my* divorce matter to God?"

Unicorn pointed at the Bible in front of her. "It states clearly in here that a woman should be obedient to her husband, and that she should not leave him unless he commits adultery."

Camellia blinked her eyes and held back her question: "Would the Bible allow divorce to a woman who had committed adultery?" Instead, she asked another one. "Am I still supposed to obey my husband if he tortures me?"

It was a simple issue to Unicorn, like one plus one equals two. Words flowed fluently from his lips. "Just follow the example of our Lord. Conquer evil with benevolence. If someone hits your left cheek, offer him your right cheek; if someone takes away your coat, take off your shirt and give it to him as well; if someone forces you to walk with him for one mile, follow him for two miles ..."

Camellia sat numbly while Jade joined her husband in trying to convince her. Their preaching was blowing around her ears like wind on winter days, so distant was their message from her immediate concerns and secret desires. To her, the two bookworms knew nothing about real love but blabbed on about it all the time. She could never expect this couple to appreciate her burning love for Dwarf. It was obvious that here, she would have to go through the same tiring daily sermons she had become so fed up with at Mrs. Rice's home. But considering the benefits of staying here, the free lodging plus the separation days she needed for a divorce, she figured that it was wise to move along with the river's current, not against it.

Camellia changed her indifferent look into a sweet smile. "Have you ever heard that Jesus Christ's ideas were influenced by a Chinese philosopher who lived around 300 BC?"

Her sudden active participation in the theological discussion amused the couple. "Where did you get this idea?" Unicorn looked at her, his good eye opened wide.

"Lily told me!" Camellia felt proud of the effect her words had created. "She said that there was the possibility that Jesus Christ had travelled to China before he was age thirty. There is no record in the Bible of what happened to him between thirteen and thirty."

Chapter 21
Beaver-teeth and Mouse-colonel

I

"Indeed, there is a seventeen-year hiatus in the story of the life of Jesus Christ. I checked the Bible." Unicorn commented seriously to Lily when they met again a week later, at the door of Buffet Empire. She had invited the couple, along with Camellia, and Mrs. Rice, for lunch in this restaurant located in the plaza near the U-shaped buildings.

This was the first time Lily had ever stepped into the business run by her neighbour, Mouse-colonel. It was also the first time she had treated herself and others to a restaurant meal in the eight years she had been in Canada. She had just received confirmation the day before from Mr. New that she had the job as an office administrator.

"I read this idea about Jesus in a recent publication by a group of newly converted communists from China," Lily told Unicorn. "They also suggested that the story in the Bible about the wise men from the East who predicted the birth of Jesus Christ hints that Jesus Christ had actually inherited the ideas of the oriental philosophers ..."

While talking, the group entered the restaurant, which was decorated with crimson-red wallpaper and golden dragons fighting for fireballs. Lily looked at the dizzying array of gaudy colours and was surprised to see that the place was packed and there were hardly any seats.

The Mouse-colonel's tiny figure in a white shirt and black pants appeared in front of the group. With a smile on his lean face, he led them to the only table left, one by the kitchen door. Once they were seated, his sharp eyes swept everyone's face and finally stopped at Lily's.

Memories of the Mouse-colonel's blunt confession to her about stealing government funds to come to Canada crept into Lily's mind. To smooth the moment, she fumbled in her handbag and took out an advertisement. "This is a new business office in town." She put it into the colonel's hand. "My boss asked me to spread the news to the Chinese community."

The colonel's eyes shifted from the ad to Lily. Lily noticed that the piece of paper was trembling in his nicotine-stained fingers. A moment later, he walked into the kitchen and came out again with an extra plate of boiled shrimp. He put it on their table and said briefly, "A treat for my neighbours."

Grace felt uneasy seeing the man, having learned from Lily about his deeds. She pretended not to know him, concentrating on putting food onto Baby's plate.

Mrs. Rice got a plateful of deep fried chicken wings and shrimp balls from the bar. She was all smiles, "So much choices, but only $5.99!"

"That's only possible in a Chinese restaurant!" Camellia said in a low voice. "I heard that the boss hires only illegals who have been smuggled in and pays them much lower than the minimum wage."

Seeing Unicorn devouring hastily a full plate of noodles, Mrs. Rice gave some advice, "When eating at a buffet, it's unwise to fill your stomach with starchy food first. It will make you feel satiated too soon. A wise way is to start with the proteins ..."

Her words were cut short by a sudden loud bang from the kitchen.

Lily saw the colonel dart into the kitchen. The door shut behind him, but the sound of banging and angry shouts could still be heard. Everybody at the table stopped eating and looked in surprise. Lily stood up and pushed the kitchen door slightly ajar to peep in.

She was astonished. Two men were fighting and the colonel was trying hard to stop them. One of the fighters was Beaver-teeth, waving a ladle in his hand, his face and neck all red. Before Lily had a clear view, the other fighter, a younger man, picked up a cutting knife and hit the ladle with a crispy metal sound. The ladle dropped from Beaver-teeth's hand as he grasped his left hand. It was bleeding.

The colonel grabbed the cutting knife from the younger kitchen helper, screaming, "Damn you all! Is your life cheaper than the five-cent bottles? I will fire all of you if I lose business because of this!" He kicked harshly at an empty beer bottle on the floor. It rolled towards the black garbage bag at the corner of the kitchen. Beaver-teeth bent down quickly and picked it up.

II

Lily didn't expect Beaver-teeth to be her first client.

The man walked timidly into her office early one morning. His bloodshot eyes avoided Lily and his dark face reddened.

She started her new job on the 8th day of the 8th month, on the 8th floor of a big office building in downtown Mapleton. Mr. New had chosen this auspicious number deliberately. In Chinese, "eight" is a homonym with "get rich fast."

The auspicious number first brought good luck to her mother's application to stay longer in Canada. Grace's visitor's visa would expire soon. To extend it, Lily had to show the financial ability to support her mother.

Mr. New stayed in Toronto, coming to Mapleton only once a week. Lily's tasks were to take phone calls from potential clients, collect information, and send it on to the main office in Toronto. Once clients were accepted, Lily would teach them some basic English and accompany them to the meeting with the immigration officer or citizenship judge when they were summoned.

Beaver-teeth had the typical humble manner of a Chinese peasant. Sitting in a chair across from Lily's desk, he confessed how he had come to Canada as a refugee claimant.

Someone from Canada came to his village in Fujian to recruit people. The man boasted about the luxurious life he had been enjoying in Toronto, where everyone had a car and lived in big houses. Many young people had already left the village and Beaver-teeth was one of the few still left in the rural area. His wife pushed hard for him to go. He sold every household item worth any money, borrowed from relatives and friends, and finally paid the smuggler the first half of the US$40,000 smuggling fee. On the day of his departure, his wife rushed home from the yam fields, her hands muddy. He asked her to stop weeping. "Once I am in Canada, you won't have to get your hands dirty in the yam fields anymore."

Beaver-teeth and his group were taken across the border with Vietnam. From there, they entered Thailand, where they stayed in the jungle for months until they were transported by air to Spain. He worked in a restaurant there for almost two years until arrangements were made to come to Canada. On the airplane, he and others were told to tear up their passports and flush them down the toilet. At Pearson Airport, however, they were stopped by the immigration officers. The person who led them there had disappeared, but they had their stories prepared to make a case for claiming refugee status.

Lily had never imagined this quiet man could have gone through all this. "Do all the restaurant's workers come this way?"

"No. Some came by boat and that's worse. Many have seen companions die on the sea and their bodies become fish food. Some smugglers are heartless creatures. They starve the women on the boat, not providing them with food or drink for days, to force them to pay with their bodies for a bottle of water or a piece of bread ..."

Once they were in Toronto, the smugglers showed up again to collect the second part of the fee. They locked the newcomers in a small basement. Beaver-teeth had no money to pay them immediately. They first burnt his chest with cigarettes, then cut off the little finger on his left hand and hung it around his neck as a warning to others. When they threatened to cut off another finger, he phoned his wife at home to borrow again.

"What can you do?" Beaver-teeth said to Lily, his face remaining impassive. "Actually, it's easier for the men than the women. I could manage dirty, tiring, low-paying jobs to pay back the debts. But some of the women were forced into prostitution when they failed to pay the fee."

"Why didn't you report it to the police?" Lily cut him off. She was beginning to realize how much better her life in Canada was compared to that of many others.

He gave her a wry smile. "Why should we? It's not easy for the smugglers to make money either. They have to bribe all kinds of officials in different countries. It was our own choice in the beginning to pay for the smuggling. If you don't keep your promise, it serves you right to be punished."

"What excuses did your people use to claim refugee status?" she shifted to the next question, aware that most of the smuggled-in people were poorly educated peasants, unlikely to be targets in China.

"The smugglers taught us excuses. Most of us claimed to be persecuted Christians. A Chinese man from a Toronto church came to our place and handed a Bible to each of us. We had to first promise that we believed in God. The Bible was printed in our Fujian dialect. We were told stories about Jesus, about how the world was created

by God in seven days, and how a snake fooled a woman into eating
an apple and we all had to die. When we were brought before the
judge, we all claimed we were Christians. But one man from my village was too nervous. When the judge asked him what God's name
is, he answered 'Adam'! Of course his application for refugee status
was refused. He had studied for only two years in a primary school.
But I have finished Grade 6, you know."

"What kind of excuse did you use?"

"Well, I have three children. That was illegal in China."

"I guess the first child is a girl, so you broke the law the second
and third time."

"Not really," the kitchen helper smiled in embarrassment. "My
first child is a boy."

"Then, why did you still ignore the law?"

"It was not only me. Everyone in my village did. The girls have to
be married off eventually. I was told to blame the Chinese government for its one-child policy. But my application was also refused,
since I could not provide any evidence that I had been persecuted."

Lily looked at the documents he had brought over, which had been
prepared by some lawyers in Toronto. "Did your family really suffer
the situation recorded here?"

Beaver-teeth blushed. He lowered his head and twisted his hands.
"Not that serious. The policy only works in cities, not in the coun-
tryside. When the government workers came to inspect, we would
simply run away and hide in the forest for a few days. They took
away a few household items such as the TV and furniture as punishment. But we still have our children."

"Do you still owe any debt?"

He raised his head, a confident smile appearing. "No, I have paid all
my debt. I don't drink or smoke. I share a bedroom with two other
co-workers so I pay a very low rent to my boss, and I sell the bottles
and cans I have collected, too. I am already sending money home. I

haven't seen my wife and children for five years. The younger ones may not even remember how I look ..."

His voice stammered as he lowered his head again and rubbed his nose. "I hope your lawyer can help me win my case. I dream every day about my family coming to join me in Canada. We are neighbours and I trust you, so I came." He put his palms together and shook them towards her, pleading in the old-fashioned manner.

The hand with a missing finger and an inch-long scar burned her eyes.

III

Mr. New came into the office the next day to negotiate the fee with the client. Lily felt bad when she heard Mr. New bargaining for a $5,000 service fee and requesting half as a non-refundable deposit.

"Can we charge him less, or let him pay after we handle his case successfully?" she suggested to Mr. New after the client was gone.

Mr. New responded with a smile, "Who is going to pay for the rent, the office equipment, and your salary?"

A fat case like this came only once in a blue moon to a small town like Mapleton. For the next few weeks there were hardly any clients, only a few fruitless inquiries asking for charitable services.

One Vietnamese woman, a single mother weighed down by two teenage children and financial debts, wanted to find a fake husband who would be willing to pay her $40,000, the current rate, to marry so he could come to Canada. Afraid that the poor mother would be trapped once again, Lily turned down her inquiry politely.

A thirty-four-year-old hairdresser who was visiting from Singapore wanted to find a real husband in Mapleton. Lily searched her mind and remembered Master Iron. She found his business card and made a phone call.

"Could I speak to Master Iron?"

"Who are you looking for?" the male voice sounded unhappy.

"Master Iron," she repeated.

"There is only the Grand Master Iron!" The man stressed the word "grand."

Lily controlled her laugh and invited him to meet the hairdresser in her office, acting as a go-between during their hour-long meeting.

Grand Master Iron came, dressed the same as he did at the Dragon Boat Festival, a black T-shirt with a bright yellow logo in the front. Obviously interested in the fashionable woman, he listed all his titles in one breath, and without a break, went on in detail about his achievements.

The hairdresser crossed her arms and legs, listened patiently, and nodded now and then in a calm manner. Afterwards, when the Grand Master had left, she informed Lily that she was willing to pay him only as a "shadow husband" so she could stay in Canada.

Lily's effort failed, since the Grand Master refused to consider a fake marriage which would destroy his image as a virgin. "I don't want to add the title of a divorcee!" he shouted on the phone.

A tall, plump senior, a white man living in retirement in his country home outside Mapleton, walked into the office with a young Chinese beauty. They had married during the beauty's last visit to Canada, but her application for permanent residency had been refused by Immigration Canada, on the grounds that they had married for convenience since they had known each other too briefly and the beauty spoke hardly any English.

Lily checked the beauty's documents and found she had been married three times in the past seven years. Her first husband was in China, the second in Hong Kong, and the third one here in the office blowing off steam.

"Everyone is jealous that I married a beautiful young lady. Jealous! I need a lawyer! I want justice!" The senior citizen banged his thick palm on Lily's desk.

IV

Business was slow, which allowed Lily plenty of free time to write during her office hours. In the world she had created, hours went by like minutes.

Scenes woven with wordless songs and everlasting dreams flowed out of her fingertips like a running stream. Her cheeks were often smeared with tears and her vision blurred as images of unforgettable men and women from the past were revived in her sentimental eulogy. There were often times, however, when she would stare at the screen for a long time without jotting down a single word.

Is it too cruel to expose the private lives of people, particularly those who are closest to you, to the public's eyes just to reflect the truth and reality of history? Are my observations and memories objective enough not to distort and damage the characters? Are real feelings about life worth expressing if they are not lofty and honourable? Which is the best thing to do, to create attractive and respectable heroes and heroines, or to portray honestly the complications of human nature?

Once in a while, she couldn't help but wonder: in the frivolous, impetuous, and materialistic world of today, are there still readers keen on serious literature?

These questions constantly bothered her and prevented the writing from going smoothly. There was also the fundamental question, raised by her mother: "What's the meaning of your writing? What is it for?"

Indeed, there was no clear purpose. She had been writing mostly because she had so many whys in her life. She wrote down the whys she had figured out for others and also the whys she had failed to understand in her own life so that others might help her.

In the evenings after supper, Lily would take Grace and Baby for a walk along the riverside road. Bathed in the soft light of the setting sun, she would raise some of the questions that had long bothered her and try to probe her mother's inner world.

The quiet and tedious life in this isolated foreign land allowed Grace space to examine the thistly path she had trodden during her life. She no longer hid herself behind shining slogans, but often admitted calmly her flaws as a human being.

When Lily's cautious antennae touched on sensitive areas, Grace would remain silent, totally lost in memories sealed to outsiders. When she eventually opened her mouth again, however, the truth often shocked Lily.

Bit by bit, from Grace's reluctant but courageous recollections, Lily saw her mother as a different person. She was deeply touched by the desires and disappointments, the pains and sorrows, and the weaknesses and regrets of an ambitious but innocent young woman caught in history's chaotic years and torn by struggles.

Grace became very emotional when talking about her young English teacher. While reciting in a melodious voice to Lily the poems he had written to her, tears oozed from her wrinkled eyes as she gazed dreamily into the distance.

To Lily, however, the verses treasured so dearly for fifty years displayed no special talent. Grace had been seeking "true love, not stained by any selfish desire," as she described it, all her life, but had been disappointed to find none that fulfilled her hopes except the very first one. Probably Mother would never understand that her "true love" remained glamorous and fascinating simply because she had never achieved it.

As Lily felt closer to her mother day by day, she sometimes forgot her position and even made critical comments on Grace's past.

"Why did you marry a man if you didn't love him at all?" she questioned the issue about her love theory.

"How could you betray your good friend by turning him in to

the authorities, even if you were under pressure?" she challenged Grace's moral standard.

Lily's increasing criticisms irritated Grace to such a degree that she lost her temper one day. "I wanted to tell you things truthfully. But when I am being honest, you start to attack me! Are you interrogating me as others did in the Cultural Revolution? I don't deny I made mistakes. But won't I ever be forgiven? How dare you blame me like this? What's your purpose in knowing all this anyway?"

"I need these for my writing."

"Couldn't you choose some positive topics? Don't you know that in rehashing these stories you are making Chinese people lose face?"

"I don't think that way! A nation or people can progress only if they can see their own problems clearly."

"No! A truly patriotic person should always feel proud of his or her own nation and culture instead of belittling it!"

"Being blindly patriotic and proud of one's own race may simply make one look ignorant. I'd rather be an internationalist than a narrow-minded patriot."

"You simply have no sense of what is decency and what is shame! You have lived in disgrace, and your writing describes disgrace, too!"

"How do you know I am writing only about disgrace?"

"Do you think I am a fool? Do you think I don't know how you portray me in your writing?"

"Then, how do you think I should portray you in my writing?"

"You should first acknowledge that I am a great mother!"

"Mother, you have to admit that no one is perfect in the world. Besides, Canadian culture and literature does not worship heroes, since there is no real hero in life."

"No hero? Then what was Norman Bethune?"

Lily told her something about Norman Bethune that she had heard from a few Canadians, including Helen. "In Canada, unfortunately, he was known as an alcoholic and a womanizer instead of a hero."

Helen was born in the Montreal hospital where her aunt was a nurse during the time when Norman Bethune worked there. Story had it that once a nurse had been missing for quite a few days from the hospital. When staff reported her case, the head nurse, reading medical records, said calmly without even raising up her head, "Check where Norman is."

"That actually answered my long-time question of why his wife had divorced him twice," Lily added.

"Oh, no!" Grace shook her head in suspicion. "The story we heard about his divorces was quite different. Accordingly, the first divorce was suggested by him, after he had contracted tuberculosis and was dying. The second time was brought on by his wife, since she couldn't tolerate his zealous devotion to medical work."

"Those excuses reflect the Chinese people's absolute love for him," Lily said. "Of course, Helen also emphasized that Bethune was known as an excellent surgeon, a creative genius, and an energetic and very attractive man. Most women would fall in love with him easily, though it was a very hard thing to live with such a man."

When Grace remained silent, Lily added, "To me, however, a man like Norman Bethune, with striking gifts, flaws, and a complicated personality, is a real man, and worth loving and remembering. That would also be true for a woman like that, Mother."

V

Lily received a surprise phone call from Helen one morning. Helen had always been interested in antiques. She had spotted an old Chinese vase in a store on Saturday. It was priced at sixty dollars, but Helen had no idea if the vase was a real antique.

"The store is downtown, near the building where you work. Could you find time to go take a look and let me know what you think?" Helen asked.

During lunch hour, Lily went to the antique store and found the vase. It was brass, about a foot tall, and engraved with plum blossoms and a sika deer in the traditional Chinese style. Lily checked the bottom of the vase and found two Chinese characters. She knew they must represent the reign of an emperor, but couldn't remember which emperor. The storeowner, a white man, noticed her examining the vase and came over.

"I got it just a couple of weeks ago. What do the characters mean?" He pointed to the bottom of the vase.

"They represent the year when it was made," Lily told him honestly. "The characters seem to be the title of an emperor who lived about four or five hundred years ago, but I can't remember exactly and have to check for it."

"Could you please let me know when you find it out?" The owner gave her his business card.

Lily returned to her office and checked her dictionary. Her estimate was right. The vase was made during the reign of a Ming dynasty emperor, between 1426 and 1435. It was more than five hundred years old.

"Oh, my goodness!" Helen's voice on the phone was excited. "I will go and buy it after work today!"

The following day, Lily phoned Helen again. "Have you got the vase?"

"No," Helen sounded disappointed. "The owner took it off the shelf and said he is waiting to confirm its value."

Lily hadn't expected things to turn out this way. She told Helen what had happened in the store and asked seriously. "Do you want me to tell him the truth?"

Helen seemed to be trapped in a dilemma. "Well, I ... I understand ... You decide what to do."

Lily felt Helen's awkwardness. "Helen, you have been my professor. Tell me what you want me to do, really. I am willing to help you if I can."

She had put the ball back in Helen's court. There was silence. Helen seemed to be struggling. Finally, she said, "I really like that vase, Lily. But I think you should tell him the truth."

Lily did. When she got home that evening, she told Grace everything.

"Canadian people are very honest, aren't they?" Grace asked.

"Most of them. Or most of them try to be, I think," Lily nodded.

"Is this because they are mostly Christians?" Grace seemed interested in digging into the issue.

"It's hard to say," Lily replied. "Statistics say only twenty percent of Canadians go to church. Helen is not a regular churchgoer, but there is no doubt that she has been brought up in the Christian faith."

Grace smiled. Lily noticed an unusual light shining in her eyes.

Predictably, the vase reappeared on the shelf marked $360. Helen gave up on buying it. "I have to curb my spending on my hobby," she explained to Lily on the phone the next day. "I am saving to buy a house and, I haven't told you yet, I am in the process of adopting a baby from China."

Lily found out that Helen got help from the same Chinese geophysicist who had been Lily's co-worker at the hotel. Adopting from China was the fastest way of getting a child, since there were many baby girls in the orphanages. Helen had joined a local organization, the Rainbow Club, started by a group of Canadian couples who had adopted baby girls from China. The group met regularly and supported each other.

When Lily showed interest in the group, Helen invited her to come and celebrate the Chinese Autumn Festival with them in a few weeks.

At home, Grace told Lily that the Chinese government was readjusting the policies now. A "Saving Baby Girl Campaign" was launched, which awarded money to parents who decided to keep their female fetus instead of aborting her. Besides, if both parents were single child, they would be allowed to have a second child now. In the rural areas, if the first child was a girl, then the couple would be allowed to have a second child.

"So the refugee claimants in Canada have one less excuse," Lily said, and somehow, felt a worry about Beaver-teeth's case.

VI

Lily didn't expect that Beaver-teeth's boss had also become her client.

One morning at nine-thirty when Lily got out of the elevator on the 8th floor, she spotted a tiny figure waiting outside her office door. It turned out to be the mysterious colonel. He was in his usual kitchen dress, and his shifty eyes showed anxiety.

"How are you, Colonel!" Lily greeted him while opening the door. She remembered seeing him last Sunday in church. He sat in front of her and threw a pink fifty-dollar bill into the offering bag when it approached him. She did wonder at that moment what had brought this man to God. Could it be the sense of guilt?

"Have you started going to church recently?"

The colonel gave her an elusive smile. "I would pray for Buddha if I were in China. But the Divine in Canada is the Christian God!"

Glancing around the office, he asked, "How many cases have you handled successfully?" His eagle-sharp eyes studied her with suspicion.

"This office has been open for just a month," Lily picked an indirect answer, offering him a seat. "What can I do to help you?"

He insisted on standing in front of her desk and took some folded papers out of his pocket. "The situation is urgent, or I would never come to a lawyer's office." He paused and looked around again. "Where is the lawyer?"

"The boss will come from Toronto today. He should arrive before lunchtime."

"Is your boss a lawyer? I am only interested in seeing a lawyer!" The colonel stared her in the eye.

Remembering Mr. New's warning about how slow business was, Lily answered carefully. "It all depends on what kind of help you need. If it's necessary, my boss can pass your case to a lawyer. But he is a very experienced consultant and has handled many difficult cases successfully."

"I can't wait too long. I have to be at my restaurant at eleven o'clock." He scratched his scalp, and walked back and forth like a caged leopard. Finally, he stopped pacing and put the paper on the desk.

"Fine! The situation is this. My daughter has been admitted to Mapleton University. Here are the admission documents. Classes start next week, but she is still in China waiting to get her visa from the Canadian Embassy in Beijing. She has completed all the required checks, but the embassy officials are arrogant, sluggish, and inefficient!"

He was so angry that he clenched his teeth and waved his trembling fist in the air. His eyes flashed with light sharper than the edge of a sword. Lily felt he was ready to jump all over the immigration official, had he been there, and wring his neck.

The colonel lit a cigarette, took a deep breath, and forced himself to calm down. At that moment, Mr. New came in. Lily was relieved.

"If you can contact the embassy and get my daughter here before September 15th, I am willing to pay you a big sum! I have a lot of money and I will pay you cash. See … See … " The colonel said, reaching into his pocket and bringing out wads of money, waving it under Mr. New's nose. "If you have no connections at the embassy, don't waste my time! My time is precious. Don't expect me to pay you a deposit! I promise I will pay you if you can help!" The colonel thrust the money back into his pocket and stared at Mr. New.

Mr. New didn't look disturbed. He accepted the colonel's case and saw him to the elevator, a smile always on his face.

"Do you have any connections at the embassy in Beijing?" Lily asked in worry.

"We'll just treat the dead horse as if it were alive," Mr. New replied.

VII

After lunch, Lily went to the downtown immigration office. Before she finished her question, however, the immigration officer, a white man with a brandy-nose and a beer belly, pushed her document back across the desk and said impatiently, "We have many cases waiting to be processed. There is nothing we can do to help. Tell them to stay home and wait patiently!"

"This is an urgent case, since school starts next week. Can't you help?" Lily pleaded.

Brandy-nose lost patience. "Missing a class is no disaster, Madam! Millions of people in the world are dying of famine, pestilence, and war, and millions are victims of robbery, rape, murder, and drug abuse!" His lips moved fast and the loose muscles in his cheeks twitched. "The immigration office is not just for the Chinese! Next!"

Back home in the evening, Lily told Grace what had happened. Grace suggested, "Maybe you could ask Helen to help. She is a Canadian professor. The immigration officers might treat her differently."

When Helen came with Lily to the immigration office on Monday, the problem was miraculously solved. Brandy-nose sent an email to Beijing and received a fax from the Canadian Embassy two days later confirming approval of the colonel's reunion with his family in Canada.

The colonel reappeared in front of Lily, gazing at the faxed letter and listening attentively as she translated it into Chinese for him.

"Finally!" He took a deep breath, though there was no trace of a smile on his pale face. "How much do I owe you?" His hand reached into his pocket.

"$1,200," Lily answered, her face reddening. She had phoned her boss this morning.

The colonel looked stunned. The figure was clearly higher than he had expected. His hand paused and his jaw tightened. After an embarrassing moment, he pulled out a wad of cash. Silently, he counted out the money and put it on the desk.

Lily put the money into an envelope, wrote a receipt, and tried to ease the awkwardness by chatting. "The letter says your wife and daughter's visas were both granted. But I didn't hear you mention your wife before."

The man raised his eyes and stared at the white cloud out of the window. "I've never loved her."

His abrupt declaration shocked Lily once again. She caught a cold front in his eyes. He remained standing in the same place and started talking in a flat voice.

"I was born into a poor family in South China. My parents died when I was very young. I was always hungry and grew up small-boned like this. My greatest wish was to go to university, but that could only be a dream. I joined the army and worked hard for many years. I pleased all my bosses and wished to get promoted ... That's why I married. My wife was forced upon me by my boss in the army and I have never loved her for a single day."

Lily asked in suspicion, "How could someone force a wife on you?"

The colonel turned to her and suddenly raised his voice high, "Why couldn't they? If you were a young man in the army and dreaming of a brighter future, of course you had to please your bosses and do everything they asked of you!"

Lily was taken aback. "Was she ugly?" she asked sympathetically.

He regained his calm and resumed his flat tone. "No, as a matter of fact, she was very pretty. Young, beautiful, and also in the army."

Ignoring her curiosity, the man went on, slowly. "I was applying earnestly to become a Communist Party member then. The condition, of course, was that I marry her, although I felt very bad about it ... They talked me into it ... What else could I do, as a helpless young man without any background?"

Lily was confused by his explanation. What was wrong with the man that as a poor young soldier he would feel pain at marrying a pretty young woman? Drawing a deep breath, the colonel brought his emotions under control and returned to his normal manner. "Anyway, I love my daughter. She is mine. And, for the sake of her happiness, I have to bring her mother to Canada as well."

He bit his thin lips, nodded his sharp chin, and shot her a complicated glance. Without any farewell, the colonel turned his back and walked towards the door.

Lily gazed at his narrow shoulders and noticed that his back was already bent, like an old man's. She was struck with the odd impression, somehow, that the man was indeed, as his nickname "Mouse-colonel" suggested, like a frightened mouse, ready to run away at any moment.

Chapter 22
Girls of the Rainbow

I

The next day, Lily phoned Helen to thank her for helping with the colonel's case. Helen reminded her to join the Rainbow Club in celebration of the Mid-Autumn Festival, a traditional Chinese event. It was held on early Saturday afternoon in a Canadian church hall located on the shore of Moon Lake.

"Please bring your son, too," Helen said. "They need a few boys to make the party more balanced."

Lily invited the four-year-old grandson of the Vietnamese woman upstairs and asked Grace to come, too. Grace, as always, was eager to participate in any church activity.

The church was decorated with red lanterns and colourful streamers, all very Chinese, since all the fifty-some daughters were adopted from China. Most of the girls had arrived in their Canadian homes when they were only a few months old.

The oldest girl had been in Canada for six years, and the youngest one had arrived just a week ago. They were all beautifully dressed, either in traditional Chinese jackets of bright red and green silk, or in elegant Western-style black and white skirts. Many parents had put on the *cheongsam*, a close-fitting woman's dress with a high neck and slit skirt, to add to the Chinese atmosphere. The tape deck was playing lyrical Chinese music. Up on the stage at the back of the hall, a woman was leading a few children running with paper lanterns in their hands.

The two boys brought by Lily seemed to be the only boys in this big hall. Baby followed Lily closely and seemed timid, while the Vietnamese boy was quite independent. He ran to the food table and helped himself to popcorn, chips, and sweet cakes. Lily watched him and realized the advantage of growing up with siblings. She put a piece of shortcake into Baby's hand and asked Grace to help herself to some food. Grace snorted as she declared, "No, I don't like to eat free food! I've told you many times to be more decent!"

Blushing, Lily turned away from the food area and took Baby and Grace to the large table where some parents were teaching their children some handicrafts. There, her attention was drawn by a man who was showing a paper crane to a baby boy in his arm. The Chinese boy looked pale and sick, leaning his head weakly against the man's chest.

"Your child seems to be the only boy in Mapleton adopted from China," she said, trying to start a conversation.

The man nodded, and told her that he was an artist and his wife was an accountant at a senior citizens home. This boy was their third adopted child from China.

"Is he sick?" Lily asked with concern, looking at the boy in his arm.

"Yes. There were only a few boys in the orphanage, and they all had health problems, some minor, some serious. He has a heart disease. We believe we can get him treated in a Canadian hospital when he is old enough for that kind of surgery."

At that moment, two little girls, one about four, the other maybe six, rushed over and held the man's legs, trying to get his attention. He touched their heads and said to Lily, "See, we have a big family!"

"How lucky these children are!" Grace exclaimed in admiration, after Lily interpreted everything for her. "I am sure their biological parents are peasants in China. Those peasants would never believe that their abandoned children would be spoiled like this in Canada!" She then asked Lily, "Do you think he really likes them?"

"Like?" the artist's large blue eyes showed his surprise when Lily translated the question. "I love them! It's odd, but we have met many Chinese who have asked us the same question."

The artist admitted that he and his wife had both enjoyed travelling around the world when they were younger. But since they had adopted three children from China, they had cut travel out of their budget. "Being an artist doesn't do much for our financial situation," he said honestly.

Grace asked Lily to interpret another question to the man, "Don't you find the children a lot of trouble?"

The artist shrugged and asked Grace, "If they were your own children, would you feel they were troublesome?" Hearing no answer, he raised another question. "I wonder why there are hardly any Chinese families adopting the children in China."

Lily explained to him that Chinese society was strongly influenced by Confucianism. It stressed the ultimate importance of family relations and it was a big issue for most Chinese to accept children not related to them by blood.

An idea struck Lily and she went on. "Christians emphasize the concept that everyone in the world is God's child. Therefore, Western people don't have as strong a sense of family defined by blood, and it's easier for them to accept other people's children as their own. Do you agree?"

The artist shook his head slowly and said, "My wife and I disagree with many church practices and do not participate in them."

Lily smiled. "Whether you acknowledge yourselves as Christians or not, when you were young this was a predominantly Christian culture, and those values naturally have permeated your lives."

During their conversation, Baby had been standing by the table trying to grab the colourful papers on it. Grace kept pulling him away and Baby was getting frustrated and starting to whine.

The artist picked up a piece of paper from the table and patiently showed Baby how to fold it, still holding the sick boy in his arms. A warm current flowed through Lily's heart. She took the little boy from his arms, stared at the long, flexible fingers of the artist, the graceful lines of his nose and lips, and the rapt attention in his eyes. She couldn't help but envy the three adopted children who could share his attention and love every day.

Grace asked Lily, "Don't you think he will feel sad when these children grow up and find out he is not their real father? You know, it's impossible to conceal it, since they look so different."

"We have never concealed it from them," the artist said after Lily translated Grace's comment. "Even before they started talking, we showed them the pictures we took in China and told them where they were from, why they were in the orphanage, and how we brought them into Canada to join our family."

One day, the artist said, he was driving the girls to school. On the way, the older girl suddenly asked from the back seat, "Why would God create children without moms?" Her voice sounded unusual. The artist stopped the car by the roadside and told her calmly, "I don't know either." She started sobbing. He knew she had to go through the sadness and he waited. A few minutes later she calmed down a bit and said, "I don't want to be alone." At that moment he told her, "That's why we were there to adopt you." She then asked, "Did God send you for me?" He said, "Yes."

Lily's eyes were moist.

"They will ask more questions when they reach puberty." A slim tall woman joined their conversation. Lily realized she was the woman leading the children running on the stage. The artist introduced her as his wife.

While helping her two daughters with crafts, the accountant pointed to the older one and whispered to Lily, "She started to ask a lot of questions when she was only four."

One day the girl came to her and said, "I want to know what my birth parents look like." She held her in her arms, took her into the bathroom, stood in front of the mirror and pointed at the girl's reflection. "Look," she whispered into her ear, "that's what they look like!"

Lily was silent. She imagined Baby asking her questions, some day, when he could talk fluently. What am I going to tell him?

Lily looked at the girl, who was folding a crane carefully. When she finished, she showed it proudly to her mother. After the couple came back to Canada, the accountant said, they wrote letters to the orphanage and asked them for every bit of information available about the child. Eventually, they were informed that she had been left at someone's doorstep in a village only one day after she was born. The couple then paid someone to go to the village to take pictures and mail them to Canada.

"Why did you go to such lengths to find out about her birth parents?" Lily was curious.

"I want to be prepared in case one day she wants to find out more about her origins. I'm trying to get as much information as possible now when people's memories are still fresh," said the accountant, her eyes looking straight ahead as if she were facing a girl as tall as she was.

"How would you feel if she wants to go back to her birth parents then?" Lily asked, imagining her own possible future.

The accountant replied calmly, "I will take her there. Her desire would be natural, wouldn't it? As a mother who has brought her up and loves her, I want her to be happy."

II

As they were talking, Helen entered the room. She had been to the shopping mall to purchase some baby furniture and had it delivered to her new home. "I have booked my ticket to China at Christmas time!" Helen told Lily.

A middle-aged woman holding a small baby in her arms came over and greeted Helen. Helen introduced her as the current coordinator of the club, a schoolteacher who had also adopted two girls from China.

The coordinator was glad to know that Lily was from China, and started to talk about her exciting experiences there when she and her husband went recently to get their second daughter.

They met with a warm welcome everywhere they went, because they had put a sign in Chinese on their backpacks: "We are from the homeland of Norman Bethune!" The sign was written by the geophysicist and it worked well. Not only were they treated nicely, they also got quite a few free meals from restaurants. The owners simply refused to accept payment. They visited a famous Buddhist temple one day and the monks offered them free admission, too.

"It's hard to believe Norman Bethune's name is still so popular so many years after his death!" Helen said emotionally.

Lily suggested, "I can write the sign for you before you go."

An idea hit Helen. She said to the coordinator, "Lily is a journalist from China and knows a lot about Chinese culture. Shall we ask her to talk to us about the traditions of the Mid-Autumn Festival?"

When most people had finished eating and making crafts, Lily started her talk.

This day in China has always been related to the moon. In ancient times, emperors would hold musical ceremonies to worship the moon and celebrate the autumn harvest. For ordinary people, it is a time for families to get together, sit in the yard, and eat fruit and sweet cakes while admiring the beautiful full moon in the clear autumn sky. Old people often tell the children the legend of the lady on the moon.

Once upon a time there was disaster on earth. Ten suns appeared in the sky and the weather got too hot. Rivers dried up and crops died. Then came a brave archer who shot down nine of the suns and the world returned to normal. People respected him so much that they asked him to stay as their king. He was also married to a very graceful and beautiful lady named Chang-E.

As years went by, however, the archer started to worry that he would get old and eventually die. To seek immortality, he travelled for ninety-nine days on horseback to the west, where a goddess in the mountain gave him the magic elixir which would send the drinker up to the heavens. It was priceless and hard to acquire, since it was refined from fruits of a tree which bore fruit only once every three thousand years. The archer didn't drink it there and then, as he was unwilling to forsake his beautiful wife for the heavens. So he brought the elixir home and kept it for the day when he would get old.

However, one beautiful, full-moon evening when the archer was not at home, his wife took the elixir secretly herself, in the hope that she might be able to go to heaven. She then felt herself becoming light, so light that she floated and drifted in the air, flew out of the window and rose towards the night sky. The husband came home at that moment. Shocked to find his wife flying, he realized what had happened. When he saw her eventually landing on the moon, he took out his bow and shot arrows at the moon repeatedly.

"Oh ... No ..." The audience made sounds of disapproval at this point.

The moon shook, but didn't fall as the husband had hoped. Chang-E fulfilled her dream to live forever, but it was a lonely life in the moon, the price of her greediness.

"Is this story used to educate children not to be greedy?" asked the accountant.

Lily shook her head. "No. We think of it as an expression of people's wish to live forever and never die." On second thought, she explained further. "However, one can see similarities between Chinese culture and the Bible in this story."

"Yes?" The accountant looked surprised.

"Think about the fall of Adam and Eve," Lily said to her. "In both stories, women were selfish creatures who cheated and trapped their men, although the punishment for Eve was leaving the garden and eventually dying, while for Chang-E it was going up to the moon and living alone forever."

"Are there any other Chinese legends with similarities to Bible stories?" the artist inquired.

"Yes, quite a few," Lily answered. She was getting excited about the discussion. "For example, the Bible tells the story of a man named Abraham who was willing to kill his only son to satisfy God's wish and was rewarded with a lamb for his absolute obedience. Did I remember that story correctly?"

Seeing a few people nodding, she went on. "The Chinese also have an old story about a poor man who attempted to kill his newborn baby because he wanted to save food to support his aged mother ..."

"Oh, no!" The audience made sounds of disapproval again.

"Don't worry!" Lily waved her hand to calm them down. "While the man was digging a hole in the yard to bury his baby alive, he discovered a pot of gold! Thus, the whole family was rescued and nobody had to die. The gold is interpreted as a reward to a faithful son. So you see the striking similarities! A lamb and a pot of gold."

"However, in our culture," commented the artist, "if someone has to be sacrificed, it would be easier to consider the man's aged mother instead of the baby."

"That's a real difference between the cultures," Lily explained.

"Because there has been no God in Chinese culture, traditional society would put the older generation, particularly one's parents, in the top position, to be respected and worshipped. In western culture, you would sacrifice the young for God while in Chinese culture we would sacrifice them for the sake of our parents. One culture stresses the supremacy of religion while the other stresses secular ethics."

III

Grace had been taking care of Baby and the Vietnamese boy while Lily was speaking to the group. She stood in the back, watching attentively as Lily talked and laughed with her audience.

"You haven't lost your vitality yet!" Grace said to Lily, after Helen dropped them at home early in the evening. "I could feel it as you talked today."

The words came as a surprise to Lily, as she seldom heard praise from Mother. She suspected that Mother might simply be trying to give her confidence.

The scenes at the party reminded her of a couple of blurred memories she had as a little girl with her grandmother and inspired a strong impulse in her to learn more about her own childhood.

"How did my grandmother feed me when I was a one-month-old baby?" she asked, when the family was sitting down for supper.

Grace told her that Lily was sent to the home of a woman who ran a home business selling spicy rice noodles by the roadside. Grace would send twenty dollars, which was a quarter of her monthly salary then, from Beijing to the woman in this remote town, for taking care of Lily. The woman had a baby girl a few months older than Lily. She was a smart businesswoman, so she paid a peasant woman five dollars a month to nurse her own daughter and made a fifteen-dollar profit.

"What was her name and what did she look like? I mean the noodle seller?" Lily imagined a stout, red-faced woman with an apron around her waist busy making noodles in a dark, smoke-stained shop. "Where did she live?"

Grace sensed something from her inquiries. "There's no point in trying to locate her," she said. "It was your grandma who supervised everything."

Lily's grandmother would drop in at the noodle woman's home once in a while to check on the baby girl. One day she noticed that Lily's little mouth was red and swollen and found out that she had been fed with leftover spicy noodles. Grandmother was unhappy that they were feeding a small baby unsuitable food, so she took Lily home.

"No wonder I have always had a craving for spicy pickles!" Lily laughed bitterly. "I heard that one can develop a lifelong attachment to food one has become used to as a baby. Anyway, what happened to me after I was taken away from the noodle seller?"

Grace shook her head. "You were an unlucky person right after your birth. Your grandma told me that it was very hard to find you a sitter. You were passed through a number of women's hands. Finally, when you were able to walk, you were sent into a government-run boarding nursery."

Lily stared at the steaming kettle on the stove and felt at a loss. A mysterious old scene which had surfaced in her memory a few times since her childhood loomed again.

A group of small children was led by a couple of young nannies into a misty area to take a bath. The bathroom was full of hot steam and children's laughter. Suddenly, the young women screamed in horror and started to push the children out of the place. While running downstairs with the other children, Lily saw a skinny old man, his upper body naked, with a long knife in his hand fighting with a young nanny at the door. Deeply scared, Lily fell on the staircase

while the young woman shouted, "He is crazy! Please run! Run!!"
Lily fell in panic and rolled off the staircase.

Did that really happen or was it only a dream? How old was I when
that happened? Did it take place in that government-run nursery?
Lily tried to figure this mystery out for years with no success, since
she had no one to ask about it.

She then remembered the nightmare she had early this spring,
during which a bunch of men chased her with waving knives.
Where were they from? She asked herself. Were they from the
images of the old man in her childhood bathroom, or Grand Master Iron and the Mouse-colonel who were dwelling in the same
building as her now?

Chapter 23
Values of the Law

I

Shortly after the Mid-Autumn Festival, the charming mild season in Mapleton was over. Around the same time came the sensational news that Buffet Empire in the downtown plaza was shut down.

Its owner, the colonel, vanished mysteriously, like a startled hare disappearing into the bush without a trace. Also gone were Beaverteeth and the other kitchen helpers.

There were no more midnight quarrels in the old building. As Lily gazed at the tightly shut window, the colonel's fleshless pale face and his sharp, dark eyes loomed behind the glass like a ghost. She was sure the man was trying to hide from danger. He must have been anxious all this time for his family to join him before he had to run away.

She then remembered a curious story she had heard not long ago. A Canadian house builder in Toronto had signed a contract to build three houses for a new immigrant from China. Each house was valued at half a million and the young immigrant wanted three houses for the three women he had brought with him. A huge deposit in cash had been paid and the builder had already broken ground when an international police organization arrived and took the man back to China for trial.

Compared with that man, Lily thought the colonel at least deserved some respect as a responsible father and a responsible, if not loving, husband. The man's painful and elusive accounts of his marriage once again floated into her mind.

Suddenly, a fresh idea hit her. Could it be that the man's wife had been a toy his boss in the army had finished with? To protect the boss's reputation, the colonel—no, perhaps just a sergeant then—had to marry her, sacrificing a young man's pride and romantic dream of innocent love for a strategic promotion. Yes, that must be it.

At this thought, pity arose in her for the fading shadow of a tiny man with narrow shoulders and a bent back.

II

The ripple of the colonel's disappearance was soon wafted away by the cool autumn breezes. The focus of attention among Mapleton's Chinese community quickly shifted to the news that Old Chia was being brought to trial.

On a gloomy, rainy morning, Lily arrived at the court on her bicycle. She had recently passed the government test and had been registered as a freelance interpreter through the Multicultural Centre of Mapleton. She was quite excited, as this was her first professional job in Canada, though the on-call case-by-case work hardly changed her financial status.

At ten o'clock, a car brought Camellia, Unicorn, and Jade to the courthouse. Lily greeted them briefly and then moved away, keeping a distance from the group to preserve neutrality, as required of interpreters.

A moment later, Mrs. Rice walked in the door with a Chinese man. She waved to Lily happily. "Hi, Lily. Why are you here today? Are you going to be their interpreter? That's wonderful! The Lord is helping us! Have you met Old Chia before? No? Let me introduce you ..."

Old Chia raised his eyes, glanced at Lily timidly, and then lowered his head again to look at his toes. The muscles on his lean
cheeks tightened and he gave a brief and awkward grin. Lily
thought that he had probably been good-looking when young, but
the fine features of his face were marred by a nervous expression
and a clumsy manner.

From a distance, Camellia's voice echoed. Lily caught Old Chia's
lips trembling.

Such a man seems more a victim of domestic violence than an
abuser, thought Lily. Does Old Chia love Camellia so deeply that he
would forgive her everything? Or is he simply a vulnerable man too
weak to face up to reality?

"Lily, be careful about your words! Don't spoil things! We all need
to help the family stay together," Mrs. Rice warned her.

Remembering her status as the interpreter, Lily excused herself
and stepped away from the two. As she paced up and down the hall,
she saw Mrs. Rice run to Camellia. "Remember what I told you to
say and say it exactly as I told you! Don't say anything against him!
Tell the judge that you need him and want to live with your husband
and son!"

Camellia's troubled eyes shifted from left to right, right to left,
looking indecisive. Mrs. Rice persuaded desperately until Camellia
finally nodded her head.

III

During the past few weeks, the warm-hearted Chinese Christians
of Mapleton had reached out their hands in a great effort to recon-
cile the estranged couple.

Camellia was disappointed to find she had no support from the
Christians for her plan to divorce. Nobody felt sympathetic to her

passion for Dwarf, and everybody exaggerated Old Chia as being lovely as a shining star. To Camellia, the Christian attitude toward dealing with domestic conflict was just the same as the old-fashioned one in traditional China. They both saw dismantling a family as the greatest sin, no matter what went on in that family.

When she said she wanted to go back to the workers at Diana's Hall and ask their help in getting a divorce, Mrs. Rice expressed her contempt for the feminist organization.

"For God's sake, please keep away from them! Their only purpose in the world is to create more broken families, the more the better, to get more government funding and keep their jobs. A trivial matter such as a quarrel between a couple often ends in divorce in the hands of those women."

Old Chia, on the contrary, was extremely grateful for the reassurance of Christian principles. He started to be a churchgoer. Like someone drowning in a sea, he was greatly relieved to find that the church in Canada actually functioned like the Communist Party's organization in China. The minister of the church was just like the Party secretary. He took care of his parish, made decisions on behalf of its members, and solved their domestic problems. At first, Old Chia thought all church ministers were paid by the Canadian government to carry out these duties, just as party secretaries were paid to do so in China. He poured out all his sorrows to Minister Wong, relying on him totally to rescue his overturned boat.

He liked the feeling of sitting among "sisters" and "brothers," surrounded by the warm atmosphere of the hymn singing. He had no sense of music and didn't know what they were singing. As the parishioners sang, he would often close his eyes and murmur "Mom, Mom" tearfully, feeling as if his mother's soft hand were patting his crumpled chest. The words of a popular song he learned as a young man flipped out of his mouth with the music.

Heaven and earth are great,
but greater still is the kindness of the Party.
Father and mother are loving,
but loving more is Chairman Mao ...

Old Chia shared his idea that in Canada, the church had replaced the Party, and God had replaced Chairman Mao. Although Minister Wong didn't feel flattered by his complimentary comparisons, he was eager to recruit someone looking at him in a submissive and grateful attitude.

IV

After a long, exhausting wait, they were finally called into the courtroom. It took less than ten minutes, however, for the judge to make his judgement. Camellia's cooperative attitude saved her husband from being jailed, but the evidence submitted by Short-hair, from Diana's Hall, meant the couple had to live separately for six months. In addition, Old Chia was required to attend a training course to learn how to curb his violent behaviour.

As the group was leaving the courtroom, Short-hair approached Camellia with a piece of paper in her hand. "Your case is a typical one for new immigrants and we need to submit a report on it." She asked Camellia to sign the paper.

After Lily interpreted Short-hair's words, Camellia grumbled to Lily: "I am not going to sign that paper. They are now ready to use my case to get more money from the government. Look, all I am asking for is just a divorce, but what have I got after all this hustle and bustle?"

Outside in the yard, when Mrs. Rice was talking with Jade and Unicorn, Camellia stopped Old Chia by the sidewalk. "Where is

Dragon today? Did he go to school? You must watch him closely and not be fooled by him!"

Old Chia looked uneasy talking with her, after she had displayed the family's dirty linen in court. Hesitating, he said in a low voice, eyes avoiding her, "Since you want to abandon us, why do you still care?"

"Hey!" Camellia stamped her foot at his challenge and grumbled to Lily, "Now you see! How can I communicate with him?"

Old Chia seemed sorry for his attitude and said, "Dragon quit school two weeks ago."

"What?" Camellia raised her voice, horrified. "Why didn't you tell me this before? Oh, without me, everything will be a complete mess! Didn't you tell him that his life would be ruined if he quit school?"

"Our life is already ruined, because of you ..." Old Chia murmured, concentrating on rubbing a pebble under his shoe.

Camellia bit her lower lip, staring at him. "What has he been doing now that he's not at school?"

"He wants to make money dealing with stamps."

"But that won't help him get into university!" Camellia shouted.

"Ah," Old Chia let out a heavy sigh. "Dragon said there is no use in being highly educated. He said his father has a PhD, but ... He looks down on me and won't listen to me, you know."

V

In Camellia's eyes, the court order was no more useful than a piece of toilet paper. In any case, her worry about her son was much greater than her worry about the law. She started going straight home each night after work at Fatty's Wok. While Dragon was enjoying the food she had brought from the restaurant, she would sit by the table and tell him tales about hard-working young men who eventually won honour for their parents by passing state exams and earning prestigious titles.

"Enough of those out-of-date clichés!" Dragon banged his spoon on the plate and sneered in contempt. "If you move back home and live peacefully with my father, I will study hard and go to university!"

Camellia saw through him at once. "You are blackmailing your mother! Your future is in your hands, not mine!" She pretended to sound indifferent but her voice became higher and higher in her distress. "Really, I would be a fool to expect you to be somebody! Are you and your father the type of men to be relied upon? No. You ask me to come back to this home. It's only because you're missing all the good food I prepare for you. All you want is to keep me as a slave to you. No doubt you're also dreaming of keeping me on as your babysitter after you get married!"

To keep her coming back, Dragon sometimes acted like a wolf at the full moon, hitting, biting and howling, and other times as a pampered cat, holding onto her neck and begging for her caress.

One night, Dragon slipped under her blanket when she was sleeping on the sofa. "Oh, Mom, please come back! I need you!" He curled up in her arms, weeping. "My father is so weak, vulnerable, and incompetent. People look down on us and nobody wants to be our friend. With you in the family, we both feel stronger and more confident because you are sociable and good at making friends."

Always at those moments, Camellia's heart softened and her determination to get a divorce was badly shaken. But hot letters and phone calls kept coming from China, reminding her of the crazy times she had had with Dwarf.

She rocked back and forth painfully on a seesaw of emotions. As a result, she would sometimes stay home with Dragon and Old Chia, but other times, when she remembered the one-year separation requirement, she would go to Jade's home to spend the rest of the night, no matter how late it was.

Jade felt her kindness as a burden now. Camellia's random arrivals in her home well after midnight bothered not only the couple, but also their son, who had recently arrived in Canada and shared his small bedroom with Camellia whenever she dropped in for a night.

Dwarf's phone calls disturbed their peace as well. They were often wakened by the loud ringing of the phone at midnight. Camellia would hide in the bathroom and whisper for an hour on a cordless phone she had bought at the Salvation Army store. In the quiet of night, the vigorous male voice on the line vibrated throughout the small apartment. One moment, Jade would get goosebumps when Dwarf was singing his lustful songs, but at the next, she would quickly pull the blanket over her ears when Dwarf started his bad-tempered swearing.

Unicorn's self-imposed fast seemed to work well for him. He was oblivious to the assault, his snores competing with Dwarf's roaring on the phone.

"You are cheating me, slut!"

"Zzzzzz ..."

"You were sleeping with Old Chia, the bastard! Why couldn't I reach you last night at this number?"

"Zzzzzz ..."

"You felt the itch! I know you too well! Then why not come back at once and let me ..."

Jade would turn restlessly in bed while listening to Camellia's marathon promises of her love and anxious pleas for Dwarf's understanding and patience.

"Don't you think we should advise Camellia to move back to her own home?" Jade grumbled to Unicorn one morning after another sleepless night. "Zhixin is only nine. I don't want him to hear something he shouldn't. It's worse than an X-rated movie!"

Unicorn shook his head. "We can't push her out if she is not ready. Besides," he said, "haven't you noticed that she is participating in our Bible study now? God is already working on her, in our home."

God's work came in an unexpected way.

One day, Camellia picked some lovely mushrooms in the woods and cooked them with pork shreds for Dragon and Old Chia. After finishing the delicacy, however, the three of them suffered from vomiting and diarrhea at midnight and ended up in the hospital.

While they were receiving intravenous drips in the emergency room, a bunch of church friends came and prayed for them by their bedsides. Mrs. Rice stated that the poisonous incident must be God's warning to the family and a punishment for not following God's wishes.

When the family was out of hospital three days later, Camellia still returned to Unicorn's home to collect her separation days, stubbornly ignoring the warning. Old Chia, however, declared formally to Minister Wong his determination to become a Christian.

VI

Not long after this event, Lily received a phone call at work from Jade. After a brief greeting, Lily inquired about Camellia. "Is she fully recovered from the poison?"

"She is, and too soon!" Jade sounded sour on the phone. "I will find a time to talk with you about this lady. Right now, I need your help urgently for my son's sake!"

The trouble bothering Jade and Unicorn was Zhixin, their son. Having been separated for years, Zhixin had grown into a stranger in his parents' eyes. Mischievous and disobedient, he had been spoiled by his grandparents. He showed no interest in academics and refused to go to church with his parents. The couple decided to send Zhixin to a Catholic school, since Unicorn insisted, after observation, that the Catholic churches seemed closer to the principles of Christianity than the Protestant churches.

He stated that the Fathers of the Catholic churches got no salary and stayed single all their lives so they could serve God wholeheartedly, while the ministers of the Protestant churches got salaries and married like ordinary people do. Besides, many of the charities in town were sponsored by the Catholics who helped the poor and the needy. He felt it was strategically important that they expose their son to the influence of authentic Christians from the very start.

When Jade mentioned her concern about the sexual abuse scandals related to Catholic priests, Unicorn argued that a tree could not represent the whole forest. His fervour was dampened, however, when the local Catholic school informed him that it accepted only baptized Catholics. With no other choice, the couple had to take Zhixin to a public school nearby.

Since the couple found that Canadians had difficulty pronouncing their son's name, they decided to choose a new name, Moses, for him. During Easter, they had watched an old Hollywood movie about Moses on TV and had been deeply impressed with the great leader who had conquered all difficulties and brought peace to his people under the guidance of God.

Registration for Moses at the public school didn't go smoothly, either. The school noticed that all his legal documents indicated the boy was seven years old instead of nine, as the parents claimed. He was therefore put into a Grade 2 class.

Since the couple's arguments failed to convince the school authorities, Lily, as the Mandarin interpreter for the Multicultural Centre of Mapleton, was approached for help.

Lily went to the public school after work to meet with Jade and the schoolteacher. The ESL teacher showed Lily Moses' documents and stated, "The school has to register students according to their legal documents. Moses can't go into Grade 4 if his papers indicate he is only seven."

Jade lost her patience. "I have told you many times that he is nine, not seven! I am his mother!"

The teacher replied calmly, "Then why do his passport, immigration papers, and his birth certificate all show him as seven?"

"I told you they were all wrong!" Jade stared at the teacher. "Why don't you believe me?"

"In Canada, we have to follow the law." The teacher's voice remained calm.

Jade turned her face away from the teacher, looking helpless. Lily examined Moses' legal documents carefully and finally found out how this had happened.

The couple met each other during their last year at university. Upon graduation, the government assigned a quota to their university for two engineering graduates to be sent to Tibet. Unicorn was chosen and, as a rule, he would be allowed to reunite with his family in eastern China only after he had served for eight years in Tibet. Though Jade was assigned to work in Beijing, she still married him, though the couple could see each other only once every two years.

When the couple finally united, Jade found herself pregnant without having first obtained a "Certificate of Birth Permit." There was an annual birth quota for the number of certificates available, and the policy was handled very strictly by the government administration to keep a low birth rate in China. Anyone who became pregnant accidentally had to have an abortion. Jade was thirty-three that year. She and Unicorn decided to keep this baby and conceal her pregnancy from the authorities. Long before her due date, she hid herself in a relative's home far away from Beijing and left the small baby there until two years later when she managed to acquire a Certificate of Birth Permit.

"Only then were we able to register him, and we had to register him as a newborn or everybody, including my boss, would get punished for breaking the regulations," Jade finished her story with a long sigh, "but we could never have the document corrected in China."

After Lily had translated the whole story for the teacher and guaranteed its credibility, the teacher moved Moses to Grade 4, although she still felt the story too strange to believe. "You can have as many children as you wish in Canada!" she told Jade. "We have two families in our school who came from Africa a few years ago. One family has fourteen kids, the other has nine ..."

"Wow!" Both Lily and Jade were stunned. "How could the parents manage to feed so many mouths?"

"There is no problem." The teacher smiled and added, "They get everything from the government, including regular help to clean their homes for free."

"Canada seems more like a communist society than China!" Lily laughed.

"But that isn't fair!" Jade exclaimed. "If the parents want to have so many children, they should be responsible for supporting them!"

"Well, those are their human rights," explained the teacher. "Besides, the birth rate in Canada has been dropping continuously."

Jade sighed. "Oh, what a pity! On the one hand, some people in the world are forced to have only one child, while some others ..."

The teacher asked Lily to sign a piece of paper, stating that the story of Moses' birth was true. While Lily was writing, the teacher expressed appreciation for the Chinese boy's new name. Trying hard to conceal her amusement, she told Lily, "We have quite a few Chinese students these days and their names are all very interesting. One boy in Kindergarten is named Darwin, and another one in Grade 3 is named Socrates. I wonder if we are going to meet Aristotle or Einstein as well."

Chapter 24
Close to God's Light

I

The joke about Chinese children's new names amused Grace, too, when Lily told her the story of Moses' birth that evening.

"Do many Chinese people change their names when they come to North America?" Grace asked with great interest.

"Many," Lily nodded. "Not only do they adopt English names to make it easy for others to pronounce, but some also change their Chinese names to show their love of God, after they have become Christians. I know quite a few people who have done that!"

"Is that so?" Grace raised her eyebrows in surprise. "How do you know these names aren't their original ones?"

"It's obvious!" Lily listed some of the Chinese names she had met at the church or read in Christian publications. There were Favours-proof, Forever-faithful, Glad-tidings, Manifest-splendour, Laud-blessing. "Those names show a distinct Christian flavour, quite different from traditional Chinese names."

Grace became silent. She was staring blankly at the glass lamp-shade above the table, her eyes reflecting its colours, bright blue, light gray, orange yellow and pinky red. Lily had purchased the lampshade for two dollars at a garage sale. The bright colours added some warmth to their plain, blank apartment and made the kitchen the coziest part of the home.

That night, Lily was disturbed in her sleep by some strange sounds.

"Oh ... No ... No ... I didn't ..." It went on and on until finally Lily opened her eyes, searched in the darkness for seconds, and realized that the creepy noise was coming from Grace lying beside her.

She turned on the lamp and looked at her mother closely. Grace was breathing hard and sobbing, her mouth half-open, her brows knotted, and her voice full of despair, as if she were pleading to someone for mercy.

Lily was overwhelmed by pity. She had never seen Mother displaying weakness and vulnerability. She pushed Grace on the shoulder gently. "Mother, it's a dream. Wake up!"

The mournful sound stopped. Grace opened her eyes, looked around, and let out a breath. "Oh, I was dreaming ... Are you scared?"

"What did you dream about?"

Grace shut her eyes again, murmuring. "It was ... for so many years ... it still hurts ..." As Lily turned off the light and settled back down beside her, Grace began to talk.

II

In the spring of 1957, the Communist Party called on all people to express different opinions about the government's work, showing a willingness to adopt a more flexible and milder policy. For a period of three months, an explosion of opinions swept through the country. But the government soon found it was time to silence the voices, for some had gone so far as to demand for free elections and a multi-party government system.

The wind started to blow in the opposite direction in late summer.

The government started a new campaign to expose Rightists who had attacked the government. In the fall, the press reported daily the names and crimes of the Rightists, ranging from high-ranking officials to doctors, teachers, editors and writers, almost all intellectuals.

Grace was caught in the web, since she had made a couple of negative comments on the government's policy. After she was forced to sign a document which labelled her as an "anti-party and anti-socialism bourgeois-Rightist," she had to undergo a series of punishments related to her "crime."

Frost came together with the snow. She had been married for just over a year and was pregnant. Her second husband, a loyal Communist Party member, required a separation and made her move out from their home and into a dormitory.

"After your brother was born and was one month old, his father came to my dormitory." Grace's voice trembled in the dark. "He asked for a divorce ... I begged in tears. That night after he was gone, I wandered along the city river for hours in freezing wind, with a desperate desire to drown myself ... There was no love, no pity, no understanding, even from the closest relationship ..."

Lily felt stuck, not knowing what to say to console Mother's wounded heart. She now understood better why Mother had repeatedly initiated separations from Father at seemingly trivial matters. Mother's coming to Canada to stay with her and leaving Father alone at home also became explainable. It takes more than one cold day for the river to freeze three feet deep, as an old Chinese saying goes.

She wrapped herself tight with the blankets, her mind alive with the sad picture of Mother wandering along the river bank on a moonless night. Had Mother lost her hope in life at that moment, I would have been left alone in this cold world. What held Mother back from the seduction of death? Love? For whom? Her mind was busy with all these thoughts when Grace's voice broke the darkness again.

"Do you think … he might have changed his name as well? Are you sleeping, Lily?"

III

The next Sunday morning, Grace urged Lily to go to the church, for she had missed services many times in the past couple of months due to her busy schedule.

Arriving at the church, Lily left Baby at the children's Sunday school in the side wing and then led Grace to the church library in the basement.

"My mother would like to borrow some books from your collection," she told Jade, who volunteered in the small library.

Jade was tidying the books on the shelves. She apologized for not having the books in good order and greeted Grace with a smile. Lily scanned the shelves and was surprised to see that the number of books available was much larger than the Chinese language collections in Mapleton's public library, but with a different focus, though. The public library had a kung fu theme, while here, the focus was evangelical. But nowhere could she find the literary quality that nourished her thirsty soul.

Jade recommended to Grace a few popular books written by new converts from China. Grace put on her reading glasses and looked at the books. She seemed to have no interest in their stories and started searching the shelves.

"Where is Moses? Didn't he come with you to the church?" Lily asked Jade.

"He stayed home. It will take some time to convince him to come with us."

"But he is only nine and it is illegal for him to stay home alone," Lily reminded her.

"We know. But our income is very limited and we don't have the budget for a babysitter," Jade replied. "Anyway, he got used to being alone for long periods in China."

"Your neighbours may report it to the police if they find him alone at home!" Lily warned her.

"We told him to keep quiet in the apartment, not to pick up the phone if it rings, and not to answer the door if someone knocks."

"But good Christians should be law-abiding citizens!" Lily teased.

"Good Christians follow the laws of God, not the laws made by humans," Jade responded quickly. Lily felt that Jade was quickly becoming another Mrs. Rice, but on a higher level than her teacher.

The choir from the assembly hall streamed into the basement. "The sermon will start soon." Lily called to Grace, "Mom, it's time to go upstairs."

"You can go ahead. I will join you later."

IV

Entering the assembly hall, Lily frowned. The air in the church was never fresh, but it had gotten worse as the weather turned colder. She wondered why nobody else seemed to mind the stuffy air.

Lily searched among the rows for Unicorn, then went over to the back row and sat down beside him. "Did Camellia come with you today?" she asked.

"No, she has to work in the restaurant," Unicorn replied. "But I will study the Bible with her when I see her this evening."

A few empty seats away were Mrs. Rice and Old Chia. Mrs. Rice waved at her with a quick smile. Old Chia buried his face in the hymn book as if he were reading attentively and didn't see her. Lily understood he was embarrassed to face her.

Old Chia had started taking his compulsory training course every Saturday in a downtown high-rise. Lily had been summoned there once as an interpreter at the request of the course instructors, who felt Old Chia didn't fully understand their lectures.

In a small room, she had sat at a big table with thirteen men accused of domestic abuse. They looked either gloomy and fatigued or resentful and ready to bite, like a group of defeated gamecocks. Old Chia stood out among them as the only Asian. He kept his head low all the time and avoided looking at anyone.

The instructor was a young white man with the perfect features often observed in Michelangelo's paintings. However, Lily's appreciation of his charming looks dropped away when he uttered the "F" word during his instruction on how to control anger and create a peaceful atmosphere at home. Throughout the three-hour lecture, the "F" word burst out of his finely curved red lips at least a dozen times, like bullets shooting into Lily's spine.

When the morning was finally over, the young instructor blamed Lily for not interpreting efficiently to Old Chia. Obviously, Old Chia was not following the lecture. He had scared his classmates a couple of times when he had dozed off and banged his forehead noisily on the table.

Lily rubbed her stiff neck while telling the handsome face that she was not going to come again. Catching a puzzled look in the blue eyes, she explained, "I don't have the nerve for this kind of company and I am not familiar with the vocabulary of your lecture. Please look for someone else who is tough enough for the job."

V

Lily was wondering if Old Chia had gained any knowledge about dealing with women from his workshop when Jade rushed into the assembly hall. She sat next to Lily and whispered, "I left your mother in the library. She wants to look at all our books!"

On the platform, Minister Wong was preaching on the topic,

"How to be like our Lord." His sermon was fairly long and rambling, but the main point, to Lily, could be summarized in two sentences. Amassing wealth on the earth is useless. Smart people should donate their wealth to the needy on earth and claim their wealth in heaven.

In the end when he reached out his arms to conclude the sermon, Lily listened to see if he had taken Unicorn's advice about the ending. He hadn't.

Minister Wong then called for contributions for a few events. He first introduced a young student who asked the congregation to support his evangelical trip to Turkey, where he planned to play guitar to spread the gospel among the heathen.

Lily felt it was not necessary to make the effort. "The people in Turkey are mostly Muslim. They already have a faith," she said to Jade. "I think the boy should go to China instead!"

Jade made no comment. She was watching Unicorn attentively. There was a tense look on her face.

A strong voice distracted Lily's attention. On the stage was a middle-aged man talking with a Cantonese accent. He announced that a Hong Kong based evangelical radio broadcaster was planning to establish a new station in Toronto and financial support was greatly needed.

"It doesn't matter how much you can contribute. One thousand dollars are not too little and ten thousand dollars are not too much …"

Lily was scared by his expectation and turned to talk to Jade, only to find Jade's eyes burning with flame, at Unicorn. Unicorn had taken out a pen and a cheque book and was fumbling with them while glancing at his wife out of the corner of his eyes. Although Jade remained silent, he hesitated under her sharp stare and finally put the cheque book back into his pocket with a sigh.

The black offering bag was passed again. It was the second time today that money was being collected. Mrs. Rice got the bag from the person in the front row and thrust her fist into it quickly. Before anyone could see clearly, she had passed the bag to Old Chia. Old Chia held the bag awkwardly. Lily had seen him put a dollar into the bag in the first round and figured he must be debating about a second donation.

At that moment, Unicorn reached over and took the bag from Old Chia. Passing over Lily, he put it directly into Jade's hand. Jade took out twenty dollars from her purse and dropped the money into the bag, explaining to Lily, "We have agreed to this amount as our weekly contribution to the church."

Lily knew the proper amount for the offering was ten percent of one's income, as the Bible recommended. She knew she was far from being a disciplined follower. Like Old Chia, she had put only a dollar into the bag in the first round.

VI

After the service was over, Lily went out of the assembly hall to pick up Baby. In the hallway, she bumped into Minister Wong. An idea hit her so she followed him to his office.

Minister Wong sat down heavily in an armchair, took a mouthful of tea, and asked, "What can I do for you?"

"The air in the church is very bad," Lily said, standing by the door. "Would you ask them to open the windows in the morning so people could enjoy fresh air when they are in church?"

Minister Wong uttered a dry laugh. "I'd love to, but that would increase the heating costs." Seeing her confused look, he explained, "To save money for heating in the winter time, I often have to work in the cold early in the morning and late at night. Most people have no idea of the cost of running a church like this, particularly when there are so many newcomers or onlookers who come for the service but hardly contribute anything. Some people put only coins in the offering bag, as if they are dealing with a beggar!" He opened the drawer, took out some sesame crackers, and started eating.

Lily felt uneasy about his comment and looked away from the chewing mouth. She was not sure what to say to him when she heard someone coughing and found Unicorn standing behind.

Unicorn stepped into the office and said, "If they put only coins into the bag, they have a very limited income." It seemed he had heard Minister Wong's statement.

Glancing at him, Minister Wong said, "The average people pay only about one percent of their income to the church. Suppose the average income for a person is $30,000 annually, then one percent will be only $300! But if everybody doubled his contribution to two percent, we would be able to do a lot, not only having fresh air ..."

"I have come to make a suggestion." Unicorn cut him short. "Can we stop passing the bag along the rows?"

"Why?" Minister Wong stopped chewing, his eyes alert.

"Many newcomers to the church are observers and not yet Christians. If we keep on passing the bag to them every time they come, they might think we are forcing people to contribute money and some of them might be scared away," Unicorn explained.

"Contribution to God is totally voluntary. No one is obliged to offer anything if they don't want to."

"But you know, for the Chinese, it is embarrassing not to give when the bag is put into one's hands in public," Unicorn insisted. "Besides, many newcomers are not financially stable. To save a couple of dollars, some of them even walk an hour to come to church instead of taking the bus, such as Lily ..."

"What do you think the church should do?" Minister Wong asked, throwing another cracker into his mouth and giving it a crispy bite.

"I have been to a Canadian church, which is right beside my home.

I like the way they leave their offering box in a corner. Anyone interested in contributing can simply go over to the box and put an offering in it. Why can't we do the same?" Unicorn asked, looking at Lily for support. She nodded.

Minister Wong grinned, his eyes not smiling though. "Your suggestion sounds ideal, but it is easier said than done. The church you mentioned is probably a well-established one. If we adopt their method, I bet we would collect no money at all! Many people come to the church just for free services. Do you know that even the money we collect now is not enough to run the church? Do you know even my wife has to work outside the home?" His fair face turned red. He stood up from his chair, but sat down again.

"If there is no money, it means the service is not good enough," Unicorn's voice was low but firm. "With a box system, whatever money collected is purely voluntary, and therefore, a true contribution to God. As long as our church is doing a good job, the offering in the box will increase."

Minister Wong sneered. "Are you suggesting that I am not giving a good service?"

"Good or not, everyone coming to the church has his own opinion," Unicorn said. "By the way, I have noticed that you are still using the same words in your final prayer, after I mentioned the impropriety ..."

"Please get it clear here!" Minister Wong shouted. "Who is the minister in the church? You or I?"

Unicorn's eyes opened wide. "Isn't this a democratic country? Aren't we allowed to express our opinions freely?"

"As long as you are not spreading the communist ideology!" Minister Wong hit the table with his palm. "I warn you, don't think nobody is watching you! If you destroy my reputation, you will have to pay for it! Just like you would have to pay with your life if you killed someone!"

He stood up, led them out of the office, closed the door, and walked down the hallway, leaving Unicorn and Lily behind.

Unicorn stood speechlessly in the hallway, crossing his arms. Lily looked at him with sympathy.

"Hi, what are you up to here, Unicorn? Can you give me a ride to the Chinese grocery store? They got in fresh, big, king-sized crabs from Toronto last night." Mrs. Rice came over.

VII

Lily went to the side wing, but found the children's Sunday school class was not yet finished. A few parents were chatting outside the door. She peeped through the door glass and saw Baby sit on the floor among a group of children between two and five years old. He was watching with great interest as a couple of ladies performed a mini drama in front of a whiteboard. Drawn on the board was a colourful tree, with green leaves and large red fruit.

Lily looked at the ladies in exotic costumes and was amazed to find one of them was Madam Jewelry, the Tongue-speaker from Hong Kong. When did she start to teach in the Sunday school? Is she going to teach her magic skills to the children? Lily wondered. She could hardly hear clearly what the ladies were saying, but she saw Madam Jewelry take out a red delicious apple from somewhere and pretend it had just been picked from the tree. She then passed it to the younger lady and said something to her.

The younger lady bit into the apple, chewed, shut her eyes and fell on the floor motionless, as if she were dead. Then Madam Jewelry looked down at her friend's body with an exaggerated scary expression. She opened her eyes wide and said something serious to the children.

Lily had figured out that they must be telling the children the story of Adam and Eve in the garden of Eden. When the class was over, she entered the room and greeted Madam Jewelry. But the lady didn't recognize her since she had been to the jewelry stand only once with Camellia and had never shown up again.

"Are you not working in the mall on Sunday anymore?" Lily asked.

"My husband and I take turns to come to the church so we can both serve the Lord," Madam Jewelry answered with a wide smile.

"Do you think, at such a young age, the children would understand the Bible message you were trying to communicate in class?" Lily asked curiously.

Madam Jewelry nodded confidently. "Of course they can! Children may not talk, but they understand what you are saying."

Lily was about to inquire if the teaching of the Tongue was also part of Madam Jewelry's volunteer plan in the Sunday school when Baby came over and took her hand. His little face was as red as an apple and his large black eyes shining with excitement.

"Apple! Mom, Apple!" he said to Lily, his tiny finger pointing at the half-eaten apple left by Eve on the table.

"See! He understands everything! He is very smart!" Madam Jewelry commented to Lily. Lily took Baby by the hand, thanked the two lady instructors, and left for the library in the basement to look for Grace.

VIII

In the library, she found Grace waiting while Jade was recording the books borrowed by her.

"Did you find anything interesting to read, Mom?" Lily asked.

"Yes." Grace pointed at the pile of books on the table, hardly able to control her excitement. "I spent hours checking all the books in the library and finally found him!"

"Who?"

"My teacher." Grace showed her the book in her hand. "I never imagined he had changed his name! But fortunately, one of his books has a picture and it is him!"

Lily noticed the pink in her mother's cheeks and an unusual tremble in her voice. She took the book and looked at it. It was not a new one, having been published at least twenty years before. On the back was the photo of the author, an elegant looking man in a tie and a western suit. It was hard to tell his age, from late forties to early fifties. His oval face was crowned with neatly trimmed hair parted on one side. Behind the white-framed glasses was a pair of thoughtful eyes.

"He looks handsome," Lily commented, flipping over the pages. The emotional story Grace had told came back to her. The contents of the book, at a quick glance, however, were no more than the usual clichés in church publications.

"Be careful not to damage it!" Grace warned her, and took the book back. She gazed at the photo again, and whispered, "He hasn't changed much. I recognized him at first sight! Were you saying he is handsome, Lily? ... Yes? ... But I don't think he was when I was young, you see. I remember his lower lip sticking out a little bit more than his upper one. But this picture doesn't show that ..."

Lily found Grace talkative as a young girl, losing a bit of her usual composure.

"Isn't this another miracle?" Jade said excitedly to Lily when she finished taking care of the others. "I never expected that your mother would know him! Did you notice that most of the hymns in our choral book were translated from English into Chinese by him? No? Look at them carefully. The verses are beautifully done. The author is a very famous minister. I met him once when I was in Montreal ..."

Grace raised her eyes from the book and asked Jade, "Does he live in Montreal?"

"No," Jade shook her head, "I don't think so. Some people said he lives in Hong Kong, but others said he lives in New York. Probably he lives in both places. He was on a speaking tour in Canada, and Montreal was one of his stops. He is regarded almost like a cardinal of North America's Chinese Christian world and enjoys great fame and respect. You just can't imagine how charming and how touching his speech was!"

Grace's eyes sparkled. "I wouldn't be surprised!" She tried to talk calmly but her voice sounded uneven. "Do you have any idea when he will come to Canada again? Would he come to Mapleton?"

"It's a pity, I don't think he will ever come to Mapleton since this is such a small city." Jade shook her head. "He seems to be quite mysterious. We can understand that. He is in such an important position that his schedule and address are confidential. Besides, he must be in his late seventies and may not travel very much these days."

At this moment, Unicorn entered the library. "Have you found the book I mentioned for Camellia?" he asked Jade.

"It has been borrowed by someone else." Jade's enthusiasm waned as she replied to his question. "She hasn't even touched the books you have borrowed for her last time."

"Those might be too deep for her," Unicorn explained. "And that's why I asked you to look for this one instead."

"Is it worthwhile for you to care so much about her?" Jade's voice sounded sour.

Unicorn's face darkened. He made no reply but walked to the shelves to start searching himself.

Lily smelled tension. She looked at Grace, but found she was paying no attention to the couple's conversation.

Chapter 25
Temptation from Satan

I

Lily's suspicions were proved correct days later when Unicorn appeared at her door unexpectedly at midnight looking for Jade.

"She didn't come here," Lily told him at the door. She was already in bed when Unicorn knocked on the door. "What has happened?"

The smile on Unicorn's face failed to cover his anxiety. "We had a minor quarrel and she ran out of the apartment." He turned away and walked towards the building entrance hastily. "I've got to look for her."

The next day after Lily got home in the afternoon, Grace told her that Unicorn had phoned to say that Jade was staying at Mrs. Rice's residence and refusing to go back home.

Lily sensed that Unicorn meant to ask her for help in convincing Jade to come home. She dialled Mrs. Rice's phone number immediately and asked to talk with Jade.

"Come on over, Lily. I have talked with her for a whole day and my throat is dry." Mrs. Rice sounded in high spirits, though. "I would like to ask Minister Wong to come and talk to her, but she refused."

Lily took off on her bike to Mrs. Rice's home.

Jade looked a different person, with sunken cheeks, dry lips, and swollen eyes. Barely had Lily sat down on the sofa, when Jade began to pour out all her sorrow. Just as Lily had anticipated, the source of the trouble was Camellia.

To help Camellia become more independent, Unicorn had started teaching her to drive. Camellia had passed the written test in Chinese and had had her learner's permit for quite a while, but was not willing to pay for private lessons to get ready for her road test.

She was grateful to Unicorn and decided to reward his kindness by helping the family with housework and cooking in her spare time. Jade had felt uneasy when Unicorn commented to her a couple of times that Camellia's cooking was better than hers. Indeed, Camellia was quick at making tiny steamed buns and they were very tasty, with variety in their stuffing, meat and vegetable, salty or sweet.

In comparison, Jade's shortcomings stood out. In the couple's earlier years of marriage, they had been separated, with Unicorn serving eight years in Tibet. Then, when they were roaming Moscow and Montreal, mere survival was their priority. The fact that Jade had never been much of a housewife had never been a problem in the couple's relationship before.

After settling down in Mapleton, however, things changed. Though she could find no suitable job in Canada, Jade enjoyed her evangelical work and visited newcomers' homes almost every day. Using her skills and feeling a sense of worth through her volunteer work, she didn't spend much time on domestic chores. Her home was often untidy and the food she brought to the table was almost always old bread, sold at four bags for a dollar. Sometimes when Jade was out of the house for too long, Unicorn would come home and fill his stomach with cold water and bread. He had mentioned a few times that he missed home-cooked Chinese food. But Jade's confidence in the Lord's protection of her family led her to neglect her man's stomach.

Besides her cooking skills, Camellia also impressed Unicorn with her sweet manner. To please Unicorn, she showed interest in the Bible. Each time Unicorn talked about his new discoveries in the Bible, Camellia would listen attentively, her eyes sparkling with admiration, and she would ask naïve questions which made Unicorn laugh. Her curiosity, and only God knew whether it was genuine or calculated, never failed to encourage him, and he would often spend hours chatting with Camellia, sometimes even after Jade had gone to bed. They also discussed the Bible during their driving lessons and sometimes continued after the lesson was over. A couple of times, Jade spotted them sitting in the car laughing, ignoring the world around them.

Jade found the situation uncomfortable because Unicorn spent considerably less time with his wife than with the questionable woman. But she felt reassured in recalling that Unicorn, raised by strict parents who were both high-school teachers and had impressed on him that sexual activities were the dirtiest thing in the world, had no idea how to attract or love a woman. After she had been introduced to him by a common friend, they had liked each other and agreed to marry. He was no longer green, but acted like an immature calf, since she was his first girlfriend. Instead of kissing and embracing as most lovers did, he would pinch her hand, arm, or thigh to express his love, or rather, to control his excitement, during their dating.

On their wedding night, after the initial performance was awkwardly completed, she heard Unicorn sighing tearfully in the darkness, "I wouldn't regret even dying right now!"

Although Unicorn had always been a faithful husband, and Jade had now the double guarantee of the Ten Commandments, she still felt uncomfortable seeing a charming woman so close to her husband day and night—especially a woman with a record of adultery. Camellia's frivolous laughter and swinging hips filled the small apartment and her presence had become increasingly unbearable.

One day, Jade decided to raise the issue to Unicorn in a subtle way. "I don't mind the expenses for gas while you teach her to drive. We can consider it a contribution to God. But you are not a licensed driving instructor and our car is not equipped with double brakes. If she has an accident, who is going to pay for the damages? Can we ask her to pay? And if she were to be seriously injured or even killed, how could we compensate?"

Unicorn replied calmly, "I don't have double brakes, but I have God with me. How else could I have had no trouble at all being in the car with her more than twenty times? I believe God has been holding the steering wheel for us!"

Jade paused for a moment and took a different track. "You spend too much time talking with her. If you spent more time on your research, you might please your boss and secure your contract for next year."

Unicorn laughed at her suggestion. "The Lord used to point out to Martha that she worried and got upset about many things, but only one thing was needed. Her sister Mary had chosen the better way and it would not be taken away from her. Don't you see that what I am doing now is the one thing needed, serving God?"

Jade was stuck. Though she spent most of her time in Mapleton spreading the Gospel, she had to admit that she was no match for Unicorn now. His capabilities in theological debate were growing rapidly. He could recite a story or phrase from the Bible without hesitation whenever the situation called for it.

Her frustration intensified when she discovered a new initiative going on between her husband and the foxy woman. Besides driving, Unicorn had started teaching Camellia English and computer skills, too.

One night after she returned from a home visit, she found the two of them sitting side by side in the large bedroom in front of the computer, while Moses was playing guitar in his small bedroom.

Camellia was in a short-sleeved red wool sweater which nicely accentuated her round breasts and small waist. Her long black hair was wet and spread down her back, and her face shone with a pink glow after her shower. She was talking excitedly and her chin almost touched Unicorn's shoulder when they both looked at the computer screen. Unicorn was explaining something to Camellia patiently and paying almost no attention to his wife's return.

The muscles in Jade's face tightened. She bit her lips while hanging her coat slowly in the doorway. She then picked up Camellia's jacket and passed it to her, trying her best to talk in a normal voice, "Don't you feel cold wearing so little?"

Camellia shook her head, smiling. "No, the apartment is very hot."

"If you put on more clothes, we could lower the heat and better protect the environment," Jade reminded her calmly.

"You don't pay utilities for the apartment, do you?" Camellia asked.

"But the landlord has to pay!" Jade raised her voice a little bit.

Camellia blinked her eyes and seemed to have noticed the tense tone. "Oh, it's late! I've got to get up early in the morning." She said goodnight to the couple and went into the small bedroom next door. Jade smelled perfume as Camellia swung by.

Jade closed the bedroom door tightly and asked Unicorn, "When did she get home from the restaurant?"

"I don't know." Unicorn answered briefly, his eyes still searching on the screen.

That night, Jade lay awake in bed until dawn.

The next evening before Camellia got back from the restaurant, Jade prepared supper, carefully making stir-fried leeks with pork shreds, and spicy tofu, favourite dishes of her husband.

She might have smoothed the tension if Unicorn hadn't asked her, at the dinner table, to give her *Advanced Oxford English-Chinese Dictionary* to Camellia.

The spark finally turned to flame. "Why?" She refused his demand. "I need it for myself!"

"We can buy another one for you later," Unicorn insisted. "Camellia needs a good one. Her pocket dictionary is too old and too simple."

"Something is wrong, Unicorn!" she shouted out.

"What?"

"You never have the patience to teach me computer skills! And now you are giving my dictionary to her!"

Unicorn nodded. "Yes, something is wrong. It's your attitude! Don't you see that Camellia needs help? We have the responsibility to help her stand up. I can't understand why you are so stingy!"

"Yes, I am stingy!" Jade lost control and shouted. "And I don't make tasty buns, either! I never flatter you and I don't know how to pretend to be sweet!"

"She has her merits! She works hard and tries to support herself. This kind of person is worth our respect."

"Are you suggesting that I am depending on your income to survive? Don't you think what I have been doing is the most valuable thing in the world, as Martha's sister Mary did?"

Unicorn simply shrugged.

"I want you to stop being so close to her, or I will have to send her out of my home!" Jade threatened.

Unicorn's face turned red. "Don't you understand it doesn't work when you try to control a man! The tighter your control, the farther away you push him!"

"If divorce is what is in your mind, you'd better say it directly!" Jade wouldn't give in.

To her surprise, Unicorn remained silent for a few seconds, nodded, and said slowly, "If two people don't feel happy together, a divorce might be an acceptable choice."

Jade was stunned. Unicorn sounded like a total stranger now, no longer her trustworthy husband. She also realized that Unicorn hadn't quoted any Bible sayings during their quarrel, and the phenomenon was intimidating.

"You are talking all the time of influencing Camellia with Christianity," she sneered, "but don't you see who has eventually influenced whom. Fine, I will leave you alone with her and stop getting in your way!"

II

"You are making a fuss over a trifle," Lily commented after Jade had finished. "I don't think there is really anything going on between him and Camellia."

"I don't believe that either. The problem is, he doesn't realize that the foxy woman is just using him. He might think she loves him!"

"He is a very nice man," Lily said.

"He is only nice to others!" Jade responded, and poured out more of her sorrows.

Unicorn's research in the school lab had stalled recently. He suspected it might be a test from God of his faith. Besides helping Camellia, he also donated his savings to as many missionary projects as possible, in addition to the family's regular offering to the church. For example, he had given $100 to a missionary group to China, and $300 to help purchase a piece of property for a church in Africa.

"Last time when the fellow from Toronto called for contributions to a new evangelical radio station," Jade said with anger. "I watched him closely and was determined at that moment. If he had dared to write that cheque, I would have torn it into pieces right in front of his face!"

"No!" Lily shook her head. "You should appreciate his generosity. I actually admire people like that."

Jade frowned. To save more for such contributions, Unicorn limited Jade's freedom to spend a dollar. He never bought any clothes for her and denied her requests to purchase things such as new curtains or bed sheets. He even asked her to do the laundry by hand instead of using the pay washer in the building. The family had not been to a restaurant in a year except the once when Lily invited them to the colonel's buffet.

"I think he is actually a selfish man," Jade concluded. "He is concerned about his life after death. He has quoted to me more than once a Bible saying that it is hard for the wealthy to enter God's paradise. He dreams that if he wants to go to paradise, he needs to deposit his wealth there, at the sacrifice of his wife's pleasant life on earth."

"Come on!" Lily laughed at her notion. "I wonder what attracted you to marry him at first. He is such a monster now!"

Jade replied without hesitation, "To be honest with you, I didn't love him that much even then. It was simply that I was on the edge of being an old spinster but still hadn't found my ideal man."

"What kind of man do you think is ideal?"

Jade blinked her eyes, looked around, but produced no answer. "What do you think?" she kicked the ball back to Lily.

"Norman Bethune, of course." Lily lost no time in replying.

"Right." Jade said with a serious look in her eye. "He is also the type of man I would love."

The two of them stared at each other, feeling they were closer than before, at finding one more important item of life in common. "I used to wonder why you don't marry again," Jade again broke the silence. "Now I understand. It is hard to find anyone like the model in your heart, isn't it?"

Lily was about to discuss the issue further when Unicorn arrived.

Mrs. Rice opened the door and brought him in. Standing silently in the middle of the living room, he looked worriedly at Lily. Jade changed her expression to an indifferent stare at the blank wall, ignoring his presence.

"I have boiled some noodles for dinner." Mrs. Rice broke the awkward atmosphere. "Let's eat while we continue to educate Unicorn."

Jade refused to eat anything and stayed on the sofa. In the dining room, Mrs. Rice started blaming Unicorn after her children had left the table. "Don't you know that you are not supposed to praise another woman in front of your wife?"

"But Camellia has her merits, indeed!" Unicorn argued.

"Okay." Mrs. Rice threw him a contemptuous glance. "What about if Jade tells you that she thinks Minister Wong is smarter and more handsome than you are?"

Leaving Unicorn speechless with a numb look, Mrs. Rice went into the sitting room to work on Jade.

"What do you think I can do, to convince her to come home?" Unicorn asked Lily in a low voice.

Lily thought for a while and suggested, "Maybe you can write a letter to her instead of talking face to face."

Unicorn nodded. He looked around and found a piece of paper and pen. Lily left him alone to compose the important letter.

In the sitting room, Mrs. Rice was talking excitedly. "Your worry about your husband is totally unnecessary. He is not that type of man at all. I can tell from the way he looks at me. Trust me, I know too well! His eyes never fall upon my chest, unlike many other men ..." She giggled.

About half an hour later, Unicorn walked into the room, holding a piece of paper in his hand. He put the paper on the coffee table in front of Jade. "For you."

Jade turned her face away, not to look at him or the paper. After Unicorn walked away, Mrs. Rice picked up the paper, scanned it quickly, and exclaimed, "Oh, my! Look what he has for you, Jade!" She put the paper into Jade's hands.

As Jade looked at it, the muscles in her cheeks relaxed. Lily was wondering what magic sentences were written on the paper when

Jade threw it back to the coffee table and said to Unicorn, "Read it aloud!" There was a sense of triumph in her voice.

Unicorn blushed and hesitated, but finally picked up the paper after Mrs. Rice poked him.

It was a poem Unicorn had composed for Jade, confessing that he had been led astray by Satan hiding in his heart and only rescued thanks to the holy splendour shed by the Lord. He regretted being blind to the wonderful wife bequeathed to him by the Lord. He was determined to wash away his sins using the Lord's precious blood and travel together with his wife as His humble servant.

Lily looked at the ceiling, trying hard to control her impulse to laugh. The verse was full of familiar vocabulary readily picked up from the church songs. She wondered how someone as pious as Unicorn could ever become tempted by worldly seductions. Jade's threat of divorce didn't seem serious either. She needed his financial support, anyway. And the poem served as a ladder for her to get off her high horse.

"I need your signature!" Jade said, after he finished reading the poem, not looking at him though.

Unicorn picked up the pen Mrs. Rice gave him and the tension was eased. Jade folded the signed poem, put it in her pocket, and insisted that Unicorn must have Camellia move out of their apartment before she would return home.

Unicorn bit his lips. Seconds later he opened his mouth. "I think we should let her stay. I promise I will never be alone with her again."

Jade shook her head firmly. "No! We have to get rid of this troublemaker." She then said to Lily, "You don't know what else has happened, Lily."

According to Jade, the couple had been receiving anonymous phone calls at home these days. The caller whispered in a fake, low voice, "I will kill you! Kill you!" repeatedly and left them scared.

"Was it a man or a woman?" Lily inquired.

"It was hard to tell." Frowning, Jade recalled. "It seemed that the caller was trying to sound like a woman."

"In that case," Lily smiled, "it must be a man!"

Both Jade and Unicorn nodded. "Right. That sounds logical."

"Who could it be?" Lily pursued.

"I suspect the caller is Dwarf," Jade said.

"But Dwarf does not speak English!" Unicorn reminded her. "I wonder if it is Old Chia."

"No." Mrs. Rice shook her head. "That guy is too timid to make such threats. I am sure of that."

"Are the phone calls still coming?" Lily asked.

"Not any more, after Unicorn told the caller that we were going to report them to the police," Jade said.

A pair of flame-burning eyes above a mouth chewing hard on crackers flashed in Lily's mind. She felt that the things going on in the small community were like a TV soap opera. "Could it be Minister Wong?" She spoke her suspicion out.

Unicorn looked stunned. Then he said with a dry smile, "No wonder! The other day my advisor told me that someone in the Chinese community has 'concerns' that I was sent by the Chinese government as a spy to Canada. I thought he was joking! Do you remember, Lily, that we had discussed the sin of capitalist society at the school's café in front of my advisor? I did try to talk to several people on campus to make sure that the leftover doughnuts are sent to the student residences. I have never thought that the rumour might be from Minister Wong. My Lord!"

"I wouldn't think Minister Wong is that mean," Mrs. Rice said in doubt.

"If that was true, I won't come to his church anymore," Jade declared. She seemed to have forgotten her pain over the domestic disputes.

III

After all the dust had settled, Lily returned home, eager to tell her mother that the thorny issue was finally solved.

Grace was wrapped up in reading the books she had borrowed from the church library and showed little interest in what was going on around her. At night, when Lily and Baby were in bed, Grace would stay a long time in the kitchen, writing something under the glazed lamp.

One day, when Lily came home earlier than usual, after completing a translation job for the Multicultural Centre, she found Grace out with Baby and the apartment empty. As she prepared supper in the kitchen, she noticed the notebook Mother left on the table. Out of curiosity, she flipped through the pages and was shocked to read of the everlasting flames burning Mother's aged heart.

Word after word, line after line, I studied every detail of each description and pondered each choice of phrase to catch any hint of the moments he and I had shared in our youth.

To my disappointment, I found none. Throughout the books, there was little trace of his personal life, present or past. Page after page, every bit of the books was filled with fanatic praises and love inspired by God, whom he referred to as "Father."

I felt the heat of his emotional rhetoric, and my vision was blurred by the image of a tearful man embracing the sunlight with open arms, just as his new Chinese name, Close-to-God's-light, suggested.

I gazed at his photo for hours. The ambiguous smile at the corner of his lips hid a hundred riddles. The light reflected from his dark pupils held a million unsolved mysteries. Occasionally, the sophisticated look of the mature man became blurred, turning into a young face silhouetted against the moonlit sky scented by the aroma of the flying reed catkins. My heart sobbed.

Perhaps he simply never loved me.

For the first time, that suspicion snuck into my mind, like a snake biting the tender tip of my heart. I remember my stubborn competition with other classmates, my unyielding struggle with the other editors of the school newspaper, and my sneers at the love letters composed by naïve suitors.

He might have been turned away by a girl of that type. My arrogance and relentless striving to be the best must have seemed distasteful in the eyes of a devoted Christian, who sings about universal love, forgiveness, and humility before God.

No! He loved me, definitely! There were countless traces of it in his words, his eyes, and his heart. But in the end, he chose to make all the space in his heart available for his God alone, his God.

In one of his books I found a poem, which, I deeply suspect, was meant for me:

I caught your tears behind people's back.
I heard the sighs from your chest.
In the empty world full of vanity,
you refuse to cheat yourself
but look honestly for the meaning of life.
You are dreaming for the day
to open the window and breathe the air fresh.
Yet I could hear your moaning
after fruitless searching.
Aren't you aware of the old myth
woven with love and forgiveness?
The dewdrops in early morning
drive sorrow away and heal cuts in souls.
Please give me your hand,
I have been waiting for you!
I see your eyes wild with joy,

and your bosom rising like tides.
You've found your goal and
Gone forever is your sorrow ...

He is worthy of everyone's respect as a man free of worldly pleasures
and faithful to his holy ideal. He is unique and outstanding compared
with all the lowly ones, like me, whose time and energy are wasted on
trivial matters throughout our aimless lives.

IV

Lily was deeply touched. She also felt guilty for peeping into Mother's
inner world without asking her permission. She had no courage to
bring out the issue for discussion with Mother and had to pretend to
know nothing. Secretly, however, she couldn't curb her strong desire
to look into the diary whenever Grace was not at home.

Most days during late autumn, Grace took Baby to the park. She
left him in the sandbox as she climbed to the top of the hill and
gazed at the cloudless sky to the south. The fallen yellow leaves
covered her shoes and the piercing wind tousled her gray hair.

Is he writing another beautiful article under soft morning light in
a quiet cottage in the woods at this moment? Or is he delivering a
fascinating speech to mesmerized crowds on the sunny Californian
coast? Would I see sorrow, pity, or regret in his shocked eyes at our
first encounter after more than half a century?

She had long ago prepared the first words she would say to him
at their reunion. She had a river of sorrow accumulated during his
mercilessly long absence.

As a seventeen-year-old, dressed in white pants and an apple-
green shirt, she had stood in the rain at a small town station, waiting for the bus which never arrived.

As a young wife seven months pregnant, she had visited the jail to request a divorce from her first husband, who had been accused of being a political dissident.

As a middle-aged professional woman, she had been shoved onto the platform at a public meeting, condemned by mobs shouting slogans, forced to confess her alleged affairs with her boss, and kicked to the ground by her colleagues and friends.

As a mother of three children, she had stood in the cold winter wind, swallowing her pride and begging forgiveness from her second husband, and was left alone in the frost-bitten, barren fields.

Would you understand all this? Do you know it was all for your sake that I survived all the trials?

But her mood changed when she saw herself in the mirror with a wrinkled face, missing teeth, and gray hair. The dandelion-blooming golden fields, the flying turtledoves, the sound of the ox-drawn cart, and the red tangerine woods were gone forever, with her lost youth.

No, I will avoid meeting him. The best way is to just send him a note.

She read out the words written in her heart as she walked slowly down the hill. "Your student of more than half a century ago sends her regards to you. I have no luxurious expectation of meeting you face to face. Hearing your voice again in my life will satisfy my soul ..."

A drop of old tears fell onto the handle of Baby's stroller. She rubbed her eyes and moved her heavy legs.

Let the romantic night with reed catkins dancing in the moonlight live forever in his mind. When he receives warm applause and excited cries from the audience, I will stand at the back of the crowd, in the last row of the church, and gaze silently at the pair of gentle, black, lamb-like eyes.

Chapter 26
Myth of Lamb Girl

I

With the fall winds blowing harder and colder, Lily's attention to
her mother's emotional state waned, for she was worrying now
about the security of her new office job. Her three-month trial
period would soon be over. Business in Mapleton had proved to
be slow, with literally no clients for the past month. In sharp contrast, Mr. New's main office in Toronto made an annual profit
of $200,000 handling refugee claimants alone, although most of
them were fake claims.

The only refugee case handled by Lily in Mapleton came on trial.

With Camellia's help, Lily found Beaver-teeth at Fatty's Wok. He
had worked in a couple of different places after the Mouse-colonel's
buffet had closed down. His loyal capacity for hard work meant that
Fatty could fire a few other workers once he had Beaver-teeth.

Beaver-teeth showed up with Lily at the immigration office, his
hair cut, his dark-gray shirt having been pressed flat under his pillow, and his eyes red, the result of a sleepless night.

The brandy-nosed officer glanced at the document in his folder
and stared at Beaver-teeth, who had started trembling long before
he stepped into the office for his fateful appointment.

"Are you sure you will face persecution if you go back to China?" asked Brandy-nose, with a burp.

Even before Lily translated the question into Chinese, Beaver-teeth's lips had already started quivering like a flying hummingbird. He was too nervous to utter a sound. Lily looked at him sympathetically as he lowered his head towards his thighs and held his knees with trembling hands.

She wanted to say something to calm him down but restrained herself in case her words aroused unnecessary suspicion in Brandy-nose. Those few seconds seemed unbearably long in the windowless room.

Finally, Beaver-teeth raised his head a little, so his eyes were even with the edge of the desk. "I think, the situation ... has changed ... in China today. It's better, for sure." The words came out of his quivering lips with difficulty. "Perhaps ... I will ... not meet ... severe punishment ... anymore ..."

Oh, no! Lily cried in her heart, fixing her eyes on Beaver-teeth's flushed face. She struggled hard with what to say. How should I translate his reply? As my boss's employee, I am supposed to correct the serious mistake he has made. But as an honest person, I should tell the truth. Her eyes swept over the officer's face before her and her thoughts fell on Helen's attitude about the antique vase. She made up her mind.

After she finished her faithful translation, slowly and heavy-heartedly, Brandy-nose closed the file and stood up yawning. "We will let you know the decision soon."

"Please wait a minute!" Lily stood up in a hurry, reaching out her hand to stop him from leaving. "This applicant has lived a decent life in Canada for three years. He has worked hard, paid taxes, and never committed a crime. Please take this into consideration ... Please!"

Her efforts were too late.

A week later in the morning, Lily collected herself and went to

Fatty's Wok again. She had struggled hard the night before after receiving the letter from Immigration Canada.

The restaurant was not open yet. She went around to the back door and found Beaver-teeth in the dark, damp basement. Among the crowded jars and boxes emitting mixed smells of pickles and salted fish was a mattress on the floor and an old blanket. The light bulb hanging from the low ceiling showed a faded picture on the wall beside the pillow. Lily looked at the picture and her eyes grew damp. In a studio decorated with green sofa and red plastic roses, the man exposed his protruding teeth fully by his smiling wife and their three small children.

She held her breath and asked the man to come outside with her. From her serious expression, the man sensed his devastating fate. He followed her upstairs silently, with heavy footsteps.

Outside the back door in the parking lot, she informed him of the immigration office's decision, and he was crushed. Squatting on the ground, he twisted his hand with the missing finger and grasped his hair in despair.

"What can I say to my wife and children!" he sobbed. "Day and night, they have been waiting to join me in Canada ..."

Tortured by guilt, Lily informed him that he would soon receive a deportation notice.

Someone shouted loudly in the kitchen. The front door had been opened. A black cat sneaked out of the greasy backdoor, gave Lily a skeptical look, and disappeared behind the garbage can.

Finally, Beaver-teeth stood up and wiped away his tears with his rough hands. He looked up at the cloudy gray sky and let out a heavy sigh. "As a man, I have to face reality. I am used to a drifting life anyway. There is nothing else I can do but cross the Niagara River to the U.S. before the police come for me!"

II

With the failure of his case, Lily anticipated the arrival of her un-avoidable fate.

Later in the morning, she was startled by the ringing of the tele-phone, which sounded extremely loud in the quiet, empty office. The caller declared himself to be a student of the Mapleton Kung Fu Academy. The Grand Master died a few days ago and a funeral was being planned for him by his disciples.

Lily's mouth was half open before she uttered any sound. A heart attack? She searched her mind but didn't remember seeing the Grand Master recently around the U-shaped building.

"The logo on our black T-shirt was originally designed by the Grand Master. We need to find out the meaning of the Chinese character in the sign and we got your phone number from the Mul-ticultural Centre," said the student.

Half an hour later, a young man showed up in the office with a black T-shirt in his hand. Lily found the Chinese character to be "woods," composed by the symbol of two trees, with water waves in the background.

"Oh, my!" Hearing her explanation, the young man raised his brows. "He did die in the woods, by the lake! We took him camping in the country to celebrate his fiftieth birthday, since he didn't want to spread the news in town. While he was swinging in a hammock, however, one of the two trees to which the hammock was tied fell and hit his head."

Sending the young man away, Lily sat heavily in her chair. There must be a predestined fate for everyone, she thought, or why would the man design the T-shirt logo that way? The water waves behind the two trees must also have embodied an inexpressible desire. Could it be that he wished his ashes to be sent back home across the Pacific?

At this thought, she stood up and chased after the young man.

Outside the building, however, she could not see any trace of him. Standing at a loss by the sidewalk, she looked into the cloudy sky, wind tangling her hair.

After going back ino the office, she found it was hard to concentrate in her writing. She sat idle until Mr. New pushed the door open and walked in with a couple. The couple was visiting from Hong Kong. The husband had a wide, frog-shaped mouth, and was Mr. New's childhood friend. Since the couple spoke no English and Lily spoke no Cantonese, they simply greeted each other with smiles.

"There isn't much to do today. You may go home early," Mr. New told her smilingly.

While Lily was clearing up her desk, Frog-mouth examined the pictures on the wall, moved the plants on the shelf, and rearranged the chairs. Frowning, he pointed up and down the office and talked loud and fast. Lily had no idea what he was saying, but found Mr. New's long face growing longer as he listened to the croaks from Frog-mouth.

Frog-mouth must be a devotee of feng shui, Lily guessed as she walked out of the office. The ancient practice had been popular in Hong Kong and Taiwan, where many people believed in the magic influence of the environment—even the placement of furniture— over the fortunes of a business or a family. In Mainland China, however, feng shui had been regarded as a superstition of the old, decaying culture.

When she got home early in the afternoon, no one was at home. Mother must have taken Baby to the park again, she thought. She walked into the kitchen and found Mother's notebook on the table. As she reached for it, the telephone rang. Somehow, her instinct told her it was her boss.

"Hi, Lily!" Mr. New giggled as if he were quite embarrassed to go on. "May I ... May I know the date of your birth?"

Her mind swirled with possibilities. Is he going to send me a birthday present or hold a surprise party? The cleaning workers in the hotel used to do so for each other. But she didn't want her boss to bother, so she lied. "Well, it has already passed."

"Already passed?" He giggled again but insisted further, "Would you please tell me the date?"

All of a sudden the image of Frog-mouth jumped into her mind. It must be that amateur wizard who is pushing my boss to find out, she thought.

"My birthday is the 18th day of the 8th month." She provided him with an auspicious number.

"Okay," Mr. New repeated the number and then whispered something in Cantonese, obviously talking with the wizard standing by.

"Is that all?" Lily was ready to hang up the phone. Now you can't blame me for the slow business anymore, she thought.

"Wait a minute! There is one more question. In what animal year were you born?" The boss giggled again. This time the giggle sounded like a sharp knife cutting through her skin. She kept silent for a few seconds, struggling, but finally decided to tell him the truth. "Lamb," she said calmly. "I was born in the year of the lamb."

She hung up the phone and sank into the couch, her limbs starting to feel numb. At this moment, she would rather her boss had been a Christian. In that case, the symbol of lamb would be an auspicious image rather than an ominous shadow.

Her thoughts flew back many years ago to when she was a young woman of twenty-one.

III

It was a bitter winter day and she had travelled many hours by train to a large city in northern China. Grace had been diagnosed with coronary heart disease that fall. Alarmed that she might bid farewell to the world at any moment and leave Lily alone, Grace had contacted a few friends and searched hurriedly for a suitable man as

Lily's fiancée. Soon she had arranged a meeting and forced Lily to make the trip north.

It was a nerve-shattering experience. As the young man, accompanied by his mother, entered the matchmaker's home, Lily was too scared to raise her head. She took in only his two legs as he was asked to sit down across from her. After the meeting was over and she was on the train back home, she could remember hardly anything about him except his big thighs. He was too fat, she felt, deciding that matchmakers must all be blind.

On second thought, she realized it was not the matchmaker's fault. The matchmaker had selected the young man according to Mother's criteria. And Mother always insisted that marrying a man who was inferior to her daughter in every respect would guarantee Lily's happiness for the rest of her life.

Lily received a letter from the young man three days later. After discussing warfare in the Middle-East and attacking American imperialism for three pages, he concluded, "I hope we will hold hands and march together on the road of revolution, dedicating our lives to the great ideals of Communism!" In those days, this was the typical way of saying "I like you and want to marry you."

The matchmaker's letter arrived in Grace's hand the following day, however, declaring that the young man's mother disapproved of the match because Lily's face was too round, and, even worse, she was born in the year of the lamb.

After that, Lily learned the old myth associated with those born in the year of the lamb. It had been passed down for generations, along with many other aspects of traditional culture. A woman born in the year of the lamb is doomed to go through many hardships in her life and will bring bad luck to the man she marries.

Grace could not tolerate this insulting failure. She asked Lily to reply to the young man's letter, inviting him over for the weekend.

He came and spent the day with Lily watching monkeys chasing each other at the local zoo. The next morning, after he went back home on the train, Lily mailed him a letter, dictated by Grace sentence by sentence, pointing out the huge gap between them and the impossibility of marching together on the road of communist revolution.

Lily had long felt it odd that Mother never seemed to be concerned about Lily's feelings when she abused her daughter emotionally or physically, but on the other hand, she could never tolerate the least bit of unfair treatment of her daughter by other people.

In the following months, Lily received a few more letters from different young men indicating their willingness to hold her hand and fight together in the struggle to realize the beautiful communist dream. Needless to say, none of the young men chosen according to Grace's inferiority principle were the least bit appealing to Lily.

IV

Even after Grace came to Canada, she still blamed Lily for her refusal to accept one of these men when she was a good and presentable young girl.

"Your brother and sister followed my advice and are enjoying happy family life now," she said. "My heart aches whenever I think about the garbage you have chosen to put into your basket and the life you have destroyed with your own hands!"

Garbage? The sparkling eyes of Prince flashed through Lily's mind, followed by the thick, knotted brows of Majesty. She stood up, walked into the bathroom, and examined herself in the mirror.

The woman in the mirror looked hardened and tired, with puffy eyes and loose skin. Her youthful glow was fading, and a few gray hairs flecked her temples. They were particularly noticeable in her black hair. She picked up the scissors and cut them off carefully one by one. It made no difference, however, to the tough outlines reflected in the mirror. A shadow crept over her eyes.

She stared at herself and shook her head. It was strange to realize at this moment that she had never had a clear goal in her life. As a little girl in kindergarten and primary school, she used to hear Mother sighing with disappointment, "How could you be so plain, with your flat nose and yellowish skin? How come you don't take after me at all?"

Lily would lower her head to avoid Mother's stare, but a strong sense of inferiority remained deep inside her for the rest of her life. She always studied hard and tried to be at the top of her class, wherever she went, in the hope that Mother would feel proud of her one day. She was not smart, and had to spend more time and work harder than others to get extra marks. Year after year, her instinct was to always strive to be outstanding, at the sacrifice of comfort and pleasure. She had never asked herself why.

In her early days in Canada, she felt thrilled when one of her suitors, a Chinese professor from a university in Beijing, had declared that he would keep her as a housewife at home if she agreed to marry him. It was the first time she had ever heard such an idea. The novelty made her feel valuable and adored. Grace's reply to her excited letter, however, poured a bucket of cold water on her rosy plan.

"He's not suitable for you," Mother pointed out, "because you are neither gentle nor charming, and you have no sense of how to please a man, and therefore, you are not the type to be someone's housewife."

Indeed, I am not the gentle type, Lily thought. But how did I get to be this way?

A light-pink pearl necklace shone in her mind. That was a gift from her grandmother for Lily's sixth birthday. She wore it only once and never saw it again. When she wondered at its whereabouts on her following birthday, Grace replied with a stern look in her eyes. "Your grandma shouldn't have sent such a gift. I don't want to bring you up with any bad influence of bourgeois lifestyle!"

The training to become a hardened proletarian was not an easy one.

During the upheaval years of the 1970s, the whole family spent years in an isolated area in West China. Chicken was the only delicacy they could get from the local peasants' household. The first time Mother brought a live hen home, she ordered Lily to kill it.

Lily took the hen in her shaking hand and a knife in the other. She let the knife touch its neck but let it go at once when her mind was tortured by the scared look in its eyes and its horrified trembling.

The next month when Mother brought home another hen, Lily fed it a sleeping pill, mixed with cooked rice, hours before she carried out the execution.

After putting more than a dozen hens to death, her hands no longer shook.

When Majesty learned about her killing experiences, however, he frowned. Where were the men in your family? he questioned.

It was only then that Lily ever felt it odd. "Of course my father was not supposed to do it, because as a man, he had never done any kind of domestic chores," she explained. "My brother, as a future man, was not expected to receive any domestic training either."

A career woman would often end up competing with other men at work while also carrying on her back the wok, the children, and her man. Mother certainly has experienced this and that is why she wants a new lifestyle for me, Lily figured out.

I have been shaped, consciously or unconsciously, by Mother, to fulfill the dream she was deprived of in her prime. The new lifestyle, unfortunately, would include no children and no men, or at best just a secondary man.

Chapter 27
The Hunt for Decency

I

The law office was shut down as anticipated. Lily had no complaint. Mr. New had been kind enough to allow her ample time writing during office hours. She now stayed home and concentrated on her writing project, while receiving unemployment insurance.

Grace knew that writing, though a decent career, was not practical. Repeatedly, she warned Lily, "You'd better take advantage of my staying in Canada and learn how to stand on your own."

It was getting cold, making it impossible to stay outside for long. To create a quiet atmosphere for Lily, Grace took Baby to the public library nearby whenever it was open. When Baby was tired of going to the same place day after day, Lily suggested Mother take him to the shopping plaza for a change.

"I don't want to bring up your son in that unhealthy way!" Grace responded. "Wandering around in a commercial environment would cultivate bad habits in him. Besides, I feel bad when he makes funny noises as we pass by the candy stands and I can't afford to buy him even a bar of chocolate!"

Lily remembered the five dollars left from Mother's writing income, but she didn't mention that. She understood that Mother was actually worried about her poor financial status. She could see in Mother's face the anxiety and impatience growing day by day. Mother's visa would expire again in a couple of months, but her secret search for her severed love was still unsuccessful. If Lily hadn't found a good-paying job by then, Mother would have to leave.

The more Lily read Mother's diary, the more she was sympathetic with her lifelong wish. She was determined to try her best to help Mother realize her secret dream.

Lily started her job hunt again. To save money, she walked to the public library to read help-wanted ads in the newspaper.

One day in the library, she read the news that police had arrested four Chinese people who were trying to cross the border at Niagara Falls. They had been hiding under the bottom of a truck and found unconscious from inhaling too much carbon monoxide. No names were given for those who had attempted to sneak into the U.S., but the report mentioned that another Chinese man had been drowned not long ago trying to cross the Niagara River in a canoe.

She was struck by the news. The protruding front teeth, the hand missing a finger, and the trembling lips like a hummingbird loomed in her mind. Had he been drowned in the river currents, or had he been lying unconscious in the truck? Would someone inform his wife and children who were still looking forward to joining him in Canada? She shook her head and tried to push away these miserable thoughts. Who knows? He might have crossed the border safely and could be washing dishes in New York in an inconspicuous corner of Chinatown right now, she comforted herself.

When an ad for a Chinese language news reporter at the British Broadcasting Corporation appeared in the paper the next day, Lily's heart bounced. Her old profession back in China now seemed as remote as planet Venus in the night sky.

Under Mother's encouraging eyes, however, she borrowed a tape recorder from Helen and practiced reading a couple of articles selected by Grace from the Chinese newspaper.

Late at night, after Baby was finally asleep, Grace sat face to face with Lily and corrected every detail of her tone and expression, word by word, line after line. Lily trembled with a sense that she hadn't seen Mother so attentive, dedicated, and professional for a long time.

"The wind is blowing hard and snow has covered the ground …" She tried to read with a variety of tones and adjusted her expressions in different style, but Grace kept on shaking her head with a serious look in her eyes. Hours went by until finally, in the early dawn, Grace passed a version Lily had recorded. When the post office opened in the morning, Lily sent it to London, England, by courier.

II

While waiting for news from London, a human resource official advised Lily to seek help in the job search from the local MP. She mailed a letter to the MP's office listing all the wonderful professional experience she had had in China. To impress the MP further, she attached to the resumé her only photo, taken for her passport before she entered Canada.

She was thrilled when the MP responded quickly, inviting her to a meeting in his office at ten o'clock the next day.

Grace, in particular, was excited, believing her daughter's miserable fate was about to end soon with the precious help of the honoured and distinguished. "You should have done this a long time ago!" she sighed with regret.

After breakfast in the morning, Lily looked in the mirror and worried. "The photo I sent to the MP was taken many years ago. If he is expecting to meet a pretty young girl with innocent eyes and an energetic bounce, he will surely be disappointed."

She worked on her hair for quite a while, parting it on the left side, in the middle, then on the right. Nowhere could she find any trace of the brilliant girl in the photo. It had been months since she had visited the hairdresser. Her hair was long and definitely needed a new cut. Realizing the unnecessary cost of keeping a fashionable hairstyle, she had tied her hair into a short ponytail again, like she used to.

Grace was watching her from the sitting room. Without a word, she must have sensed the reason for her daughter's worry. Opening up Lily's trunk, she went through it, searching for something suitable for her to wear to the important interview.

"Oh, look at the rags you have collected all these years!" Grace grumbled, throwing on the floor the old clothes Lily had acquired from church sales.

Before Lily finally stepped out the door, Grace examined her daughter from head to toe. Her eyes rested on Lily's face and she suggested hesitantly, "Perhaps you could use some makeup, like face powder or lipstick? That would help."

Lily shook her head. "I've never had any." She felt dismay and realized reluctantly that most women talked about confidence all the time, but when facing a man, they still couldn't forget they were women. "Don't worry, Mother," she comforted Grace as well as herself. "It is my knowledge, not my face, that matters."

Indeed, the MP showed no sign of surprise, when Lily walked into his office and sat down in front of him. "What can I do for you?" he asked, his manner polite, his smile charming, and his voice gentle, all matching with the cozy, clean office bright with large windows.

Lily told herself to look calm and started talking about the difficult situation she was in and the professional skills she could contribute if given the opportunity. The MP listened attentively, with a sympathetic nod now and then. She was almost touched. But somehow, she perceived in the neatly shaven face a subtle hint of hidden tolerance, coming, perhaps, from the tedious routines of his role.

"What kind of job is most suitable for you, in your opinion?" The words rolled out of his lips fluently. Obviously he must have repeated these thousands of times.

All at once, she felt that her anxiety all morning had been as silly as her presence in that office. "I would like to work in the Ministry of Foreign Affairs in Ottawa," she said abruptly, her nervousness totally gone. She had decided to cut short her interview and free the poor man from the boring roles he had to play.

The MP must have become accustomed to office-seekers who always overrated themselves. He showed no contempt at her ignorance and, instead, kept the same graceful look on his face.

"Let's see," he said, rubbing his smooth chin, "how about this. You write a letter indicating your qualifications and interest ..."

"To whom?" Lily asked, her voice doubtful.

"Naturally, you should address it to the Minister of Foreign Affairs. And I'll deliver it to his office when I go to Ottawa."

Lily thanked him and went home in despair. Of course, she wouldn't bother to write the futile letter.

III

Grace proved her strength by hiding her disappointment. "It seems we are too naïve for the politicians."

When Grace accompanied Lily to the grocery store that evening, she was drawn by the sight of many people waiting in line. Lily told her that they were buying lottery tickets, with the prize jumping to $10 million for the coming Wednesday draw.

Grace stopped walking and stared at the eye-catching display at the lottery stand.

"Have you ever bought a ticket?" she asked.

"Yes, a few times, when the hotel workers purchased tickets jointly. But I never won."

"How many tickets can I buy with five dollars?" She asked in a serious look. "Okay, help me with it." Her voice sounded determined.

Lily helped her to fill out four groups of numbers on the slip for Lotto 649 and checked the encore. Grace didn't conceal her careful choices of numbers, which were the birth dates of everyone in the family except Lily.

"I have to choose only the lucky ones," Grace explained, her eyes avoiding Lily's.

On Wednesday morning, Grace tried to control the pleasure in her voice as she told Lily, "I had a dream last night that I won the top prize! I always had the feeling that I am going to be a lucky person!"

"What are you going to do with the money if you really get it?" Lily asked, feeling that her mother still possessed the heart of a little girl.

"Me?" Grace's eyes shone with a rosy dream as she talked in smile. "First and foremost, I'll get you back to school, to do your PhD degree, while Baby can be sent to a good daycare. As for the rest of the money, I have always dreamed of the day when I would have a lot of money to give it freely to whoever needs it, as I wish, without hesitation!"

Though Grace was deeply disappointed on Thursday morning after learning the lottery results, her hope in the gambles of life was ignited once again, when a letter came from the BBC in England that same afternoon. Lily was informed that she had been selected for the short list and asked to come to Toronto for a written test and an interview.

Another sleepless night. Lily got up before dawn to catch the bus. When she arrived at the gorgeous hotel in downtown Toronto in the morning, she found she was the only female candidate among the eight people on the short list.

All of the men were dressed like professional businessmen, with elegant suits and polished shoes. Lily hid herself in a corner and avoided talking with anyone. She was wearing the same outfit she had worn for her meeting with the MP, her mother's navy blue wool sweater and a pair of dark pants. She felt like a crow hiding in the woods and observing magpies flying around singing happily under bright sunshine.

The test took two hours and was followed by an interview. Though Lily was not nervous facing the two women from the BBC, she realized her incompetence immediately when she was asked to comment on current news. She didn't even have a TV in her small apartment. When questions focused on her personal life, her confidence drained away totally. Pale-faced, she admitted she was a single mother with a little boy.

"Who's going to look after your son if you move to London?" one woman asked. "You would be required to work different shifts, including night ones."

Lily was stuck, her heart filled with a miserable feeling at the thought of separating from Baby. Looking through the window at the crowded high-rises competing with each other for space under the gray sky, she finally answered in a weak voice, "I'm afraid I would have to send my son to Beijing and have my mother take care of him so I would be able to work in London."

The BBC women eyed each other silently, asking no more questions.

IV

On her way home on the Greyhound bus, Lily felt deeply depressed. She had never regretted having Baby, though the role of being a single mother constantly hindered her career and life. Lily felt it was a pity that, unlike Mother, she had no man worth devoting her life to. But the child, whose arrival was her own choice, filled up the gap in her soul.

She recalled the last night in the beautiful, natural estate when Baby was conceived. All of a sudden, a warm feeling rushed into her chest, reminding her that actually the most pleasant and relaxing time she had had in Canada was that period, although she had worked as a servant.

Four years had gone by since she had left that house by the riverside. What had happened to the old lady? Did she still indulge in vodka? Has she been getting along well with her new servants related to the royal family of England? If not, would she welcome me back at her side? Would she agree to take in my mother, too? She had stated that she would not tolerate a baby crying in her house, but Baby was now grown up and seldom cried.

Lily was excited by the fresh idea. When the Greyhound stopped in downtown Mapleton late in the afternoon, she stepped directly onto a city bus going towards the riverside.

Her throat was choked with nostalgia as she walked through the familiar stone entrance, across the concrete bridge, past the deep valley, and along the winding driveway. Many fading memories revived.

Dusk was falling and her vision became blurred. She seemed to find a lively black dog rushing into the dark woods under summer's setting sun. She saw a white-haired old lady in pink pajamas calling her pet in a worried voice in the quiet orchard. She also saw the handsome figure of a Chinese man climbing up a big tree overlooking the snow-covered valley, trying to connect the hydro line broken in a fierce snowstorm.

Her sentimental reflections reached their climax as she finally came to the front of the white house standing alone on the hill.

She saw butterflies dancing around the fountain and bees buzzing among the roses. She saw a fair old lady standing at the marble doorway and greeting her smilingly. She saw a young Chinese couple singing emotionally in the snow-lit library....

She held her breath and knocked on the door. It was opened by a slim, brown-haired lady with a cell phone in one hand and a cigarette in the other.

"I am sorry," Lily apologized for her surprise visit, wondering how long this young woman had been working in this residence. "Is Mrs. Fortune at home? I worked for her years ago and have come back to see her."

"No," the young lady shook her head. "This is my home."

"Your home? Where is Mrs. Fortune, then?"

"I have no idea. I moved into this place in the summer." Seeing the disappointment in Lily's face, the young lady added, "Someone said that she was taken into a nursing home a couple of years ago."

"Do you know which nursing home?"

"I don't know."

"So you have bought this house?"

"No, I am just renting it. Somebody owns the whole estate and is turning it into a new residential development," the young lady replied. She then greeted someone on the cell phone with a joyful laugh and closed the door.

Turning around slowly, Lily noticed the changes that had taken place in the winter dreamland. She was shocked to find a winding sandy road through the meadow which used to make so much hard work for Majesty. She left the house and walked down towards the farther end of the estate. The bronze statue in the drained fountain had disappeared. The orchard had become flat ground. The duck pond and the swampy area where Victor chased deer and foxes had been filled in. The old cottage in the woods hanging above the running stream was gone, leaving only a dark fireplace and a chimney pointing to the sky. Far down the new sandy road was a huge, yellow bulldozer.

She shivered with cold. In the spreading dusk and the freezing winter air, she cast a last glance at the isolated house on the hill and bid a silent farewell to the vanished wonderland.

V

The snowy season had started and there was absolutely nowhere to go. Grace stayed at home with Baby now.

Lily noticed Mother staring into space for long periods. But her meditation was often interrupted by the little boy who refused to sit quietly reading the old cartoons Grace had brought from China for him. He attempted to open the door all the time, ran out of the apartment to the yard outside, or climbed up the staircase whenever Grace lost sight of him. While chasing him back, Grace would grumble that the boy was especially disobedient when Lily was present.

Lily looked at Baby but said nothing. The boy didn't talk much, but he understood a lot. He could easily figure out who was willing to spoil him. For the first few months after he was born, he slept very little and cried day and night. She would pick him up at his first cry, hold him in her arms, and walk around the apartment with exhausted steps until he fell asleep again. The unconditional love was formed this way, as she touched every inch of his tender body and watched his growth with wonder and surprise day after day.

Had I been with Mother when I was a baby, she might have spoiled me the same way, Lily concluded.

One day Grace discovered a new way of occupying the boy by encouraging him to jump down from the couch to the floor repeatedly, holding his hand.

Six, seven … fifteen, sixteen … twenty…

With Grace's counting and the thumping at her back, Lily tried hard to fix her eyes on the computer screen. Yet for a long time she could not write a single word, her mind occupied by a robust image of a man from the past.

Reflecting on the paths she had trodden, she realized that the anonymous letter many years ago accusing her of having been the "mistress" of the American instructor had been her Waterloo. Without that letter, she would not have had to marry a man she didn't love and eventually unroll a life tapestry full of unharmonious colours.

The American Bear and his lonely roaring in the empty sports ground came fresh in her mind. She wondered what had happened to him after all these years. If he returned to China today, he might not feel his lust for flesh so frustrated anymore, with the situation changed in that puritan land. On an impulse, she sent a letter to the home address given to her before he left China.

Within a week, his response arrived in her mailbox. It was a long one, depicting his wanderings in all corners of the world and some reflections on his China days.

Curiously, I look upon my years in China with great nostalgia and longing, and they seem like years of adventure, though when I was there they often seemed terribly lonely and difficult. I have only myself to blame for much of the difficulty, especially my failure to learn Chinese.

I am not very happy with my American life, which seems flat and tedious compared to life in Asia. I don't want to get older but obviously there is not much I can do about it. Asia seems more interesting to me but maybe that's a reaction to America which seems to have no place for me.

When I look at myself in China during those years, mostly I feel ashamed and embarrassed by what a proud, ignorant, loud-mouthed fool I was. With performances like mine, it's no surprise that many Chinese distrust and are appalled by the empty-headed arrogance of Americans and Westerners. If I saw myself now as I was then, I'd probably hate myself—though it's true, I can't remember much.

China seemed difficult and cold but now, in retrospect, I see just how incredibly generous and kind most people were.

Are you studying in Canada on a Canadian scholarship? I am interested in how you finally got the opportunity to study abroad after all these years. You were always incredibly strong-willed and focused. You impressed me with the inner resilience and strength of your nature. It shouldn't surprise me that this strength of character and willingness to struggle hard to achieve goals has brought you success. Best wishes, always.

Just as China has changed, he has changed, too, she mused. The image of the bear, a lovely bear now, stayed in Lily's mind.

Baby was finally exhausted by the jumping game and sat quietly on the floor playing with his puzzles. Grace fell back in the sofa and sighed heavily, her eyes shut, looking more exhausted than the little boy.

Lily turned and looked at her in concern. "Are you tired, Mom?"

Hearing no response, Lily tried to focus her attention on the screen again. A moment later, she heard Grace's voice in a sad tone. "You can write whatever way you like now. I have thought it over."

Lily's fingers stopped typing and her ears perked up.

"For your sake, I will have to sacrifice my own dignity..."

Lily's throat became tightened. Mother's pride had slowly eroded away as she endured the humiliation of their depressed life.

Since the family now lived on the limited income from Lily's unemployment insurance, Grace calculated carefully to save every dollar she could. When Grace's birthday came and they went shopping, she bought as usual only the cheapest vegetables—cabbages, carrots, and potatoes. Lily suggested they buy a live fish which was Mother's favourite, but Grace turned it down. Lily found Mother's eyes attracted by the new crop of Red Delicious apples shining on the shelf so she put a few into their cart. Grace compared the prices and noticed that green Granny Smiths were fifty cents cheaper. Without a word, she put the Red Delicious back. She also brought home a giant pumpkin, cut it into small pieces and stir-fried them with rice.

"They may not taste very good, but they are nutritious," she said encouragingly. "Don't you think we are eating much better than the peasants did in the 1970s?"

As Lily looked at Mother, she remembered a small incident. A warm current flew over her heart, and her eyes moistened.

VI

Government policy of the day required all intellectuals in the cities to be re-educated by the rural peasants. The family was separated. Father went to a farm in central China with Lily's brother and sister, while Mother took Lily to a small village deep in the mountains outside the Great Wall.

The village of about thirty households was on a piece of barren and stony land. Besides Grace, there were three other intellectuals sent from Beijing. The four of them worked in the fields with the peasants during the day and read newspapers and government documents to the villagers at night. This new way of life was designed by the government to improve the backward rural society.

Grace and her colleagues took turns cooking and shared the cost of food. The food was meager and simple. For months, there was only cornbread, pickles, and gruel on the table. The intellectuals followed the strict rules, and worked, ate, and slept the same way the peasants did. But the villagers were still jealous of them, since the city people were given wheat bread and rice by the state.

Lily lived in a residential high school in town and came to join Mother during holidays. At fourteen, she was still as short and skinny as a twelve-year-old. Grace worried. There was no place to buy good food, and it would create sensational, envy-inspiring news in the small village if she cooked anything special.

Most peasant families in the village raised a couple of hens in their homes, but the eggs were saved to exchange for table salt. On a rainy day when everyone was staying indoors, Grace walked miles across the hillside to another village and found nine eggs.

"How do you want to eat the eggs?" she asked Lily, voice gentle and smooth as the egg in her hand.

Lily's mouth watered as she said, "Deep oil fried!" She had not eaten an egg for at least two years. Turnip soup with cornbread was the year-round menu in the school. Grace hesitated, afraid that the smell of the cooking would bring attention and criticism. But seeing the desire in Lily's eyes, she finally decided to run the risk.

After dark, Grace's colleagues sneaked into her room secretly. Grace closed the door and told them in a constricted voice, "I have a treat for you today."

Lily sat down in front of the mud stove and helped Mother look after the fire. She added dried corn stalks to the dancing flames and watched with happy excitement. Mother poured some oil into the wok. Happy sizzling noises and a good smell filled the air to produce the gold-laced eggs.

The first six eggs went to Mother's colleagues waiting on the brick bed. They ate quietly, nodding in satisfaction. Then they snuck out as silently as they had come. Lily waited anxiously as Mother took the last three eggs out of the wok and put them neatly into a bowl. It's our turn at last! She exclaimed in her heart.

Just at that moment, the door was pushed open. Mother raised her head, fear in her face. Standing in the drizzle were two small children in dirty rags. They were peasant children who lived next door.

Obviously, the smell had brought the unexpected guests. Mother calmed down, waved them in, closed the door, and gave each of them an egg. Standing by the stove, the children gobbled up the delicacy hurriedly and reached out their small hands again.

Mother's eyes fell on the remaining egg in the bowl. Lily's heart sunk.

"Lily ... Could you wait for next time? I will cross the hill again ... some time later ... " Mother asked hesitantly. Her eyes looked uneasy, but her chopsticks had already reached into the bowl to separate the egg into two parts.

Lily bit her lips and nodded silently. Tears of disappointment gushed out of her eyes and down her cheeks.

"Come on! How could you cry over such a small thing?" Mother said. Her hand stopped. She looked at the two kids and looked at Lily again. Finally, she cut the egg into three pieces.

Chapter 28
The Wish of the Departing Hero

I

When Lily typed the last sentence of her book, Christmas was at the door. She printed the first three chapters and mailed them to a few prestigious Canadian publishers. The rock in her heart was not removed, though, as she started the anxious wait for replies, the final test of her search for a more meaningful life in Canada.

On Friday morning, Jade's phone call broke the heavy atmosphere in the small apartment. To concentrate on her final draft, in the past few weeks, Lily had avoided all social activities and Grace had turned down all visitors. Lily was surprised to hear from Jade that dramatic changes were taking place in the small Chinese community during her absence.

Ever since gossip about Unicorn's alleged affair with Camellia had permeated every corner, the couple had stopped attending the church services. Madam Jewelry, the Tongue practitioner who had been advised by Minister Wong to pick another church, came to the rescue and introduced them to Minister Yu in Toronto.

Yu had come from Hong Kong years ago. He started his first church in Toronto single-handedly by stopping every Chinese passerby on the sidewalk. Summer in the river and winter in the bathtub, he washed every single soul who had been conquered by his tongue. Gradually, he had established nine churches with Chinese followers in Toronto.

A week after Unicorn and Jade had been baptized by Yu in his bathtub, they started the tenth church for Yu in Mapleton, with Madam Jewelry's assistance. The first service held in his home attracted more than twenty participants. The new church doubled in size weekly after Yu's magic prayers cured one man's headaches and brought an unemployed engineer back into the job market. Madam Jewelry contacted the mall and secured the community room there for the group's Sunday services, for free.

Since many of the participants were from Minister Wong's congregation, the situation drove him crazy. In the following Sunday sermon, he read from the Bible and preached, "Don't be seduced by heresies! Whoever leaves our church is an ungrateful traitor! Those who dare to participate in heretical activities will be expelled forever, I warn you!"

Mrs. Rice had also been to the new church, for she felt her insomnia became better after Yu had massaged her forehead with his hand in praying. She stopped going, however, after Minister Wong's warning.

Yu's reaction was considerate. He advised Unicorn not to take away lambs from other people's sheepfolds, but to look for missing ones on the roadside.

To solve the couple's concern about the heresy label, Yu flipped over pages in the New Testament and assured them that the Tongue had received no objection from the Good Shepherd.

For Unicorn's dream of going to the famous theological institute in California, Yu's praying worked well again. Five thousand dollars were raised miraculously in one week from his churches in Toronto. Unicorn quit his job at the university without a second thought and the family was to leave for the west after Christmas. That night,

Mrs. Rice was holding a potluck farewell party for the couple in her home.

Grace was alerted by the news. "A theological institute in California? Which one? Is it famous?" she asked.

Lily caught the light in Grace's eye. She was hit by a fresh idea.

II

In the late afternoon, the sky hung dark with heavy clouds in the cold air. Unicorn and Jade drove to Lily's home to pick them up.

Lily chatted with the couple while Grace prepared food for the party. Grace had made a vegetarian pizza. After almost a year's practice with the oven, she had become a semi-expert in baking.

Jade was surprised to see the Bible theme puzzles Baby was playing with on the floor. "Ah, he is a smart boy and puts together the complicated picture so well!" She pointed at the puzzle showing the city of Sodom destroyed in burning flames while a good family picked by God was escaping.

"Familiarity leads to skills," Lily responded and asked, "Why didn't you bring Moses with you to the party?"

"He prefers staying home alone. He still feels indifferent to us, for having left him for so many years with his grandparents." After a pause, Jade added, "I will bring up my second child totally by myself."

"Are you pregnant again?" Lily asked in surprise.

Jade nodded. "Please keep it a secret! You know, at my age, forty-three, it is very risky to bear a child, and I don't know if the pregnancy will be successful or not."

Lily thought about the dispute the couple had a while ago and wondered if the pregnancy was Jade's secret attempt to strengthen the marriage. She remembered Camellia and asked about her.

To Lily's surprise, Camellia had left the couple and moved back to Old Chia a few weeks ago. "Mrs. Rice claimed this as one more proof of her excellent service to God. But God knows how much Unicorn has done to help Camellia," Jade stated, glancing at Unicorn. He seemed to be devoted to observing Baby working on the puzzles and was paying no attention to the conversation.

"Doesn't she want a divorce anymore?" Lily asked.

"Who knows? But Unicorn must feel sad when she left with all her belongings except the Bible he gave her."

While Lily was trying to figure out what had made Camellia change her mind, Grace appeared at the kitchen door. "The pizza is ready. We can go now."

III

"Are you going back to China after your graduation?" Lily asked Unicorn as they drove out of the parking lot.

"Yes, I will go back to my hometown and try to set up a church there with my own hands. You know, it's one of the most backward areas in west China. All these years in Canada, I have felt uneasy whenever I think of the peasants there. Year after year, they live like ants, toil in the yellow earth, and die hopelessly. I know I could bring some happiness to their lives!"

"How?" Lily asked.

"It's simple. Just telling them the facts—that Jesus Christ died for us and will come back to take us with him, as long as we believe in him."

"Would they believe your words?"

"Why not?" Unicorn asked. He told her that he had met a visiting composer in Toronto recently. She was a country girl who didn't even finish Grade 7. She had become a Christian when someone brought her to church and told her the story of Jesus Christ. She had never learned music, but miraculously, she started to compose beautiful, lyrical hymns with Chinese melodies. Tens of thousands of peasants were touched by her singing and have become Christians. She composed more than nine hundred hymns, though she didn't even read musical notes. She would sing, and somebody else would record the notes. Her songs were made into CDs and were hot sales in Mr. Yu's churches.

"If she, as a semi-illiterate, was able to convert people with her music," Unicorn said, "why can't I, with my knowledge of the Bible, achieve even greater results?"

Lily let out a heavy sigh. "Many people left China originally for the material riches in North America. But eventually, we find that what keeps us here is more the spiritual wealth, something China took great pride in for thousands of years but which has been totally destroyed by the materialist bombshell."

"It's never too late!" Unicorn replied in an encouraging tone.

"Would Jade and Moses be willing to go back to China with you?" Lily asked. Jade was talking with Grace in the back seats and paying no attention to their conversation.

"I understand they both like Canada much better and would rather stay here," Unicorn answered. "I am not going to force anyone to join me. Among the people who really need me, I won't feel lonely."

The words struck Lily as familiar. "Are you taking Norman Bethune as your model?"

"In a way," Unicorn nodded. "But he was there to treat the wounded flesh of the Chinese, whereas I am planning to treat their wounded souls!"

Chapter 29
Unfit for the Threshold

I

Outside Mrs. Rice's residence, the driveway and the street were already full of parked cars. Lily got out of the car and shuddered at the cold air.

The sitting room was lit up by a huge chandelier. While Jade was showing Grace some new church publications, Lily took Baby into the family room and left him to watch cartoons with a few other children. Looking around, she found Mrs. Rice busy talking with guests. She went into the kitchen and found Camellia by the counter.

"Hi, Lily!" Camellia greeted her with an uneasy smile. "I haven't seen you for so long! Mrs. Rice said that you were very busy and refused to talk to anyone. What are you up to these days?"

"Nothing serious, just looking for a job. What about you?" Lily asked.

Camellia pointed at the crabs in a large bowl and a roll of soy-sauced roast beef on the counter. "I came here this morning and prepared some dishes for Mrs. Rice ..."

"Are these crabs? They are more like spiders!" Lily looked at the mini crabs, laughing. "They should still be in a daycare."

"There are king-sized ones in the store, but those are much more expensive!" Camellia lowered her voice, "Mrs. Rice is undergoing financial difficulties and could hardly afford to buy delicacies anymore. She complained a couple of times to me that her husband hasn't been sending money home from Taiwan for quite a while. It's funny, she asked me to call her every day before Christmas. I suspect she just wanted to remind me to send her a gift!"

"Does she really mean that?" Lily asked, wondering if it was Mrs. Rice or Camellia who had been over-smart.

"Of course she does! She had mentioned a few times that she liked my cashmere sweater very much!" Camellia claimed as she picked up the knife and sliced a couple of pieces of the roast beef. "This was brought in by a guest. It tastes pretty good. Try some!"

While Lily was trying the beef, Camellia changed the subject. "You must have heard that I have returned home, haven't you?"

Lily nodded. "Yes, I just heard that today. Don't you want your divorce anymore?"

Camellia put down the knife, and looked at Lily with a serious look. "Something happened and my staying at Jade's home has been totally worthless." She crossed her arms and shook her head.

It turned out that Camellia's lover, Dwarf, had been arrested recently and accused of involvement in a pornography business which had trapped more than ten school girls, aged twelve to fourteen.

Dwarf's Tiger Power Pill business had gone bankrupt almost overnight when Viagra came onto the Chinese market. As a way of making quick money, Dwarf and his new girlfriend worked as pimps forcing his victims to sell their virginity to the newly rich and powerful. The cost to the buyers was the equivalent of six hundred Canadian dollars per virgin, but more than half went into the pocket of the pimps. The buyers were either rich businessmen or corrupt officials who could have their costs reimbursed as business expenses. Business was good since a popular myth among those men believed that sleeping with one virgin would bring three years of good fortune.

The alarm sounded when one of the victims became pregnant and went for an abortion. The investigations ferreted out not only the rich men and the pimps, but also a city police chief!

Camellia was shocked. Her mother had told her on the phone that the big scandal had been widely covered on Chinese TV, with Dwarf's sickening image on the screen over and over.

Her mother's voice like piercing police car sirens, Camellia's crazy passion for Dwarf vanished like smoke. Her flesh crept when her thoughts fell upon her stupid struggle to become the wife of an ugly toad. After her initial panic was over, she destroyed all her souvenirs of him. Flushing them down the toilet, she suddenly realized there was no reason now to build up a year of days separated from her husband when she no longer planned to marry Dwarf. Without a second thought, she left Jade and Unicorn's apartment.

Camellia ended her accounting with a long sigh. The thick makeup failed to disguise the tiny wrinkles around her eyes and the clouds inside them. The cruel truth, like autumn winds, had swept away the last trace of youthful charm of the mature woman, who now looked her age.

Lily was still troubled by the sensational news. "You should have noticed his salacious tendencies long before this."

Camellia admitted, twisting her fingers nervously, that she had known of Dwarf's affairs with other women, but she didn't like the feeling of being defeated by the other competitors and couldn't tolerate the insult of being abandoned. Besides, Dwarf had pictures and videotape of her naked, and she had been afraid that he might release them to others if he was irritated. After learning about the scandal, Camellia urged her mother to look for the photos at Dwarf's residence, but it was too late as the police had already seized his nest.

Lily suddenly remembered her doubts about Dwarf's secret sign on Camellia and mentioned it, believing it wouldn't be sensitive now. It turned out that Dwarf had learned a folk prescription recorded in an ancient Chinese book composed during the fourth century.

You would start by feeding a lizard with cinnabar until its body turned completely red. Then smash the lizard into red paste and spread it on a girl's body. She wouldn't be able to wash the sign off for a long time unless she had sex with a man. It claimed to work well on virgins, but its effectiveness on experienced women was hard to prove.

Lily held back her curiosity about its function on Camellia and inquired about her current status at home.

Old Chia and Dragon were happy about Camellia's return. They still felt humiliated, however, about the scandals Camellia had caused. Dragon pushed his father to look for a job elsewhere, and Old Chia had started sending resumés. Camellia was indecisive about her future, but at least she could enjoy the temporary peace of a place she could call a home.

"I just need to wait one more year. Once I get my Canadian citizenship, I will go back to China! With a Canadian passport in my hand, I can choose anyone I like!" Camellia looked around and whispered, "There are a few men in China who would like to see me and I have started communicating with them on the phone."

Lily couldn't help but to admire Camellia's high efficiency in handling love affairs. "Be careful not to be caught by Dragon when you talk on the phone," she warned her.

"With my cell phone, I can make calls anywhere outside home now …" Suddenly, Camellia remembered something. "Oh, Lily, I forgot to tell you. I got a call from Big Brother a couple of days ago. Do you still remember him?"

Lily nodded. "Yes, the one in New York, right? What's new?"

"He talked about half an hour, advising me on this and that, as casually as before. But in the end he told me that he was diagnosed with cancer and had prepared a parcel, which he felt should be left to me," Camellia paused, her eyes moistened.

Lily sighed. "If I were you, I would go to New York and stay with him for the rest of his life."

Before Camellia responded, Jade came into the kitchen. Camellia changed into all smiles, as if nothing had happened.

Lily helped them put all the dishes out on the dining room table and went into the sitting room. "Dinner is ready. Shall we start eating?" she asked Mrs. Rice.

"Wait a little bit longer." Mrs. Rice waved her hand. "Minister Wong has not arrived yet."

"Is he joining us tonight?" Unicorn looked surprised at the news.

"Yes," replied Mrs. Rice. "He is at the church having a final talk with the people who are going to be baptized at Christmas ..."

Before she had finished, the doorbell rang. Minister Wong entered with five more people. Among them was an all-smiles Old Chia.

Lily found Unicorn's eyes lit up. He was obviously touched by Minister Wong's presence at the farewell party, taking it as an olive branch from the arrogant man. He walked over to the doorway and shook Minister Wong's hand warmly.

II

After the meal, Lily helped Camellia bring cups of ginseng tea into the sitting room for everyone. Minister Wong sat in the middle of the couch in a relaxed manner, cleaning his teeth with a toothpick while chatting with Unicorn about his trip to California. Lily could see that Minister Wong was relieved that a thorn had been pulled out of his throat.

"Are you going to come back to Mapleton when you finish your studies in California?" asked Minister Wong.

"No," said Unicorn. "I have decided to go to China."

"China?" Minister Wong raised his voice. "It's going to be very hard for your family to survive there. Apart from the government's problematic attitude, the congregation there will not be able to support you well financially."

"I don't mind," Unicorn replied. "Our generation experienced living among the peasants in the 1970s. The worst is that you don't have meat to eat for weeks, you might sleep in a mud house with snakes and mosquitoes, and you have to climb up mountains and travel on muddy roads. What else?"

Minister Wong smiled. "Of course your sacrifice is respectable. Being realistic, however, you could easily find a clergy job in North America. You are aware of the shortage of Mandarin-speaking clergymen these days. Quite a few churches in Toronto are hiring at the moment and the pay would be much better than ..."

Unicorn cut in impatiently. "But I feel China needs me more than North America does."

Minister Wong made no more comments. He took the ginseng tea from the coffee table, tasted it, and nodded with satisfaction. "Hmm. The taste is just right." He looked around for Camellia. "Hey, Camellia! Did you soak the ginseng in lukewarm water first before chopping it into pieces for boiling as I told you? Yes? A perfect job!"

As Camellia was adding more tea to his cup, Minister Wong asked her, "Have you made up your mind yet? Old Chia is going to be baptized the day after tomorrow. I hope you will join him."

Camellia gave him a sweet glance as she replied. "I am afraid I need more time to think about such a significant step."

"Come on!" Minister Wong seemed to enjoy teasing her and said playfully, "Think about the hours I have spent trying to wash a scarlet stone whiter than snow. Some people will never be ready until the day they are leaving this world. Remember, we do it only twice a year. If you miss this time, you will have to wait till Easter."

Camellia giggled. "Let Old Chia go ahead, then. I will wait till

Easter. Oh, dear, I forgot the red bean soup! Lily, would you come and help me with it?" She made her escape smartly.

In the kitchen, Camellia whispered to Lily, "Minister Wong is so pushy. When he talked with Old Chia in our apartment last time, I treated him with courtesy and good food, expecting that he might help Old Chia find a job. But I am not willing to be enrolled as one of his soldiers."

"Why not?" Lily teased her. "Didn't you hear him bragging that he had already washed you whiter than snow?"

Camellia shook her head. "There are too many restrictions in life for Christians. I'd rather swim in open water and breathe freely for the rest of my life, not be smothered in a fish tank."

Lily and Camellia carried the red bean soup into the family room first, where Grace and a few other women were listening to hymns on the CD player. Jade had just told them the story of the country girl and her miraculous music. Lily helped Baby with the sweet soup while the music filled the house.

A nail-scarred hand knocks at the long closed door.
A gentle voice draws my heart to follow.
Grateful tears run like streams,
Words from my bosom rush towards you.
Fully aware the road leads to a cross,
Windy, rainy, and hard to travel,
Yet held by the loving hand of our Lord,
There is no reason that I won't go.
I hear you calling from over the sea.
China, China, come to me.
Oh, Lord, we have found you.

When the music stopped, Lily exclaimed to Jade, "No wonder it was so successful. The colloquial language and folk music are much more adaptable to the Chinese ear and tongue than the rigid trans-lations and western music in the conventional hymns."

"It all depends," Grace disagreed. "The conventional hymns are also nicely translated. But they probably appeal more to the educated."

Lily kept silent. She knew that Grace had read through all the verses in the hymnbook translated and edited by her teacher.

Unicorn was standing by and watching. He suddenly remembered something and talked to Jade in a low voice. Jade smiled, nodded, and waved Lily to come over.

"Unicorn and I would like to see you baptized before we go as our farewell souvenir to you," she said.

"Baptized? Didn't you complain that no church has enough quali-fied Christians around?" Lily joked.

Unicorn replied with embarrassment. "Minister Yu told me that the church is not there for only the righteous man ..."

Jade whispered to Lily, "Would you come to our home on Christ-mas and let Minister Yu wash you in our bathtub?"

Lily shook her head. She couldn't forget the scene when Madam Jewelry demonstrated her Tongue skill in the mall, and felt it diffi-cult to appreciate the practice. "I would rather be baptized in a more normal church, if I have to be."

Unicorn and Jade discussed for a minute and said, "Okay, let's talk to Minister Wong about it."

III

Although the suggestion had arisen rather abruptly, Lily felt there was no harm in having a discussion. She left Baby to Grace and fol-lowed the couple into the sitting room and sat in a chair across from Minister Wong, who was chatting with Old Chia.

Unicorn waited until Old Chia had left and brought up the issue with Minister Wong. "I think Lily is ready to become a Christian now. She has always shown great interest in studying the Bible and in being a real Christian, not just one who pays lip service. We would be happy to see her baptized before we leave Mapleton."

Minister Wong was surprised at his request. He remained silent, but his gaze flickered from one to the other, as if he was trying to figure out if this was a trap. Finally, he said to Lily, "I haven't seen you in church for quite a while ..."

"She has been very busy recently," Jade explained for Lily. "But I am sure she is sincerely persuaded of the truth of God."

"How long have you declared yourself a Christian?" Minister Wong asked.

"I have been deciding to be a Christian for a long time," Lily said. "I ... I think declaring out loud and truly believing in your heart are two different things."

"In that case," Minister Wong replied, "you can make an appointment with the secretary and wait till I find time to talk to you ..."

Unicorn seemed unhappy at his attitude. "Minister Yu of my church baptizes people whenever one is ready. He has the record of baptizing more than a hundred people in one month ..."

Minister Wong waved to him impatiently. "But our church does not work in that careless way. I need to talk with you first before I can make any decision, Lily."

He sipped at the tea, straightened up his body, and asked seriously, "Why do you want to become a Christian?"

Lily thought for seconds before she spoke her mind slowly. "For many years I have been looking for a beautiful faith. I came to Canada because this is Norman Bethune's home country. To me, he was the embodiment of that beautiful faith. After arriving in Canada, however, I eventually found out that Norman Bethune was the ideal man because he had been brought up in the Christian culture ..."

"Wait, wait!" Minister Wong stopped her. "Whom are you talking about? Who is Norman Beth—?"

"He was a Canadian," Jade explained to him. "He died in China and was held up by Mao as a role model for the whole Chinese population ..."

"Fine, let's move on." Minister Wong changed the subject. "Do you accept Jesus Christ as the only God?"

Lily nodded. "I think I can accept that. At least the ideas he promoted are the best ones I have found so far."

"Do you acknowledge that he was born of a virgin?"

Lily thought for a moment before she answered. "Why not? There are many ways for women to get pregnant without having sex."

Minister Wong frowned but went on with the questions. "Do you accept that he was crucified for our sins and that he rose again three days after his death?"

"There are many things we cannot understand, but I am willing to accept it, since it is encouraging to think that way."

Minister Wong asked again, "Are you willing to put yourself into the Lord's hands?"

"Sure," Lily nodded. "And not just me. I wish to put my son's life into the Lord's hands as well." She looked at Unicorn and Jade and suddenly felt overwhelmed with thoughts she would like to share with them. "As first generation immigrants, many of us came here alone, without family and relatives. Before I became a mother, I was fearless. But since I have had Baby, I have changed ... It is really painful to think that when you gave life to someone you love the most, you were also giving him at the same time the unavoidable fate of death down the road. On many lonely nights, when I look at Baby while he is sound asleep, I am seized by a terrible fear. We all have to die sooner or later. It's a pity that Chinese philosophy is secular and provides no consolation related to death—although it deals very well with the issues of life. That's why I'd like to bring up Baby in the Christian faith."

She paused for a few seconds, twisting her fingers to control herself, before going on. "It still remains a riddle what will really happen to us after death. But I hope, when that unavoidable day comes, Baby will not be crushed by a hopeless sorrow at losing his mother forever, the only person close to him in this world. The Christian faith that his mother is living happily in heaven with the Lord and that he might see her again would comfort his lonely soul and help him go on with his own life ..."

Her nose twitched. She bit her lips hard to stop her tears running out. Jade held Lily's hand in hers. Unicorn buried his face in his palms.

When she had calmed down a bit, Lily went on. "Probably my reasons sound too pragmatic and not as lofty as they should be. But I'm being honest."

Minister Wong remained in silence. He cleared his throat, and said slowly, "I don't mind adding one more person to our list on Sunday, although this comes at very short notice indeed." Seeing their attention focused on him, he continued. "However, some problems have to be cleared up before we can go on."

Lily rubbed her eyes, wiped her nose, and asked, "What kind of problems?"

Minister Wong's sharp eyes swept over her face. An embarrassing moment passed before he asked in a low voice, "Have you ever been divorced?"

Lily blushed. How does he know about my private affairs? It must be from Mrs. Rice. She looked down awkwardly at her knees, telling herself to be calm. Finally, she decided to be honest. She raised her head and faced him. "Yes, I have."

Unicorn and Jade shot glances at each other, both recognizing a huge obstacle in her path to getting baptized. Minister Wong's face remained serious, but there was a glare behind his glasses. "Good, you have acknowledged this. Now, you must explain to me clearly who was the one at fault, you or your ex-husband?"

"Sorry, what do you mean?" Lily failed to understand. In most divorce cases, including her own, it was rather difficult to distinguish who was in the right and who was in the wrong.

Minister Wong cleared his throat again and raised his voice. "If your ex-husband committed adultery, then he would be the guilty one in the divorce. If you committed adultery, then you would be the guilty one."

At this point, Jade cut in smartly to remind Lily of the proper reply. "I think it was the fault of your ex-husband, wasn't it, Lily?"

Lily ignored her help, trying to make a quick analysis of her relationship with Prince. When Jade patted her on the shoulder, she was startled, wakened from her thoughts.

"No, he didn't commit adultery. Neither did I." She shook her head. "Before I got in touch with Christianity, I used to think it was all his fault." She looked bravely at Unicorn, Jade, and then Minister Wong. "But after studying the Bible, I no longer think the same way. Honestly, it would be fair to say that neither he nor I were at fault."

"Okay, now tell me," Minister Wong continued, "were you abandoned by him or were you the deserter?"

"I ... I was the one trying to leave the marriage," Lily replied, her back moist with sweat.

"In that case," Minister Wong's voice turned stern, "you would have to acknowledge that you have committed a serious sin. Such a sin is not unpardonable, but it could hinder your service to God. You also have to convince me of your sincerity in promising never to commit the same sin again."

Lily felt irritated. "Sin? I have never felt regret for the divorce. I don't understand why I should acknowledge any sort of sin in that respect. I have learned lessons from the divorce, but I can't guarantee that I would never do the same thing again in my life."

Minister Wong leaned back in the sofa, let out a brief laugh, and said, "Well fine! I am afraid I cannot baptize you under these circumstances."

Lily was stunned. She opened her mouth a few times, but uttered no sound.

"Wait a moment!" Unicorn tapped his fingertips on the coffee table and asked Minister Wong hastily, "Could you please tell me which part of the Bible says that people who have divorced cannot be baptized?"

The question sounded provocative. Minister Wong's face dropped. "Well, I thought you knew everything!" He looked into the distance as he gave his sarcastic reply. "Listen. God hates divorce. He hates the hardness of the human heart. That is the primary factor leading to the destructive sin of divorce. This is clearly indicated in the book of Matthew. The Lord rejected the Pharisee's request to divorce. He said, if your wife has not committed adultery, you must not divorce her to marry someone else. If you do, you are unfaithful. A woman who divorces her husband and marries again is also unfaithful. Don't those words mean anything to you?"

Unicorn had no intention of giving in. "Still, there is no indication that a divorcee cannot be baptized!"

Minister Wong raised his eyebrows. "Sorry, sir. As the minister of this church, I am responsible for the dignity and reputation of my church and parish."

Unicorn's tolerance reached its end. He hit the coffee table hard with his fist and stood up. "Okay, let's see! We will find out if the Earth still turns on its axis without you!"

As Unicorn pulled Lily up from her chair and led her out of the room, Minister Wong sneered behind their backs, "Fine, why not check with the Tongue practitioner who baptized you? I'm sure he collects not only communists, but divorcees as well!"

Chapter 30
The Dream's Signal

I

Snow arrived on Christmas Eve and lasted well into the new year. The sky remained heavy with clouds, and the old streets in downtown Mapleton lost their charm, with messy slush and dog dirt on top of snow piles.

For days, Lily stayed despondent at home. She had received disappointing responses from the publishers she had contacted. From the form letters she received—the kind sent to unknown writers like her—she knew they hadn't even bothered to read her manuscript.

One evening, she stood by the window and stared at the snowflakes flying outside. The apartments where Mouse-colonel and Grand Master Iron had lived before were occupied by new tenants now, with different curtain patterns, nicer. She was standing there soaked in a nostalgic feeling when she heard Grace murmuring behind her in a soft tone.

"I had a dream last night. There were blooming reed catkins flying allover the sky ... everywhere ..."

Lily looked back. Grace was leaning against the couch. Her eyes stayed fixed in space, her mouth half open as the words slipped out with a gentle, tremulous sound.

Here bloom winter jasmines.
There buds weeping forsythia.
Bathed in waves of rotating hues,
My soul sweetened by intoxicating aroma …

Lily felt her neck swelling and stomach pinching at the sound of the familiar lines. She lost her patience and asked in a sarcastic tone, "Is that all he has written to you? That doesn't sound appealing at all."

"Of course he has written many others." Grace seemed happy to start on this topic. She cleared her throat, raised her voice a little bit, and recited more to Lily.

At the wooden pavilion ten miles out of town,
I bade farewell to friends and together we sang.
Among the crowds my eyes searched for you,
I caught smiles in your face yet tears hidden byond
Silently I begged the wind passing through,
To bring you blessings along …

Seeing Lily listening attentively, Grace went on with another one.

Expecting your letter,
As a sleepless man no longer young,
Waiting for Venus to appear at dawn.
Tortured by endless missing of thee,
I silently call, Grace, Grace, in plea …

Grace's voice faded. Lily was touched by the nostalgia in her eye. She saw a seagull hovering over and kissing the broad surface of dark water, searching for a long lost treasure. Mom was lucky, she thought, for at least she has enough happy memories to last a lifetime, while

my youth was a piece of barren land, with not a single flower blooming. The thought made her even more dismayed.

Late that night, Lily started to feel a pain in her abdomen. Drinking cups of hot water didn't relieve it. It came on without any reason, since they hadn't had any special food for dinner, and Grace and
Baby looked fine. Grace worried. She found the only pain pill left in
the bottle she had brought from China for her toothache, and urged
Lily to take it. As soon as her head hit the pillow, she fell into a deep,
exhausted slumber.

II

Lily saw herself in a brownish-red sandy ground like on the Mars.
On the bumpy horizon, a huge sky-high bulldozer loomed menac-
ingly. She looked around and searched for her family members but
found no one.

Then she saw herself hovering above the globe and looking down
on the continents yet finding no sign of human civilization. Seized
by loneliness, she drifted down and immersed herself in the deep
engulfing ocean, with piercing cold blue waves.

The next moment, she saw herself with a small group of people
walking in a jungle. They were all in rags, skinny and exhausted,
staggering aimlessly towards nowhere. She understood they were
survivors of the last civilization. Everyone was a stranger. Life was
meaningless without her loved ones ...

Somehow, she sensed the warm attention of a man. The expression in his face was so familiar that she felt relieved that her long
lost love was finally back. Abruptly, however, there came a fierce
movement in her abdomen. She felt a baby kicking hard inside and
her heart sank. She realized painfully that she couldn't explain how
she had lost her virginity and become pregnant.

When Lily opened her eyes, it was dawn. She let out a sigh. Lying still under the blankets, she tried to piece together the fragments of her strange dream, which was drifting away fast.

She stared at the furnishings in the room.

The asparagus plant on the drawer had totally recovered from its dryness and thrived over the months with nothing but water. The greenness felt precious in the barren winter.

She got up and looked outside. The snow had stopped but heavy clouds had blocked the sun and the sky looked gray. She remembered the tough interview she had to deal with in a few hours, and her abdomen cramped again.

III

This opportunity had come quite unexpectedly. On New Year's Eve, she had taken Grace and Baby to the recreational centre in downtown Mapleton. They joined thousands of people for a grand celebration in the huge complex, which echoed with deafening music and children's shrill laughter. There was skating and swimming, and free popcorn and soft drinks were offered to everyone. They sat on the chairs and watched the people packed in the pool.

Lily had phoned Camellia in the afternoon and asked her to join them. Unfortunately, she couldn't come. Old Chia had been sick with a serious cold for a few days. Camellia blamed his illness on his clumsiness during the Christmas baptism.

"Nobody had any trouble except him!" she complained on the phone. "He has always been scared of water. When Minister Wong pushed him into the tank on the platform, he was so nervous that he forgot to hold his nose as the others did. He started choking and couldn't get out of the water. What was worse, he got Minister Wong's new wool suit all wet ... Oh, it was so embarrassing!"

Among the crowds, Lily bumped into the Jamaican woman who had been her co-worker at the hotel. She had brought her children for the free swim. She told Lily that she had been promoted to be the sub-leader of the cleaning team since all the Chinese doctors had left. Lily felt happy for her and they exchanged their phone numbers.

While watching people play in the pool, Lily also bumped into the artist and his family whom she had met at the Rainbow Club. When they learned that Lily was looking for a job, she informed her that the seniors home where she worked was hiring a nurse's aid. After learning that Lily had experience working for a senior lady, she encouraged Lily to apply for the position.

IV

Lily dressed carefully for an interview, but at breakfast time, the cramps became serious. They came and went every ten minutes. Grace suggested they go to the family doctor immediately, but there was no time left. Lily had to be at the seniors home for nine-thirty. She put on her overcoat and rushed out the door.

An hour later, she got off the bus and walked towards the flats along the riverbank. The location of the seniors home, in country woods far away from the city centre, prevented many qualified people from applying for the position, she realized. When she was about a hundred yards from the entrance, the cramps became worse. She had to slow down, struggling to move step by step towards the building. The gnawing pain made her legs shake. She felt so weak that she could hardly move an inch further.

I can't present myself like this to the manager, she realized. Biting her lips, she stood stiffly on the ground and looked up at the sky. The gray clouds were getting thicker and heavier.

She felt she was smothered by the thick clouds overhead and the whole world around her was suffocating. She rubbed her eyes, clenched her teeth, and moved towards the entrance.

The manager opened her eyes wide, to see Lily standing by the door, her face so pale and her voice hardly audible. Lily gripped her fingers tightly to try to restrain a new wave of cramps. She raised her face to smile but tears rushed out instead.

V

After Lily had gotten out of the hospital's emergency room and rested for two days at home, she picked up the phone and dialled the number of her Jamaican former co-worker. She learned, however, that business was slow in the season and the hotel was not hiring at the moment.

Though the never-ending snowfall prevented them from going out, the family learned what was going on in the Chinese community through Mrs. Rice. Without Unicorn's car, it became inconvenient for Mrs. Rice to drop by people's homes freely. But she phoned almost every day.

According to Mrs. Rice, Minister Wong was quite annoyed since more than a hundred people had left his church recently. In addition to joining Yu's Holy Spirit group, those who were young and understood English were also attracted by the Canadian-run Baptist church where Unicorn used to drop in. The Canadian church was so amazed at the fast-growing number of Chinese converts that a long-time volunteer was turned into a paid employee to lead a newly established Chinese branch. But Lily was not impressed, remembering her own experience there. On the Sunday morning after Unicorn and his family had left Mapleton, she had walked into the church, sat in the front row and listened attentively to the minister's sermon. Afterwards, she approached the white-bearded gentleman.

"No, we generally don't baptize divorced people," the minister informed her.

She was not satisfied with the simple answer and inquired further.

"Then, who do you think is more qualified for baptism, a woman who is divorced but has not committed adultery, or a woman who has committed adultery but hasn't been divorced?"

The minister looked up at the ceiling, blinking his eyes for seconds, obviously searching for an authentic answer, before he replied, "We can probably baptize the latter."

The family had become used to Mrs. Rice's regular calls. When the phone didn't ring for a few days, they felt it odd. Finally, Lily picked up the phone and called Mrs. Rice herself.

She was shocked to hear Mrs. Rice weeping at the other end of the line. It turned out that her husband in Taiwan was having a love affair with a young lady in his office. Mrs. Rice had actually suspected this for quite a while. For months, her husband had not sent any money. After a friend in Taiwan told Mrs. Rice the shocking news, she had made numerous calls to Taiwan but could find no trace of her man. She left a voice message on his phone asking him to send money or she would be forced to sell their lovely house immediately. A fax came, written by the girl, declaring "the crystal of our love is solidly formed," which implied a pregnancy well on its way. The fax also stated that Mrs. Rice should be prepared to sign the divorce papers to be delivered by mail to her soon.

"I'm flying to Taiwan tomorrow!" Mrs. Rice finally stopped crying. "And I will tear that witch into pieces!"

Chapter 31
Inedible Apple

I

The day after Lily saw Mrs. Rice onto the bus for the airport, she got home in darkness and found Baby playing with puzzles silently on the sitting room floor. There was no dinner on the kitchen table and the stove was cold. She sensed something unusual and rushed into the bedroom.

There she found Grace lying in bed in darkness. Was Mother sick? Her heart started beating fast. Turning on the table lamp, she bent over Grace, and asked worriedly, "Mom, are you all right?"

Grace made no movement. Lily touched her hand, which felt cold, and asked again, "Are you not feeling well, Mom?"

Grace opened her eyes, shook her head weakly, and closed her eyes again.

Lily looked around and found a few pieces of paper under the lamp on the night table. She picked them up, scanned them quickly, and found it was Jade's letter addressed to Lily but already opened by Grace.

Dear Lily,
How are you? How are your mother and Baby doing? I miss all

*of you very much. Unicorn started his classes in January and every-
thing is going smoothly with our life here. The weather in California
is much warmer than in Mapleton and we haven't had any snow yet.*

*First of all, I am going to give you the good news: I am three
months pregnant with twins! Medical tests show them to be healthy,
and my wish to have a second child has been over-granted by God!
Now Moses will have two relatives in North America after his
parents die. Secondly, I have never forgotten your wish. Ever since
we arrived in California, I have been searching for your mother's
beloved teacher, as you asked me to before we left. The theology institute Unicorn attends enjoys much prestige and attracts many famous
ministers. I made a lot of inquiries but nobody seems to know the
exact address of your mother's teacher, or rather, nobody seems willing to tell an unknown person like me.*

*But God must have noticed my efforts and finally led me to him!
When I saw in the newsletter that he was coming here for a speech
during his honeymoon, I was excited!*

*On the day of his visit, he walked into the school hall accompa-
nied by his wife. She spoke first, talking for almost an hour in her
loud voice to call for contributions to the evangelical organization of
which she is currently the chair.*

*The old gentleman, who looked weak and fragile, talked for less
than five minutes but was warmly applauded. While the couple was
sitting in their seats, I rushed over to talk with him before I was
signalled to leave.*

*When I asked him if he had been in central China during World
War II teaching English in a high school, he nodded. However, when
I asked if he remembered a girl student named Grace, he looked
confused. "Grace ... Grace ..." he repeated the name several times
and seemed to be searching his memory hard. I then showed him the
old picture you had given me. He looked carefully at it and seemed
to remember something. "This girl looks somewhat familiar ..." I*

told him quickly that Grace had been looking for him all her life and that she clearly remembers everything about the precious moments she spent with him. I gave him your phone number and told him that to hear his voice once again was the greatest and only wish in Grace's life.

At that moment, his wife, who had been watching us on full alert all this time, took the note from him and told me that he was tired.

I was disappointed by his response. I wanted to ask him more and squeeze out something worthwhile for you, but there was no time. He was escorted out of the hall …

I have been hesitating whether to tell you his news or not, since I feel so sorry for your mother! I am sad to think that we are women, anyway, so different from men …

Lily put down the letter and found a newspaper clipping that had been folded into the envelope. As she spread it out, the headline caught her attention: "Fifty years of devoted family life. Beloved wife returns to God's home. All Christians celebrate our reverend minister's blessed new marriage!"

Beside the article was a picture of a neatly dressed, smiling old man with a robust younger woman holding a bunch of flowers. The story told of the courtship between the bride and the groom, shortly after the first wife passed away. She was from Taiwan, a Buddhist turned Christian, and was promoted to her current high position after her marriage with the old man.

Lily stared at the picture. The groom looked much older than the picture printed on one of Mother's treasured books. Remembering Grace's awkward efforts to cover her year-long search in North America for traces of her youthful dream, she shook her head. Fifty years of happy marriage! So it turned out that the man either lied to Grace or to God. For a man's lying declaration, Mother had destroyed the simple happiness she could have had in her own life.

"Mother," Lily said gently, "I have read your diary, secretly. Sorry I didn't ask your permission."

Grace opened her eyes. She didn't look surprised. Lily suddenly realized that Mother probably wanted to tell her the love story this way, without embarrassment.

Gazing at the ceiling, Grace talked, "If he doesn't remember me at all, he must be a hypocrite. True love would never be forgotten." Her voice sounded miserable.

Lily decided to tell her true feeling. "I think you have idealized him, year after year in your waiting and searching. He has become an idol, a God-like perfect idol created by your imagination over numerous sleepless nights. From his side, there has been nothing between you. If there was something, it was indeed a 'pure friendship,' as he has indicated, I am afraid."

"No, it was certainly not a pure friendship." Grace shook her head. "How could he forget everything?" Her voice became emotional. The night before he departed, we wandered along the wild creek outside the western city gate ... He kneeled on the ground and carefully picked off the reed catkins blowing in the wind and sticking to the hem of my skirt. Under the silver moonlit, he held my shoulders and asked to kiss me. I was so shy and refused. He did, anyway, on my forehead, my cheeks, and my lips ... He asked, 'did you eat garlic for supper? I could taste it.' Oh, I was so embarrassed ...

"Didn't he know that his action and words took away the soul of an innocent young girl for the rest of her life? ... On the way back to school we dropped into a store still open late at night. Under the flickering candlelight, there were all sorts of plastic combs. He asked me to choose one as his souvenir for 'our love.' I picked an elegant one, ivory coloured. Somehow, I found the comb turned out to be a gaudy pink one the next morning under the sunshine ..."

In the dim lamplight, Grace kept on murmuring. She looked old, her wrinkled face under the messy gray hair shrunken and pale, like frost-bitten reed catkins blown by autumn wind.

"How could he forget everything? Could someone forget the verses floating out from his heart? Or were they simply products written for everyone? Aren't Christians not supposed to lie?"

II

At Pearson Airport, Lily helped Grace with the check-in process. Her luggage was light. The bulk of the nice clothes Grace had brought to wear in Canada were now left for Lily.

They sat down in the waiting area. Lily took out a few Red Delicious apples she bought from the store and tried to put them into Grace's backpack. But Grace insisted on putting the bag of apples back into Lily's hand and said, "Take these home with you. I will have plenty of good stuff in Beijing."

They sat numbly, watching passengers passing by.

The night before, Grace had a long talk with Lily after Baby fell asleep.

"It has always been my wish to spend a period of time living with you, just you and me, to make up for something you didn't get," Grace said, "and the year in Canada helped me to accomplish my wish. I wanted to give you a mother's love, but the road of my life was never a smooth one and I was an impatient mother from the very beginning.

"All my life, I have been wronged, misunderstood, unappreciated, by all whom I cared for and loved. I was often angry and took it out on you when things seemed too hard to bear. You were the victim of my bad temper, I know."

She recalled her first unhappy encounter with Lily when the girl was about four. "Your grandma brought you back to me in Beijing, and then she left. I wasn't prepared. You were such a gloomy child, rarely smiling, and you refused to eat the food I put in your bowl. That was the first time I hit you."

"I don't remember that, Mother," Lily assured her.

Grace let out a long breath and continued. "Your grandma had no idea that I was in a very difficult situation then. Because I had been labelled a Rightist and sent to the labour camp, I had to make myself humble in front of everyone, including my husband. I pleaded with him for so long not to divorce me, stressing that our son was only a few months old. I had finally convinced him to keep the marriage when your grandma brought you to Beijing without warning. Your presence added more frost to the heavy snow around me then.

"To be considerate to your father's feelings, I was always more strict with you and blamed you more than I did your siblings. How much I hoped that you would turn out to be outstanding in all respects so that you would win admiration and love from others! But you could never understand my expectations and always disappointed me."

Lily listened quietly as Grace recalled one event after another, all of which had unfortunately been engraved on her memory. Finally, Grace came to the point where Lily could feel that Mother was probing cautiously to see if Lily still remembered that horrible rainy evening in her childhood.

"People threatened to put me on display as an adulterous woman. I felt totally insane. I wanted to kill myself rather than be humiliated in public. I was not myself. But you were not a sensitive child, and you made me lose my control ... Do you remember that night? Do you remember what happened after I got home?"

The horrible event floated up clearly in Lily's mind, but she shook her head.

"I know you were deeply hurt," Grace went on, her eyes fixing on the ceiling. "For so many years, I have lived in sorrow and regret. But life is not a round trip, and there is no return ticket. Nothing I could do would ever heal the scar I left in your tender heart ...

"I know you must also remember the time, when I slapped your face so hard that your nose bled and blood soaked the blanket. I wanted to teach you to learn to keep quiet in those absurd years. I hated your outspokenness! In the most difficult times, I thought more than once about taking your hand and jumping off the high rise, dying together and leaving this world ... "

"I am sorry I failed to be a loving mother in the way you have hoped, but I have tried in my own way to help you become strong and successful. You might feel lonely without me. But after a while you will get used to it.

"Don't tie your hopes to anyone else, including your child. He is going to grow up and leave you alone eventually and probably disappoint you. Rely on yourself to find happiness if you don't want to be disappointed one day when you realize it's too late.

"The life you have chosen is a hard one. But there is something interesting you may like to know. After my father passed away in the early 1940s, a geomancer in my hometown selected two sites as suitable burying grounds for him. The one on a hillside was said to bring good fortune to his son's offspring, and the one by a streamside would bring prosperity to his daughter's descendants. My mother hesitated, for she had one son and two daughters. But finally she picked the streamside ..."

III

Lily looked at her watch. It was nearly boarding time. They stood up and walked towards the security checks.

Outside the gate, Grace stopped and stared at Lily. Her eyes moistened. "If you find it too hard on your own, you may choose to believe in God, as you have wished ..." she said, her voice trembling. Tears welled up in her eyes.

Lily's heart split into pieces. This was the first time she had ever seen her strong Mother in tears. She had a strong desire to hold Mother in her arms and comfort her. But never before in her life, as far as she remembered, had she had any intimate physical contact with her. She twisted her hands, and finally held Mother awkwardly. She was sad to find Mother so fragile and trembling in panic.

Suddenly, Mother slipped out of her arms, cast a last glance at Lily, turned her back abruptly, and walked towards the gate.

Lily burst into tears as she was seized by the fear that this might be the last time she would ever see her mother. She buried her face in her hands, forcing back the sorrowful tide tearing open her chest.

"Oh, Mother, you are a wonderful mother, I know, my wonderful mother!" Lily screamed silently. She rubbed the tears off her cheeks, and looked through the security check door.

All of a sudden, she dashed off towards the security checks. Stopped by guards, she stretched her neck and searched anxiously among the people who had passed the check and were walking in different directions. From afar, she caught sight of Mother's gray hair down the long corridor and started shouting, "Mom, wait! Mom, please wait!"

Mother seemed to have heard something and turned her head briefly. Failing to see Lily, however, she continued to move ahead. Learning against the bar, tears blurred her vision again as Grace's lonely figure disappeared from her sight.

IV

Late in the evening, Lily returned home and knocked on the door of her upstairs Vietnamese neighbours.

Baby and the Vietnamese boy were playing with cards on the floor.

Other members of the large family were watching a Vietnamese video on TV and cracking peanuts. The room was filled with smoke, and the air smelled stuffy but pleasant with the cozy atmosphere of a family.

The skinny lady told her in sign language that Baby had eaten supper and that he had eaten a lot. Lily thanked her, gave her twenty dollars for babysitting, and took Baby home, down to the basement.

She opened the door. The apartment felt empty and cold without Mother.

For a full year, she had been used to life with Mother beside her. Her warm encouragement, her sarcastic comments, and even her severe reproaches now seemed precious and indispensable. With Mother gone, gone too was Lily's self-confidence. She sank into the couch and closed her eyes, her mind as blank as the room.

Some time later, Baby came over and pulled on her arm. She opened her eyes and stared at him, realizing that the quiet, dumb life between the silent little boy and herself had now returned to the home. Baby pulled her again and pointed at the telephone on the computer desk, his large eyes wide open. Lily stood up, walked over, and saw the red flashes showing messages. Who has been calling me? She wondered and pushed the button.

"Hi, Lily! This is Eva of The Eden Press in Toronto. I was happy to receive your manuscript and I enjoyed reading it very much. Would you please send us the rest of the manuscript as soon as possible? I can be reached at 416 ..."

Lily held herself tightly, her mouth open wide. After all the rejections from the large publishers, she had lost her confidence as well as her hope. But urged repeatedly by Grace, she had printed five more copies of her first three chapters and mailed them to a few small publishers just a week ago. She hadn't expected a response so quickly.

She started to tremble at the unexpected news, and walked around the sitting room like a startled deer. Baby must have sensed her unusual mood. Sitting on the floor, he put down the puzzle in his hand and stared at her with questions in his clear black eyes.

She needed to share her complicated feelings with someone. But who? ... Helen jumped into her mind. Lily dialled her number quickly but heard only Helen's answer machine. Then she remembered that Helen had gone to the beach in Florida with her new daughter for the school's study week.

She put down the phone and looked around the room. Her eyes fell on the table and the Red Delicious apples Mother had given her to bring back. With trembling hands, she took two out of the bag, put one into Baby's hand, and bit into the other shining fruit with a crisp sound.

"No, Mom!" Suddenly, Baby burst out crying, his large eyes full of fear. "No eat apple! I don't want you die!"

She stopped chewing, her jaw hanging open as she realized that Baby, now three and a half, was finally able to speak in full sentences.

Acknowledgements

I acknowledge the generous support from the Ontario Arts Council for my literary pursuit. I would like to express my sincere thanks to the following people:

Susan Hodges Bryant, for your unending encouragement and the golden touches in editing my first draft;

Dr. Judith Miller and Dr. Lynne Van Luven, for your professional guidance; Catherine Voight, Dr. Laifong Leung, and Dr. Ed Jewinski, for your caring support.

All staff at Canadian Scholars' Press/Women's Press, for your great effort to bring this book to the public;

And finally, Dr. Gail Cuthbert Brandt, for your genuine trust which formed my most valuable experience in Canada and gave me immense confidence to complete this meaningful work.